MAGGIE MASON

The Fortune Tellers

SPHERE

SPHERE

First published in Great Britain in 2023 by Sphere

1 3 5 7 9 10 8 6 4 2

A CIP catalogue record for this book is available from the British Library.

ISBN 978-1-4087-2815-4

Typeset in Bembo by Hewer Text UK Ltd, Edinburgh
Printed and bound in Great Britain by Clays Ltd, Elcograf S.p.A.

Papers used by Sphere are from well-managed forests
and other responsible sources.

Sphere
An imprint of
Little, Brown Book Group
Carmelite House
50 Victoria Embankment
London
EC4Y 0DZ

An Hachette UK Company
www.hachette.co.uk

www.littlebrown.co.uk

Maggie Mason [illegible] eudonym of author Mary [illegible] d. Mary began her career by self-publishing on Kindle, where many of her sagas reached number one in genre. She was spotted by Pan Macmillan and to date has written many books for them under her own name, with more to come.

Mary continues to be proud to write for Pan Macmillan, but is now equally proud and thrilled to take up a second career with Sphere under the name of Maggie Mason.

Born the thirteenth child of fifteen children, Mary describes her childhood as poor, but rich in love. She was educated at St Peter's RC School in Hinckley and at Hinckley College for Further Education, where she was taught shorthand and typing.

Mary retired from working for the National Probation Service in 2009, when she took up full-time writing, something she'd always dreamed of doing. She follows in the footsteps of her great-grandmother, Dora Langlois, who was an acclaimed author, playwright and actress in the late nineteenth–early twentieth century.

It was her work with the Probation Service that gives Mary's writing its grittiness, her need to tell it how it is, which takes her readers on an emotional journey to the heart of issues.

Also by Maggie Mason

Blackpool Lass
Blackpool's Daughter
Blackpool's Angel
Blackpool Sisters
A Blackpool Christmas
The Halfpenny Girls
The Halfpenny Girls at Christmas
The Halfpenny Girls at War

As Mary Wood

An Unbreakable Bond
To Catch a Dream
Tomorrow Brings Sorrow
Time Passes Time
Proud of You
All I Have to Give
In Their Mother's Footsteps
Brighter Days Ahead
The Street Orphans
The Forgotten Daughter
The Abandoned Daughter
The Wronged Daughter
The Brave Daughters
The Jam Factory Girls

In remembrance of Thalia Proctor, an editor with an insight of my work that was second to none, a kind and considerate lady, always ready to encourage and inspire. A joy to work with. Will always be remembered and missed. Rest in peace.

PART ONE

A Lasting Friendship is Forged

ONE

Martha
Dublin, 1916

'Whist, woman, a man can't hear himself think!'

Martha cringed. She hated to hear her pappy angry and wished her granny would stop nagging him. She'd seen Mammy tense as she stood at the sink drying the dinner pots, her back to them as they sat around the kitchen table.

This room, their living-kitchen, in a small farm cottage outside Dublin, was a place Martha loved. It was bright and welcoming with its constantly roaring fire flickering behind the thick iron and glass door of the stove – the beating heart of their home, kept so by her pappy's long treks to Kilbarrack to find driftwood, and on to the bogs to bring home peat to make briquettes.

The fire not only served to keep them warm but heated the hotplate for cooking and kept the kettle boiling for the umpteen cups of tea the family drank. Then, once a week, Mammy would boil the washing in a huge tub of water on its almost white-hot plate, before filling the tin bath for their weekly ritual.

Martha sighed as she looked around her. To her, the walls were pitted with the memories of happy, funny times, and dark times too, when Pappy was in drink. For then his mood could swing from dancing around the table to throwing things at anything and anyone.

His anger always centred on the British and their treatment of them and their fellow Irishman. Today, he hadn't taken a drink, but was tense like a coiled spring.

'It is that I see a bad outcome, Michael, and want you to be calling off the rising.'

'I can't, Mammy. For the love of God, will you listen to yourself? It is time, Mammy. We must get rid of the British pigs and be regaining what is ours.'

Granny sighed.

Martha loved her granny. At sixteen years of age, she took after her with her hair a vibrant red – the colour Granny's used to be. And the same flashing green eyes – all-seeing eyes, people said.

This was true of Granny as she saw things before they happened and could tell anyone's fortune.

'I'll not be quietened, Michael, for I know it won't go well.' Granny shivered. Turning to Martha, she said, 'It is for being true what I say, isn't it, me wee child?'

The thump on the table made them all jump.

Mammy dropped her tea towel and came over to Pappy. She patted his shoulder gently. 'Sure, it is that your mammy knows, Michael. Will you listen to her?'

Martha felt her granny's eyes burning into her. A shiver slithered down her back. She didn't want to see the vision that was trying to come to her. Pappy's angry voice broke the spell. 'I'll not be standing for her filling our daughter with her witchcraft nonsense. Martha, away to your room.'

Martha couldn't move. She stared into the leaping flames of the fire.

'Close your eyes, Martha. Be telling us what it is that you see.' Granny's voice, gentle and yet compelling, became a surreal echoey presence. Martha closed her eyes. Visions flashed, like an incomplete jigsaw. Everything glowed red. Faces, dripping with blood. Burning buildings . . . and her pappy and mammy standing holding hands. Their clothes scorched, their faces a fleshy mass of torn skin. They stared ahead. Gunshots rang out. They dropped to the floor.

The scream filled the space around her. Martha knew it had come from her. It rasped her throat and stretched her mouth wide.

Arms grabbed her, held her. But they couldn't stop her mind shutting down or her knees sagging as she sank into the terrifying blackness that consumed her.

When she came to, she was lying on her bed. Granny sat on the wooden chair next to her and Mammy lay on the bed with her, still holding her as she had done before the dark place had claimed her.

Unsure of what had happened, Martha could only stare up at the ceiling, wanting the blankness of the whitewash that covered it to be all she saw.

'To be sure, it is that you're all right, me wee darling. It is the gift that your granny always knew you were for having.' Granny took hold of her hand. 'It's a curse the women of me family are clothed in. Use it for the good of folk,

Martha. Then it will be for being a blessing. That is, if they have a mind to listen to the sense you try to tell them.'

Mammy sighed. 'We have to be doing what is right for our family and for our fellow countrymen, Mammy.' The strength of this conviction told Martha that the doubt Mammy had expressed to Pappy was gone without trace. 'The British are weakened by their fighting in France, and now is the best time for us to rise up.'

Martha looked at her mammy. Slender and dainty, her dark hair held off her face in a bun at her neck, her vibrant beauty in her sculptured face showing nothing but love. How could she speak such words of hate – even think of killing others, or of holding a gun in her delicate hands?

'When?' Granny's voice sounded resigned. Martha didn't want her to give in.

'You will die, Mammy, please don't do this. Do as Granny says: let us all leave tonight on the ferry for England. Granny is for knowing of a lovely seaside town – Blackpool. She has heard that the streets are lined with gold . . . Please, Mammy.'

Mammy's gentle stroking of her hair didn't soothe Martha. She didn't know how she knew, or why the horrific pictures had come to her and given her an insight into the future, but she believed what she'd seen in the vision, and was desperate to stop it happening.

'England is at war, me wee darling. None of their streets are lined with gold, only poverty and dilapidation. They are a nation of suppressors, they are for taking all we have – our farms, our food. Our own have been dying of the hunger at times and no mercy was shown. Mammy and Pappy must be taking up the fight for a better Ireland for you and all the folk of our Emerald Isle.'

Martha lay her head on her mammy's breast. Her heart was heavy with the knowledge that soon she would lose her, and the thought was unbearable. And yet, there was truth in what Mammy was saying. 'The Cause' was a worthy one. But that didn't help to alleviate her fear.

How she wished for everything to be normal. But then, what was normal? Living in a cottage and her father working his fingers to the bone on what used to be his father's land but was now owned by a rich English family – the same family that she worked for, helping the upstairs maid?

Martha shuddered as she thought of how her many duties included the emptying and cleaning of the pots from under the beds – a stinking job she hated. Her favourite was helping to keep the clothes of all the ladies of the house clean and in good repair. She loved sewing and was exceptional at it, often chosen to carry out any delicate stitching on a special frock that had a tear in it.

Granny interrupted these thoughts. 'Martha, me lovely, it is the gift that you have that is telling you the future. But I want you always to remember that people's destiny is their own. You can try to help them to change it, but you cannot change it for them.'

'Oh, Granny, I'm not wanting to see the happenings of the future.'

'I understand.'

Tears filled Granny's eyes. Martha felt lost between the world she lived in – a sometimes troubled, but happy world, as though poor and downtrodden, the folk pulled together

– and the life that was to come that she felt helpless to do anything about.

Two days later, Martha stood on the deck peering down into the depths of the Irish Sea as it lashed the side of the boat seeming to angrily mock her. For her granny's sake she'd agreed to go with her and live in Blackpool until it was safe to return home.

It seemed to her that life had suddenly been turned upside down. Her heart was heavy with fear and sadness.

An urge took her to jump into the Irish Sea and let the swirling water win her soul and tear her body to shreds.

Looking heavenward, she called on whatever God ruled those like her – for surely it could not be the good, loving God that the priest told her of? He wouldn't give this cursed power to her . . . Maybe it was the devil? Was she a daughter of the devil himself?

'Come away from the railings, Martha. I fear a sudden lurch will take you.'

Martha glanced over her shoulder at her granny, saw the fear in her face – had she seen that happening? Shaking herself mentally, she told herself that this new part of her was possessing her and she mustn't let it. Older folk were wary of anything happening to those they loved; that's all this was. But she moved away, suddenly fearing that she might be swept away, as now she didn't want to be.

'Come and sit with your granny and keep me warm.'

Sitting huddled into her granny's soft body, she asked, 'Granny, is it that I can rid meself of this curse?'

'No, child. It is with you till you die. But it won't always be present. You're not seeing anything this good while, until now, are you?'

'No, Granny.'

'No. Everything must be in its place. When you had your vision, you were open to it. You were imagining what it was that your mammy and pappy proposed to do. This left your spirit guide a clear path and she was after taking her chance. She gave you the future of the two people who you were focusing on.'

Granny had told her about her spirit guide many times. Martha hadn't really understood, but now she did. 'So, if I want to see something, I have to concentrate on the person it is that I want to read the future for?'

'That's right, but suddenly, at times, it can happen when you're not asking for it to. Me own granny told me that those times are for when it's important for you to be having a message.'

But for the vision happening, Martha wasn't sure she believed all her granny told her. It sounded like a lot of mumbo jumbo. Often Martha heard her pappy say, 'Mammy, it is that you think you are like your gypsy forebears, but you're not, for didn't you up and leave the clan? No true gypsy would be for doing that.'

A week later when they came out of the boarding house where they had been staying in Liverpool, a man called her name. 'Martha! Will you be Martha O'Hara then?'

Granny's face turned deathly white. Martha felt her grip on her arm as if it was a vice.

'She is, and I am her granny. What is it you want, Eamon Finlay?'

'You're remembering me then, Mrs O'Hara?'

'You'll not be forgotten, Eamon. Wasn't it you who always took the coward's way out and that is why you're here now and not fighting alongside your fellow men?'

'Not the coward's way, it is wrong that you are. But come, I have news, and this is not the place.'

Martha wanted to yell at the man. Tell him that she didn't want to hear what he had to say, but in the depths of her heart, she was already grieving as she knew her vision had come true.

A strange howling noise came from her. She had no control over it. It sprang from her deep shock and despair.

'Will you come with me now? It is that the young lady has guessed me mission and it isn't good for us to draw the attention of others to us.'

They learned that everything had happened as Martha had known it would. Her lovely mammy and pappy had been killed in what amounted to an execution in broad daylight.

The following weeks were a blur of pain and misery for Martha. Granny kept herself together and had somehow managed to find them a terraced house in Blackpool to rent, even though Martha knew her hurt was just as deep as her own. And now, they were on their way to take up their new residence.

The train would take them to Preston and from there they had to catch another to Blackpool.

Villages whizzed by the carriage window. None of them registered with Martha.

The only thing she noticed was that there wasn't the destruction Mammy had spoken of. No sign of poverty, only a noticeable number of young men in uniform to give any hint of this country being at war. The everyday folk she saw seemed to be going about their business as if life was the same as it had always been.

The names of the villages declared proudly on signs on each station platform as they either stopped or passed through sounded strange to her – Wigan was one and Leyland another. They seemed to mark in her that this had truly happened, and she was being taken further and further away from all she'd ever known.

At last, they reached Blackpool. The hurry and scurry of people, either alighting from or boarding trains, zinged an excitement through the air. How different from any station atmosphere she'd ever known as everyone lugged cases and excited children were shouted after to bring them to order.

Though tired and hungry, this all lifted Martha for a while, but her spirits plummeted when she saw that they were a long way back in the queue for a cab. She felt drained, but Granny still looked strong and fresh. 'Nearly there, me wee darling. Our new home and a new beginning.'

Martha didn't want a new beginning. She wanted to go back to the only home she'd ever known. To have her mammy hold her and her pappy call her his wee Irish *colleen*.

She swallowed back the tears. Tears didn't help, they only made her feel wretched.

She didn't stay this way for long. Swept away by all around her as the horse and cart taking them to their new house swayed and bobbed down the promenade, she felt as though life had burst into being. The noise of the waves breaking on the beach a backdrop to the vendors calling out their wares from gaily coloured tent-like constructions. The people, some strolling, some sitting on the promenade wall, giving off a happy, relaxed feeling and yet an air of anticipation.

It all served to transport Martha from her doom and gloom to a place of hope, and she had the feeling that this was where she was destined to be.

She looked at her granny and smiled. Slipping her hand into Granny's gnarled one, she told her, 'Sure, it is that everything's going to be all right, Granny. I'm going to look after you.'

Granny grinned a one-tooth grin. 'It is, me wee darling. I can see it in me mind. *Beidh an ghrian ag rís ar maidin.*'

With these words, Martha felt even safer and more settled in her heart as Granny had said, 'The sun will rise on the morrow' – words she always spoke to combat sadness. And Martha knew that her granny could always make happiness happen.

TWO

Trisha
Blackpool

Trisha stroked her ma's bird-like hand.

It will happen today, the doctor had said as he'd left an hour ago.

'Oh, Ma, I don't want you to leave me.'

Ma made no sign of hearing her. Not because of the noise of the train rattling by on the railway lines opposite, something they were used to in Enfield Road, Blackpool, but because she was in a deep, last sleep, as the doctor had called her ma's state.

Ma lay on the bed they'd brought downstairs for her that used to be Trisha's until she and Bobby had married – a shotgun wedding, last December.

Everyone said they were too young – she was only sixteen and Bobby seventeen. Most said that it wouldn't last, but they were doing all right – or had been until Ma took ill not long after the wedding.

Now, she knew she'd been foolish. She'd been besotted by Bobby with his black, curly hair and the makings of a handsome moustache from the moment she'd met him on the tram going to Fleetwood. She had been going shopping and he'd been going to work on one of the fishing trawlers.

Always rebellious since her da had been killed by a runaway horse and carriage, she'd disobeyed her ma on many occasions to be able to wait on the port in Fleetwood for the boat to come in.

When Bobby received a good share-out, he asked her to go to the King Edward picture house with him to see a Charlie Chaplin film. They didn't see much of the film as they sat in the back row snogging all through it. She hadn't stopped Bobby's hand wandering and had loved the feelings his touch had given her.

Once outside, they'd snuggled together in a doorway in a quiet alley, and she'd let him go all the way after he'd told her he loved her and wanted to marry her. She'd loved what he'd done to her, screaming out when he'd entered her – not because it had hurt, but because an exquisite feeling had gripped her, making her forget everything but her love for Bobby and her need to have more of the same.

Many lovemaking sessions followed this first time and last summer became a haze of clandestine meetings whenever they could manage them. Looking back on it now, she felt ashamed of all she'd brought down on her ma. The scandal had been such that they'd almost been hounded out of the street. But then came the wedding and everyone got as drunk as skunks, and she was forgiven.

Life after that hadn't been all she'd wanted it to be. Bobby had become sullen and bad-tempered. Ma said it was the responsibility. That he was too young to take on the thought of becoming a dad and she was to be patient with him.

She didn't feel very patient when he punched her, as he had a few times in the privacy of their bedroom – the one they'd taken over from her ma. Always over nothing – or so she thought, but he didn't.

Like the other night when the boat had had a good haul and he didn't come home but had gone drinking with his mates. She'd told him she'd been worried about him, and he'd grabbed her neck and threw her backwards onto the bed. He'd punched her arm – he knew no one would see the bruise – and then had done to her what she thought rape must feel like. Hurting her and the little one in her belly.

Thinking of this, Trisha touched her bump. A small movement reassured her. She loved the child inside her so much it made her heart ache for the birth so she could hold her – she always thought of her baby as being a little girl.

A knock on the door brought her out of her thoughts. Father O'Leary stepped inside.

'Me heart goes out to you, Patricia. It is that the Good Lord is calling your mother and she will need me blessings to help her on her way.'

Trisha knew the doctor would have sent him and that he meant to give her ma the last rites – a ritual of the Catholic Church. A sacrament, they said it was. And anyone who received it went straight to heaven. She wanted that for her ma.

'Now, let me be getting what I need out of me bag, while you say your confession to me so that you can take the holy communion and offer it up for the soul of your mother.'

This shocked Trisha. She didn't think she would be part of the ceremony. She didn't want to confess to a man who wouldn't even carry out her marriage service as she wouldn't make a full confession of her sin of already having had 'marital relations', as he called it – Bobby had called it sex – before the sacrament of marriage had taken place.

Bobby was having none of it. He didn't want a church wedding and so she'd brought more shame on her ma by marrying in a register office.

'Come on, now. It is that you must tell me all. Then we can tell your mother that you will come to the church and say your vows before God.'

Thinking he might not bless her ma if she didn't, Trisha knelt on what used to be a beautiful green rug with a pattern of flowers woven into it but was now so threadbare that it felt no different to kneeling on the stone floor, which she did often to scrub it.

'I confess to all me sins, Father. Amen.'

'That won't do. Was Bobby after touching you here?'

His hand squeezed her breast. Shock sent her bending backwards, causing a terrible pain in her back. She stared up at him. His face showed his desire. Her eyes went to the bulge in his trousers. Twisting herself, she scrambled onto all fours and crawled away from him till she was under the table.

He sighed. 'Don't you be getting silly ideas now, Patricia. The Good Lord directed me to help you to tell your sins so that you can be forgiven. Come away out of there and let me be helping you some more.'

'Go away! I'll scream!'

'So, you'll put the final nail into your poor mother's coffin, will you? For isn't it you and your sinful ways that has caused her to be dying?'

The pain of these words made Trisha gasp. These thoughts had visited her, but now Father O'Leary was making them the truth ... *Oh, Ma, Ma, I'm sorry. I'm sorry.*

'And now it is you that will be sending her to hell, for without me blessing, it is doubtful she will get through the pearly gates ... Maybe, as it is a good woman that she is, she'll make it to purgatory, but there she'll feel deep unhappiness until the time the gates are open to her, which could be a thousand years from now, we are not for knowing. And yet, you can be making a difference to that, Patricia. Is it that you will do that for your mother?'

He knelt in front of her. 'Come on now, isn't this what you like?' His hand came out again, aiming for her breast once more. Trisha cringed away from him.

'Go away! You're a beast – the devil!'

The door opened. Edna from two doors away popped her head around, took one look and stepped inside, closing the door behind her.

A formidable woman, Edna glared at Father O'Leary as she crossed her arms over her ample bosom. 'By, you're up to your old tricks again, I see, Father. Well, you knaw what happened last time, man. You were told that if you did it again, we'd go to the bishop!'

Though he looked shocked, Trisha was surprised to see how composed the priest was as he straightened himself, stood up, and pulled his coat around him. Not that he had anything to hide now as being caught out had visibly put paid to the desire that had bulged his trousers.

He coughed. 'Mrs Wright, this isn't what it looks. I – I was after coming in to find Patricia where she is now. She'd dropped something and has the cramp. Wasn't I just about to help her out?' He bent down; Trisha saw a glare in his eyes as if he could see into her soul. 'Now, give me your hand, Patricia, so I can help you, and then I'll be after helping your mother on her way. Mrs Wright can help with her prayers too.' His voice seemed to take on a threatening note as he said, 'It is what you want for your dear mother, is it not?'

Trisha nodded. To her, he was saying that if she came out and didn't make a fuss, then he would see her ma off to heaven. This was her dearest wish. Taking his hand, she let him help her out.

Edna stepped closer. 'Eeh, lass, are you all right?' Almost shoving the priest, she told him, 'You get out of the way, Father. Let me help her. Come on, Trisha, lass, hold on to me.'

When she stood, Trisha was grateful for the strong, supportive hold Edna had on her and then felt comforted as Edna put her arms around her. 'There. This ain't a good day for you, is it, lass? . . . Aw, me love, don't cry. You've been brave up till now. Let's do this for your ma, eh?'

Trisha could only manage a nod. Her body trembled and she felt sick to her stomach, but yes, she would do this for her lovely ma.

When the ritual was over, Ma's face took on a different appearance. Every part of it relaxed. Her mouth dropped open. A loud breath left her body, never to be drawn in again.

'There, it is that she is with the Good Lord. Just look how peaceful she is for being . . . Well, I'll be off. I'll be sending the doctor along to write the certificate . . . Oh, and Patricia, I'm sorry for your loss, so I am. I'll be seeing you at mass no doubt, as is tradition on the first Sunday after death? Then it is that we will talk about the funeral . . . I'll be booking Monday afternoon for the requiem, so you can be making all the other arrangements for then. God bless you both.'

With this he was gone. Edna snorted but didn't speak.

Trisha felt as if her heart had turned to stone. She stared at her ma.

'Aw, lass. Go and hold your ma. Her soul is still in the room.' Edna shook her head. 'Eeh, there were never a nicer lass on this earth than Joan.'

As she took a step closer to the bed, Trisha knew her head was shaking a denial, then suddenly on a moan came the words, 'Naw, naw, I don't want her to leave me. Eeh, Ma, Ma!'

Edna's hand patted her back. 'Let her go, lass. Let her go.'

With this, Trisha knew her ma needed her to do that for her. She took her ma's hand. 'Eeh, Ma. I love you. Ta for all the love you gave me.' A sob caught deep in her throat. 'And . . . and I'm sorry, so sorry . . . I did sommat bad, didn't I, Ma? I'm sorry.'

The patting on her back started again. 'Now, now, lass. Don't be taking this on your own shoulders. Your ma was taken by the cancer ravaging her body. Nothing you did accounted for that. Anyroad, you ain't the first and won't be the last. Half the women in this street had a young 'un early. Ha, you've never known so many premature births in your life as happened down here. Then they had the bloody cheek to hound you as if you were a sinner. Bloody hypocrites, the lot of them.'

The urge to giggle took Trisha. It was funny to hear, but not only that, it was as if a huge weight had lifted off her shoulders. 'Ma will go to heaven, won't she, Edna?'

'If she doesn't, then God ain't all He's cracked up to be . . . Don't you worry, lass. Now, say your goodbyes, and she can get on with her journey. Tell her you'll be all right.'

Trisha turned back to her ma. She bent and kissed her still-warm cheek. 'I love you, Ma. Go to your rest. You're out of pain now and that's all I want for you. I'll be fine. I'll look after your grandchild like you looked after me. And she'll always knaw you, Ma. And she'll love you like I do. You knaw that, don't you?'

The tears were streaming down Trisha's face as she crossed her ma's arms across her breast.

'There.' Edna nodded her head as she touched one of Ma's hands. 'She looks lovely. Like you say, her pain has gone.' To Ma, Edna said, 'You rest in peace, lass. You've a good girl here, who'll carry on as you taught her.' With this, Edna bent and kissed Ma. When she straightened, her face was wet with tears. 'I'll put the kettle on, love. You go upstairs and get your ma's Sunday-best frock, and after we've had our tea, we'll give her a good wash and lay her out. She'll want to look nice for your da who'll be waiting for her. And to see that Saint Peter an' all. By, he'll not be able to resist letting her in the pearly gates. He'll knaw what a beautiful person she allus was.' As Edna went towards the kitchen, Trisha heard a sob. She turned towards the door that led to the stairs, at peace with herself now, and glad to have something to do for her ma.

Choosing the right frock was easy. The light grey cotton one that Da had loved Ma to wear. She hadn't worn it since Da had died, but now, if it was true what Edna had said, that Da would be waiting for her, then Trisha knew this was the frock she'd want to be wearing as she went to him.

Ankle-length, with a bell-shaped skirt and a neckline that, but for the lace inset, would show just a little cleavage, the frock had a fitted bodice and long sleeves.

As Trisha gazed at it, she could see her ma coming through the door clutching her purchases from the spring jumble sale, excited to show Da the frock. He'd loved it and had taken her to the pub for a drink that night to proudly show her off wearing it. Their giggles when they came home echoed around Trisha. She smiled as she knew in her heart that what Edna said was true. Once Ma was ready, she'd go to Da, and she'd giggle all the way.

Trisha hadn't realised she was crying, but now had to sniff as she became aware of her nose running. Gathering the frock, she went downstairs.

Edna had the teapot at the ready and poured two steaming mugs of tea as soon as Trisha appeared.

'There, now, let's sit a moment and have this, lass. I've some news for you.'

Trisha waited.

'Well, I've two bits as it happens. One led to the other.' She took a sip of her tea. Trisha did the same, not thinking the news affected her and not really interested in it. The tea tasted grand and helped her, warming the cold place that had been knotted inside her.

'Eeh, you're going to be pleased. I've spoken to Hattie Hargreaves.'

Trisha sat up and took notice. Hattie was their landlady. Her heart thumped against her chest.

'Eeh, don't you be worrying, lass. Hattie ain't going to put you out. She's going to sign the tenancy over to you and Bobby. Mind, she did say that she'd have to think about the rent as Bobby's earning good money. She said she ain't raised it in a while as she knew your ma was struggling with having no man.'

Relief mixed with anxiety as Trisha thought of the pittance Bobby gave her for her housekeeping.

'Anyroad, that ain't all. You're to have new neighbours.'

Before Trisha could digest this news, Edna said, 'Eeh, I don't knaw what the street's coming to. Irish they are. Escaping the Troubles. Well, they'll find worse here if they try their violent ways on us. Hate the English they do, but they soon come crawling to us when they need to get out of their own country.'

'Aw, Edna, they ain't all bad. Let's give them a chance, eh?'

'By, you've a kind heart and a good head on your shoulders, lass. I said to Hattie that they couldn't wish for a better neighbour than you . . . Apparently, there's a grandmother and her granddaughter. The granddaughter is about the same age as you as it turns out, so if you get on well together, she'll be company for you. Someone your own age, instead of all of us around you who're old enough to be your gran.'

The idea appealed to Trisha. At just seventeen she would love another young woman of a similar age to befriend. That's if they could even be called 'young women'. But then, like her, she thought, this Irish girl had probably had to grow up fast too.

With her ma washed and dressed in her Sunday best, Trisha began to feel a little better. The task had helped her. Made her feel that she was still looking after her ma as she had done these last few weeks since Ma became so weak. A labour of love, though it had been tough as sometimes the lifting of her ma and the endless washing had had her in tears with the aching of her back and the sheer exhaustion.

Bobby had spent as little time at home as he could, taking extra shifts on the trawler and then helping in the fish huts, gutting the fish and packing it for transporting to the markets and regular customers. He stank to high heaven when he did deign to come home, and often that would only be to wash, change, dump his stinking clothes for her to see to and go out for a drinking session.

'That were a big sigh, love, but I know how you feel. It's all become real to you now that you've got your ma ready. Well, she looks grand ... Let's open the door and let her spirit escape, shall we?'

This sounded like a strange ritual and one Trisha struggled to think of as really happening. Her ma's unresponsive body whilst they had seen to her had given the truth of it being an empty shell. Ma had left. Hopefully to go to her da. Well, that's how she'd think of them from now on. Together.

'Right, lass. I'll get the collection going around the streets tonight. I knaw we'll get enough for her funeral, so don't you be worrying. So, what about the wake? Will you do that here? And what about relatives? Is there any you need to tell?'

All of this was so far from what Trisha had been thinking about that she felt lost for a moment. Taking it in at last, she shook her head. 'No. Ma were an only child and me da's four siblings all died before they reached five years old.'

'Aw, that's sad. Eeh, a lot of youngsters went when I were growing up. You'd see a woman with her belly up, but you didn't ever see her pushing a pram. If you did, when a lot of them young 'uns got to be toddlers, sommat or other got them. Me ma suffered the same, only rearing four out of fifteen of us. Broken-hearted she was . . . Aye, and bodily broken. Me da would be at her the moment she dropped a young 'un.'

Trisha felt her cheeks redden. Never in her life had she heard Edna talk like this in front of her. Though her ma had often giggled over something Edna had said. Then she'd say, 'It's not for your ears, me little lass, but eeh, that Edna's a one.'

Well, it seemed it was all for her ears now as she was to find out with Edna's next words:

'I expect you knaw how it is that you can stop yourself having one after the other, don't you, Trisha, lass?'

Trisha nodded, but she hadn't a clue. She just didn't want to be told, not here, not now with her ma lying there, and not ever from the mouth of Edna!

'Good. As you'll be in the same boat if not, 'cause the bloody men won't take any care. Once they get going, nowt's going to stop them.'

The sound of a horse-drawn cart pulling up outside shut Edna up. Trisha felt glad of the distraction. They went to the open door. Two women were climbing down from the cart that had drawn up next door.

They both glanced towards Edna and Trisha. The younger one was the most beautiful girl Trisha had ever seen. The sun seemed to light her red hair up as if it was in flames as her ringlets caught its rays. She smiled and her eyes sparkled. Trisha smiled back.

The old woman spoke then.

'It is good to meet you, but it is sorry I am for your loss.'

This surprised Trisha, as she saw it did the girl. Trisha heard her say under her breath, 'Whist, Granny.'

The old woman looked at her granddaughter. 'It is that I saw the beautiful spirit float up to the sky as we came into the street, me wee darling. This grieving young woman should know that, as her mammy was on her way to heaven, so she was.'

She looked over at Trisha. 'She's happy now and says she is with your pappy, so you're not to be worrying about her, dear.'

Trisha felt her skin prickle. Edna just stared at the old lady. Her jaw seemed that it would touch the ground as her mouth gaped in awe.

'I'm for being Mrs O'Hara – Bridie – and this here is me pride and joy, Martha, me granddaughter. We're pleased to meet you and want you to know that it is no trouble that we'll be. But our door will always be open to you.'

'Ta, love. This is Edna, she lives two doors down. And I'm Trisha. And aye, me ma did just pass. She had cancer. There was nowt as could save her. I did me best.' Trisha couldn't stop the tears flowing.

Martha hurried over to her and took her hands in her own. 'I'm knowing your pain, Trisha. I lost me mammy and me pappy just a few weeks ago.'

'Oh, Martha. I'm sorry, lass.'

Then, even though they had only just met, what happened next seemed natural and right as Trisha found herself in Martha's arms. Both were sobbing.

Edna once more resorted to patting Trisha's back. But all that mattered to her was the comfort she felt from Martha and the hope that she was giving her some in return for the loss she had suffered too.

It felt to Trisha that her life was going to change with these two coming into it and as she held on to Martha as if she was a lifeline, she just knew that a bond was forming between them that would sustain them both.

Suddenly, she had a friend, something she hadn't had since school days, and the feeling this gave her filled a huge void inside her as now she could carry on. Martha would make life bearable.

THREE

Martha

When they opened the door of their new home, Martha was surprised to see it was furnished. She'd been worrying about this but hadn't wanted to question her granny.

'The agent said that all the furniture and bed linen is still in place after the woman who lived here was taken to live with her daughter,' Granny explained. 'They were for saying that if I wanted it, I could buy it, or they'll remove it if I don't. It would be helping if we were to keep it, Martha, so what is it you are thinking?'

Martha looked at the shabby sofa against the wall opposite the window. A faded blue, she could just make out a pattern on the cushion where she thought that maybe no one had sat for a good while, as the one that was more faded was sunken a little.

Standing against the wall on her left was a dresser of light oak, and in front of the fire a rug that had seen better days with an armchair to one side of it to match the sofa. A table and four chairs stood under the window which was hung with thick brown velvet curtains. The whole appearance was drab and aged, and a musty smell hung in the air. And yet, Martha felt welcome, and the love that had been within these walls conveyed itself to her.

'I'm for liking it, Granny, and for sure it will give us a good start. Have you the money to be buying it?'

'I have. Don't you be worrying about us affording to live now. For haven't I been stashing away a nest egg this good while for you, me wee darling.'

Martha wondered about this. There were times when getting enough to eat or to pay the rent had worn her pappy down, and yet Granny had money?

'I am knowing your thoughts, Martha, but I knew a time would come when you would need it more than we needed bread on the table. That time is on us and me savings are for funding you to safety and a new life. It's just glad I am that you're feeling the same about the house as I am. This has been a happy home. The couple were for loving each other and their children. And I'm thinking we'll be happy here too.'

Not sure she agreed with Granny over the money, when she thought of her pappy with tears running down his face at not being able to provide, Martha didn't comment, but carried on exploring their new home.

She found the door opposite to the entrance led to the scullery which housed a pot sink under a window overlooking a yard. A cupboard was next to this with two drawers; one of these held cutlery and the other cloths for drying up and holding hot dishes, besides two tablecloths. The cupboard held crockery that was more than enough for their needs. Opposite this was an iron gas cooker. Light green, it seemed to be welcoming her and she imagined herself cooking lovely Irish stews and apple dumplings for pudding on its hob.

At the end of the kitchen, a door led to a pantry with a cold slab and through the back door they found a small yard with a coal house and an outside lav.

It all seemed homely and as if the old lady that had lived here was opening her arms to them. *And I have a friend already, right on me doorstep!* This thought helped Martha to settle in her heart that this was the right place for them. Here, they would be safe. But what the future held . . . She stopped this thought as she didn't want to see it. She wanted to live each day as it came, taking care of her granny and hoping the pain in her heart would ease as time went on.

'It's perfect, Granny. Is it that you are happy with it all?'

'I am that. Though we'll need to brighten it up. We'll cover the sofa and the chair and make some cushions and get a new rug. I just hope the stairs are not for being steep. I feel the ache of climbing them these days.'

The stairs were steep, but Granny managed them well. A strong woman, Martha knew Granny liked to play the old lady at times. Though she did look tired after the journey and her legs seemed to be dragging.

'Sit yourself down in that chair, Granny. I'll be for finding fresh sheets and making the beds up. I'm thinking this room is for being perfect for you and you can be having a rest while I go to that corner shop we passed and get us some groceries. I'll be for bringing you a nice cup of tea when I come back.'

* * *

The street was quiet when she went out and most of the curtains were closed in the front windows, as they would be in respect of Trisha's mammy.

Martha was glad not to meet anyone – she couldn't face a lot of questions. It was all she could do to keep her body and soul together.

The shopkeeper, a small woman with a round, shiny face and a huge bosom, greeted her.

'Well, you're a stranger around here, lass. Have you just moved into the Coopers' old house in Enfield Road?'

'I have. It is me and me granny, and I'm wanting to buy a few essentials, please.'

'Here, let me fill this for you with the things you'll need to get you started.' The shopkeeper bent and retrieved a brown paper bag from under the counter and shook it open with a snapping sound. 'You keep an eye on what's going into the bag and stop me if it's not to your liking, lass ... I'm Mrs Philpot, by the way. What's your name, love?'

'Martha, and it's grateful to you that I am.'

'Well, I'll do me best for you but eeh, we're short of a lot of stuff as there's a war on, you knaw.'

Martha nodded. To her, the little shop looked well stocked. Its shelves were lined with jars of preserves, and on the floor next to where Martha stood there were sacks of potatoes, flour, sugar and oats. Behind a glass-fronted counter she could see open boxes lined with wax paper containing loose biscuits. Another shelf held jars of sweets and the cold slab behind the counter was stacked with blocks of butter and a joint of ham.

'Will there be a butcher nearby, Mrs Philpot?'

'Naw. You'll have to be going into the town for that, and for fresh vegetables. I've a few mangy carrots left, and some onions that are past their best. I'll drop them in and not charge. At least they'll make you a broth with the Oxos I've packed for you. Allus makes a meal does an Oxo.'

'That's kindness itself, so it is. Thank you.'

'There, that'll get you going. Now, if you have your weekly order in by Thursday every week, me delivery boy will bring it around to you, Martha.'

Martha watched her lick the end of her pencil and then add up the column of items.

'I'll put a copy of yesterday's newspaper in an' all. It'll stand you in good stead in the lav. No charge . . . Right, that's two bob, all told.'

'I can't be thanking you enough, Mrs Philpot.'

'It's a pleasure, lass. Me old man were from Ireland, and it's good to hear the lilt again. You take care.'

Martha felt her spirits lift as, weighted down with a bulging carrier bag, she left the shop. It seemed to her that she'd received a welcome as all shopkeepers were known for their gossiping ways and that meant Mrs Philpot might give a good account of her and help others to accept her.

As she walked home, she was already planning to make a meatless stew for Granny's tea, but wished she had some bread to give her. And for herself too, as she could feel her own tummy grumbling for the want of a meal.

Checking on her granny and finding her snoring her head off, Martha busied herself unpacking the food. Under the sink she'd found a rusty tin full of grated soap so used this to wash the shelves of the pantry, not taking long to do this task as the one thing about the house was that it was spotless.

By the time she heard a movement upstairs, Martha had prepared the potatoes, onions and shrivelled carrots and had them simmering on the stove.

When she went back upstairs with the tea, Granny was fast asleep once more. Martha stood and looked down at her, worrying that the shock they'd had, and the deep sorrow, had maybe begun to take its toll on her granny as she'd been so brave and so strong to get them this far.

Feeling lost, Martha left the tea on the table by the bed and went downstairs. Loneliness clothed her and made her heart feel even heavier than it had. Sighing, she picked up her own cup of tea and opened the door that led onto the street, then lowered herself onto her front step.

The hot tea soothed her as she looked towards Trisha's door. At that moment, as if she had willed it to, it opened, and a man she assumed was a doctor and Trisha stepped out. Trisha said her goodbyes to the man. Martha saw him take some money from Trisha's hand before touching his bowler hat and walking away.

Trisha's smile when she turned towards Martha was tear-filled. Martha patted the step next to her. 'It's for being cold on your bum but brings the outside world in and that will be making you feel better. And I'm for having a drop of tea in the pot that you're very welcome to.'

Trisha just nodded.

As she got up, she told Trisha, 'Though it is that we have no milk.'

'It don't matter, ta. I often have it without, but I think I'll bring a chair out as me back's aching and I'm a lump for anyone to pull up if I get stuck down there.'

'You're for looking bonnie, so you are, Trisha. But don't you be for lifting a chair, I'll bring one out for you.'

They sipped their tea in silence for a while, and Martha felt it wasn't an uncomfortable silence, just one of those where you knew you weren't alone and that there was no need for words.

Trisha broke it. 'Do you reckon as you're going to be happy here, Martha? Is it a lot different to what you've allus known?'

'It is. And I'm for wondering how the rest of the neighbours will be with us. Will they be accepting us?'

'Well, Edna did after she got over the shock of your granny knowing me ma had died. How did she know that? Did you chat with anyone before you arrived?'

'Me granny is for knowing what happens before it does. She has a gift. I – I'm for having it . . . well, at least it did visit me and told me what was about to happen to me mammy and pappy. It is for deserting me now, though, as I'm at a loss as to how to earn money to keep me and me granny going. Granny has savings, but a rainy day may be on its way. What is it that you do for a living, Trisha?'

'I work on the beachfront. I stand one of the stalls in the gardens of the bed and breakfast houses and sell rock. I used to work in the rock factory but when I got me belly up, I were retching at the smell of the sugar boiling. This job ain't so bad, though there's days when the wind cuts through you rather than goes around you, and it's no good in the winter when the visitors don't come, but I'll have me babby then so'll be staying at home.'

Martha wanted to say how young Trisha was to be having a child, but guessed it was a sensitive subject. But then was surprised when she spoke openly about it.

Pushing a stray curl of her mousy-coloured hair back under the mop cap she wore, Trisha looked down, shielding her hazel eyes from Martha's gaze. 'I'm only seventeen, you knaw. And to tell the truth, I'm scared. I – I let me ma down badly by getting pregnant when I were unwed . . . Oh, I'm wed now. Me husband's called Bobby.'

The while she spoke, Martha could feel Trisha's unhappiness as her over-long face seemed to lengthen more with her sadness, which Martha guessed wasn't all because of her mammy having gone. On impulse, she put out her hand. Trisha took it.

'I'll be helping you all I can.'

Trisha smiled and squeezed her hand before she let go. The smile changed her, rounding her cheeks and showing beauty in her otherwise plain-looking face. Her cheeks flushed with obvious embarrassment and Martha thought she must curb her own natural way of showing her feelings with gestures as maybe the English didn't like that. She'd heard they were 'stiff upper lip'.

A woman came out of the house on the other side of Martha's. Her dark hair scraped tightly back off her face, she had a pinched expression and cold black eyes. 'So, your ma's gone then, Trisha, lass?'

Trisha nodded.

'Well, I'm sorry to hear that, but she's at peace with your da. If you need owt, I'm here for you, love.'

'Ta, Mrs Higginbottom. The funeral's Monday.'

'I know. Edna's been along the street collecting and told me she went to the funeral director's and arranged it all. I'll be there and I'm on with doing some baking for the wake. I told Edna that I would see to making some scones as I've been making jam with that fruit my Bill brought home from the market.' She nodded her head but didn't look at Martha. 'I see you've a new neighbour.' Without seeming to change her tone, she finally acknowledged Martha. 'So, you're Irish then, lass?'

Trisha answered. 'She is, and lovely with it.'

'Huh! Well, we don't want no trouble in the street. Is it just you and your gran?'

This shocked Martha. She had thought to encounter prejudice against them, but now it had come, it hurt. But then, the Troubles at home were all because of the English and they may be wary of her and Granny.

'We'll not be any trouble, Mrs Higginbottom. Me and me granny are for the quiet life, so we are.'

Mrs Higginbottom humphed as she went back in and pointedly closed the door.

'Don't mind her, love, she likes to think this is her street. Though she has a job on with how Edna likes to run things around here.'

This all sounded strange to Martha, and she wondered what 'things' Mrs Higginbottom and Edna liked to run. Trisha enlightened her.

'They're both busybodies, but Edna's kind with it. Mrs Higginbottom ain't always. She'll be mad because Edna got to me first and did all that needed doing. But between them they'll support me . . . Do you go to church, Martha?'

Taken by surprise, Martha wasn't sure how to answer. Was Trisha a religious sort? She wasn't herself, though had always attended mass for her mammy and pappy's sake and she did believe in God. It was just the rituals of it all she didn't like. She knew Granny felt the same, though like herself, Granny had conformed – you had to in Ireland.

'Why? Do you?'

'Naw. I ain't for all of that, but me ma were. Only, I must go on Sunday. It's tradition with me losing me ma and there'll be prayers said for her. Would you come with me?'

'I will and I'll be glad to . . . anything that will help you, Trisha. I can be saying some prayers for me mammy and pappy, too.'

The pain of her own loss cut deeply into Martha and she involuntarily took a deep breath. It was Trisha who offered her hand this time. Taking it, Martha didn't speak, but the gesture meant such a lot to her and seemed to cement the friendship she knew would grow between them.

'Well, I'd better get in and get me spuds done. Bobby said he'd come home early tonight, as he could see how things were with me ma . . . It smells like you have yours on. Did you manage to get any meat?'

'No. I daren't be for taking the time to go to town.'

'I have a bone from our joint – it's got plenty of meat on. I've cut off what we'll need. Only Bobby exchanges some fish for meat, so we do well – he's a trawlerman. Ha, you'll smell him before you see him coming.'

They laughed at this, but stopped abruptly when Mrs Higginbottom opened her door and looked at them with disdain, before slamming it shut again.

Trisha grimaced. 'Another black mark in me copy book. Eeh, lass, you've to watch yourself around here. If they think you're not behaving in a proper fashion, they'll let you know. She'll be thinking as I was disrespectful to me ma, but me ma loved a giggle.'

'And she'll love you having one too . . . She's for being at peace, Trisha. I can feel how it is for her.'

'You're doing the same as your granny now. The pair of you should set a tent up on the beach as fortune tellers – you'd make a packet in the season. There used to be one till last year. The queues for it stretched almost back to the sea. Gypsy Rosa Lee, she was called . . . Your granny ain't a gypsy, is she?'

'She does come from a family of gypsies. Her grandmother was a gypsy princess. But Granny married a farmer – she met him when her clan stopped to help with the potato picking. Her family were for being called Lee too.'

'There you are then, "Gypsy Bridie Lee". I can see it now. Eeh, she might knaw Rosa.'

Martha giggled again, though was careful to put her hand over her mouth to stifle any sound.

But as Trisha disappeared inside, the idea she had planted began to take root. If folk liked knowing their future and would pay for the knowledge, they could do no better than ask her granny what was in store for them. And if it went well, she'd make sure she practised the talent her granny said she had, then maybe they would make the fortune Trisha had spoken of.

Suddenly, there seemed an answer and Martha determined to talk to her granny about it the moment she woke.

With this thought brightening her, she looked up and down the street and thought, *Maybe me life won't be so bad here.* But the thought was whisked away as a train seemed to appear from nowhere and fill the air with the sound of it chugging past. Martha wondered if she would ever get used to living opposite a railway line. But then, there were worse things – living with the sound of an uprising, for one.

Her body shuddered. Taking a deep breath, she dispelled the images and sounds that wanted to haunt her. She had her granny to see to, and a new life to begin, and she would do her best at both.

FOUR

Trisha

'What the bloody hell! It stinks in here. I take it she's gone then? And you've kept her rotting body here all day! Are you mad?'

Bobby's anger permeated the kitchen walls and even though Trisha couldn't see him from where she stood at the kitchen sink in the scullery, she could feel his presence and cringed away from it.

He appeared at the door. 'You bloody idiot, why didn't you get Ronnie Stanton to take her away, eh?'

'I – I want to keep her here. The neighbours have been calling in to see her and pay their respects. I want to look after her here, Bobby.'

'Naw, naw, bloody, naw.' His head shook from side to side. 'That ain't going to happen. You're a stupid bastard at times. I'm going to fetch Ronnie this minute. I ain't sleeping in a house with no dead body.'

'Please don't, Bobby, please. I can't let her go. She'll be all on her own . . . Please.'

Bobby strode over to her. Her head rocked on her neck with the stinging slap across her head.

'Naw!' Trisha gasped in the sob.

But the blow she'd seen coming landed in her stomach, bending her double. She sank to her knees.

'I don't know why I ever shagged you! You were easy. After me all the time, waiting till me boat come in – an easy lay. But I didn't fancy you, just what you've got between your skinny legs. Now I'm stuck with you. Trapped with an imbecile with her belly up. You're ugly! Ugly and I hate you!'

This last cut Trisha in two. She was glad when he stormed out, but desperate as this meant her ma would be taken away to the morgue. She couldn't bear the thought. Everyone kept their loved ones at home after they'd died.

Pain gripped her. She couldn't get up. Couldn't see for the tears that ran down her face and mingled with her snot. Nor could she breathe, only gasp in air that didn't fill her lungs. 'Help me, someone help me.'

'Will I come in, Trisha? I was for hearing everything. Where are you, me wee love?'

'Martha . . . Martha, help me.'

'Oh, Holy Mother of God, what has he done to you? Trisha . . . Oh, Trisha!'

'Pain . . . so bad . . . help me.'

'I can't be lifting you on me own, I'll fetch me granny and Edna. I'll not be long, me love.'

It seemed no time at all before there was a crowd around her. Hands came under her arms, soothing voices coaxed her, while other voices cursed the daylights out of Bobby.

One voice was different in tone to the others, that of Mrs Higginbottom. 'You brought all of this on yourself, Trisha! The lad weren't ready for marriage, him not long being out of short trousers. You behaved like a hussy and now you're paying for it.'

Edna turned on her. 'Get out, Agnes! Get out before I clock you one!'

No one could humph like Mrs Higginbottom – it spoke volumes that she didn't have to voice. But it was followed by her exit, which Trisha was glad of. Not that she could feel any gladness, or anything other than the terrible pain that gripped the middle of her and the sticky wetness of her knickers.

'Oh, Edna, it is that she is bleeding!'

'Aw, Trisha, love, I don't like the look of that. I'll nip outside and get one of the young 'uns to run for the doctor. Has he been yet and given you the certificate for your ma?'

Trisha nodded her head.

'Well, have you the money to pay him, lass?'

Again, all Trisha could do was to shake her head as the pain in her stomach seemed to grow in its intensity and leave her crying out.

'Let's get her onto the sofa, Martha. You hold her under her arm, lass.'

A bleary-eyed Bridie came through the door as they reached the sofa. She took over from Edna as she went in search of help. Trisha felt Bridie take her arm firmly and yet gently.

'I'm heart sorry, so I am, Trisha, but your child will be in your mammy's arms shortly.'

'Naw! Naw! Don't let it happen . . . please . . . please.' Though she hadn't stopped crying, Trisha felt her sobs deepen as her mouth went slack and she hollered out the pain in her heart.

'We cannot be stopping it, me wee love. How far is it that you've gone?'

'Si . . . six months . . . Ooh, it hurts . . . please do sommat. Save me babby, please!' These words went into an almighty pain that compelled her to push down into her bottom.

'Be helping me to take her knickers off, Martha, I think the child is coming.'

'Naw . . . naw!'

A hand wet with her own blood took Trisha's. She held on to it for all her might, knowing it was lovely Martha's hand and thinking it a lifeline to her. Already she knew she loved Martha and that she would be the saving of her. But she knew in her heart that no one could be the saving of her child as a pain worse than any she'd experienced gripped her and her whole body dispelled her child.

Bridie's voice came to her. 'Will you have some scissors handy, me wee darling?'

Trisha could only point towards the dresser.

'Support the child, Martha. I've to cut the cord and we have to be helping the afterbirth to come, so we do, so be massaging Trisha's stomach firmly.'

Feeling calm and accepting, but not knowing why, Trisha went along with everything they did to make her comfortable and to dispose of the afterbirth, even answering without hesitation when Bridie asked what name she wanted to give her child.

'Patricia Joan Martha.' Where it came to her from to call her child after her new friend as well as herself and her beloved ma, she didn't know, but somehow it felt right.

Patricia had been her granny's name too, her ma's lovely ma, who'd cared for her so much as a child and beyond, till she'd passed away three years ago.

Martha clutched her hand tighter. 'Oh, Trisha, I'm for being honoured to give me name to your beautiful little girl.'

Trisha tried to smile, but at that moment, Bridie said, 'I baptise thee Patricia Joan Martha, in the name of the Father, the Son and the Holy Ghost,' causing hot, fresh tears to run down her cheeks.

'There now. Where is it that we'll find a shawl for the little one, Trisha?'

Before she could answer, the door opened and a panting Edna came back. 'I couldn't find anyone, I had to go to the corner shop. Nora Philpot sorted it out and the doc . . . Oh, my God!'

Trisha, feeling calm once more, heard herself say, 'Me little Patricia Joan Martha, she's here, Edna.'

'Aw, lass, lass . . . I – I don't know what to say.'

Bridie still held her child. Trisha didn't know what to do next.

'A shawl, Trisha?'

'Oh, aye, sorry. In that bottom drawer of the dresser. I – I were going to put all her clothes in there, but only the shawl has made it so far. Me ma crocheted it.' Still she could feel nothing as she mentioned her ma's work – work that she'd laboured over as she became increasingly weaker during the last months.

'You be for getting that for me, Edna. I'll take the child and wash her.'

A hope entered Trisha's heart. Was her child alive? But she hadn't heard her cry, nor could she see her as Bridie whipped her away towards the kitchen.

Then almost as if no time had passed, she had her child in her arms and knew she had lost her. Holding her close, her tears bathed the child's face. Feeling for her tiny hand, she held it in her own and stroked the fringe of dark hair that protruded from the shawl. 'You're beautiful, me little lass.'

The quietness around her seemed to leave her floating alone with her still child, but then a sob broke the silence, and the truth came crashing into her. 'Naw . . . naw, I don't want me babby to be dead . . . Save her . . . someone save her, please!'

She looked frantically from one to the other, but no one offered to bring her child back to life. She felt Martha's arms holding her. 'Your mammy will be taking care of her, so she will, Trisha. Shall I help you to be putting wee Patricia into your mammy's arms?'

'I don't want her to go, Martha.'

'I know, me darling, I know. She's so beautiful that she isn't for this world. Sure, it is that her soul is already in heaven, she just needs to be nestling in your mammy's arms where she will be safe and loved for eternity. You want that for the wee mite, don't you?'

Trisha knew a feeling of hopelessness and despair, but she also knew this was a lovely thing for her child, to be going with her granny and not on her own. She stood on unsteady feet.

'How long is it since your mammy passed, Trisha?'

Edna answered. 'It were around eleven this morning.'

'It is that you may just have to lie the child on her breast, me wee darling, but even if we cannot put your mammy's arms around her, I know it is sure that she will hold her close to her for ever, so she will.'

Trisha knew Bridie was talking about rigor mortis having set in. But though her ma felt cool to the touch, she wasn't stone cold, and they were able to move her arm and lay it across her little granddaughter's body.

Martha had her arm around Trisha as they stood gazing down at what to Trisha was the saddest sight in all her life.

'Let me be helping you to a chair, Trisha, love. It is that Granny is busy cleaning the sofa.'

Trisha had only just sat down when the door opened again. 'In here, she's over . . . What the . . .?' Bobby's head bobbed on his neck as he looked from one to the other. Trisha felt the hate rising in her as Bobby's glance fell on the bed in the corner. His mouth slack with shock, he looked at her.

'You killed her, Bobby. You killed our babby!'

'Naw . . . naw . . . I – I . . . Oh, God!' He looked from the baby to her. 'I – I didn't mean . . . Trisha, I wouldn't . . .'

'But you did! You thumped her that hard she let go of her grip on me and her life . . . I hate you!' The last came out like a growl which rasped her throat.

Bobby sank to his knees in front of her. Tears filled his eyes and his voice held a plea. 'You made me so angry!'

'By wanting to keep me ma with us? Why? You knaw it's how it's done.'

'I – I'm sorry.' He put his head in her lap. His sobs racked his body. 'I – I'll never hit you again, Trisha, I promise.'

Trisha felt cold. As cold as a block of ice must feel. 'I wish I'd never met you.'

'Come on, lad. Leave her alone now, she's been through a lot today.'

As he rose, Bobby asked Edna, 'What can I do? How can I make it right?' He caught sight of Martha and Bridie. 'Who's this?'

'We're for moving in next door to you. We'll not be any trouble but be for helping you all we can.'

Bobby looked as though he didn't know how to take this from Bridie. Martha spoke then. 'I'm Martha and this is me granny, Bridie. We're heart sorry for your loss, so we are.'

Trisha held her breath. Bobby never had a good word to say about the Irish. She prayed he wouldn't insult them.

He didn't. He just turned back to Edna who told him, 'If I were you, I'd tell Ronnie Stanton to come back on Monday afternoon to take them to the church. We'll let him knaw the time. Don't send her ma and babby away, Bobby, her heart's broken. Don't be stamping on the pieces of it.'

Bobby surprised her then as he said, 'Will you tell him, Edna?' Then as Edna went out, he crossed the room and went to the bed where Trisha's ma lay holding their babby. He put his hand out and touched the babby, before sinking to his knees and sobbing his heart out.

'I'll be for putting the kettle on. I think a cup of tea is in order. Will you be helping me, Martha, me darling?'

As Bridie and Martha went through to the scullery, Trisha sat staring at the man she'd loved so dearly and realised for the first time that he was only a boy. Nineteen years of age now. She'd brought a lot down on him with the passion she'd had for him.

A trickle of regret entered her, and an understanding. Not that anything he'd done to her was right, but they were the actions of a young person, still rebellious, who'd felt he'd been trapped into a life he hadn't planned for. Oh aye, he was as much to blame – that's if you could blame anyone for acting according to their age. 'We can get a divorce, Bobby.'

She didn't know where that had come from but now saw it as the best thing.

He shocked her then. He stood up and stared at her. 'I don't want to . . . I've been a fool, Trisha. I've behaved like a spoiled kid. I – I'm sorry . . . If you'll wait for me, I'll be a better husband when I come back.'

'Where're you going?'

'They were recruiting at the town hall when I went to get Ronnie. That's why I've been an age . . . I joined up. They said I'll get papers for a medical soon, and then go away for me training before being deployed, most likely to France.'

Shock held Trisha rigid. She hadn't expected this, and yet, wouldn't it be for the best?

Seeing his lost look, she felt a trickle of compassion for him. She couldn't understand why but as he stood there, no more than a boy, his guilt weighing him down, she knew she had to help him in some way. He had a lot to face.

'Come here, Bobby. I want you to knaw that I'm proud of you.'

He came and lifted her to her feet and held her close. 'I'm so sorry, me little lass. I didn't mean owt of what I said. I love you . . . I just couldn't cope. It were all so different – living with your ma, then her being ill and taking all your time, and you with your belly up and not being so . . . well . . . Oh, God! I made a muck up of that an' all. I weren't gentle. I've been so angry . . . I'm sorry.'

Trisha heard the scullery door open and close and then saw over Bobby's shoulder the same happen with the back door as Edna came back, nodded and went out again. Patting Bobby's back, she said, 'We'll get through it somehow.'

'But I'm going—'

'I knaw. Let's take the time you're away to help us both. I need time. I don't knaw how I feel.'

'You mean, there might be a chance for us?'

'We'll see. Just keep safe, eh? Keep safe and come back to me.'

Trisha felt surprised how much she wanted him to keep safe. The alternative was too awful to think of. But she welcomed this chance to be apart and knew it would be the best thing for them both. Sighing, she held him closer, soothed his sobs and felt inside her that both had grown up by years in the last half an hour. She would hang on to that and hope that somehow she found a way to come to terms with what he had done. She had to. What other choice did she have?

* * *

Trisha had had some bad days in her young life, but when Monday came it was the worst day she'd ever known. She stood looking at the closed coffin, thinking how a huge part of her was inside this simple-looking casket.

Bobby squeezed her hand. Tears flowed down his face, but she couldn't cry. She knew if she did, she would never stop.

As they lowered the coffin into the ground, she shuddered. Her babby should still be in her belly, not going down into the earth.

An arm came around her. 'Look up to the sky, Trisha, for it is that I can see them floating. Your mammy is twirling your baby around. Mammy is giggling and Patricia looks happy in a calm, peaceful way. Look, they are for waving to you.'

Bobby shifted uncomfortably by her side, but Trisha looked up to where Martha pointed. The clouds drifted away from the sun and in their formation, she did see what Martha had described. A warmth filled her heart. She lifted her hand in a small wave that Bobby wouldn't have seen. A smile stretched her face. 'They're safe, Bobby, they're safe.'

His hand tightened on hers. She looked into his eyes. His searched hers and it seemed to her he needed reassuring. Telling him, 'We'll be all right, lad, I promise' was all she could manage as the icy cold fingers around her heart tightened every time that she looked at him.

As they walked out of Layton Cemetery, he pulled her close to him. 'You're beautiful when you smile, Trisha. When I come back all of this will be behind us. I promise . . . I love you, me little lass.'

As she felt his sincerity in this, Trisha hoped that with that to hang on to, this feeling of deep hate she had for him would leave her while they were apart.

Somehow, she had to try to suppress her anger, or at least try to show she had. For there was a part of her that wanted to claw at Bobby for having caused them to lose their child . . . But for all that, she had loved him once.

Maybe, she thought, she would heal while he was gone. She had to, as she had no other home, nowhere to go. Staying with Bobby was her only choice.

The wake went off well. A good send-off, they all said. Trisha wanted to scream that she hadn't wanted to send her ma and babby off, but she just kept herself calm. She felt years and years older than she did a few days ago when she'd sat with Martha and told her she was only seventeen. Now, she felt she could cope with anything.

This resolve was tested three days later when Bobby passed his medical and had notification and a rail pass to travel south the next week.

'I wish I hadn't done it now. I were a fool. I needn't have gone.'

'You knaw it's what you want in your heart, Bobby.'

'Not any more, not now. I want to be with you. I love you, Trisha. I've only just found you, really.'

Trisha's heart dropped. She wanted to say, *So killing our babby made you realise what you had?* But she swallowed hard. 'You'll be home on leave in six weeks. It's not so long.'

He took her in his arms. 'You will wait for me, won't you?'

Stiffening, she forced herself to say, 'I will, I promise.'

He kissed her on the lips. A gentle, loving kiss which deepened, showing her his love and his need. She was glad when he let her go and smiled. 'I think I'd best go for a walk. I've to go to the docks and let me skipper knaw as I won't be coming on the next trip, or any, for a long time. You have a rest, lass.'

He kissed her nose. Then left.

Trisha sighed. Inside she still felt cold – shut down. His kiss had done nothing for her but being held and loved, she had to admit, was something she needed.

Would her love for him ever come back? She couldn't ever see that happening, but for now, she would humour him and long for the day he left. After that? She didn't know.

FIVE

Martha

The last six weeks had been busy. The house now looked more like home. Granny had bought a second-hand Singer sewing machine, a beautiful thing to look at with its shining brass filigree design on its main body and its brass wheel that glinted as it turned.

Martha loved it and was never happier than when she was sat sewing. Already she'd used the machine to make covers for the sofa and chair and new curtains to match and a smaller curtain in bright yellow gingham for around the pot sink in the scullery, with curtains to match for the window looking over the yard.

On the wall of the living room hung a picture of Mammy and Pappy taken on their wedding day, when life was much better as the farm Pappy ended up working on had still been in the family and food and money had been enough for their needs.

It was sad to think of them being turned out and of Pappy having not known anything but owning his own farm.

Granny sighed. Glancing at her, Martha saw a tear in her eye. She too was looking at the photo. Not wanting to get too morose, Martha thought to tackle Granny about their future. Neither had spoken of it.

'Granny, is it that your savings will last much longer?'

'I was after trying to find the right moment to talk to you about that, me wee darling, but no, they are dwindling fast. But I wasn't for asking you to go out to work when you're still grieving and coping with poor Trisha's grief too.'

'Well, we can be helping all the situations. Trisha needs to get back to work, or she'll be for losing her job, and she was for making a suggestion for you and me.'

'So, you'd put your granny out to work, would you?'

'Ha, yes, it is that I'm going to wave the whip at you.' They both laughed, but after Granny had heard her out, she became serious.

'So, folk would be after paying good money to hear their future?'

'Yes, Granny. We'd need a tent with a chair in it for you to sit on and a table with anything on it that is for giving your clients confidence in you being authentic.'

'I am knowing what you are meaning – a crystal ball and some playing cards would do the trick. This Rosa Lee, she's after being a relative of mine. Does Trisha know where it is she lives?'

'I can ask her. Why?'

'For it isn't for me to just step in. Rosa will have to be giving me the right, so she will. Also, she may have the family crystal ball and be willing to pass it to me. It is for enhancing the special powers of the Lees.'

Granny was quiet for a moment, then said, 'If Rosa retired, they wouldn't be knowing where to find me. I used to see them when they travelled to Ireland but haven't this good while.'

'I'll pop and ask Trisha; she was for getting very friendly with Rosa Lee. But if we can't find her, what then?'

'I'm feeling she is close by.' Granny closed her eyes for a moment. 'Yes, she is looking for me, which bodes well, so it does. And you are saying that there is no one telling the fortunes now?'

'No, Trisha said not.'

'Well then, I must be the next in line and it cannot happen until I am found. I'm thinking we have our solution, me wee darling. For I will be taking this on and making you me next in line. You are to hone your skills. Let the spirits in to guide you, then they will help you to be of help to others.'

Martha wasn't so sure. She didn't even like the sound of looking into others' futures. Suppose she got it wrong?

Trisha greeted her with a smile, but a watery one. Martha thought better of probing. Like herself, Trisha had many moments when she just cried. She wouldn't want to always share those.

But the reason became apparent.

'I've had a letter from Bobby. He's being posted. He will come home for a week first, and then go with his regiment to France . . . Oh, Martha, how will I cope? . . . I mean, well, I do feel a bit different. I don't hate him as much.'

As Martha comforted Trisha, she wondered how this could be so. She could never see herself feeling anything but hate for any man who had done to her what Bobby had done to Trisha. Especially as Trisha had told her that this wasn't the first time he'd been violent. So, how could she be sure he wouldn't do it again? But she didn't voice this.

'I'm heart sorry, love. It is that you've been through two lifetimes of sorrow. Maybe getting back to work will be the saving of you. Are you still of the mind to do that?'

'I am. I had an inkling that Bobby would come home about now. It's the normal thing to happen with the lads going away, so I arranged to go back after he leaves. Have you thought any more about doing the fortune telling? It'd be lovely to have you down the front with me.'

'It is that I popped around to talk to you about it.'

After she'd explained the rituals of Granny's gypsy family, she was pleased to hear Trisha say, 'Aye, I do knaw. Her clan have a camp in a field near to Lytham. They'll be there for the season. I can take you both there if you want. I'd like to see Rosa again, and ... well, just to get out other than going to the shops.'

'Thanks, Trisha, and it is that you'll be welcome to come with us.'

'We can walk to the front and then get on a tram.'

'I'd love that. Ooh, I'm excited now. I'm after being ready meself to get out and about ... I'll tell you what, would you come and have a cup of tea? Are you for feeling up for some company today?'

'I am. It will lift me spirits. I need to get meself going for when Bobby comes home. I've to find a way to get through that. For his sake an' all as I've to think on what lies ahead for him.'

Martha didn't comment but her thoughts were that Bobby didn't deserve to be allowed home, let alone have Trisha trying to make it a calm time for him. But then, if she did anything other than make him welcome, who knew what he would do. Besides, she knew that Trisha feared being made homeless on top of everything else. She needed to be where her ma was still around her.

The next day the walk to the tram stop took longer than Martha thought. Granny looked as though she couldn't go another yard by the time they reached the end of Pleasant Street and crossed over Dickson Road to the promenade and the tram stop.

But it was worth it as she loved the bumpy, swaying ride on the tram. Martha could feel her granny's excitement as she pointed out this and that that she'd spotted. A boat out at sea. A lovely hotel with folk sitting outside enjoying the sunshine. The North Pier that seemed to stretch endlessly out to sea, lined by long benches and crowded with people. The women, their long frocks blowing in the breeze and each with one hand on their hat to keep it from going on a merry dance without them. The men, smartly dressed in three-piece suits, or some with their trousers tucked into gaiters, a look that Martha loved and, to her, made them look dandier than a suit did.

Blushing at herself admiring the males, she giggled.

'You sound happy, lass.'

'I am for feeling so today, Trisha. Everywhere feels full of hope . . . Oh, look, the vendors!' They crossed over to sit on the other side of the tram. 'Which stall is the one you work on, Trish?'

Trisha gasped. 'Eeh, Martha, lass, naw one's called me that since me da used to. Me ma hated it, but I loved it.'

'Oh, I am for being sorry, me love. I . . . it just came out.'

'Naw, like I say, I love it, less formal . . . well, Trisha's less formal than Patricia, but Trish, it's like only those who love me'll use it.'

Martha looked at Trisha and knew she did love her as if she was her own sister. She found her hand. Trisha didn't reject her grasp but held on to her.

'It is that I'm glad you were there to greet us when we came to Blackpool, Trish. I were feeling afraid and lost. You were like a bright light shining through me fear.'

'Naw, I'm glad you came into me life when you did, Martha. I were sinking fast and had more to come with how Bobby were with me. You saved me – you and your granny.'

They squeezed each other's hands and smiled tear-filled smiles at each other.

Trish broke this as she suddenly said, 'There it is, look, down there. That's where I work.'

'Oh, there's still an empty spot beside it in the same garden! Granny, look! And look how busy it is.'

'Me bones are for being too old to jump from one seat to the other, me little darling. I'll be for seeing it all soon. I'm resting till I've to walk over to the caravans from the road.'

'What was it being like, living in a caravan, Granny?'

'A vardo it is, not a caravan really. And it's lovely – cosy. A moving of your surroundings, not your home. And it is that you do so with your community, no one is for being left behind.' Granny sighed. Martha felt her pain. They'd left their loved ones and community behind and were now in a strange place. She herself was finding it difficult to adjust, but for Granny, it must be heartbreaking.

She whispered to Trish, 'Will you let me pass, love? I think me granny is for needing me.'

When she was sitting next to her granny, Martha clutched her hand, and put her head on her shoulder. 'It is that we're still together, Granny, and now you're going to see a relative of ours. I'm excited to meet her. Does she look like you?'

'No, she's dark-haired, or was, and she's for having the Romany nose – a beautiful slender nose. Yes, it is that Rosa was the most beautiful girl to look at and beautiful inside too.'

'She's still beautiful, though her hair's grey now, Bridie.'

'Was she for telling you your future, Trisha?'

'Naw, I wouldn't let her, but she once met me ma and she shivered all over and said she felt in the presence of an angel. It unnerved me ma, but now I knaw what it was she was trying to prepare me for.'

'Well, she shouldn't have voiced that feeling in front of your mammy, love.'

Trish didn't answer.

Martha thought to change the subject. 'I'm having a new name for Trisha, Granny. I like "Trish", it sounds sort of special.'

'So it is, me wee darling. Trish it is then.'

'And did you hear when I was saying there's a vacant spot where Rosa Lee used to tell fortunes? Well, it's still there!'

'That's good, so it is. Let's hope she receives me well. None of them were best pleased when I married a *gorger*.'

Sometimes Granny talked a whole different language. To her question of what a *gorger* was, Granny told her it was what they termed those who weren't travellers.

'It doesn't sound complimentary.'

'No, it is never said in that way.'

Thinking these questions were helping Granny, Martha asked, 'So, what is the relationship between you and Rosa Lee?'

'We share a *curara* – a grandmother, of a few generations back. I have been remiss in not to be teaching you the Romani, but it is of no consequence, they all speak the English today. It is just that we should not let our traditions die with us.'

'I would like to learn. Already it is that I know what a *gorger* is, and a *curara*.'

Granny smiled a wide smile, and Martha felt that some of the nerves she was feeling had settled and was glad to see it was so.

'We have to get off the tram now, it doesn't take us all the way. We need to get a cab, as I don't think you'll be able to walk to where the camp is, Bridie. There's plenty of them come past here as they knaw folk can't get any further on the tram.'

They were soon in a landau and feeling the jogging along of the horses. Granny looked in her element.

'So, you want the field on the way to Little Plumpton, just as you leave Lytham? What's your business there? It's full of gypsies in the season.'

'It is them I want to see. They're kin.'

'Oh? You're a Lee, are you?'

'I am.'

'Me grandfather was a Lee. Frederick Lee.'

'I know him. A good upstanding man, always one for the horses. Many a time he gave me a bareback ride when I was for being a kid. Where is it you and your family are living? Are you not with the clan?'

'Naw. I'm a Lancastrian now. Arthur is me name, Arthur Boswell. Me ma were a Blackpool lass. Me granddad brought me ma and da a field up top o' Marton. We have a house there, and I make me money running a fleet of cabs. Best job in the world.'

'Well, I married a *gorger*, so I'm hoping the clan will accept me in.'

'This lot will. They love to have a chat with me and ride me cab. They all do a good season an' all. They have some rides going on South Shore Beach, stalls selling all sorts, and the young 'uns sell the lucky white heather in the streets. Then there's shoe shiners and peg sellers. Oh, and a basket maker who does a good trade. Keeps them going through to the winter, I reckon, as they disappear then.'

Martha found it lovely to hear about her ancestors carrying on their way of life, and thought the journey was over all too soon, as she'd enjoyed watching the sand dunes pass by and seeing the big houses that lined the other side of the promenade. And listening to the conversation too, with the sound of the gentle rhythm of the horses' hooves clip-clopping on the tarmac in the background. She sighed contentedly as she got up from the padded bench to climb down from the landau.

'Right, it's this way. Look, you can see them from here.' Trish opened the gate. The screeching sound of its metal hinges sounded eerie in the now quiet landscape where only birds tweeted.

'Martha, run forward and tell them a Lee princess is coming.'

Martha didn't really want to do this; she felt wary of these people. Always the tales about them had been of their wrongdoing, until she'd met Trish, who spoke of loving Rosa, but for her granny's sake she did as she bid. 'Come with me, Trish. If Rosa is sitting outside, she'll remember you and welcome you.'

'You daft ha'peth, you'll be all right. They ain't monsters, you knaw. Just people like us who live a different way of life.'

Reassured, Martha went deeper into the camp.

'What is your business here?'

'I'm having me granny with me and she's a gypsy princess.'

Trish had caught up. 'Hello, Rosa.'

'Ah, it is me lovely Trisha. How are you? I've missed you, so I have. Tell me, who is that making her way towards me?'

'A distant cousin of yours, Bridie O'Hara, was Bridie Lee.'

'Bridie!' Rosa stood. Her face lit up with the huge, toothless smile that creased her cheeks even more than age and the weather had done over the years.

Martha would describe her as a magnificent woman with a presence she couldn't define. Her silver hair was pulled back into a bun and her coal-black eyes were piercing and seemed like Granny's – that they could see into your soul. Her features still had a beauty about them, though wrinkled. They were chiselled and Martha could see what Granny had meant by her long but perfect nose.

She went to meet Granny. 'I saw in a vision that you would come, my dear Bridie. I didn't know when, but knew it was for being a great tragedy that brought you to me.'

Granny bowed her head. Rosa took hold of her gently by the shoulders. 'Welcome to your rightful place, my dear Bridie. It is that you've come to take after me, when it should have been you there all the time. I am a lesser relative but had to take your place.'

'It's good to see you, Rosa, so it is. But no. I'm not coming back into the clan. I have a house in Blackpool. It is right you are that tragedy brought us here.'

As Granny told of what had happened, Trish held Martha in a hug. A hug that softened the blow of hearing it all.

'Well, that's an awful happening, but you should be proud of your son and his wife, they stood for what is right. That is the way of the Lees. So, it is that you want to take my place on the promenade? It will be my pleasure to hand over to you. This is the last of me rituals, I can go to me maker in peace now.'

'Are you for being ill, Rosa, love?'

'Yes. I am not long for this world. I've tried all the cures but am ready now that I have found you.'

‘Oh, Rosa!’ Trish went up to Rosa and put her arm around her.

‘Don’t be sad for me, Trisha. I have had me time on earth and hope I’m deserving of me place in heaven. I’m ready to go. I don’t want to be a burden to me clan.’

A tall young man, who’d stood a little way away listening, came over to them then. ‘Granny, you’ll never be a burden, so you won’t. Rest now.’

‘This is me grandson, Handsi. He is a good man and heads the clan now.’

‘It’s pleased I am to meet you, Bridie, I have heard a lot about you. You were forgiven a long time ago and are always welcome amongst us or can call on us for help if you need it. And that goes for you, Cousin Martha. Come and meet me wife and me bairns.’

By the time they left, clutching the crystal ball Rosa had given to them, Martha liked them all, but still it didn’t feel as if she was one of them. Maybe that would come in the future as she got to know them? She hoped so, as they were her heritage, her granny’s family and, so, hers too.

SIX

Trisha

As she waited on the station, Trisha thought about how her life had changed since Martha and Bridie arrived. She loved that they now called her Trish, her da's pet name for her. It put them where she viewed them, as special in her life.

Deep in thought, she became aware of a change in the atmosphere. Folk who'd sat on the benches had stood and now looked eagerly along the line. Bobby had said there had been a few from Blackpool in the squad he'd joined and that all would come on leave together and then go off to France together too. 'Pals', the government called it – grouping together lads who had a history with each other. Their theory was that it would help them to have familiar faces around them and that they would watch each other's backs without being told to.

It frightened Trisha. She worried that the lads would take more risks when with their mates. Show off, even. And feel it more if one got killed.

The sound of the train in the distance pulled her out of these thoughts. She looked along the line. Seeing the smoke puffing out of the engine gave her a feeling of excitement, mixed with trepidation. How would Bobby be? Would he still feel the way he did before he left? She hoped so, as though she dreaded even having to look at him, she wanted the week he had at home to be a good one for him so he could take happy memories with him when he went to France. She couldn't live with herself if she didn't make that happen and Bobby was killed.

Handsi came to mind and how happy he was with his bride – the respect he gave her and his kids. Such lovely kids. Trisha sighed. If only it had been like that for her and Bobby, she'd still be carrying her babby then. A stab of pain threatened to weaken her resolve to give Bobby a good week.

But there was no time to think about this more as the train pulled in and soldiers spilled from every door, laughing, looking around anxiously, joking with each other and collecting their haversacks from a pile on the station that the porter had dumped out of the goods van.

Then she spotted him. Her heart dropped as memories of their last couple of weeks together flooded her – the humiliation and the pain.

Nerves clutched her stomach. Bobby walked towards her. He looked so different with how his hair was now shaven at the sides and back, but his grin was the same. It showed no sign of him remembering, or of him having suffered as she had. Nor did he seem to have a care in the world – not even for the loss of their unborn.

Brushing this bitter thought away, she forced herself to smile back. He dropped his rucksack and opened his arms, but Trisha felt as if she'd turned to stone.

When he reached her, he took her in his arms. His lips were on hers and all she wanted was to kick him and keep on kicking him until he begged for mercy.

As the kiss went on, the noise of the station faded until a cheer went up. Bobby laughed as he pulled away from her. A crowd of lads surrounded them. 'Get in, Bobby, lad!' 'Get her home first, lad!' 'We won't be seeing you at the pub tonight, lad!' were some of the catcalls. Bobby laughed and swung her around. Trisha allowed Bobby's joy, trying to remember how sorry he had been and all he, and the men cheering him on, had to face.

When they reached their home, everyone was out in the street. The atmosphere was as if they were famous as Edna began the applause and everyone followed suit. Mr Jackson, from three doors down, brought a bottle of beer for Bobby. 'There you go, lad. Enjoy that, you deserve it. We're right proud to have you live in our street and will all be rooting for you when you go to France an' all.'

'Ta ... I'm grateful. I'll enjoy that.' Bobby blushed. He looked at Trisha as if asking her to save him, and yet she could see he was loving the attention.

'Eeh, lad, you get inside and get your feet up. We won't all be bothering you on the last days you and Trisha have together before you go. You're a very brave lad. We all knaw you needn't have gone as your job made you exempt. So, we just wanted to show our appreciation.'

'Ta, Edna. And everyone.' Bobby raised the bottle in the air. 'And cheers, Mr Jackson.' He grinned at them all, then went inside. Trisha followed him, aware that she had tears in her eyes. Bobby hadn't been accepted in the street and he'd known it. But now he was one of them, and she knew it pleased him.

She only wished that Martha and Bridie had been at home – they understood how she was feeling and would have steadied her. But they were out making arrangements for their stall. She hoped they would secure it as going back to work next week would be so much easier having Martha there in the tent next to her stall. Though she dreaded the work and the commitment as she'd got used to being housewife at home and had made a lot of changes over these last six weeks.

Second-hand Lil – the woman who dealt in all cast-offs, and who folk pawned goods to when in a tight corner – had collected Ma's bed and given her a bob for it and this had made the living room look much bigger.

'By, it looks different in here, lass. You've been busy.'

Despite her dry mouth, Trisha managed to say, 'Martha made those throwovers. They give the sofa and chair a new life, don't they?'

'They do. And new curtains . . . The whole place looks and smells different.' He looked towards where the bed used to be and sighed. 'I liked your ma, lass, she was a good 'un. We got on well, she understood me. I often came down in the night to check on her and have a chat. She tried to guide me, but I didn't listen. I'd love to tell her now that all she said has sunk in.'

Trisha couldn't believe what she was hearing. She hadn't an inkling this had happened. But then, she'd always been so exhausted that she'd fallen asleep as soon as her head had hit the pillow . . . or rather, after Bobby had had his way with her in his rough manner. She shuddered.

'Eeh, lass. I knaw it hurt you badly to lose her . . . and . . . Eeh, me lass, I'm sorry . . . I'm so sorry.'

He took her into his arms, bent his head on hers and sobbed. They clung together. His tears and remorse broke her own grief. But this was different to the times she'd lain in bed crying in anguish, desolate and alone. This grief was laden with blame. She clenched her fists, trying to control her feelings.

After a moment, he lifted his head and looked her in the eyes. 'Eeh, lass, I shouldn't have hit you . . . I don't knaw what got into me back then. I knaw it were only a short while ago, but it feels like a lifetime with all I've been through. And every minute of every day, it hasn't left me. I – I used to feel so angry, so trapped. I hadn't got marriage and having a kid in me mind at all when we did it all them times . . . just the sheer enjoyment of it. I couldn't get enough of you.'

She sighed. 'I knaw. I were the same and let it happen . . . made it happen by making meself available. I weren't brought up like that, but it was sommat you did to me, Bobby. You consumed me.'

'And now? I bet you wish you'd never met me.'

'Naw, Bobby, naw.' This wasn't what she wanted to say.

'Oh, Trisha.'

His lips came on hers. With a cold heart she allowed his

kiss. And didn't resist when he broke free and took her hand leading her towards the stairs.

Once in their room, though, she looked at the bed and wanted to scream and scream, but fear of what Bobby might do stopped her.

When Bobby entered her, she felt nothing.

After a moment, he stopped his frantic pounding and rolled off her. His sobs shook the bed. She reached out and touched him.

'What can I do to make things better, Trisha? Tell me! I can't go on like this. I thought everything would be all right.'

A small compassion for him seeped into her. 'Just hold me. Nothing else.'

'But I love you, lass.'

'I knaw. I'll try.'

After a moment of holding her, he kissed her cheek and then her mouth. Some of her coldness melted. She couldn't keep on punishing him for ever. He was sorry. Not that any sorry was enough, but it was all she had – all he had. She wanted to be loved. Bobby loved her. Maybe they could build something together once more.

With these thoughts she turned to him and accepted him.

Not allowing her bitter thoughts in, she began to enjoy the sensations, shocked that she could, but past the point where she could allow anything to stop them she welcomed them. Used the exquisite building of sensations to take all other feelings from her – to soothe her and help her to feel alive once more.

Then it happened. Wave after wave of extreme pleasure washed over her.

When it passed, she flopped back exhausted, leaving Bobby to pound her while she emptied her heart of tears.

His sobs joined hers as his own release happened and they clung together. With this came some healing.

When Bobby rolled off her, they lay still and quiet. After a moment, Bobby said, 'I love you, Trisha, I love you with all me heart. I'll never hurt you again. I've grown up. I'm not pretending to be a man now, doing what men do but then behaving like a lad. I am a man, and I'll take care of you . . . after I've won the war, that is.'

Him laughing at himself lightened the moment. She rolled over to place her arm over his naked, firm body. Her own body felt heavy with the aftermath of her breaking down. Her nose was blocked, her eyes swollen, but the bitterness had eased a little. 'I still need time, Bobby. But I reckon we've made a start.'

'I'm glad, lass. By, I missed you so much. It shocked me how much and made me realise that what we have ain't just sex, not like it was. I missed that, of course I did, but more than that, I missed being with you. I reckon we were meant for each other. As young as we were, we were meant.'

She didn't answer. It wasn't that clear to her yet.

'You knaw, Trisha, I don't knaw how I'm going to get through it.'

'You'll have your mates to keep you going, Bobby. And the future to look forward to – we're all relying on you lads to make it a better one an' all . . . And things'll improve for me with time, I'm sure.'

His answer didn't seem to fit what they were talking about. 'Oh, Trisha, I didn't take care!'

'What do you mean, Bobby?'

'I – I might have made you pregnant again ... Eeh, Trisha, I'm sorry, lass.'

For a second, a chill went through her, but then she thought, maybe if he had, some of the void inside her would be filled.

Her answer was to make him feel less anxious. 'There's nowt you could do about that. I was willing.'

'There is sommat I can do. The lads have been talking, and they told me ... well, they were all joking about me being wed so young and not keeping it in me trousers out of harm's way like I should have done ... you knaw what lads are like. Anyway, they started talking about how we can make love without getting the girl into trouble – that's if they're willing to do it, which don't happen often ... I mean, well, me and you were different, there was a strong attraction between us which we both gave into.'

Trisha found she liked this new Bobby, which was a different feeling for her. She hadn't liked him for a long time, if ever. Yes, he'd been like an addiction, but he hadn't been easy to like. 'So, what did they say you could do?'

'I'd have to pull out before ... Well, you knaw ... It's the end bit that makes you have a babby.'

'Oh? I didn't knaw that, but I reckon there's other things that can be done an' all.'

She told him what Edna had said and how she'd blushed.

'But you knaw, I'm on different terms with Edna now. She treats me like a woman, not a girl. I've been sort of accepted as changed from the kid they've all watched grow up. I think I could ask her now. Tell her that I'm sorry to ask her, but I've got no ma to ask. That way, maybe we'll find out that it is sommat as I can do, not you.'

Bobby stiffened. She could sense a change in him, but he took a deep breath and relaxed a bit as he said, 'I don't want you to do that. Promise me you won't.'

She couldn't think why, but felt he was on the verge of being angry. Feeling afraid, she agreed.

But then he grinned. 'It's my job to protect you.'

She detected a sternness in his tone. Guessed its basis was in fear of her being unfaithful to him as he said, 'I don't want you knowing things like that.'

They were sitting on the step enjoying a cup of tea when Martha and Bridie arrived home. Trisha swallowed hard, nervous as to their reaction to Bobby. She sensed that neither of them trusted him to be all he'd promised to be. But she needn't have worried, they both greeted them cheerily, excited to tell them that they had secured the stall for a year, renewable each year at the discretion of the council and the owner of the boarding house whose garden they were to set up in next to Trisha.

'Eeh, you've no need to worry about Cissy – that's the boarding house owner – except that she can talk you to death!'

They all laughed at this.

'All she worries about is her rent for the pitch and as for the council, we never see them, but if we do, it's to check on litter and making sure that we are trading legally, but it's only once in a blue moon that they suddenly turn up.'

'Well, it is that we have no litter, Trish, so that's not for being a problem.'

'By, it's going to be grand having you next to me. Mind, you'll need earplugs, as some of them are shouting out all day . . . "A farthing a go – knock all the skittles down and win a prize!" Or "I've a hot spud to warm your belly, thou knaws!" Then there's the clowns that are up and down doing cartwheels and the candyfloss sellers. By, that's a delicious treat, but not everyone can afford it, only the posh lot who come "to take the waters", as they put it. By, they're a fussy lot. They like it strictly adhered to that the men are not allowed on the beach when it is their bathing hour. You've never seen such a palaver. They have their maids set up little tents for them to change in. But they can giggle as loud as any of us when that cold sea tickles their toes.'

'It all sounds exciting, so it does. Me granny cannot wait.'

'It'll be the posh lot you get your money from, so don't be afraid of charging. They all seem to like having their fortunes told. Anyway, I've a pot full of tea if you'd like one?'

Bobby shifted uncomfortably next to her. She could sense his irritation. Bridie must have too as she refused. 'Ta, me wee love, but I need to be getting inside to take the weight off me feet.'

As she turned to go inside, Martha said, 'I'd better be for seeing me granny's all right, but ta, Trish. And it's nice to see you, Bobby. Enjoy your leave. We'll not be bothering you, we've a lot to sort out.'

Trisha was pleased when Bobby smiled up at Martha. 'I will, ta.' He put his arm around Trisha. 'We've made a good start, haven't we, love?'

Trisha felt her cheeks blush. Martha giggled, but then her expression changed. She stared at Bobby. Her body shuddered. Her face went deathly white. Turning abruptly, she said, 'Well, I'll be seeing you, I've to go in now,' and hurried inside.

'What were all that about? I tell you, Trisha, I ain't keen on them. They're a strange pair. I'd rather you weren't so friendly with them. You never knaw with folk, and they're virtually at war with us according to a newspaper I picked up on the train. One of the officers must have left it in the lav. Anyway, it had an article on that uprising a couple of months ago. It were a blood bath as the Irish turned against British rule. They were brought into line, but they're now causing all sorts of atrocities to happen. You can't trust them, so you be careful.'

Trisha shrugged. She decided not to bother to argue with him but knew she would never do as he said. She loved Martha. Her world had changed with her coming into her life. She could never shun her; she just wouldn't say so.

Standing up, she said, 'I thought we might go for a walk, Bobby, what do you reckon, eh? We could go along the prom and get a fish supper for our tea.'

'Aye, I'd like that, lass.'

It was five o'clock by the time they were strolling along the promenade eating fish and chips out of newspaper. There weren't many folk about; most would be in the hotels and boarding houses having their evening meal. It was what the traders called the 'lull' and lasted for a couple of hours, but come seven o'clock, the strollers would be out again and that could be a busy time as with not much else to take their attention the visitors flocked to the stalls for their entertainment.

'It feels like we've got Blackpool back instead of sharing it with every Tom, Dick and Harry.'

Trisha knew exactly what Bobby meant. Sometimes, she dreaded the summer with its crowds and charged atmosphere. It was like sharing it with all and sundry.

The tower came into view. To Trisha, it was magnificent. She loved it.

A clown, trying to drum up business for the evening performance of the circus, came up to them. 'Now then, soldier, are you going to bring your missus to the show?'

'Naw, not tonight. We're locals and can't afford your prices.'

'Here, anyone fighting for our country deserves a treat, lad. Have these on me.'

Trisha couldn't believe their luck. How many times she'd seen the huge elephants on the beach and heard of their antics in the ring and longed to be at a performance. She hoped with all her heart that Bobby would say yes.

'Ta, that's grand. I'll take them and be grateful to you.'

Trisha felt excitement zing through her. 'Eeh, Bobby, the circus!'

He squeezed her hand; she could feel he was containing his own excitement. They'd been born in and lived in Blackpool all their lives, but treats like this had been out of their reach and only enjoyed by those who visited.

As they came out of the circus later that night, Trisha felt she was in heaven. She'd loved the animals – the naughty chimps, the roaring, performing lions, the magnificent horses with their bareback riders doing acrobatics as they rode around the ring, and the elephants – these were her favourites, linking their trunks around the tail of the elephant in front and walking around the ring as if holding hands. Then kneeling as if bowing at the end of their act. She'd wanted to go up to them and hug them.

As she sighed her happiness, she thought of how today had been a funny day. Her grief had clothed her when she'd stood on the station and she'd thought she would have drowned in the hate that had welled up in her, but now she felt she had found a path she could tread if she had to tread her future with Bobby. It wouldn't be an easy path and she knew there would still be times when her bitterness would rise up, but knowing the remorse he felt and how he was trying to put things right, and with her choices so limited, she felt that maybe there was a way for them. She could know peace once more. She hoped so.

It seemed no time at all till she and Bobby stood on the station. Other couples were cuddling, and she knew Bobby wanted to do the same.

The week had been like being on a roller-coaster. For most of it she'd coped, but then, last night, Bobby had wanted to make love and she hadn't, and he'd been fine with her – kind even – and she'd known that though she was glad he was going, his coming back was important to her.

'Eeh, lass, I wish I hadn't to go. I want to do me bit, but I want to be with you. You will write, won't you? And . . . well, you'll wait for me? You'll not find anyone else, promise?'

'Don't be daft, Bobby. 'Course I won't. I . . . I don't want anyone else.'

He looked deep into her eyes. Then his lips were on hers. She could taste his tears and wished with all her heart that the violence he'd shown towards her hadn't happened and the world could be a normal place to live once more. Maybe after this new offensive that was raging in somewhere called the Somme, it would be over. She hoped so. She hoped so with all her heart. For this last year her own world had been torn into shreds – everyone she loved had been taken from her. And the love she'd had for Bobby was tarnished.

It came to her then that if it wasn't for Martha coming into her life, she wouldn't want to live.

SEVEN

Martha

Martha held Trisha's hand. The winds she'd heard so much about being Blackpool's autumn signature howled around them as she tried to reassure her. 'It is fine that you'll be, Trish. Me and Granny will help you all we can.'

'I knaw. I just feel so alone when I close me door at night. Everyone in me life has left me.'

Martha felt deeply for Trisha and sought to find a way to distract her. 'It would be doing me a favour if you'd be showing me some of the sights of Blackpool. I mean, experiences. I'm seeing it all now, but haven't been inside the tower, nor have I been on the big wheel, which is looking terrifying, so it is, and yet I want to try it!'

'You daft ha'peth! But aye, I'd like that. There's dancing at the tower, and a circus, which is wonderful, and they say you can see for miles from the top of the Ferris wheel. And we can have a fish and chip supper . . . My treat, as with me dependence money, which is better than what Bobby used to tip up, and me wages an' all, and only me to feed, I'm in clover.' Her jovial tone turned to a wistful one. 'But, you knaw, it ain't without guilt that I take me weekly dues, as at times they feel like a payment for relieving me of having Bobby to keep happy all the time and having to fight me inner feelings of hate.'

They were sat on the sea wall opposite their pitches. Martha closed her eyes against the visions that talking about Bobby conjured up. She unwittingly trembled, then turned it into a laugh as she said, 'Well, if it will help your guilt, you'll have to pretend I'm him when we go out.'

Trisha laughed with her – knew she was trying to stop her from getting maudlin again. 'Well, you'd better get your wellingtons on then and get out to sea in the trawler if you're going to imitate Bobby.'

Giving Trisha's shoulder a playful slap, Martha had to then grab her as she lurched forward causing them both to gasp in fright. But with Trisha safe again, they bent double with laughter. Trisha sobered first. 'Eeh, I thought I were going to land on the beach then, you daft ha'peth!'

Their relief at this not happening drove them into each other's arms.

The evening sun beamed down on them, taking any sting out of the blustery wind. Martha loved it when they hugged like this. It helped the part of her that for ever felt lost without her mammy. As Trisha released her, Martha smiled as she saw her love returned and how much their friendship meant to Trisha, too.

They both turned back to the sea. To Martha, it was as if an unspoken knowledge and calm came to them.

Everywhere matched their mood as just then, the wind died into a breeze and the angry waves calmed to a gentle lapping onto the sand. As she looked over at the setting sun, gradually turning everything a fiery red, she thought how quickly the weather could change on this coastline.

Martha loved this time of the day the most. Very few people milled around as they would be having their evening meal. Usually, she and Granny would make their way home for their own meal and a peaceful hour, Granny nodding, and herself either sitting on the step watching the children play and the women gossiping, or just sitting wishing she had some needlework to do. But tonight, Granny had a lady client who'd been booked in by her maid for six-thirty and so they would be late going home.

With the thought of the needlework, an idea she'd had came back to Martha. It was something she'd been mulling over in her head since Granny had wrapped the shawl around the body of Trisha's baby. The memory hurt Martha's heart but gave her how she'd felt so sorry that the little mite had no other clothes and how she'd had the fleeting thought at the time of how she would have loved to make a gown for her.

'Trish . . . is it that you are any good at needlework?'

'Naw, I've never been taught. But I can knit, me Granny Pat taught me . . . and she started to teach me how to crochet, and me ma tried to continue that, but I found it more difficult than knitting and wanted to be off out, so didn't bother with it.' Trisha looked out to sea and almost as if she'd known Martha's thoughts, said, 'I would've made me babby things, but there were never any spare money to buy wool.'

Martha gently touched her back. It seemed that all roads led back to their grief. But she hadn't meant for this to happen and decided to say what was on her mind.

'Well, how about it is that we start to make baby clothes now?'

'What? Now I know you're mad, ha! Babby clothes! Who for? . . . You're not having visions that I'm . . . but I can't be, me monthlies have been regular since they started back!'

Martha laughed. 'No! That isn't what I am thinking . . . I mean . . . I—'

'Naw, don't worry. It's just that you made me belly do a tumble then, with you seeing things . . . How lovely that would have been, eh? I mean . . . well, even if it was Bobby who gave it to me. Not a replacement for little Patricia, no one could ever be that, but . . . Oh, I'm not making sense.'

Martha grabbed her hand. As she did a feeling shuddered through her. She closed her eyes, heard Trisha say in a scared voice, 'What? What can you see, Martha? I knaw you can see sommat.'

Compelled to speak, Martha told her, 'You are destined to have another child. A girl. She will bring joy and yet . . .' Martha clamped her mouth tightly. She must not speak of what she saw, but then there was something she knew that she could speak of, so cleverly made it sound as though this was what she was going to say all along. 'And yet, anguish, as she will be courageous above words.'

'Will she live, Martha?'

Martha opened her eyes, the vision having receded. The answer was something she didn't know, but she could pretend. 'Oh, yes, she will live and she will give you many grandchildren . . . Ha, Granny Trish.'

Trisha burst out laughing. Her face looked full of joy. 'Eeh, a heroine and a babby machine! Well, I can't ask for more than that, can I? By, you've made me day.'

Martha laughed with her, relieved and yet still shaking inwardly from the knowledge of what she hadn't told Trisha. Changing the subject, she said, 'So, to get back to what we were talking about, it is that you'll need to be skilful with the knitting and the crocheting – I can be for teaching you the last.'

'So, you're thinking that we need to start now? By, just how many kids is this daughter of mine going to have?'

They bent double. Martha's sides ached and her eyes streamed with tears with the laughter that went on and on . . . Oh, how she loved Trisha, she was so funny!

'No, you . . . what is it now that you are for calling me that is for sounding better than eejit? . . . Daft ha'peth, that's it – you're a daft ha'peth!'

This set them off even more. Trisha was bent over the sea wall with the agony of their giggles. At last, they sobered.

It was then that Martha could voice her idea of them making baby clothes to sell. 'We can be spending our evenings doing it. Wouldn't that brighten your life, Trish?'

'It would. And I tell you sommat else, I've bought one of them gramophones so we could play that while we work. I got it second-hand, so it's ancient, but I like listening to the records that came with it. I got it mostly for the winter months as I dread the quiet in the evenings. When everyone's gone in, I thought it'd be company for me.'

'To be sure, it would make a jolly evening of it as it is that I love music. We can be knitting and sewing in time to it!'

This time when they giggled it was just a short burst as the first of the magical electric lights along the prom began to flicker into life, taking their attention. They both fell silent as they gazed at the wonder of them.

'Eeh, it'll be time to get back to work in ten minutes. Your granny will be looking for you. Is she all right on her own?'

'Yes, it is that she was going to have a wee nod.'

'Aw, she loves that wing-backed chair you insisted on getting for the tent.'

'Yes, she does, though it was a trial to get her to agree to it. But look, it is that we have a few more minutes. No one has opened their stalls again yet, and the prom is still empty of people. I have a longing to do something about our plan to make layettes. Come on, let's go along to the haberdashery stall. Lisa is for knowing you and may let us browse as she sits having her mug of tea.'

'Ha! You're a one. Anyroad, what's a layette when it's out? It sounds French.'

'It is! The Romanis always use that word too. It covers all that new babies need. Sure, I can be making little gowns and we can embroider the bodice on each. And I can crochet some matinee jackets, and you can too, when you learn how to do it. And oh, blankets too . . . I'm going to love doing them as it is that sewing, and all needlework, is me first love.'

Jumping down from the wall, they ran together to a few stalls down to where Lisa Mathews, a widow with five children, had a stall selling wool and materials for dress-making, besides pins and needles and all kinds of things they would need.

Martha had admired it from the first time she'd seen it, and thrilled that she now had an excuse to handle all the fine cottons and silks. To her, this was heaven.

Between them they chose some lovely lawn cotton in white and lemon. 'It is that these colours are for being a good choice as both can be worn by a boy or a girl, Trish, so will be good sellers. And from these two pieces of cotton, I can make four gowns – oh, look, there is for being some lemon ribbon. Shall we be buying a yard of it?'

'Aye, why not . . . Look, Martha, lass, I knaw we said we're going halves, but as I told you earlier, I've never been better off so I can put in the lion's share . . . Eeh, Martha, lass, you've perked me up no end. Not just thinking of all them grandchildren, but for the promise that I could be part of our very own business . . . Mind, we're to talk about that side of things. Where are you thinking we can sell all that we make?'

'I haven't. It was being just a fleeting idea and a desire to be getting back to me needlework. I loved making the curtains and chair covers, so I did, but they didn't challenge me. I know it is that I can make things of beauty. And it is the baby things that are a pull on me to make.'

Trisha grinned. 'It's got to me now an' all. Eeh, get a yard of that ribbon. We can use it for umpteen things. We can thread some through the waist of the gowns, and some will come in for tying the matinee coats I knit. By, I can't wait to get started.'

'Ooh, I'm so glad. I am loving this and feel so excited.' Putting the ribbon on the pile of the items they intended to purchase, Martha said, 'There, that's being all we need to get started . . . but it is worried I am, as I think of it all. Are you sure you will be for coping? I – I mean, it seems almost cruel now to have you even thinking of baby clothes, let alone buying the material.'

'Naw, you've given me an aim in me life. Aye, it will make me sad sometimes that I ain't making them for me own little babby, but I'll be making a new life for meself – I'll be giving meself options.'

Martha didn't have to ask what options she meant; she knew Trisha was only trying to make things work with Bobby because she didn't have any other choice.

'And if that prediction is true, I'll be able to build good prospects for me future daughter and all them grandchildren an' all.'

Trisha gave a lovely smile, which put Martha's mind at rest.

'So, we're getting this done, lass?'

'We are, love.'

'Good. Besides, I have some patterns for me knitting. I – I used to take them out of magazines that the ladies left lying around. There was once one blowing along the prom and I put me foot on it to stop its progress. It has loads of baby patterns in it.' Trisha sighed. 'How I longed to get started on them.'

This was the very thing that had worried Martha, but before this reminiscence could take Trisha deeper, she told her, 'And it is that I can draw what I want to make and cut a pattern from newspaper to the design.'

With this, ideas tumbled around Martha's brain as designs came to her – a little gown in white with lemon petals embroidered on the bodice and the lemon ribbon threaded through the waist. She could visualise it and clutched her breast at the thrill it gave her to think of working on such a garment.

Trisha was just as excited. 'Eeh, it's a wonderful idea. The whole thing!' She twirled around in a happy dance.

But suddenly something occurred to Martha. 'What is it you will do about getting some wool?'

'Hmm, we've spent enough now on materials and things, but wait a mo . . .' Trisha went quiet, but then said, 'Would it be bad of me to unravel some of the cardigans and jumpers me ma knitted for herself and use the wool? She loved to knit, and she always used soft colours.'

Martha saw the uncertainty and the slight tremor of Trisha's lip.

Jumping in, she said, 'No, it would be wonderful, so it would. It would make your mammy a part of what we are doing, and you can put the first one away safely in tissue paper for that little girl you are going to be blessed with. Then it will mean she is part of her too. For she will be wrapped in the wool your mammy lovingly fashioned for herself. It would be like she is wrapping her little granddaughter in her arms.'

Trisha's smile lit her face. The unshed tears released and glistened on her cheeks. 'Aw, that's a lovely way of looking at it and a lovely thought. Ta, Martha, ta.'

They hugged again, but only briefly as a voice hollered, 'Martha!'

Startled, Martha turned. 'That's Granny. Can you be seeing to paying for these and we'll settle the bill between us later, Trish?'

'Aye, of course. You go to your granny.'

As she went to turn, Trisha grabbed her and hugged her. 'Ta for all of this, Martha. It's going to be grand.'

Martha patted her back. 'It is. It can be for changing both our lives.'

They parted then. But for Martha, the feeling wouldn't leave her as she ran along the prom that yes, they would be successful, but they had a lot to go through first.

EIGHT

Martha

Martha's heart was in her mouth as to why her granny had called out so urgently, as she hurried along the gardens to their tent. Though a small part of her was glad of the distraction halting any further insight. She didn't want to see into her own future.

'What is it, Granny? Are you for being all right?'

'Ooh, I've cramp in me calf, Martha ... Ooh, help me, me wee darling.'

Dropping to her knees, Martha rubbed her granny's leg vigorously, making the fat wobble. She could feel the tightened muscles and willed them to release. 'It is that you've been sitting too long, Granny. Let's be getting you up and then you can walk around and that will release the cramp. And to get warm too. We cannot be doing these late readings now it is that the nights are drawing in.'

Poor Granny hollered out as she stood, then sighed a sigh of relief as the pain subsided. 'It is thankful I am for such a sensible granddaughter; your pappy would be proud of you.' Granny sniffed. Then plonked back down into the chair. Tears rolled down her cheeks. Martha swallowed hard, trying to dispel the lump that had tightened her throat as her own grief lay just below the surface. She'd felt it when Trisha mentioned her ma's cardigan, for her own lost mammy had knitted cardigans and jumpers for her and her granny too, and now it threatened to leave her in floods of tears as Granny bent forward, weighted down by the loss of her son. Martha cradled Granny's head. She had no words and couldn't have uttered them if she did. All she could do was to smother her granny in love and hope the moment passed.

'It is an old fool I'm for being, me darling. I'll be all right. Will you pop yourself along to Macie's and get me a mug of tea?'

'I will, and I'll get a bun for you too, Granny. You always get low when it's time to eat. It may perk you up. You need energy to be tapping into the spirits for the lady that's coming to have her fortune told.'

'That's for being part of the problem, Martha. Since speaking to the lady's maid earlier when she made the appointment, I've had a feeling that her mistress had trouble coming to her in abundance. Till I'm sat with her, I cannot decipher what, but it is for upsetting me.'

This worried Martha, for the lady she'd never met and for Granny. Granny hated bad news to visit her, even when it was coming to strangers.

Hurrying along the road to where Macie, a woman in her thirties, ran a little café and served mugs of tea to take onto the beach, Martha wished for the umpteenth time this cursed gift would go away. More and more she was seeing snippets of the future and she found it disturbing. Granny had spoken lately of her taking over now and again to get her used to it, but she didn't want to, nor did she like when she sat in on a reading and she saw what Granny saw.

Sighing, she greeted Macie who always had a cheery word.

'Hello, lass, you look as though you've the troubles of the world on your shoulders. What's making you so glum, eh?'

'It's just that I'm worrying over me granny, Macie.'

'Aye, it must drain her telling the fortunes of others.' Macie giggled. 'Mind, I'd like to knaw what was going to happen to this bloody Kaiser. Would she knaw? Only, I want me man back to keep me warm in bed.'

Martha blushed but giggled with her. 'It is that Granny would want five minutes with him and then she could tell.'

'What about you, love? Ain't you one for seeing things?'

'I am, but don't want to be.'

'Practise on me, eh? Tell me what you see. Am I going to make a fortune in me little café? Is me man coming home? And when he does, will we have that babby we longed for but didn't happen?'

Macie had become very serious and leaned forward, staring into Martha's eyes. Martha knew the strange feeling that took her just before she saw into the future to grip her and seem to transport her into a hazy existence. She saw a child on Macie's knee – a little girl – and Macie looking blissfully happy, but she couldn't see a soldier returning, only the image of Joe, a man who was missing half an arm and had a coconut shy along the promenade. He was standing behind Macie, smiling his huge smile.

'Well?'

'You will have a little girl, Macie.'

Macie sighed. 'Ta, love, you've made me day. So, me Tommy will come home then?'

Martha couldn't speak. She didn't want to tell Macie any more. The door opening saved her till she turned and saw that it was Joe. Had she conjured him up?

'Hello, Martha. Macie, the apple of me eye, pour me a mug of your delicious tea, lass.'

Macie giggled.

Joe turned to Martha. 'She should have married me, you knaw, lass, but along came Tommy and swept her off her feet. Took her from under me nose. Broken-hearted I was.'

'Get away with you, Joe. You're too slow to catch a train. A girl would wait a lifetime for you to fall in love with her. Well, me Tommy came along, and you were too late.'

'I'm steady but sure, Macie. You broke me heart, now I'm destined to be a bachelor all me born days.'

Macie laughed, but to Martha there was more in the laugh than Macie realised. To her, it wasn't a brush-off to Joe, but a sign that Macie wanted to keep Joe's interest.

As she clutched the steaming mug of tea Macie had handed her and paid for that and the currant bun she'd selected, she said her goodbyes. Martha felt happy for them both, for though she knew them coming together would be after a lot of heartache in the first instance for Macie, she also knew that joy lay ahead for them.

Feeling cheered by the knowledge that her gift could give hope, she felt a lot better as she waved to Trisha who was back on her stall shouting, 'Come and get your Blackpool rock!'

Giving her a little wave, Martha called out, 'See you in about an hour, Trish.'

Granny gave her one-tooth grin when she arrived back at their tent.

'There you go, Granny, that'll warm you through. Now, be getting this bun down you, it won't be spoiling your supper.' She gave her granny a wry smile as they both knew nothing stopped her granny from eating. She could eat till the cows came home.

Granny looked at her quizzically. 'Something's happened to you, Martha, me wee darling. What is it that's making you smile?'

When Granny had listened to Martha's experience, she nodded her approval. 'Often life is for being that way, me darling. Bad must happen for what was truly meant to be to get its opportunity. So, did you see the death of Tommy?'

'No, I only felt a little sadness for him, just in case that was to happen and for what Macie would go through before she found happiness with Joe.'

'Well then, it might be that he isn't going to die. Macie may not have been the right bride for him. Maybe he will meet someone and fall in love and not return to Macie. You were for making assumptions that as he is for being at war he will be killed. It is good that you weren't for voicing this. Never tell anything that you only surmise. You knew Macie was in for heartache, so you did, but you didn't know why. You knew she would be happy again with Joe, so you are happy for her, but you only told her she would have a little girl – not who with. You did well.'

Granny sipped her tea, then sat back munching her bun. 'I am wanting you to sit in with me and to read the lady client I am to have. You may be knowing more than comes to me.'

Martha didn't want to do this, but she wouldn't upset her granny by saying so.

When the lady arrived, she was beautiful. She wore a beige coat with a brown fur trim around the collar and down the length of the front. It was an unusual shape, being buttoned across her breast and then cut away and falling from her hips. Underneath it was a long brown dress, but it was her shoes that caught Martha's eye. They were a shiny tan and brown, with a lacy pattern cut out of the leather, and they had a small dainty heel. On her head she wore a brown hat of the shape of the one the legendary Robin Hood is said to have worn.

Martha put her age at around the same as Macie at the café.

As soon as she sat down and asked anxiously, 'Is it true that you can see into the future?' Martha felt the strange feeling coming over her. She didn't fight it, nor did she look to her granny for guidance. She had no need to.

She gasped as she saw a child lying bloodied in the road and a man with a whip about to bring it down on the lady's back.

Granny's hand clasped hers.

'What is it? What have you both seen? Please tell me nothing bad is going to happen.'

Martha felt Granny tremble. As she did, Martha saw more of her vision. The lady very ill but recovering and then holding the boy and smiling.

Granny's voice shook as she said, 'You have a son, who is not for being fathered by your husband, but he doesn't know?'

The lady looked shocked and then afraid. Granny told her, 'Take care at all times as someone will harm the boy and you.' But then went on to say how she will find happiness and so will her son with her true love and the boy's real pappy, as those hurting her now will be punished and she will be free.

The lady had tears running down her face. She stood. Thanked Granny, crossed her palm with a guinea and left.

Granny didn't speak for a moment. When she did, she said, 'You saw?'

'Yes. I saw it all. How can we be saving her and her child?'

'We can't. I said before that people's destiny is their own, we can only help by informing them. If she believes me, she may be able to make different choices, I don't know. Just hang on to how happy we saw her in the long run. She is now forewarned. That's all we're able to do. Rid yourself of the memory of it now, Martha. You're a channel, not the saviour of the world.'

Martha found this surprisingly easy to do later when she and Trisha were sat together in Trisha's living room planning their first layette.

She was to make the gown she'd dreamed of earlier, and Trisha a matinee jacket to go with it. The wool of one of her ma's cardigans was perfect for it.

Martha loved drawing the pattern, and then laying the material out on the table ready to cut around the shapes she'd made. She'd drawn and cut out her design on a copy of the *Blackpool Evening Gazette* – a paper Trisha bought and devoured from beginning to end to keep her entertained. She had a stack of them. Martha had deliberately chosen an older one and had rubbed it well with her hands to check the print wouldn't come off onto the lovely cloth. She glanced over at Trisha, worried that now she was unravelling the lemon jumper she might feel the pain of doing so, but she seemed quite happy winding the wool around the back of one of her dining chairs into a skein. When she'd done this, she would need to soak the wool to straighten it, and then when dry, wind it into balls that were of a size that would be easy to slip into her pinny pocket while she knitted.

Trisha looked up and smiled, a smile that held pain, and Martha knew it was the memories assailing her, but then it quickly turned to a grin as she said, 'Ooh, I knaw, let's get the music going, lass.'

'I'd love that. I've been looking at that contraption in the corner on the dresser, is that it? It looks like a box with a big brass tulip coming from it.'

'Aye, it is. I'll wind it up and get it going. I'll put on sommat to get us jigging.'

Martha laughed. 'Jigging? Sure, that's a bit hard to do when doing what we're doing.'

'Naw, we can have a break. Me ma used to play piano, you knaw. She were good at it and every Christmas we'd have a sing-song and a jig. But she had to sell it when me da died.'

Trisha went quiet as she wound the machine up and selected a huge rubber disc to put on the turntable, and Martha allowed this. She had to let Trisha feel and deal with her own emotions at times. She did herself, so knew what it felt like to have a sudden memory attack you – as that's what memories could feel like, as though they were out to break you at times. But at others they were welcome and kept you going.

'I like this one. It's a bit crackly, but it makes me smile.'

As she placed the needle in the groove of the record, the tone of a man filled the room as he sang:

'When you caressed me,
T'was then heaven blessed me,
What a blessing no one knows.
You made life cheery
When you called me dearie,
T'was down where the blue grass grows.
Your lips were sweeter than julip
When you wore a tulip ...
And I wore a big red rose.'

To Martha, it was magical. She couldn't help but dance with Trisha when she grabbed her hands and waltzed her around the room. Both sang at the tops of their voices, '*When you wore a tulip ... And I wore a big red rose.*' Then collapsed into a heap of giggles to the background of the needle going backwards and forwards as it had come to the end of the song.

'Eeh, that was fun. I'm enjoying meself like I never thought I would do again. I want to dance and dance. Let's do as we said and go to the tower ballroom one evening, eh?'

'Will it not be frowned on by the street? Especially Mrs Higginbottom. It is that I can see her now with her arms folded and her head nodding with that tight-lipped mouth of hers not for uttering a word, and yet saying all.'

'Ha, you have her off to a tee, lass . . . But, aye, you're right. We'd have to go in the day, though they do sometimes have a brass band playing in the afternoon and folk get up for a waltz . . . Ooh, I love dancing.'

'And you've a pretty voice too, so you have. You should be on the stage.'

'Ha, me Granny Pat allus said that. When I was little, she'd make me party dresses and get me to dance for her . . . She were lovely, me Granny Pat . . . It sort of gives me hope to think of her, as when she first died, I couldn't say her name without crying, but now I talk as if she ain't gone, and that's how it feels.' Trisha reached out and took Martha's hands. 'And it will for you for your mammy and pappy and for me for me ma and me little Patricia, won't it, Martha?'

The tears were streaming down her face. Martha knew her own face to be wet with stray tears too, but the lump in her chest didn't break. She dreaded the day it did as she felt she would never stop crying. Having Trisha to console helped. She took her in her arms and held her, but then found the knot did break and they both sobbed as they held on to each other for dear life.

Neither tried to stop the other's sobs, they just held each other with the love they had for one another and found solace in not having to excuse themselves but giving in to their grief.

After a while of telling things they remembered to each other, they calmed.

'Eeh, look at us, we're a daft pair.'

'It is that I feel better for letting it out, though, Trish. Ta for holding me, and not shushing me.'

'And you me, love. I needed that. I'd like to make it a screaming, kicking the walls and beating them with me fists session at times. But a good cry has helped.'

She gently disentangled herself from Martha's arms and said, 'I'll put the kettle on, eh? We'll have a cuppa, put the music on again, and get another half an hour at our preparation for making our babby clothes.'

Martha felt drained as she sat down while Trisha went into the scullery to put the kettle on. She looked at the cloth, half cut out, and the wool, almost completely wound around the chair, and the thought came to her they were their future. With all the posh folk coming to Blackpool in the season, they could do well selling their baby layettes. And yet, it wasn't the selling of them that was going to be their solace, but the making of them. The working together and keeping each other going. Something told her that in the future, they would both need that, but she didn't let the thought develop. She wanted to live her own life without knowing how it would pan out for her. She'd never allow her spirit to tell her her own future. It was bad enough knowing Trisha's and the pain she was going to go through. One day she would allow the spirit to give her the whole story. She wanted to know that her lovely friend would be all right in the end, but she wasn't ready for even the first bit, and her trying to stop Trisha from going dancing in the evening was part of that.

Trisha came through the door a few moments later with two steaming mugs. 'We'll have this and then turn in for the night, eh? I feel exhausted and all bunged up after that cry.'

'Yes, it is that I'm for feeling dead on me feet now, and I've left Granny for long enough, though she loves a quiet time, so she does. She likes to just think about things and to nod off. I'm often at a loss trying to tiptoe around. I used to be for the reading.'

'Really? Books, you mean? I ain't never read a book, but I like to read me paper. I love finding out about me town's goings-on, though when I read about a local lad having copped it in France, I feel bad ... In tonight's, they were saying that womenfolk should be knitting warm clothes, scarves, socks and jumpers for our boys as they could be in for a hard winter in them trenches.'

Martha wrestled with the thought that came to her that she didn't want to help such men who killed her mammy and pappy. But then, Irish men were in France too. 'Maybe that's what it is we should be doing first ... I didn't think. We're both for making enough money on the prom for our needs, maybe it is that we should put our talents to the good cause of keeping those fighting men warm?'

'My money ain't coming from the prom, but from the government, but aye, I agree, lass. We should do our bit. I'll put all this up in me spare bedroom till we've knitted a pile of two left-footed socks!'

Once more they were laughing, and it felt good. Trisha had the most wonderful way of turning things around very quickly that Martha loved. But then, she loved everything about Trisha and blessed the day she came into her life.

NINE

Martha

Martha was really looking forward to her first English Christmas. Blackpool was buzzing again after the lull they'd had, though soon she and Granny would experience their first closed season.

This worried her a little, as they hadn't yet made enough to put by as much as they might need. She wondered if any of the stallholders had, as though it seemed to her that Blackpool had been busy, with visitors thronging in, many had said that the war was affecting trade.

But for now, they had this extra boost of Christmas visitors and were hard at work, despite being hampered by winds and struggling to keep their wares from sailing across to Ireland.

How often Martha had wished to do that herself. Not to stay. Blackpool was her home now, and she loved it here, but just to see the rolling green hills and to hear her countrymen calling out to one another. With this thought came the terrible times of the unrest, and her image of her country as a fearful place. But times were changing. For now, England's war in France was Ireland's war too, and she and Trisha were doing all they could to help the poor lads fighting it.

It had been sad to her to put her idea on hold, but she loved any kind of sewing and needlework so clicked away on four pins with her grey wool and loved the long thick socks she produced. Taking them to the WRVS headquarters in Blackpool was a joy too as they were so gratefully received. And always they were given more wool from the stock that had been donated and told they were doing a grand job.

'Are you managing to keep warm, Martha?' Trisha's voice carried on the wind.

'It is that we are, our wee stove is well alight now. Come in and warm your hands, Trisha.'

As Trisha bobbed her head in, she said, 'I'm not selling much rock today, but by, I'm being attacked by starving seagulls, and pooed on by them an' all.'

As she said this, she tried to brush bird poo from her sleeve, but only managed to spread it even more.

'Come here and let me rub it with this cloth for you, you're for making it worse.'

Trisha sat down heavily on the chair reserved for clients. 'I'm just so fed up, Martha. Nowt happens in our lives. Here we are freezing to death, with Christmas just two days away, and we've nowt much to look forward to. I ain't even had a letter from Bobby for weeks and that worries me as to whether he's all right . . . For all our troubles, I don't want owt to happen to him.'

Martha knew what she meant. She felt the same way. Bobby was someone she knew out there fighting and she wouldn't like to think of anything happening to him for all his wrongdoing. And she had to agree too with the feeling of being fed up – life did seem to be humdrum and socks!

'Maybe if we were to ask to be allowed to knit them scarves now?'

Trisha burst out laughing. A lovely sound. 'You daft ha'peth! But think about it, Martha, that is what it's come to – we're like two old knitting women!

'There are things about to be happening for you, Trisha. Don't be wishing trouble to your door now.'

'Granny!'

'Naw, it's all right. I'm sure Bridie only meant the old saying of being careful what you wish for.'

Trisha smiled at Granny, but Martha felt a shudder. She knew there was truth in what Granny had said.

'But I don't care if it is trouble I'm wishing for, Bridie, I want sommat to happen before I go mad. I've too much time to think and that ain't good for me.'

As Trisha peeped out of the tent to check her stall, Granny gave Martha a look and whispered, 'Remember what I said, we cannot change another's destiny. Trisha needs something to lift her spirits, and you do too. You're both for being young and should be having some fun, so you should. Sure, you live the life of an old lady.'

Trisha brought her head back in. 'I heard that, and we do, Martha. We work hard, we do our bit. We should be allowed some fun. Please come to the tower ballroom with me tonight. We'll be safe. Only they're having a grand ball.

There's a quartet on. And I can pop along now and buy some tickets from the clown who stands outside . . . Eeh, thinking of clowns, how about the circus? That's open all year round – they don't do as many performances in the winter months, but you'd love it. Both of you would. The animals are wonderful how they perform their tricks.'

Granny clucked her teeth. 'I'm not liking how they must treat the animals that should be running wild over the plains of Africa.'

'Oh, but Bridie, they are kindness itself. The animals do what they do for treats, and for cuddles . . . Aye, the keepers often cuddle them, even the big cats.'

Granny humphed.

'By, Bridie, you could rival Mrs Higginbottom!'

They all laughed at this.

'All right then, let me be getting me money from me purse. Get us tickets for the circus on Boxing Day, will you? I'll be paying for the three of us.'

Martha clapped her hands together. 'Oh, Granny, what a treat it will be, me darling. I know we'll love it. You're one for watching the elephants when they go to the beach for their swim and to wallow in the mud baths they are for making on the water's edge.'

'I am that. I love the elephants, so I do.'

'So do I. Ooh, I'm that excited.' Trisha clapped her hands together. 'And what about the ball? You will come to that, won't you, Martha? I have money enough for our tickets.'

Martha couldn't refuse. In her heart she wanted to as she feared for Trisha, but it was as Granny said, they couldn't alter the destiny of others, and she somehow sensed that the ball might be the place where Trisha's may begin to change.

Sighing, she asked, 'What will we wear?'

'I have a frock that was me ma's. She never wore it, she said it was too posh. It were a spontaneous buy from one of her church jumbles. One of the wealthy lot had donated it. It's long and a lovely rose colour with a frill that goes around the collar and down to the waist. The material is satiny. I love it. Ma said one day I'd be able to wear it when our fortunes changed. She always said our fortunes would change one day, bless her.'

'They will. But in the future. That is a promise I can make.'

'By, that sounds exciting. I can see me now being driven around in a posh car by a chauffeur.'

Martha dispelled the thought that came to her and laughed.

'Sure, you are to be the belle of the ball, and it is me that will be Cinderella, for I'm not for having anything like that gown in me wardrobe.'

'But it is that you can run something up in an afternoon, me darling. Go along with Trisha. Sit me outside so that I can watch her stall. Me thick blanket will keep me warm and if anyone comes to our tent, then I can be making them an appointment. Get yourself a yard or so of a nice silk, then we'll away home as soon as we can and you can be making a start. You'll soon run up a simple style – simple is elegant, me wee Martha. Simple is for being elegant.'

'Oh, Granny, ta. Is it sure that you are?'

'It is. Now away with you.'

Once Granny was settled out of the wind, they held hands and ran to Lisa Mathew's stall, Martha thinking frantically of what style she could run up in an afternoon. But then it came to her that she did have a long black skirt, so maybe making an elegant top and, as Granny said, in a simple flowing style, would be easier. With this idea taking shape, she began to imagine it – something shiny, with only a frill for sleeves, and without shape, but flowing from the neckline. Yes, she could manage that. 'I am wanting a green satin. Green goes with me hair and me eyes.'

'You'll look beautiful in any colour ... Mind, I'd better not come with you, I'll go along to the tower and get our tickets. We can't leave your granny too long.'

Martha found what she needed almost immediately, a lovely mint-green satin. She could see her top in her mind and was already thinking of how to make it. And she found some lovely pearl buttons for the back too. It would be making the loops for these, she thought, that would take the most time, as cutting out a simple shape and sewing the back and front together, with darts for the front and a slit at the back of the neckline for the buttons, wouldn't pose her a lot of problems. She couldn't wait to get started. Making the top would be just as exciting to her as the ball would.

When she met Trisha, she was shivering outside the café. 'I've bought three mugs of cocoa to warm us up, but I can't carry them all. Macie will pour them now that you've arrived.'

'Me Granny isn't one for the cocoa, Trish, can you change hers to tea?'

'Aye, I just thought cocoa reaches places nothing else can. It warms the cockles of your heart – and your belly and your bum!'

They were laughing again. There was an air of excitement about Trisha that Martha latched on to. She forgot her forebodings and let the excitement in. She was going to make a posh top and go to her very first ball. She couldn't wait to do either.

As soon as the last of those milling around left for their midday meal, they all packed up, though Martha felt concerned about Trisha doing so.

'Eeh, don't worry, lass. I can't see me boss knowing, he'll be in some pub getting drunk. And besides, the takings are better than most days. Did you see that car pull up and buy practically all of me stall?'

'I did, Trisha. And the maid with the driver was for booking in a whole family for a reading of the cards in the morning. I'm going to be doing some for Granny. I'm beginning to enjoy reading the cards. It is that I have more faith in what they tell me.'

'Well, here's one whose cards you won't be reading. I'll take me future as it comes, I've decided. Though I knaw as you've looked at me tea leaves.'

'I'm not at all skilled at the tea leaf reading, but I'm learning. It's to do with the formation of the leaves around the cup, and I'm not good at knowing them all yet. But when I do, I'll keep your future to meself, I promise.'

'Well . . . you can tell me if I'm coming into a fortune.'

Martha laughed at her.

'I'll try. Though I'm not one for looking at what's in store for meself. I want it all to be a surprise that I hope I'm to enjoy living through.'

'Aye, that's how I look at it. I wouldn't mind a peek at the best bits, but owt that's going to hurt me I'll pass on and deal with it when it happens.'

They linked arms and giggled as they followed Granny's slow pace to the stand where they would get a landau. They often went home by this mode of transport now as Granny couldn't walk the full distance, and she loved the pace of the horses and the smell of them. She said it brought memories of her childhood to her. Though in the summer months they often had to catch the tram and cut up the back streets to home, as the landaus were too busy.

As they alighted, Granny asked Arthur to come back at seven-thirty to pick up what she called 'the two belles of the ball' and deliver them to the tower. 'And I'll be paying you now for that trip and for being outside for them by ten-thirty to bring them home again.'

Arthur doffed his cap. 'I'll be doing that for you, Bridie. You can be trusting me.'

'You better had, so. Or it is that I'll put the Lee curse on you, Arthur.'

Arthur laughed as he geed up his horse and gave a cheery wave as he left.

When they had Granny inside, Trisha beckoned Martha back out. As they stood on the step with the door held closed behind them, Martha saw a worried look on Trisha's face.

'What is it that's concerning you, Trish?'

'I wanted us to walk out of the street, with our coats covering our frocks, as if we were just going for a walk. I don't want to be the talk of the neighbours. Especially as Mrs Higginbottom has started to pass things on to Betty Rippon. She's an aunt of Bobby's and she tells me ma-in-law. Both of them are nosy old cows. I knaw they both write to Bobby and I don't want to give them owt bad to tell him.'

Martha didn't know what to say.

Trisha whispered, 'Look, I'll walk to the prom, eh? I'll meet you there. It'll be dark and no one'll bother about footsteps on the pavement outside, they're used to that. But one of them landaus coming along, that'd set the tongues wagging. And then when we return, we can get Arthur to drop us a couple of streets away, eh?'

'Oh, it is that Granny will worry if she thinks that I've walked home.'

Trisha sighed. 'But I can't let owt get to Bobby's ears about this. He's jealous as it is. His letters are full of me waiting for him and not going anywhere without him.'

'You weren't for saying, Trish. Oh dear, perhaps we shouldn't go.'

'Naw. We deserve some fun. And I'll go mad stuck in that house on me own. I'll be all right. We'll get Arthur to drop me a couple of streets back, eh? I'll wait a while in a doorway for shelter, and then come home.'

Martha didn't like this at all and thought the neighbours would still be curious as to where Trish had been, but then thought she meant not to be seen even going out when she said, 'I'll leave all me lights on that I normally have on, and they won't knaw the difference. I might even put me slippers on till I get out of the street, and I'll pick me moment when all the doors are shut and the curtains drawn.'

Martha sighed. She wasn't sure she liked being on a clandestine mission like this, but she'd do anything for Trisha.

When evening time came, Martha sewed on the last of the buttons at the neckline and surveyed her top. Her feelings were a mixture of excitement at going to a ball, joy at the lovely time she'd had making her top and how it had turned out so beautifully, and cobble wobbles as she felt disturbed by how they were to achieve this night out. It was as if they were thieves in the night, but then Trisha was a married woman with standards expected of her while her husband was away fighting the war. Suddenly it seemed very wrong to be doing what they were doing, but she could do nothing about it now, so determined to enjoy herself despite the trouble that might come down on them.

Granny gasped when she saw her dressed and ready with her hair hung in ringlets down her back, teased there by damping them and plaiting them with rags while she'd busied herself with her sewing.

It was a trick her mammy had taught her, and one they had often done for each other. The memory had made her heart feel heavy, but then she'd seen her mammy and pappy dancing together again on a happy cloud and had cheered.

If only she could get over the feeling that this whole outing was wrong. That she shouldn't be going to a ball unchaperoned. Well, she told herself, she was in a way as

Trisha would be with her, and Granny had approved the outing, but ... She sighed. If only Trisha's circumstances weren't such as she had to act in the way she must.

'Take that look of worry from your beautiful face, me wee darling. You're for looking like a princess, so you are. And sure it is that you're just going out for an evening. A well-deserved treat. You be enjoying yourself and be getting home safely. That's all your granny is asking.'

'I will, Granny.'

There was only time to kiss her granny before the landau pulled up outside. Many a curtain twitched as she got into it, but predictably, Mrs Higginbottom came out.

'Well! Where's Martha off to then?'

'She's for visiting a lady. Martha is getting to be known for her readings of the cards now and she is to attend a party and be the entertainment. It is proud of her that I am. She's for carrying on the Lee tradition and looking like the princess that she is.'

'Oh? I didn't knaw she were a gypsy princess.'

This was said with almost contempt as the door closed on Mrs Higginbottom. Martha just hoped that she would swallow Granny's ingenious story.

As she waved to her granny, Martha smiled. For the first time she felt relaxed and that she and Trisha could pull this off. Granny was a marvel.

The sight of the ballroom made them both gasp. It seemed to be a grotto of gold as the chandeliers glittered off the carved balconies high up around the walls. The paintings on the ceiling of cherubs picked out in greens, blues and golds held Martha mesmerised, as did the music that haunted and captured your heart.

They found the room wasn't crowded and they were able to grab a table on the edge of the shining dance floor.

Once they were settled, Trisha leaned forward. 'By, you look stunning, Martha, lass.'

'And you do too. That colour does something to you. It brings out the rosiness of your cheeks, so it does.'

'That's me excitement. Just look at the dancers. Aren't they lovely? I could sit here all night watching them.'

'They are, but is it sure that you are that you weren't seen, Trish?'

'Not a soul twitched their curtains. Mind, I ain't much for carrying a bag with me smelly slippers in. I can honk them from here!'

Martha laughed, then told her what her granny had said to Mrs Higginbottom.

'Clever Bridie, that'd shut her up, though I hope she don't go knocking on me door to check. I wouldn't put it past her.'

'I shouldn't be worrying about her. She swallowed me granny's story. I don't think she'll even be wondering about you.'

'Anyroad, I don't . . .'

Trisha didn't finish her sentence as two gentlemen had approached their table.

The tallest one with fair hair asked, 'Ladies, we see you are unaccompanied, may we act as your chaperones?'

Trisha burst out laughing. 'You can if you want, lad, but we're fine on our own, ta.'

The young man with him, slightly shorter in height and as dark as the first one was fair, said, 'Ha, you're a Blackpool lass. We don't get many in here, only the posh lot who won't look at me, and here's me off to war next week and longing for a dance with a pretty lady before I go.'

As different as chalk from cheese, the other one said, 'I saw her first, Ricky.' With this, he offered his hand to Trisha. Martha was mortified to see her take it and glide onto the dance floor with him.

'Can I sit down, lass? I knaw you're too posh for me. I thought Ralph would have gone for you.'

'I'm not for being posh. I'm from Ireland.'

'Oh? And you ain't worried about being here with us lot?'

'No, I don't think you bite, do you, Ricky?'

Ricky looked nervous as he sat down. 'Ralph's more at home with this sort of thing than me. He's the posh one, you see. He's from a banking family. They live in Lytham. He joined up on the same day as me, and somehow we landed up being mates. We've nowt in common, but we get on.'

'So, is he not an officer?'

'Naw, but I reckon he will be one day. His dad's old school and believes everyone should start at the bottom. Mind, a few of the officers knaw Ralph's family and ain't above giving him favours. Like tonight. We'd never be allowed out without uniform on, but he wangled it.'

Ricky put his finger into the neck of his collar and slid it around in a gesture that said he wasn't comfortable. When he next spoke, he voiced why.

'I'm a bit scared as folk'll judge us and think we're cowards or sommat.'

'It is that you're a worrier, and you have no need to be. As you say, Ralph's family are known. Everyone will know that he is soon to be going to war and will be deducing the same about you, so they will.'

Ricky relaxed. 'I never thought of that. Well then, would you like to dance with me, lass?'

Martha did want to. She stood and took his hand. He was surprisingly masterful on the dance floor and took her around effortlessly. She began to really enjoy the experience.

'Who taught you to dance so well, Ricky, as it is you are a master at it?'

'It were me grandfather. He used to bring me here on a Saturday morning. He'd say, "Lad, there's nowt wrong in a working-class boy learning the art of dancing. It'll stand you in good stead with the lasses." I used to feel a right dumbo dancing with him around this dance floor.'

Martha laughed out loud. She liked Ricky.

'It was me mammy and me pappy who taught me. Saturday nights was when me pappy took to the beer and to making a fool of himself – and of all of us. But all in a funny way, so it was. He was a stickler for me having the right step to the dance. And I loved it.'

'Well, you're good at it. Have you left your parents back in Ireland?'

Martha felt a pain slice her heart.

'Eeh, I'm sorry. You've lost them?'

'Aye, it is that they have gone to their rest.'

The music stopped and Ricky took her back to her seat without commenting further.

For the rest of the magical evening, Trisha danced with Ralph and Martha chatted to Ricky. He had so many tales and he liked observing people and making things up about them, making her laugh as he imagined one couple having a clandestine affair, and another forced to marry by their parents but hating one another. It was all so entertaining that Martha didn't realise how the time had passed.

Suddenly she knew that Trisha was no longer in the room. She looked around for her.

'She will have gone out for fresh air with Ralph. I hope she is all right. He is known as one for the ladies.'

Martha felt her blood go cold. It had begun. Her vision was to be fulfilled.

TEN

Trisha

Trisha shivered. She hadn't stopped to get her coat from the cloakroom, carried along as she was on the excitement of the evening and the feeling of being in a man's arms again.

Arms that were so different to Bobby's. Being held by Ralph was an exhilarating feeling. He said nice things about her hair, her frock and her eyes. And he smelled fresh, spoke well and, to her, seemed like a prince.

'You're cold, Patricia.'

She loved the sound of her name on his lips. No one ever called her Patricia.

'Here, let me put my jacket around you.'

'Ta.'

Finding herself a little tongue-tied, this was all she could manage as his arms came around her to tuck his jacket around her body. As he clasped the two lapels, he pulled her closer. 'You're a very desirable woman, Patricia.'

Her senses lit up. Her body took over her reasoning. She knew she should step away, tell him she was a married woman, but she couldn't. Her mouth had dried. The nearness of him and feeling the desire he had for her pressing against her thrilled her and left her will weakened.

Gently he manoeuvred her into the shadows of the doorway of a shop. There he looked down into her eyes, and then it happened. His lips were on hers, his tongue probing till she let him explore her mouth, his breathing heavy and his hands caressing. She was lost as he fumbled and then lifted her onto him. Her sigh holding relief as well as pleasure as he whispered, 'Don't worry, I'll take care of you. I won't make you pregnant. Just relax and enjoy.'

Clinging to him, Trisha gasped as he entered her, sending familiar pleasure rippling through her. She'd so missed this feeling.

When it was over, Ralph stepped back from her. Putting his hand in his pocket, he must have reached for a hanky as she could see he was wiping himself.

'Straighten yourself up, Patricia, I'll sort you out in a moment.'

She didn't know what he meant but she straightened her skirt, patted her hair and pulled his jacket around her. Though the cold she felt wasn't from the icy night, but from not being held and kissed, and almost feeling abandoned. Ralph had become distanced – businesslike, as if he'd hired her for a service and she'd fulfilled that . . . *Oh, my God! What have I done?*

Ralph began to fidget in his back pocket. Then he thrust something into her hand. 'Thanks, that was good for a doorway bang. I'd like to meet you and take you to a hotel room before I go to France. Are you free?'

Realising that he'd given her a coin, Trisha filled with horror. 'I ain't naw prossie! Just who do you think you are, eh? I'm a respectable married woman . . . I – I . . .'

'Ha, I don't think so. You may be married, I knew that, but you're anybody's to have who's willing to drop their trousers and give you a couple of bob! That's obvious for anyone to detect. Two minutes on the dance floor and I knew you were aching for it. I got you nice and ready and you came out with me willingly. Don't try to come the hard-done-by, scorned woman at this late stage, as it won't wash, my dear.'

With this, he took his jacket from her, turned and walked towards the entrance to the tower.

Trisha watched him in disgust. Never had she felt so dirty. So used. Tears of shame and humiliation tumbled down her face. *Why did I do it?* She slumped against the wall. Martha's lovely, innocent face came to her. She cringed against the shame the image brought her. How could she explain the disgusting thing she'd just done?

She knew she couldn't. She couldn't go back inside. She would have to walk home and wait and hope that Martha brought her coat and bag so that she had her key.

As she set off, she heard her name being called. Wanting to jump into one of the gardens and hide behind the closed stalls in it, but knowing she would distress an undeserving Martha, she stood still.

'Here, love, I have your coat. Put it on, eh? And I've your handbag too.'

'Oh, Martha!'

Turning into Martha's arms, Trisha couldn't stop the sobs that wracked her body. Martha just patted her back and waited.

'I'm no better than a prostitute, Martha ... Why? Why am I like I am?'

'You're for being a beautiful woman, Trisha. It is that you lost your way for a moment, that's all. No one will ever be for knowing about what happened. Just be forgetting it, eh? It was a wee lapse; we all have them.'

'You knaw what happened?'

'Yes, that pig of a man felt compelled to tell me, so he did. As if it was that he'd made a conquest.'

'He didn't!' Humiliation stung Trisha. 'W – what did he say?'

'Oh, it is of no matter. He is the kind of English pig who is for taking what they want and not bothering who it is that they hurt. It was men like him that took me pappy's land.'

Trisha didn't know what to say. She'd never heard Martha say anything bad about the English, not like she had expected her to. But suddenly she understood, because she felt like rising up and fighting the Ralphs of this world for taking from her too.

'Look, Macie is still for being open. She told me she often works late if there is a do at the tower, so she does. Are you feeling like a nice hot cocoa? Though is it that we should as we are trying to keep it from the neighbours that we've been out?'

'Naw, Macie won't say owt. She's a good 'un. And aye, I am ready for a hot drink ... Martha, well, I'm sorry. I shouldn't have left you. I behaved badly.'

'Maybe the truth is that we shouldn't have come. We were unchaperoned and easy pickings. Though Ricky was the gentleman himself, so he was.'

'You're right. I ain't never been chaperoned, I've allus gone out and done just what I like. I – I hurt me ma a lot for being like that. But I paid for me ways. Bobby only really wanted me for what he could get. When there were consequences, he changed . . . When will I ever learn, Martha?'

Martha didn't answer. Trisha felt this deeply. She had to know what Martha thought of her.

'Do you think me a bad person, Martha, lass?'

'No, of course not. I'm not knowing much about the workings of a man and woman coming together, but whatever magnetism it has is strong in you, Trish, love. You are to fight it if you can. It can only be leading to heartache and sorrow . . . Come on, let's be getting inside.'

When they were in the full glare of Macie's gas lamps Trisha felt Martha pull on her arm.

'Is it a handkerchief you have, Trish? You are in need of tidying up your lipstick before we go in fully.'

Trisha felt her cheeks blush with shame as she wiped her mouth and applied fresh lipstick. 'There, you look respectable again.'

Once inside Macie didn't remark on them being out this late at night, or being all dressed up, but had a lot to say about nothing much at all. This gave Trisha time to recover, so she was grateful for Macie's discretion.

Once they were sat down, her body began to shake with the disgust she felt in her actions.

'Trish, are you thinking there may be consequences this time?'

'Naw! . . . Naw, he said he'd take care.'

'How was he for doing that?'

'I don't knaw, Martha. He didn't seem to do owt that would make me safe . . . Oh, Martha, what am I going to do?'

'Though I don't know about what it is that happens between a man and a woman, I am knowing that having a baby is all to do with your monthly bleeding. We will have to watch closely for yours coming on, Trish. But try not to worry. Men like Ralph are not wanting trouble at their door. Let's forget it, eh?'

Trisha didn't think she would ever forget it, or how it had made her feel. To her, it was as if she had a demon inside of her that she couldn't control – didn't want to control – and it led her to doing what she shouldn't. Trying to change the subject, she asked about Ricky.

'He was the nicest of young men. Afraid of what he had to face by going to France, but sure he was feeling brave enough to. He made me laugh, but it was you he was having his eye on.'

'Me? But why? You're a beauty, Martha, and I'm a plain Jane.'

'Ha, never that. You've an inner magnetism, Trish, you will always be having to fight the men off.'

'Only I don't, do I?'

Martha's hand came across the table and took hold of one of hers. Trisha felt blessed to have such a friend. She wasn't judging her, just being there for her, and somehow that increased the shame she felt. It would have been a relief to have a fight on her hands, even a scratching, punching one, other than to be understood. She didn't feel worthy of being understood. She'd betrayed her ma's upbringing once again. And just as bad, she'd dragged Martha down as she'd be tainted with the same brush if them going to the tower ever got out.

Feeling mortified, she said, 'Shall we go home, Martha?'

'Yes, it is that that is best for us. Would you like to walk a ways?'

'Aye, I would.'

They walked along the dimly lit prom to the sound but not the sight of the lapping sea. The breeze tinged with an icy bite played with their hair and the moon dodged the few clouds to shine a light on their path.

They hadn't gone far when Martha stopped and walked towards the sea wall. She leaned on it and gazed into the distance across the now shimmering water that danced in the reflection of the moon's beam.

'That were a big sigh, Martha, lass.'

'I was for thinking how I would love, at this moment, to jump in and swim all the way to Ireland . . . Home.'

Trisha didn't know what to say for a moment. The statement had devastated her. It seemed that somehow she'd blighted the friendship and now Martha wanted to escape. But suddenly, she turned and grinned. 'But then it would be that I wouldn't have you by me side, and that would make me powerful sad, so it would.'

'Oh, Martha, I thought . . .'

'No, Trish, don't be crying. I'll never be leaving you, I promise. If I swim, then so it is that you will.'

Trisha went into Martha's hug. It felt to her that this was a place of safety. She sent up a prayer. *Please God, don't let me ever lose Martha, and . . . please don't let there be consequences of me action tonight.*

As they separated, Martha said, 'Do you know, I feel that I could walk all the way home. Shall we go and see Arthur and cancel our cab?'

'Aye, I'd like that. And I have me slippers for the last bit . . . Will you come into mine for a while, lass?'

'Yes, I'd be loving that.'

As they walked arm in arm, Martha said, 'Wasn't the ballroom grand? One day I am wanting to go back, but on the arm of the man I fall in love with, as I am seeing it as a place of romance.'

'Me too, unfortunately.'

Martha laughed out loud. Trisha suddenly saw the funny side of everything and laughed with her. She'd done wrong, she knew that, but she couldn't dwell on it for ever.

With the laughter and this thought, she cheered up and forgave herself. It was a slip and that was that.

They giggled when they got to within a street of home and Trisha stopped to put her slippers on. 'Eeh, the cold comes through the thin soles. We'll have to shift ourselves or they may stick to the ice.'

When they got in Trisha was glad to see the embers glowing in the hearth. The room felt warm and welcoming. 'Thou knaws, I haven't put up a single leaf of holly, let alone streamers. It just don't feel like Christmas.'

'But it is the day after tomorrow. Is it that you have some streamers?'

'Aye, they're in a box under me bed. I'll go and get them. And I tell you what else I have. A little sherry left from what I put in me Christmas pud . . . I don't knaw why I made one, but it were like it gave me hope that all would be normal again by Christmas.'

'You mean, Bobby coming home?'

'Aye. Part of me don't like the thought of him, or any of our lads, spending Christmas in them trenches that they tell us about in the news. But he don't even talk of having any leave on the rare occasions I receive post.' She sighed as she went to the stair's door. 'Anyroad, it's Christmas and it don't feel like it is. I won't be a mo.'

When she came down, Martha gave her a quizzical look. 'Are you thinking we can put streamers up looking like this?'

'Ha, I forgot. Naw, I'll go and get changed.'

'And I'll look in on me granny and let her know it is that we are home and get meself changed too.'

When she returned, Martha had two sweet tarts with her. 'I made these a couple of days ago. Sure, they are a Christmas treat – shrid pies, we call them.'

'Well, they look like mince pies to me. I've never heard of a shrid pie.'

'Yes, I have heard them called that too, but always me mammy called them shrid pies.'

'Well, it ain't naw matter, I'm sure they'll taste delicious. So, are you up for a drop of sherry to go with them? Only we can't have either till we've the decorations up.'

With the room looking lovely, its walls hung with paper-chains and dangling tinsel, they tucked into their pies around a now roaring fire.

Trisha laughed to see Martha timidly take a sip of sherry, and then shudder and squeeze her eyes tightly.

'Ooh, I'm sure it's a drop of the good stuff as me pappy used to call all liquors, but it isn't for me. It makes me want to cough. I'll have a cup of tea any day of the week, so I will.'

'Eeh, Martha, you get used to it, you knaw. Try another sip.'

'No. It isn't the killjoy that I am, but I think if I do, I'll be sick. I'll put the kettle on.'

'Go on then. And make me one an' all. I can't say as I like it, but then, it is cooking sherry.'

They giggled at this.

When Martha disappeared through to the scullery, Trisha looked around her. It seemed to her that even her own home was alien to her. As if she was a different person to the girl who'd been so excited to go to the tower ballroom. Her eyes fell on her knitting. A grey sock protruded from the four needles. Somehow, it increased her sense of guilt as it symbolised what Bobby was doing at this moment. For all the anger that still burned in her against him, she wasn't without guilt at what had happened where he was concerned. No matter what, he was her husband.

The sock had reminded her that reports had been of heavy rain and of the men ankle-deep in mud. *How I wish I could dry your feet for you, Bobby, lad. I'd rub them till they were warm and toasty.*

A feeling came to her of love – not the true love that should be between a man and a woman; Bobby had killed that when he'd killed their child. But that didn't mean that everything that had happened between them meant nothing to her. It was as if he could be a good friend now, with how hard he had tried to make amends.

And she had to admit that before she became pregnant, Bobby's lovemaking had been nice. She'd enjoyed it and wanted it, but it didn't compare to what Ralph did to her.

The self-assured Ralph, who knew exactly where to touch her, who had initially made her feel like she mattered. That he wasn't after a quick grope. He'd taken his time and awoken feelings in her.

Shaking herself, she made herself think of the awful way he had treated her afterwards and forced him down in her estimation. But try as she might to do this, she did have an ache in her heart to see him again and to have him touch her, hold her and . . . yes, to make love to her again. And she knew that if ever the chance did come, she would take it with both hands.

These thoughts weren't comfortable ones, but she couldn't deny the feelings they gave her.

'Oh, it is sorry I am. Did I make you jump?'

'Ha, naw . . . Well, I was off inside me head as me da used to allus say I do . . . Anyroad, I'm ready for that cuppa. I should have made you one as soon as we got in, it would have thawed us out a bit.'

'Your antics with bringing Christmas alive did that, love, so don't be worrying . . . So, is it ready you're feeling to have a good Christmas celebration? We could be having it together.'

'That would be lovely. I knaw we ain't spoke much about it, but I ain't been bothered till now . . . Aye, let's make it a good one, eh? Well, as good as our rations will allow. I've nowt in for it, mind. Well, except for me pudding.'

'Don't be worrying, I put an order into Mrs Philpot yesterday. I was for hoping you would join us so bought enough for you too.'

'Aw, that's kind of you, ta.'

'No, it will be making our Christmas too, as it was that we were not wanting to celebrate with this being our first without . . .'

Trisha knew that for Martha to say their names was too painful, so she thought to say something to make Martha feel better. 'I knaw, love. But in a way, it's like honouring your mammy and pappy, and me doing so for me ma and da that we are carrying on with the traditions they handed down to us.'

'That's a powerful good way to look at it. Thanks, me darling . . . So, I've ordered a beef from the butcher in town. It'll come tomorrow and it is that I planned on putting it in a low oven for a few hours tomorrow evening. And I have spuds and sprouts coming. And Granny makes a gravy that is to die for from the meat juices . . . Ooh, it is that it's going to be a lovely day and a lovely meal . . . Only, would you be after coming to midnight mass with me tomorrow night?'

'I would, Martha, and I'll be glad to. I can pray for me soul then.'

'Oh, Trish, you don't have to do that . . . I'll tell you what, it'll be better coming from me, so it will. I can ask that you be forgiven for your sins, and you can ask that I am for mine.'

'Ha, you daft ha'peth, I doubt you've a sin on your soul.

But yes, I'd like to come. And we needn't creep out either. I can tell that nosy old Mrs Higginbottom where we're going, so she'll be satisfied I'm being a good girl.'

When they were sat in St John's Church in town, Trisha looked up at the Holy Mother of God statue. In her face she thought she saw an understanding, that she wasn't condemning her, and this made her feel better.

Father O'Leary brought her attention to him as he waved the incense about, causing a right stink, and chanted prayers and she thought, *Now, there's a sinner if ever I saw one, the randy sod.*

This made her giggle – with relief as much as anything, as she was just a girl really, coping with a lot and, yes, she'd fallen by the wayside, as this lot called it, but him? *What is he then? He's the devil in holy clothing, that's what.*

These thoughts cheered her. She wasn't as bad as she was painting herself. At least she wasn't a hypocrite. She knew herself and wasn't pretending to be what she wasn't. She knew that if Ralph called tonight, she would go into his arms willingly. She wished it wasn't that way, but it was.

She looked heavenward and her usual humour came to her. *Don't blame me, you made me in your own likeness, or so this lot would have me believe. Well, you reap what you sow, mate.*

A giggle did escape her then. She felt eyes on her. Martha's in particular. But she couldn't stop herself. It was then that the giggle turned to a sob.

Martha's arm came around her and she leaned into her. She may have lost all those she loved dearly, but she'd found Martha – the best friend ever.

PART TWO

Consequences

ELEVEN

Martha

Martha sat on her step. The spring weather was pleasant, and she'd relished a little time on her own in the peace of the morning before the day broke fully and she and Granny would have to get to the prom.

A year had passed since they had arrived in Blackpool – the first anniversaries of birthdays, Christmas, and even the last time her mammy had held her in her arms had now passed. They say the first ones are always the worst, but she wondered if this pain in her heart would ever lessen.

Such a lot had happened in that time and now it felt as though more changes had taken place. Especially in her friendship with Trisha. Trisha had become secretive. She knew why, but it hurt badly that it was so.

And then there was how Granny passed more and more of the reading of the tarot cards over to her, and lately, the fortune telling too, when she told a person's future just by holding their hand – an experience that left her drained, and she still hated. Most especially when she saw something bad.

Still, it did bring in more money as they had a second tent right next to the first one now, and so the queues were kept moving, and at last they were able to keep the wolves from the door.

Once Christmas had passed, the winter had been difficult. But now those wishing to get some respite at the seaside were flocking back to Blackpool and Martha hoped to make enough to stash some away this year, as she didn't like the times when they had eaten meatless stew, and only had chunks of homemade dry bread to go with it. Granny loved her little bit of dripping on her crust, but even that had been scarce without the meats to roast and so to catch the fat from.

Thank goodness things were picking up, though, and with a good summer to go at, she determined they would be better off for next winter.

So deep in thought was she that she didn't hear Trisha's door open and jumped when she said hello. Part of her was embarrassed to look up as she knew Trisha's secret but didn't want to show she did.

It had been two days after Christmas that she'd been woken by a noise. Going to the window, she'd looked out and had seen the light from Trisha's open door splash across the pavement. A figure had come out of the darkness and slipped inside. Martha had spent the next half an hour with her pillow over her head trying to block out the moans and cries that came through the wall.

Though it had never been spoken of, it had hung

between them. Now, Trisha had a rounded stomach and always looked as though she'd been crying.

Martha's heart went out to her when she looked up at her. Once more her face looked haggard with the tears she'd shed. Patting the step, Martha sighed. 'Are you ever going to share with me, Trish?'

'Eeh, I've nowt to share, lass. I've been crying for me ma and me babby, that's all. It's a year since . . . And I had a letter from Bobby an' all.'

Martha sighed. It needed to be out in the open. The strain on them both was bad, but on Trisha, it must be terrible.

'Trish, I know it is for being more than that troubling you . . . It is that I am your friend and am here for you, me darling.'

Trish burst into tears and ran inside.

Getting up, Martha ran after her. 'Oh, Trish, is it that you are in trouble . . . the family way?'

Trish collapsed in a heap of sobs onto the sofa.

Running to her, Martha gathered her up. 'Why is it you've kept it from me? Oh, Trish, this is for being too big a burden to carry on your own.'

'What am I going to do? He said he would be careful.'

'And was he? Is it that he was careful when he visited you?'

Trisha went quiet. When she looked up, she said, 'You knew?'

'Yes, I heard and saw him, and heard what went on between you . . . Oh, Trish, me heart goes out to you, so it does. How was it he found your address?'

'Someone ... passed me a note on me stall ... It were when we were clearing down on Christmas Eve. It was from him. He begged me forgiveness and told me that they had been delayed in sailing and were to go the next week. He ... he said he loved me and could he visit me at me home ... I wrote me address down ... He said he loved me, Martha, he said he'd take me away from all this and I would live in clover with him.'

'Oh, Trish, it's sorry I am.'

'It ... it was as if he was giving me a way out of years and years of trying me best to be a good wife to Bobby – of being afraid of being homeless if I left him ... Not that I couldn't live with Bobby if I have to. It ain't like he means nowt to me. It's just that I have came to knaw I do love Bobby, but like a brother ... I – I thought meself in love with Ralph ... but I ain't heard a word from him since ... Oh, Martha, what am I to do?'

Martha had a fleeting thought that it was a bit late to think like that now, but she would never say such a thing. She wanted to ask too how Trisha could do such a stupid thing and be taken in, but she knew it wasn't her place to judge. She had known this would happen and hadn't tried to stop it. She shuddered as more came to her of what would come down on Trisha and she decided that for once she was going to go against her granny.

'It is that you must go away, Trish. You cannot be here when Bobby returns.'

'What? What are you saying, Martha? ... Martha, why are you looking like that? What have you seen? ... Martha?'

Martha shuddered again. The tremble brought her to her

senses. 'I – I'm sorry, Trish, I shouldn't have said that. I haven't seen anything . . . You mustn't be afraid or go away.'

'But I'll be hounded from the street! Oh, if only Bobby would have come home on leave, I could have made it look like it was his!'

Martha saw how her own words had shocked Trisha. A tear fell onto her cheek.

'That's a terrible thing for me to say, ain't it? Deceitful and unfair! Oh, why am I so evil, Martha?'

Martha cradled her to her. 'You're not evil, me darling. You were cruelly duped, and you fell for it. It is that the men can then disappear having had what they craved. But for you, you are stuck with the consequences. I will protect you, Trish.'

But even as she said it, Martha didn't know how.

'I – I had an idea last night. I thought to put it about that I weren't well and then make it look as though I was going into a clinic or sommat, but take meself to the nuns . . . but, eeh, Martha, I can't bear to lose me babby. Not another one, I can't.'

'Let's think about it for a while. It is that there must be a solution. But it isn't that you will have to be giving your babby up. We can go somewhere together . . . Granny would be willing to come, she is for doing anything that makes me happy. But, Trish, you must be strong, me darling. Your babby needs you to be eating well and looking after yourself, for in doing so you are looking after her.'

'Her? Am I having a girl?'

'Yes, I think it is a girl. I have seen her this good while. She will have dark hair and be strong in character. It is the daughter I was telling you of. She will be brave and will make you proud, and then she will give you those grandchildren we giggled over.'

'Oh, Martha, I love her so much already and I'll be here for her, no matter what I have to go through . . . This were me own doing. I don't knaw what it is that drives me, but I can't say naw . . . Don't look like that, Martha. It'll be all right . . . I once heard Bridie say to you that you can't change people's destiny. Well, this is mine, Martha, and I'm going to face it no matter what.'

'Oh, Trish. It is that I'll be with you every step of the way, I promise.'

'I knaw that as a given, lass. I've known it since we first met. You were like a light coming on in me life that awful day. But now, I'm a burden because of me ways. What is it that drives me to want to be loved by a man?'

'It is that you were lonely, me darling. You had lost so much, and it is that you wanted to replace it all. It's not for being your fault, Trish, it is the fault of those who sense this and prey on it.'

'I can't ever see it happening again, as now I have me little babby to love and her to love me. But, you knaw, this is why I can't like God. Why couldn't He have seen to it that it was Bobby who gave me a babby? What does He have against me?'

'Don't blame God, Trish. That will make you a bitter person. Don't blame anyone. You're human and it is as I say, you needed a love of your own after so much being taken from you.'

'Ha, I'm like everyone, nothing's our fault. Well, I reckon I do have to take this one as mine. But, eeh, Martha, I'm scared of what Bobby will do when he comes home to find a babby that can't possibly be his. And him going through what he is an' all.'

Martha closed her eyes then opened them before any more could be revealed to her. She didn't want details, it was hard enough knowing what she did, but now Trisha knew too, and was willing to face up to it, so there was nothing more to be done.

To her relief, with this thought, all the visions left her. Maybe it was like that once a person had taken charge of their own destiny and it was no longer her responsibility. She would ask Granny, but she hoped so with all her heart.

Changing the subject, she said, 'Well, it is that we will have to be getting to work, love. Are you going in today?'

'Aye, I'll be driven mad staying here . . . Eeh, look at the time! I should be there by now. I'll grab me coat and get off. I'll see you later when you arrive, eh?'

Seeing it was nine-thirty shocked Martha. Where had the last hour and a half gone?

Dashing back inside, she found Granny sitting with her coat on. Granny didn't ask where or why, but just said, 'Is it sorted with Trisha, me darling?'

'It is, Granny.'

'It'll be a wee girl she'll be having.'

'I know.'

'And a whole lot more. Did you tell her?'

'I did. Not details, I haven't let those in, I just know it is for being bad. Trish wants to face it all, so I have to be accepting of that.'

'Didn't I tell you that? Now, you must let it go. Sure, you've done all you can be doing.'

'It has gone, Granny. And I wanted to ask, can that happen when it is someone who is so close?'

'It can and has to be. If you are for delving into everything, you will be driven mad. Now, let us walk as far as the tram for it is that you need to clear your head and your heart to be allowing those spirits who will come to you today to have a clear road. It is that you are doing well, me wee Martha. Your granny is proud of you.'

Granny reached out and took her hand. When she held it, Martha felt a strength come into her that helped her to cope.

The walk to the prom was pleasant with greetings being called out from many a housewife as they scrubbed their steps and swept the pavement in front of their houses, before throwing their buckets of suds over the slabs and brushing the water away.

Everywhere had a clean fresh smell, tinged with the salt of the sea brought in by the light breeze.

A kaleidoscope of colour made the morning cheerful – all the curtains were part of this, as the winter heavies had been taken down and replaced by bright cotton, looking crisp and clean. Daffodils were dying off, but the odd one defiantly stood proud adding a dazzling yellow here and there and many bushes were in bloom.

Martha took a deep breath of the air that blew over from her precious Ireland and knew a peace to settle in her. Everything was right again with her and Trisha, and that made her happy.

Though she couldn't understand Trisha's need as she hadn't felt anything like it herself. She sometimes wondered if she was meant for marrying as it seemed most girls she saw of their own standing in life were with a boyfriend or were likely to giggle at the attention of the boys.

It wasn't that they didn't find her attractive, though she had thought a lot about Ricky and how he felt the loss of not being chosen by Trisha but just wanted to chat in a matey way with herself. Maybe it was the different vibes she and Trisha gave off. She just didn't know.

'You're very quiet, me wee girl. Are you still holding on to what you know is in store for Trisha?'

'No, Granny. It is that I am wondering what drives her when I don't see meself feeling how she does.'

'We're all different. Sure, the world would be a boring place if we weren't. What we've been through shapes us . . . Oh, will you look, it is dawdling that we are and the tram is coming!'

Granny suddenly put on a spurt and dashed into the road.

Martha's world changed in that split second. From contemplating, she was catapulted into a world of screams and of horses' screeching neighs as terror struck them. Of a crashing of metal and wood as the carriage they pulled upended, throwing their passengers hollering in fear to the ground. And, worse than all, seeing her granny's twisted body not moving, but leaking blood over the tarmac.

No sound came from Martha and yet she knew she had her mouth open. It was as if in that second she had frozen as before her she watched horses struggling to right themselves amidst a scene of bloodied bodies and the sound of moans of pain.

'Eeh, lass. I saw it all. Come on now, we have to help the injured.' Martha looked at the man who had spoken but couldn't respond.

Another voice came to her. 'I'll get the horses free, Arthur. Poor buggers are trapped with the cart being hitched to them.'

Then there were more people around and Martha became aware that the tram had stopped and folk were piling off of it. A woman's arms came around her. 'You're all right, lass, I've got you. Is the lady a relation?'

Martha nodded. 'Me . . . granny.' It was then that all feeling and knowledge came back into Martha and she heard her own voice screaming for her granny, felt arms holding her tightly, heard the man who was bending over Granny say, 'She's gone, lass, I'm sorry.'

'No . . . no! Granny! Granny!'

'Let her go to her, Missus, she needs to be with her granny.'

It felt to Martha that she floated then and, as she did, she heard her granny's voice. *Thank the Lord for not letting us know our own destiny, me wee darling. But I am for going now. It is that me spirit'll always be by your side, but the pull on me soul is too strong for me to stay with you.*

'Granny, no.' Sobs cut into her voice. 'Granny . . . don't leave . . . me.'

But as she cried this, Martha knew she had.

Above her she saw a beautiful light. It hovered and then floated away. 'Granny . . . Granny!'

But then tinny bells sounded, and the vision was gone.

'Come on, lass. We'll take care of her.'

Looking up, Martha looked into the kindly eyes of a gentleman with a uniform on.

'I'm the ambulance driver, lass. We'll take your granny for the doctors to look at and to certify. She'll be in the morgue, lass, but she'll be all right, as you saw her go to heaven, didn't you? This will only be her earthly body. But we will give it all the respect she deserved.'

'Ta . . . but what will I do?'

'You can come if you like and hold your granny's hand. I think she will see that and like that she isn't going alone.'

He helped Martha up. She looked around. Everyone was being attended to, and the bloodied scene was surrounded by ambulances and policemen. 'Is it that everyone's going to be all right? Granny wouldn't like to hurt others, or to cause the end of their lives.'

'Some are badly injured from what I can see, but none have copped it, lass. I take it that your granny ran out in front of the carriage?'

'Yes. She was seeing the tram and dashed out . . . Tell them all I am sorry, and I know it is that me granny would be mortified.'

'I will. Your granny was an old lady. She wouldn't have the quickness of thought that she was born with, lass. No one will blame her. They will all be sad that this caused her end.'

This was borne out three days later when Martha stood with Trisha at the graveside. A tap came on her shoulder and the ambulance man stood there. 'I have these for you, lass. They're notes of condolences from all the passengers and the driver.'

It was later when she and Trisha sat together on the step that they read the notes. Everyone said that she mustn't feel any guilt about them being injured and each gave updates on how they were and most were recovering well. All asked after herself, which she thought was lovely. And the driver even gave her a report on the horses, telling her that they were none the worse for their experience, that Reenie was a little shy of going out now, but was improving all the time, and Ronnie was just as sprightly as ever.

'Oh, Trish, how kind folk can be.'

'That's Lancashire folk for you, lass. They care for one another, and not about themselves. So, now you've to stop worrying about them all as this is what they want for you – to concentrate on sorting yourself out and to be all right.'

'I will be, Trish. I feel that me granny is happy and is with me mammy and me pappy, but oh, Trish, but for you, I feel so alone.'

Trisha sighed. 'I knaw the feeling, lass. Though with me little Sally growing inside me, I feel less so.'

'You're to call her Sally? What was giving you that name?'

'I was thinking of some of me Granny Pat's sayings, and it came to me that she had a best friend called Sally – well, Sarah, but everyone called her Sally. She was killed one day when she was going to the biscuit factory where they both worked at the time. Me Granny Pat never forgot her, so I was thinking I would honour her with calling me babby her name.'

'It is a lovely name, so it is. And just right for the girl she is to become . . . I see her differently now that she is in the making, Trish. I see a happy, singing and dancing girl.'

'Ooh, that's lovely, lass. I did worry about the "brave" prediction. I was thinking that I'd be out of me wits while she was off being brave.'

They both laughed. Something Martha didn't think she would do again, but suddenly she knew that she could, and she knew too that the brave girl she'd imagined would exist, but she didn't know who she would belong to.

Trisha found her hand and squeezed it. 'Laughing is very near to crying, lass. You can cry whenever you need to and I'll cry with you, as we have a lot to cry about, you and me.'

Martha nodded. The action spilled her tears, but she found comfort with her head on Trisha's shoulder and knew she always would.

TWELVE

Trisha

Trisha was shocked out of the hug by the sight of her mother-in-law, who she saw as little of as possible, striding down the street. Her voice boomed out, 'You hussy, you! Me lad's out there doing his bit, and you're putting yourself about like a common prostitute. Look at you with your belly up and it ain't naw grandchild of mine!'

The neighbour's door opened, and Mrs Higginbottom stood there, arms folded, head nodding. 'Don't try to deny it, my girl, anyone can see as you're carrying a bastard.'

'She's a slut!' Ma-in-law's screams brought out those neighbours who weren't already gawping. Some, wanting a better view, crossed the road to stand by the grass mound that led up to the railway line.

Before Trisha could take in all that was happening, Ma-in-law leapt at her and grabbed her hair. To lessen the pain, Trisha got to her feet but could do nothing about the onslaught of words spat at her.

'Look! Look at her! She ain't far off being six months having a young 'un, if the size of her belly is owt to go by, and me lad's been gone to war eleven months!'

Trisha tried to wriggle free from the tugging of her hair and the unbearable pain it inflicted on her.

'Eeh, Mrs Rathbone, let her go. You're hurting the girl.' Edna seemed the only one willing to stand up for her against this tyrant of a woman. Poor Martha just sat there looking shocked and as if she would break.

Seeing this gave Trisha strength. She yanked her head away, standing the pain until she was free.

She didn't know where it came from, but a lie escaped her tongue. 'I was raped!'

All the muttering voices and knowing nods came to a halt. Feeling she had the upper hand, Trisha looked around her. 'I knaw for some of you that still clothes me in shame, but it weren't my fault! He was strong. He grabbed me when I were walking home from work on me own and pulled me into one of the alleys. I couldn't even see his face ...' She began to sob as the lie seemed to become a truth. 'He stank! He ... he was too big for me to fight off ...' With tears now mingling with her snot and her mouth slack, she looked around at all the women once more. All looked uncomfortable. One shouted, 'Why didn't you go to the cops then?'

'They wouldn't have believed me. A lass on her own, whose man's away ... Ha, they'd have done nowt! Well, now I live in fear of the consequences every day. Afraid to face you lot as you're already being judge and jury. Look at you! You look like a lynch mob!'

None of them spoke, just stared at her. Martha stood. Trisha felt her arms come around her, then Edna stepped forward. 'Come on, lass, let's get you inside.'

But as they were almost over the step, Edna turned on Mrs Rathbone. 'And you, Mrs Rathbone, who can't even be bothered to check up on your own daughter-in-law but relies on tales from that nosy old cow' – she nodded towards Mrs Higginbottom – 'can piss off back to your own end. We don't like the likes of you around here.'

The mumblings began again, only this time they were more favourable to Trisha. Mrs Higginbottom did one of her famous humph noises and went inside. Ma-in-law calmed a bit as she crossed her arms. 'Aye, well, that puts a bit of a different light on things, but me lad'll have to knaw.'

Trisha swivelled round. 'Why, eh? Why upset him when he has a lot to put up with?'

'Well, it depends. Are you going to get rid of it, eh? If you are, then he can knaw when he comes home, but I ain't having him returning to the shock of another man's babby in his home without him knowing about it first.'

'You'll do what you want to in the long run anyroad. I don't care. I've lost one babby and I ain't losing another.'

With this, Edna and Martha pulled her inside and shut the door.

Shaking from head to toe, Trisha allowed them to lead her to the sofa.

'I'll put the kettle on, lass. Have you got any sugar, Trisha? You need a hot sweet drink; you've had a shock.'

'Aye, there's some in the tin next to the caddy. Ta, Edna.'

Sinking into the sofa, she found herself in Martha's arms. Thank God for Martha.

'You did well, me darling.' Martha whispered the words. 'You've given yourself a solution, so you have. At least it is that the neighbours won't hound you out.'

'I'm not sure, Martha. They still might. Not many folk believe there's such a thing as rape.'

Edna came back into the room then and what she said seemed to give a truth to this.

'Well, now, lass. Get this down you . . . You knaw, I've been thinking, are you sure you wanted to fight him off?'

'Of course it is that she's sure! What is it you think happened, Edna? You of all people. You are knowing Trish better than anyone, and yet you are asking her that!'

'Eeh, I'm sorry, lass. I shouldn't have. It's just hard to imagine and well, we haven't seen any signs of you having been in a tussle.'

Trisha's heart sank. 'I – I . . .'

'I cleaned her up. She came to me and Granny. She was all muddied and was for having bruises on the inside of her thighs and some on her upper arms. Granny tended to them, so she did. And as it was winter you were only seeing Trisha with her coat on, so it is that you wouldn't see these marks.'

'I'm sorry, Trisha.'

'And so it is that you should be. Trish counts you as a friend. We should be able to rely on our friends.'

'It's all right, Martha . . . I understand what Edna's thinking.' Turning to Edna, she said, 'But please believe me, Edna.

I haven't been anywhere except to work; how could I have messed around with someone? I wouldn't anyway.'

Trisha breathed a sigh of relief when Edna showed no sign of contradicting this. It seemed she hadn't heard anything untoward and hadn't realised that she and Martha had been out the night they went to the tower.

She began to relax. With Edna on her side the whole street might come round to thinking this wasn't her fault and feel sorry for her rather than condemn her, as she knew she deserved.

'Well, lass, I'm sorry to the heart of me for your plight. But, if you don't want this to come back at you down the years, I would think about going into one of them convents and giving the babby away. It can bring nowt but heartache and trouble to your door.'

'I can't do that, Edna. If I have to choose between me babby and Bobby, then it'll be me babby.'

'Think about it, lass. You can have more babbies with Bobby when he comes home. And how are you going to live seeing it every day and knowing what happened to you, eh? I knaw I couldn't.'

Martha spoke, saving Trisha having to, as she felt if she did, she would tear into Edna.

'It is that I think you shouldn't be saying such things about an innocent baby, Edna. The child is not responsible for how she got into her mammy's womb. She will need love and care, just like any other child, and she will give joy in return.'

'By, you have it down as a girl already then? Well, it's a pity you couldn't have predicted this happening and warned poor Trisha, that's all I'm saying. And now, if you're the friend you say you are, you should be helping her to get rid of it! I'll go now. I've said me piece and if you won't listen, Trisha . . . well, on your head be it!'

As the door slammed behind Edna, Trisha felt herself collapsing inwardly. Martha caught her. 'It is that you must be strong, Trish. Brave it out. Carry on as if all you have said is the truth. Then folk will come to thinking your story true and will be gathering around you to stand in your corner.'

'They won't, Martha. I can feel this is going to be bad, but I'm ready. We knew there would be trouble, didn't we? Well, it has started. But at least I have you.'

It was two days later when Trisha had a visitor at her stall. Her boss came to call.

'Well now, Trisha, I have been hearing tales about you. I will thank you to leave my employ forthwith.'

'You're sacking me? Naw, why? I need the money. I haven't done owt wrong.'

'That's not what I've heard. I'm a chapel-going man, and we don't like sinners.'

'Oh? And I thought sinners were your business, you hypocrite!'

'Go on, get off out of it. I don't want any trouble.'

Grabbing her bag, Trisha held back the tears as she pulled her cardi around her and hurried away, not daring to ask for her wages as she felt she would claw the sanctimonious face off him.

Not feeling like going home, she went across the road and down the slope to the sand. The sea was calm today and looked like a blue oasis. For a moment she felt like walking into it and not stopping till it got deep enough to swim and then to swim and swim till she could do so no more. But the thought of drowning her baby too stopped her.

She sat down on the sand. Warmed by the sun, it spread out and accepted her like a mother's arms would. She didn't try to stop the tears.

Around her a few children played and mothers sat gossiping away. She wanted to be like them, they looked as though they hadn't a care in the world, but she knew that wasn't so. They were all of the age that would mean their men were at war. That was the thing these days – no babies, or very few. No pregnant mums to be seen. For some this would be a welcome respite, but for her it wasn't. Why did she need the feeling of making love so much? But then, that feeling had gone now and she hoped it would never come back.

A voice interrupted her thoughts. 'Get your donkey rides. Come on and gee up a donkey.'

This brought a smile to Trisha's face. No matter what, Blackpool never changed. Everything was up and running again as if there'd never been a winter.

It had been the winter months that had put her behind with everything. With this thought her worries piled in on her.

She'd thought the money the government allowed her was plenty, but she'd found with having to buy more coal and use more gas that it was barely enough. Now, she was faced with having no wages again as no one would consider taking on a pregnant woman.

'Wouldn't you like a donkey ride, missus?' This was said on a laugh.

Trisha looked up at Benny. 'Naw, I don't, ta, very much. You weren't for buying me rock off me stall, were you?'

'Naw, I don't like rock. So, why ain't you there now then, eh?'

'I've been sacked for sinning.'

'Oh, your belly being up, you mean? How did that happen then?'

'It was the immaculate conception all over again, that's how.'

Benny burst out laughing. 'You should be on the stage, Trisha, you allus make everyone laugh . . . Oh, well, it's your own business, I guess. But look, you're a strong lass, how about you help me out, eh?'

'What do you mean?'

'I've got arthritis, and it gives me gyp. I could do with working just mornings. I make enough, but I don't like letting the children down with the busy season almost on us. What do you reckon, eh?'

Trisha stood. 'Are you sure? Eeh, Benny, you'd be the saving of me. And I'm not set to have me little one till September, so I could put a good season in.'

'Right. You'll do me. Why don't you work alongside me now? I can show you the safety measures we take, and talk you through the different characters. Come and talk to the donkeys and see how you get along with them. They're all wise, you knaw.'

'Ha, I am sure they are.'

'Well, that's a good start. You must like and respect the donkeys to be able to get along with them, Trisha.'

'I do like them. They're lovely. And I can see in their faces that they all have different ways with them. I shouldn't have said that.'

As the afternoon wore on, Trisha found that she was coming to love the donkeys and felt that they loved her too. It was a nice feeling. And she did find they all had different personalities and wisdom.

Shelley was gentle with the timid children, and Horace liked those who didn't mind him galloping. He seemed to love to hear them giggle and cry out with glee. Trisha could have sworn that he smiled after giving an adventurous child a ride.

Then there was Daisy, the granny of the troupe. She was lazy and often refused to budge no matter how you tried to coax her. And Lucy, the unpredictable one who could suddenly rear and seem to be very cross, but you could almost see her laughing as the kids looked scared. And lastly, Billy, the playful one. He was a proper boy as he showed when he lifted a lady's skirt up. The lady in question wasn't at all pleased and Benny had to give her children a free ride to make up for it, while Billy plonked himself down on the sand and looked pleased with himself. Trisha felt a special liking for him. He had the devil in him, a bit like she did herself. When on her own for a few minutes she told him, 'That attitude won't get you anywhere, Billy. Look what being a rebel has done for me.'

As if he understood, Billy nuzzled her tummy, only his strength was such that he made her step backwards in a hurry. She slipped and fell.

Benny leapt forward. 'He didn't mean owt, lass. He has a rough way of showing his affection. Are you, all right?'

'Aye, just me pride's hurt. I'll be fine.'

'It won't put you off, will it? Only the donkeys have taken to you, I can tell that, and you're good with the kids. I reckon if you'll do afternoons for me, I could rest up. Though I won't leave the beach. I'll sit in me chair over there and have a nod, then you can wake me if you need a break or if it gets really busy.'

'It ain't put me off, I'm loving it. I've often watched you working, Benny, and thought it must be boring, but it ain't.'

'Well then, I'll give you a quarter of everything you take. It'll be a good wage on some days, but not so good on a wet day. But then you don't do owt, so that's fair.'

'It ain't, I'd still turn up and have to stand about in the rain.'

'All right then. A couple of bob on the days you can't earn much, guaranteed. But that's all I can run to.'

'I'll give it a go. There ain't many afternoons in the summer that I don't see you working. The kids like to be entertained no matter what the weather, so I reckon I could manage that. But come August, it might be too much for me, so you'll have to look for someone else then.'

'The lads'll be out of school then so I can allus get someone. Right, you're on. Do you want to start tomorrow?'

'Aye, that suits me. I'll be here at one o'clock.'

'Good. Sundays off as I ain't got a licence for Sunday trading, but six days a week otherwise.'

'Aye, I knaw the terms of working on the prom and the beach. I'll see you tomorrow then, eh?'

As she walked off, Trisha could have jumped for joy. She knew she was going to love working the donkeys much more than standing on the rock stall, and she'd come earlier than one o'clock to work and have her snack with Martha, so it wouldn't seem as if anything had changed.

THIRTEEN

Martha

Some days, it seemed to Martha, were endless as she sat in her tent seeing one client after another, having their lives pass through her but not touching her. And yet, never feeling her own close ones. Not her mammy or pappy, or even her granny, who she felt sure would try to keep close to her and be there for her. She missed her granny so much. But it seemed to her that after suffering the grief of losing her mammy and pappy, nothing could hurt her so deeply again.

Now the year had ambled along – already they were halfway through September, business had slowed, and more trouble loomed as on top of her sadness was the worry of possibly losing her home. More than one in the street had remarked that it wasn't right for a single person to live in a two-bedroomed house when families needed them more.

With worries like this, Martha felt it deeply that there was no Trisha to call out telling her she'd a few moments and would be fetching them a cuppa from the café, or to have a natter to. All of that had to wait for midday when the promenade went quiet. Then Trisha would meet her by the wall opposite and they could chat.

Sighing, Martha tried to put her worries to one side. Surely, the landlady wouldn't evict her on the gossip of others? Not when she was paying her rent regularly?

But then a happier thought came to her as the hours of sewing for Trisha's new baby had given her so much help with coping with her loss, and with the loneliness that often crowded her when her door was closed to the world for the night.

Not that she always worked alone. She and Trisha spent a lot of time together, laughing and chatting as she sewed hems and intricately embroidered bodices and Trisha knitted a shawl, matinee jackets and little booties – no more socks. And, best of all, and what had kept Martha going when she'd gone back to her own home at the end of an evening, had been the creation of the christening gown that was Martha's pride and joy and a surprise she was planning for Trisha.

All of this had rekindled the idea of them going into business making layettes, and this had given Martha hope that her future needn't lie in fortune telling, which she still didn't like doing.

Sighing, she gathered the tarot cards and stacked them to one side of her table before emptying out her pot of money to count. Not many had crossed her palm with silver this morning – most of the coins were copper and didn't add up to much. But this was down to the time of year. The rich were leaving their summer homes and the boarding houses to prepare for the winter season in London and most of her trade now was folk just wanting a laugh and not taking anything that she said as serious.

This morning, one customer – a cockney woman who had been proud to announce she had been born and bred in the East End of London, and had made good running a market stall – had even remarked on her being so young.

'How come yer think yer can tell fortunes at your age, eh? You're barely out of nappies!'

This last had been said on a smirk, which Martha soon changed as she'd told her, 'Soon it won't matter to you how old anyone is for you won't be long of this world.'

She'd regretted the words the moment she'd said them and had almost heard Granny's voice thick with disdain for such an action.

'What? What the bleedin' hell are yer saying, girl?' The woman had leapt from her seat, horror and fear etched on her face. 'I come 'ere to escape London for just a couple of days and you tell me that!'

Martha quickly took the words back, feeling remorse as she saw the devastation she'd caused to the woman. 'I am mistaken. I – I became confused with the way you were ridiculing me. I'm sorry. It is Blackpool that you won't be long in, not life itself,' she'd told her.

The woman had scoffed, chucked a farthing on the table and stormed out.

Martha's head ached with going over the incident in her mind, and her body shuddered at the truth of what she'd told the poor woman.

Pulling the strings tight on her purse, she prepared to leave the tent but before she could get to the flap it opened and a young man stood in the doorway. His face showed his anguish and his clothes his poverty. As he looked at her, his whole body seemed to shake with the effort of standing. Martha knew her own body to tremble as the knowledge zinged through her that this man would play a huge part in her life. That their destinies were entwined.

Recovering, she asked, 'Can I be helping you?'

'I need you to hand me your purse.'

Shocked, Martha stared at him. An understanding of his plight came to her and sorrow filled her heart. 'Is it hungry that you are?'

He leaned forward and grabbed the back of her visitor chair. Martha instinctively moved towards him and caught hold of his arm. 'Be sitting yourself down. Taking me money is not for being the answer, but I will help you all I can.'

He slumped into the chair. 'No one can help me, I'm a dead man.'

Martha still had hold of his arm. She closed her eyes. 'It is that you will live till you are an old man and you will find happiness after much heartache. Not of your own doing, but because your mind needs to heal. You have seen much and it all haunts you. Let me be helping you. But first, you must let me be getting you a drink and something to eat. Then, you will be feeling better. Wait here and rest.'

She didn't know why, but Martha suddenly felt a lightness in her step as she ran to Macie's café. Waving to Trisha, who she saw sitting on the wall pulling her shawl tightly around her against the wind, she called out, 'It is only a moment I'll be.' Then hesitated for a second as she sensed all was not right with Trisha.

Making a quick choice, she dashed into Macie's. 'Three mugs of tea, and three oven-bottom muffins, please, Macie, but I'm in a powerful hurry, so I am.'

'Well, lass, I don't see any impending disaster, but if it involves me, I'd like to knaw about it.'

'No, Macie, it is that Trisha isn't looking well and I want to get to her, so I do.'

'Aw, well, in that case, I'll pour from the pot I've just made. It won't take a mo, and the muffins just came out of me oven and are ready to go. You run along with the muffins and make sure she is all right while I pour the tea. It's quiet, so I'll pop them along to you.'

Grabbing the muffins as soon as Macie had put them into the brown paper bag, Martha ran back to her tent. The man was asleep with his head on his arms which rested on her table.

Leaving him, Martha dashed between the horse and carriages, but gave way to a motor vehicle going along the prom, kicking out a stench she hated but knew was a sign of the future.

Trisha was white when she came up to her. 'Trish! Trish! Is it that you're all right, love? What is it, Trish?'

'I – I just witnessed a death.'

Martha's blood ran cold.

'A woman. She crossed the road at the tower and then over the tramlines and was hit by a tram! Someone said she was running to catch it.'

Martha didn't have to ask more, nor did she have time to as Trisha doubled over. 'Ooh, Martha, I think it's me babby. It were the shock . . . I – I've had pain ever since.'

Panicking, Martha frantically looked this way and that, hoping something, or someone, would help her. 'Oh, Trisha, is it that you're sure it is the labour pains?'

Trisha doubled over again. 'Yes . . . Eeh, Martha, help me.'

'Let's us get over the road to Cissy. Sure, she will take you in, she knows you so well and I'm still renting part of the garden from her.'

'But she'll have her guests in for their midday meal. She won't . . . agh . . . Ooh, Martha!'

Water flooded the pavement and dripped down Trisha's leg.

'Oh, Trisha, it is that we have no choice, unless it is you can manage in me tent!'

'Yes . . . take me to your tent.'

Martha worried about this. There was little room, and she hadn't yet sorted the gentleman out. Besides, it was hardly private, but rather than upset Trisha further she thought it wasn't a bad first move. 'I'm for having a client in there, but I'll ask him to move. Sure, he can go along to Macie's for the tea I've bought him.'

'A man? And you left him in your tent! . . . Eeh, Martha . . . just get me there, lass, hurry!'

As soon as they entered, Trisha's moans woke the man. Startled, he stared at them and then looked around, his expression full of confusion.

'It's all right. You wandered into me tent, so you did. I'm for helping you, but me friend needs me more. She's having the labour pains.'

He stood, and in doing so seemed to have more strength than he had before. 'I – I'm sorry. I shouldn't have bothered you . . . and, what I said, that isn't the man I am, I was just desperate.'

'Take yourself to Macie's café . . .'

The tent flap opened again and Macie appeared. 'Eeh, Martha, what on earth . . .? Trisha, lass. By, you look all in. Here, young man, take these teas. Martha, hold Trisha one side and I'll get the other.' Trisha collapsed onto Martha. Her cries told of how close she could be to having her baby. 'I was for taking her to Cissy's.'

'Right, come on then.'

When they reached the door, Martha banged on it. An irritated Cissy opened it. 'What do you want, Martha? You knaw I have me diners to see to . . . God Almighty, what's wrong with Trisha?'

'Come on, Cissy. Let us in. Trisha's in labour!'

'Good heavens, Macie. You of all folk knaw this is me busy time. What's wrong with your café? Take her there.'

'She won't make it, her waters have gone. Have a heart, lass.'

'Naw. What will me visitors think?'

'Please, Cissy,' Martha begged.

'Eeh, you bloody traders, you'll be the death of me. Anyroad, can she walk upstairs? Only I've a room free, but you tell her that if she does take it, she pays, and if she makes a sound, I'll knock her block off.'

'Aye, and then I'll knock yours off. Look, I've to get back to me café. Open your bloody door and let us in.'

Cissy did as Macie bid. 'Come on, Trisha, lass, just a few more steps, eh?'

'Naw, naw, I can't move.'

'Please, Trish, please try.'

To watch Trisha try wrenched at Martha's heart. It was obvious the pain the effort was causing her. But she persevered and somehow they managed to get her inside.

But just as they stepped through the door Trisha let out an almighty scream.

Guests came running from the dining room. One took one look and cried out, 'I'm a midwife, I'll help you, love. Take her into the drawing room . . . hurry. And fetch clean towels and hot water . . . and blankets . . . Hurry, I say!'

The flurry of activity soon resulted in Trisha being laid on the floor on a blanket.

'Right, away with the lot of you. Me and this young lady have work to do.'

'Naw, not Martha. Let Martha stay.'

The woman looked at Martha. 'Have you seen a baby born before, love?'

Martha could only shake her head.

'Well, it's up to you, but if you're prone to fainting at the sight of blood, then you can skedaddle now!'

Martha took a deep breath. She couldn't bear to leave Trisha with a stranger at such a time, even a kindly one as this lady was. She walked over to Trisha and knelt beside her. 'I'll not leave you, me darling.'

'Right, I know your friend's name. What's yours, love?'

'Her name's Trisha, though I call her Trish.'

'So, let's get on with the job in hand, Trisha, love. Let's get your baby into the world, eh?'

It seemed an endless round of indescribable cries of pain and a huge effort by Trisha put into pushing before at last, the nurse declared she had the head in her hands. 'One more push, darling girl. You can do it. That's right . . . Yes! Well done! Your baby is here, a lovely little girl!'

Martha heard a sob come from Trisha. She gripped her hand even tighter. 'A girl, a wee girl! Oh, Trish, your Sally is here, me darling.'

Martha had only just muttered the words when Sally decided to announce her own arrival with a loud cry. There was a silence when she stopped, and then a cheering and clapping could be heard from the other side of the door. The nurse giggled. 'There, I've cleaned her up. Do you want to hold her, me darling?'

Trisha's tearful 'Yes . . . oh, yes' warmed Martha. The horror of the birth, the pain, the screams, the calling on God to bring this to an end, were forgotten – for now the reward was snuggled in Trisha's arms. And Martha wondered how things would change for them both from this moment. She knew that Sally would bring them joy but didn't want to think of the consequences for Trisha.

'Now, can I present Sally to her waiting fans?'

Trisha nodded and smiled at the nurse. The smile turned to a grin and then to the loveliest serene and proud look that Martha had ever seen as the nurse took Sally and opened the door to oohs and ahhs. And cries of, 'She's beautiful.'

Cissy could be heard taking credit. 'Well, I must apologise for the disruption to your meals, everyone, but I had to take the young woman in when she were in such a predicament.'

This led to a woman protesting, 'You shouldn't apologise, you were kindness itself to do such a thing.'

Everyone agreed. Then a gentleman said, 'Let me be the first to offer a gift to the child and her mother. I think a collection is in order.'

Another gentleman's voice piped up, 'Yes, I agree, and I will pay for the mother's accommodation as she will need to stay here for a few days.'

Trisha looked astonished at this. 'Naw, I must go home. I've nowt here that I need . . . Martha, will you get Arthur to come and pick us up? . . . Please, Martha, I'll be all right at home . . . tell them.'

'That's kindness itself, so it is, but me friend needs to be in her own bed. Sure, the baby's things are all there at her home and I'm living next door so can care for them both.'

She was relieved to hear the nurse back them up. 'Yes, home is the best place for them both, but mother will need to be carried out to the landau and the same when she reaches her house. Have you someone who can do that, Martha?'

'I'm sure it is that the driver of the landau will help. He is a friend.'

'Good. In that case, I agree, Trisha should go to her own surroundings. She will recover there and have everything she needs to hand.'

Cissy piped up, all too eagerly, 'Aye, I agree, as I wouldn't be able to give her the attention she needs if she stays here.'

Martha didn't miss the relief in her voice and thought to herself that never in a million years would she subject Trisha to her bad-tempered ways.

But suddenly, the man she'd left in her tent came to mind. 'I'll not be long, Trisha. It is that I must check up on the client I left and make arrangements for another time for him.'

An urgency in her to try to find him came to Martha. Without waiting to hear if anyone disagreed, she hurried to the door and through it. Waiting outside, she found him leaning against the garden concrete post.

'Is it that you are all right?'

He nodded. 'And your friend?'

'She had a wee girl. She's for being fine – both of them are.'

'I waited, to make sure . . . Me name's Peter. I don't know me given surname, I was a foundling, I was given the name of the man who found me – Reynold . . . I'm mortified as to how I treated you . . . Are you really called Martha Lee?'

'No, it is the name of my gypsy ancestors. I'm for being Martha O'Hara. I – I want to help you, Peter. What is it I can do?'

He shook his head. 'I'm needing work and a home – you say I do have a future. Can you see me getting a job?'

'Sure, it isn't that detailed . . . but why is it you're not fighting in France?'

'I was. I became ill and was sent home. Many have ailments, but mine was on my chest. They say it was breathing in the fumes from the discharge of the guns, but I've always been prone to being chesty. They didn't bother about that when they took me in. I was sent home, but I have no home . . . I was brought up in an orphanage and lied about my age to go. I was already on the streets – abandoned by everyone and joining up seemed like a chance to be fed and cared for, but it was hell.'

In her heart, Martha wanted to take him home, but knew that would bring certain eviction down on her. She felt helpless – her own plight was enough to cope with, and yet she didn't want Peter to go out of her life. 'Look, if you come here tomorrow – midday, as I don't think I will be being here until then – it is that I will try to help you.'

'Ta, but can I stay in your tent till then? It's so cold during the night. At least that'll give me some shelter.'

Martha felt torn. If Cissy found out that she'd done such a thing, then she wouldn't like it and would surely give her notice. And yet, she couldn't think of Peter sleeping on the beach where many homeless made their beds.

'I'll be so quiet no one will know I'm there, and your winged chair will be a bed for me.'

Without meaning to, Martha found herself nodding. 'But I will have to put my padlock on – I have a chain that locks to the fence and is for keeping me flap closed. Or it is that it will be noticed that I have left it unlocked.' She dug her hand into her pocket and pulled out a key. Hurrying to her tent, she retrieved the chain that she hung from one tent post to another and wrapped it around, securing it to the fence, then padlocked it.

'Here, it is that I have a spare key.' Delving into her purse, she gave him some coins. 'And buy yourself two penneth of chips and a mug of tea . . . Now, it is that I must hurry. Don't be coming to me tent until after dark, and don't be for being seen by anyone.'

'Ta, Martha . . . Martha, you're beautiful.'

She looked up into his dark brown eyes – tired eyes, set into what she knew would be a handsome face, but for the weary lines around his eyes and the dirty, swarthiness of his skin. Nor did his hair, dark and matted, help his appearance, and yet, she had the sense that he was beautiful, and she never wanted to be out of his presence.

His eyes held hers. She didn't want to look away, but a voice came to her. 'Martha! Have you seen Arthur yet? I need to get sorted in time for me evening meal. Eeh, give you traders an inch and you take a mile!'

'Sure, I am for going now. He tethers near to the tower. I'll not be long.'

Tearing herself away from Peter, she ran for all she was worth to where Arthur usually was, but he wasn't in sight. Another landau pulled up. 'Will you be taking me and me friend to Enfield Road, please? Only it is that me friend will need help when we get there.'

'I ain't for naw lifting, lass, I've a bad back as it is.'

At a loss, Martha thought she'd have to accept and help Trisha as much as she could herself, or maybe Edna would help?

'I'll take it. Will you come down to the Primrose Boarding House, please.'

As she turned, she saw Peter had followed her. 'I can help you, Martha. I am not as strong as I used to be, but I could lift your friend.'

Martha wasn't sure. Was she trusting him too much? Already she'd given him a key to her tent! Was she mad? What was it about him that drew her to him? And yet, she knew that her guiding spirit had already informed her that their destinies were tied to each other. 'Ta, that is for being kind of you.'

'Well, jump up if you're taking the ride, lass.'

Peter held her hand to help her. His touch sent a strange feeling through her. One that she welcomed, wanted … needed. And yet, a shyness came over her, so they sat in silence as the horse trotted along the prom taking them to Enfield Road.

With Trisha safely tucked up in her own bed and Sally, having suckled at Trisha's breast, now asleep in the bottom drawer of what used to be Trisha's ma's dresser, Martha felt able to leave them for a while. 'Get yourself off to sleep, Trish, me darling. You're exhausted.'

'Aye, and so would you be if you'd gone through what I have, lass. But, eeh, it's worth it. Ain't she adorable?'

'She is. I love her as if she was me own. Sure, I've never taken care of a baby, though. Do you know what it is you have to do?'

'Aye, 'course I do. She'll be fine. As long as she's fed, kept warm and, most of all, loved, then she'll thrive.'

'Well, we'll see to it she has all of those things, so we will – though it is that the loving of her is going to be the easiest.'

'Don't leave me long, will you, Martha?'

From this, Martha detected that Trisha wasn't feeling as confident as she sounded, and that made the fear of this huge responsibility become real to Martha. But she knew she had to be strong – her dear friend had no one else to turn to for help.

'I'll stay awhile. Close your eyes now, me darling.'

'Before I do, lass. What's this with that scruffy individual? Don't be so trusting of folk. I didn't like him coming into me house, and you – who he's obviously holding a torch to – telling him you live next door!'

'I'm sorry, I am, but how was I to get you home and up here to your bed? And . . . well, I am for knowing he is unkempt, but that doesn't make him untrustworthy.'

'You've an eye for him. Eeh, lass. He's got the look of a thief!'

Martha couldn't deny this as it was what had happened. But she did defend him. 'He is homeless, Trish. Homeless and sick. Is it that you would turn your back on him?'

'Naw. I'm just saying.' This she finished on a yawn.

'Get yourself off to sleep, me wee darling, and don't be worrying.'

Trish smiled. 'I'm a ma, Martha. A ma to me little Sally.'

'You are, me darling. And a wonderful one you'll be.'

Before she'd finished saying this Trisha had her eyes closed. Martha smiled down on her and then on little Sally. They'd manage somehow. They would.

FOURTEEN

Martha

In the silence that followed, Martha heard voices drifting up from the street. 'Hello, Hattie. Are you after Martha?'

The fear she'd had earlier for hers and Trisha's new future deepened into an overwhelming worry for herself. Her landlady had answered, 'Aye, I need a word. I think I've been generous enough with the time I've let her keep the house on, but I've a family who've approached me, and they're that desperate they've offered more rent than I get now.'

'Well, it's only right a family should have a family house. Are they from round here?'

'Naw, he's moving up from the Midlands to take up a position in the tower. He's a maintenance engineer. Only, he can't bring his family till he finds a place.'

'Eeh, that sounds posh, when he probably only keeps the bloody lifts working!'

'Naw, there's a lot more to his job than that. Anyroad, they've two kids at school and need to get them settled.'

'Well, I saw Trisha being carried inside, and Martha was carrying a babby, so Trisha must have given birth.'

'Oh, she has, has she? That's a bit suspect, ain't it?'

'Ha! More than suspect. She reckons it were a rape, but she's allus been a floozy, that one!'

Unable to bear hearing any more, Martha checked that Trisha was sound asleep and then scooted down the stairs. The agony of losing her home becoming a reality gave her wings and a determination to fight this. *Surely I am for having rights?*

But if she did, she soon found they weren't to be granted to her as her landlady gave her three weeks' notice to get out of her home.

'How can it be right that you can do this? I've always paid me rent on time. I have nowhere else to go . . . Please, Hattie. Please be reconsidering.'

'Naw, you knew these houses were not for single occupation. I've every right to put you out. Three weeks and naw longer. And with that I'm being generous. Good day to you, miss.'

'But what about the deposit me granny paid you? Will you be giving that back to me?'

'Naw, I most certainly will not! Look at how the paint is peeling off the windowsills! You were told it was down to you to keep the maintenance of the house up to a standard. I'm only responsible for any major repairs. That woodwork ain't seen a lick of paint in the while you've been a tenant. I shall keep your deposit to pay for what you haven't done!'

Martha felt the tears pricking her eyes.

Loneliness had visited her often, but at this moment she felt it was her against the world and she didn't know which way she could turn.

She was soon to be homeless, and with very little money. What would become of her and how was she supposed to help Trisha?

'Ha! Bloody gypsies, you shouldn't have taken them on in the first place, Hattie, and if I were you, I'd be thinking if that Trisha is a fit enough tenant. She's brought shame on this street for the second time. It were bad enough when she got pregnant afore she were wed, and now she's brought a bastard here, and her husband away fighting in the war! She's a bloody disgrace.'

Martha felt as though a hot ball of fire had burst into flame inside of her. 'Don't you dare be talking of Trisha in that way, you vile, evil woman. I curse you! I see nothing but loneliness at your door. A cold woman who everyone avoids. It is yourself you should be taking a long hard look at, so it is.'

'Don't you come here playing God. I laugh in your face at your curse, you charlatan!' Turning to Hattie Hargreaves, she said, 'See! See what we have to put up with since you let gypsies into the street! I'd burn her at the stake if it were down to me. Bloody witchcraft, that's what she deals in. Taking folk's money for nowt but a pack of made-up lies . . . Aye, and that's the money you get your rent out of an' all. Shame on you!'

'That's enough! Martha ain't the only single occupant, you knaw. You've been on your own a good while now. It's only your age that keeps me from evicting you! So don't start lashing your nasty tongue at me. There's allus the workhouse as would take you, you knaw!'

Mrs Higginbottom visibly shuddered. Her bottom lip quivered. 'I'm sorry, Hattie. It were her and her talk of curses. It upset me, till I didn't knaw what I were saying.'

'Aye, well, think on.'

For once, there was no humph as Mrs Higginbottom meekly went inside her house, and no meaningful shutting of the door, just a gentle closing of it and silence – an oppressive silence that left Martha quivering and feeling she had nowhere to turn and no one to turn to. Not even Trisha could help her with her dilemma. Not that she would bother her dear friend with the problems she had to contend with at such a time.

As she went inside to the harsh voice of Hattie Hargreaves saying, 'Three weeks, mind. Naw longer. And leave the place as you found it!' Martha could hold the tears back no longer. The words that there was always the workhouse zinged through her – though meant for Mrs Higginbottom, Martha knew that such an alternative may turn out to be the only one that she had for herself.

Slumping onto the sofa, she let her body cry. Her tears seemed to drain her, baring her soul as she wept for her mammy and pappy, and for her granny and, lastly, for herself and the dreadful, frightening plight she found herself in.

She woke an hour later, her eyes clogged with the aftermath of her tears, and her body aching and trying to pull her back into the blessed release that sleep gave her. But the pressing need to see to Trisha tugged harder and she rose, glanced at the clock, and felt the relief that she hadn't abandoned her friend for too long.

Gathering herself together, she went into the kitchen and splashed her face with cold water, ran her fingers through her curls to make them bounce again and pulled her shawl around her creased frock.

The sound of Sally crying when she opened Trisha's door sent her running upstairs. Trisha lay back on her pillow, her face drained of colour, her eyes staring.

'Trish, Trish, me darling, what is it?'

Weakly, Trisha threw the covers off her. She sat in a pool of blood.

'Oh, Jesus, Mary and Joseph! Trish! What is it that's happening to you?'

'Doctor . . . Martha . . . Doctor . . .'

Coming to her senses, Martha ran down the stairs, through the front door and banged on Edna's front door. All the while praying that the coldness Edna had shown to them both since the public announcement of Trisha's pregnancy would melt when she learned of Trisha's plight.

As Edna folded her arms and nodded at her once she'd opened the door, Martha's heart sank. 'Help us, please, Edna . . . Trisha may die!'

'What? Good Lord, naw! What's happening? I thought she'd had the babby!'

'She has, but she's bleeding badly.'

'Right, you run for the doctor. I'll see to her and the babby. Poor mite, I can hear her from here. That's a hungry cry if ever I heard one.'

* * *

It was going dark by the time Martha sat cradling Little Sally. She worried herself sick over Trisha, who'd been rushed into the Victoria Hospital, but she'd had no news. Edna had told her how to feed Sally, sending her out to buy a bottle with a rubber teat at each end and some powdered baby milk.

She looked down at the little face so like her father's and smiled as Sally stretched herself gracefully. 'Me little darling, you have a future of trouble and strife, but you will have a friend by your side to help you. You and she will be for being as close as your mammy and me are, and she will help you. Together, you will do amazing things, but as yet, I don't know who she is. She will love you and take care of you. Never fear. And I'll do that for your mammy, so I will.'

With saying this, Martha let out a huge sigh. Before she could look after anyone, she had to have somewhere to live. Where would that be? Silently, she sent up a prayer. *Please don't let it be far away from Trisha and Sally. I couldn't bear that.*

Trisha

The life seemed to be draining from Trisha as she lay in a room of white – white walls, white ceiling, white-gowned women and men, all scurrying around her – and yet all seeming to be in a haze and at times as if she was floating above them all.

Somewhere in her mind, she knew she had Sally, but couldn't bring her little face to mind, only a feeling of deep love and not wanting to leave that behind. This was the saviour of her, as each time she drifted along a dark tunnel towards the beautiful light beckoning her, she held on to her little Sally waiting for her to come home, to feed her and to love her. *I'll be the best ma ever, me little lass. I'll be like me own ma was to me.* Her heart tugged at these words, and she knew she could float right now to be by her ma's side. *I can feel you are there, Ma and Da, and Granny, but help me to stay for me Sally. Please help me.*

It was three days later that Trisha woke. For a moment, she didn't know where she was, and then memory flooded back into her. She tried to move, but pain creased her stomach. She tried to break through the fog to call out, but her throat was so dry and sore only a croak came out.

'Now, don't you be moving, Patricia. You must keep still or you'll undo the marvellous job the doctors have been doing, so you will.'

'Martha?'

'No, it is Nurse O'Ryan. Martha is your Irish friend, is she not?'

'Aye.'

'Well, to be sure, she has been here as often as she can with looking after your wee baby, but she isn't here at the moment.'

'What's happening? My stomach hurts so much.'

'Well, firstly, me name is Theresa, and I am from Cork in Southern Ireland. There, we are taught to always be telling the truth, but are you up to hearing the truth, Patricia?'

'Yes. I want to know . . . Will I live?'

'It is that you will, but . . . you won't be the same, for sure. A powerful intervention had to take place to be saving your life. You see, you were in danger of bleeding to death, so it is that the doctor had to take away everything.'

Trisha tried to sit up. Suddenly she was wide awake and alert. 'Everything? Me ... me womb?'

'Yes, dear ... I'm sorry, so I am.'

'But I – I won't be ... I mean, me husband, he ...' Her thoughts raced as to what this meant. Would she be able to have sex ever again?

'I understand what it is that is bothering you, me darling. You're not to worry. It will all be the same, so it will. But no babies can be made as you are not for having a home to nestle them in and to nurture them ... Sure it is that I am sorry to be telling you this.'

Trisha couldn't take this in. Bobby had said he wanted kids when he came home ... *Oh, God! What will he think of me already having one?*

A tremble zinged through her body. For the first time, the enormity of her sin hit her. *This is me punishment*. Laying her head – the only part of her she could move – back onto the pillow, she allowed the tears to flow.

'Cry it out, me wee love, for crying does help, no matter what they say. It is that the Good Lord gave us this way of expressing our emotions for a reason. Never be bottling up how it is that you are feeling.'

Trisha didn't need this encouragement – she couldn't stop. It seemed that her whole world was collapsing around her.

'To be sure, you have your beautiful little girl, Patricia. Think of that, eh?'

For a moment, Sally seemed part of the troubles piling on top of her shoulders, and Trisha couldn't see her child as a solution, only making things worse. She felt so tired. Her tears had drained all of her energy. She closed her eyes and listened to the soft lyrical voice of the nurse as she soothed her with words. None of them had any meaning for her, but still, they were a comfort.

When she next woke and tried to open her puffy eyes, Trisha knew that Martha was by her side. She stretched out her hand and felt the comfort of it being taken by Martha.

Turning her head, she told Martha, 'I'm afraid, Martha. I – I can't have any more babbies, Martha . . . Bobby will go mad! He wanted us to have a babby . . . He'll never let me keep me little Sally now!'

'He loves you, Trisha. It is that you must hold on to that. Of course it is that he'll have a lot to take in . . . Anyway, let's not think too far ahead. Sure, the papers are full of things beginning to go Britain's way, but there's still for being a lot to do to bring the war to an end, so you've time to be sorting out how you are to deal with Bobby.'

'There's some days when I don't want to, Martha. I just want to pick up Sally and run. Is she all right? Is she feeding? Do you think she is missing me?'

'It's a yes to all three. Sure, she is confused with how things are, but all right. She is being well looked after. Edna has her at this moment and is treating her like her own grandchild, and I'm for becoming an expert in baby care . . . I – I . . . well, I have something I must be telling you of, Trisha.'

'What? You're not going to tell me anything bad, are you? I couldn't take that. I'm hoping you can soon tell me that me and Sally have a bright future.'

'It is bad news that I have. Ricky called. He was for being on leave and had found out where we lived by going to me tent and asking around when he found neither of us in. He – he was telling me that . . . Well, I'm sorry to the heart of me, but Ralph has been killed.'

'Killed?' Trisha couldn't take this in. Nor could she understand not having any feeling about it. It seemed to her that he'd got his just deserts, and yet she knew this was wrong. No one should think such a thing of anyone losing their life.

'Trish? Are you all right, me wee darling?'

'I am, Martha. I'm sorry for his family, but somehow I can't . . . well, I hope his soul rests in peace.'

Martha looked quizzically at her.

'I'm all right, I promise. I just cannot feel anything for anyone at the moment . . . It's strange, but that is helping me to cope . . . I can't explain it.'

'Yes, I am knowing that feeling. It's there to shield you, but be prepared for when it is peeled away you are left devastated. I will be there for you when that happens, Trish, just lean on me.'

Trisha couldn't deal with this either. It seemed to her that her emotions had been cut off and she would never feel the same again. But Martha's next bit of news did touch her and bring what was left of her world crashing down.

'Trisha, I've something else . . . I don't know how I am to tell you this, but I have to leave me home.'

'What? You won't be living next door to me?'

'I can't. The landlady is giving me notice to leave. She has a family who will pay more rent. I can't afford to match it, and no longer feel I am welcome in the street.'

'Naw . . . naw, Martha, don't leave me.' Suddenly the floodgates opened, and Trisha knew she was sobbing, she just couldn't help herself, or really feel the emotions that were tearing at her. It seemed nothing, no matter how bad, could be worse than she was already facing, and yet, she couldn't bear the thought of Martha not being next door. Never had she felt this confliction of feeling before.

'It is that I have nowhere to go, Trisha. I'm worried sick, so I am. I can only see the workhouse looming for me. But as I have a job, I'm not for knowing if they will take me. I've even thought of sleeping in me tent as Hattie Hargreaves wasn't for giving me deposit back, and I can't find that sum again to put on another rental.'

'Move in with me until you get on your feet . . . Yes, it's the answer, Martha! If we share everything, you'll soon get some money together. Please say you will, lass. We can both look after Sally, as I'm not going to be strong enough to do so on me own for a while. Even holding her might be too much for me at first.' Realisation hit Trisha of the enormity of caring for her babby when she felt so weak and lost. 'And . . . and I don't knaw how to feed her now that me milk's dried up, or even how to care for her on me own . . . I – I'm half the person I was, Martha . . . half . . .' With admitting this, the tears came again, only this time, Trisha felt every one of them rip her heart in two. Reality had flooded into her. She truly was half the woman she had been – not only physically, but in all she should be able to do. It had dawned on her that she really didn't know how to care for her child. She felt so helpless. She couldn't lose Martha as then she would be alone too.

Martha held her close and let her cry. More than once, Trisha felt a tear land on her hair. She didn't want Martha to cry, or to ever feel sad and alone.

Together, this wouldn't happen, even if it was only for a short time until she was stronger. Just the thought of them being so was helping her.

Calming a little, she said, 'Please say you will, Martha. I need you with me.'

'Really? Are you meaning it, Trish? I – I can't believe it. Yes. Oh, Trish, it would be the answer to me prayers, so it would . . . And I'll pay me way. I did manage to put a little by from the summer months – not enough to move into another home, but a little.'

'Aw, we'll manage, lass. Nowt can get at us when we stand together. With you living with me, I knaw I can cope.' Trisha sniffed and dried her eyes. 'Don't cry any more, Martha. We'll be all right and so will me little Sally . . . Eeh, Martha, suddenly I'm longing to see her, to hold her. Don't let her forget me.'

'She won't, I'm promising you. She will know you the moment you come home.'

'Well, that'll be soon if I have owt to do with it . . . So, you said Ricky came. Did he tell you how things were out there?'

'Yes, he said they were bad. He said he was afraid to go back, but knew that he must. He sent you his love and asked after the wee one. He was also for giving me a warning.'

'What? What warning?'

'He said we should never tell anyone who the father is. He knows Ralph's family now and says they are a nasty lot. He is fearing that if they get to know who Sally is, they may want to take her.'

'Naw! That can't happen, Martha.'

'I know, and it won't. Sure, there's only the three of us that know, and Ricky ain't for telling. He did ask if he could call on me when he comes home from war and if it is that I would write to him. He wants me to be telling him how you are. He was very concerned for you and disappointed not to be seeing you.'

'Ha! I hardly noticed him.'

'I know, but even on that evening I could tell he only had eyes for you.'

'Stop it! I'm a married woman . . . though whether I will be when Bobby comes home and finds out about Sally, I don't knaw . . . And I ain't sure that I care.'

Martha didn't answer this. Trisha could feel her hand take hers.

'Anyroad, sommat'll sort out, lass. It allus does. The main thing is that you get yourself moved into mine . . . What will you do with all your furniture?'

'Sure, I don't know. Maybe sell it. None of it is for having any sentimental value.'

'Well, get yourself to Second-hand Lil's. She has a place on Whitegate Drive. Next to the hospital, here. A sort of garage-cum-warehouse. She buys and sells stuff. Mind, she won't give you its value, but she's fair with her pricing. She just allows for herself making a good profit. But at least it'll be a bit for you and she'll collect the lot, which'll mean you don't need to hire a dray.'

Trisha couldn't believe how she could organise all of this, and how she felt once more part of life. But she so wanted to keep Martha close. The thought of losing her had given her a jolt – the one she'd needed as now she was looking differently on things and seemed once more to belong in the world. She squeezed Martha's hand. 'We'll do all right together, lass. I knaw we will.'

'Ta, Trish. You're saving me life. And yes, we'll do all right together.'

Trisha could feel the strength coming back into her. She hadn't come to terms with what had happened to her, but now she knew she had so much to live for and the knowing was making her want to heal.

When at last she was let out of hospital, Sally was six weeks old, and she'd barely got to know her.

As Trisha walked towards Arthur's landau on unsteady feet, helped by Nurse O'Ryan, her heart swelled to see Martha sitting in the carriage with little Sally asleep on her knee.

Climbing up the steps, helped by Arthur, proved to be a painful process.

'Good to see you're better, wee Trisha.'

She smiled up at Arthur. He'd taken them to and from work in his landau, and to that fateful night out, but hadn't spoken much to her. Mainly, he'd chatted to Bridie or Martha.

'Ta, Arthur,' was all she could manage to say.

The pain that had brought the sweat out on her brow eased when she sat on the bench and Martha gently placed Sally on her lap.

It felt to Trisha as if she would burst with the love that filled her as she gazed down into the changed, and yet the same, little cherub-like face.

'By, she's filled out. But aw, so beautiful . . . Me little Sally . . . Your ma's sorry to have left you, me darling lass. I'll never do so again.'

Sally opened her eyes. The blue they'd been at her birth was beginning to fade and they now looked as though they would be a hazel colour. She gazed up at Trisha, then gurgled. One of her hands came free from her shawl and reached out towards Trisha's face. Trisha bent forward allowing the touch and filling with a warmth that bonded her to her child. A tear of joy ran down her cheek, and her lips stretched into a smile that she felt in her heart. 'Me little Sally, me lovely little babby.' Pulling her closer, she bent and kissed the soft skin of Sally's cheek. 'Ma loves you, me little lass. I'll never let anyone hurt you, I promise.'

She looked up into Martha's eyes. 'We're going home, Martha. Really going home. The three of us against the world – well, against them in Enfield Road, Blackpool, anyroad!'

Martha, looking full of emotion, put out her hand and lay it on Trisha's arm. 'Ta for helping me, Trish. You're for being a true friend. It is that I am almost ready to move in. Lil is coming in the next week, then I can begin to pack. But any night that you're not feeling up to caring for Sally, I can have her with me.'

For a moment, Trisha couldn't speak. But then asked, 'So, Lil will take the lot, but what about your bed? You'll need that.'

'Yes, and it is that I have to sort out which bed to bring. And I will keep a bit of the linen so that we are having plenty – me bedding for one, and the covers I made for the sofa and chairs. I don't know why them, but it is that they were the only things I had that were truly mine and me granny's . . . I kept some of her clothes too. So, now I am thinking that we could use the material, then it would be as if me granny is helping us to further ourselves.'

'You're still thinking that we could make a go of selling what we make then, lass?'

'Oh, I do, for sure. There's enough trade in Blackpool to sell anything, and it is that no one is selling baby layettes, or children's clothes . . . We can design our own, so we can – make them unique and appealing to them who have money. It is that I can see us having commissions to make a full layette for a newborn and to be the main outfitters for the children as they are growing up . . . Oh, Trish, we could be getting rich!'

'Steady on, lass. You're making me feel tired just thinking about it . . . But, eeh, it's a grand idea and exciting. I've never had a chance to make owt of meself before.'

'Sure, we can be for doing it together, Trish. We can be our own bosses in the future, and I'll be able to stop telling the future of others and work on me own instead.'

Trisha grinned. 'It would help if you could look into your crystal ball and see that we're going to do all right, though, lass.'

'No! That would be taking the fun out of it. It's an adventure we are going on, Trish.'

Trisha thought her life so far had been enough of an adventure, but then she shuddered inside as she thought there was more of it to come. A fear gripped her. Martha had said there was talk of real progress towards winning the war. What then? What would life be like with Bobby home? How would he react to her having a kid, and not able to ever give him any? She dreaded to think.

Looking out at the houses they passed – the big houses of the well-to-do along Whitegate Drive – she wondered how it would feel to be like the folk who lived in them, not to have any worries, to be respected and listened to. But then she glanced down at her little Sally, and at Martha, and she knew she was rich, as rich as she ever need be to have these two by her side.

FIFTEEN

Martha

By the time they reached home, Trisha was exhausted. Arthur had helped her down, but Martha had to call Edna to help to get her inside.

'Eeh, love. What have they done to you? Here, hold on to me and we'll get you comfortable, won't we, Martha?'

'It is that we will, Trisha. Let me get Sally into her pram. You hold on to Edna, love.'

'No, I want to hold her, Martha.'

'Now, don't you be spoiling her. Martha has her in a good routine, lass. Best way with babbies.'

Trisha looked devastated at Edna saying this. Martha could feel the pain of jealousy she was feeling and thought to put things firmly back into her charge. 'No, Edna, it is that a mother will always know best . . . Sure, I'll hand Sally to you once you're sat down, Trish.'

From the look on Trisha's face, Martha knew she'd said the right thing and the air cleared.

'I were only saying. I mean, it's natural for you to want to cuddle her, you've missed out, but for her sake, think on. A spoiled child is a nasty child.'

'I will, Edna, I won't spoil her. I just need to get to knaw her again and have her knaw me an' all.'

'She will knaw you, lass. Now, tell me, what have they done to you to leave you in this state?'

Edna looked horrified when she heard. 'Well, I feel sorry for you, lass. I were never in favour of you keeping your young 'un, but now I think you made the right choice. But by, you've to hope as Bobby sees it that way.'

Martha drew in her breath. How was it that these women felt they had a right to speak so openly? She looked at Trisha, saw that she had taken this well and was nodding her head.

'Aye, well, we'll deal with that when it happens. I ain't heard from him in a good while, so naw doubt his ma felt it her duty to put him in the picture.'

'Eeh, lass, if that bitch has done that, well, you'd better prepare yourself. And now Martha tells me that she is to move in . . . well, I ain't against you doing that, but it's another thing for the lad to contend with when he does come home.'

This stayed with Martha as she prepared for bed that night. She looked over at little Sally, glad that she'd been able to persuade Trisha to let her stay the night with her so that there would be no worry over Trisha having to look after her.

Just how would they manage living together? And could she make enough money to be able to move out before

Bobby came home? *I have to! I cannot add to the troubles that are coming Trisha's way.*

Sipping the hot cocoa she'd made, she began to feel sleepy and could feel her eyes closing when a noise woke her. Something had caused her dustbin to rattle and it sounded as though the lid had come off and clattered to the ground.

Fear held her rigid. Was it a burglar? Glancing at Sally and pleased to see she was fast asleep, Martha crept towards the bedroom window. Hardly daring to pull the curtain aside, she did so in very slow movements, but it didn't help as her yard was in darkness.

As she went to close the curtain, the sound of pebbles hitting the window made her jump back and gasp in horror. Someone was in the yard!

More pebbles hit the window, giving her the knowledge that whoever it is was trying to contact her. Tentatively, she opened the window. A whispered 'Martha, it's Peter' came to her.

'Peter! What is it you're doing here?'

'Please let me in, Martha. I mean no harm, but I'm so cold and feel unwell.'

Martha hesitated. Her heart told her to open the door, but her fear stopped her. 'Go away! I cannot be letting you in, Peter, it is for being wrong.'

'No. Don't turn me away. I mean no harm. I have no one, Martha.'

This was followed by the sound of him throwing up. Concern for him deepened. Against all she believed right, Martha did up the buttons on her frock that she'd undone and ran down the stairs to the back door.

The sound of the bolt being pulled back resounded through the quietness of the night. No sooner had it unlatched than Peter gently pushed it open and stepped inside.

Martha lifted the oil lamp she'd brought down with her. The light lit Peter up, showing the violent shivers of his body, the beads of sweat standing out on his forehead and the deathly white of his face.

'Come away in. Oh dear, what is it that has happened to you?'

'I was sitting in your tent when I felt nauseous. I began to shiver, then was sick, and that has carried on. I – I didn't know what else to do. I don't know a soul . . . I came so close to ending my life, Martha . . . You have a sharp edge to your table, near to where the legs are. I ran my wrist backwards and forwards along it, hoping to cut the vein as I have seen many a soldier do. But I thought of you and . . .'

His body swayed. Martha put out her arms to steady him.

'Oh, Martha . . . Martha . . . Only the thought of you stopped me . . . Help me . . . please help me.'

She was lost as his words awoke the same feeling she'd had earlier for him. 'I will. Let me help you to a chair. I can rekindle the fire and get you a hot drink . . . and I'll be fetching you a blanket to warm you up. Come. But be quiet as the walls are being very thin and sure, I'll be hounded out tomorrow if me neighbours suspect I have a man in me house. Besides, little Sally is for being asleep in the room upstairs.'

When he sat, she asked, 'So, is it that you've been staying in me tent every night? I thought you had moved on. Has anyone seen you coming and going?'

'No, and every morning I hoped you would come – I left early and sat on the wall opposite waiting for you. Many customers came, but never you.'

'It is that I had Trisha in hospital and was looking after little Sally. Rest now, take off your shoes.' It was then that the smell of him and his terrible unkempt appearance became apparent. Why she hadn't noticed before she could only put down to the joy that had surged through her at seeing him. How often she had thought of him since their meeting but had assumed he'd left the key for her and taken off on his travels once more.

'I'll move the pan that I keep for my washing water onto the middle of the stove and heat it for you, and put fresh towels out. You can be having a wash after I have gone up to bed. Have you any more clothes?'

'No. I realise I must look a sight and must honk to the high heavens, but a wash would be great. Ta, Martha. I knew that I would be helped if I came to you.'

Martha didn't reply. As she busied herself moving the pan onto the gas flame and filling the kettle, it came to her that he may want something to eat, so she put a pan of fat on the heat too and broke two eggs into it. Cutting two thick doorsteps off a loaf, she buttered them in readiness of making a sandwich for Peter. All seemed like a labour of love to her and she felt a happiness enter her at being able to look after him. It was as she poured the boiling water onto the tea leaves that she remembered that in Lil's second-hand shop she'd seen some clothing hanging up. All had looked clean and of good quality. An idea came to her.

Taking his tea and sandwich through, she told him, 'Be eating this while your water heats up. Then in the morning, I will go as soon as I can to a second-hand shop I am knowing of that is for selling clothes and will be getting an outfit for you. Maybe then you can see if there is any employment anywhere that will help you to get a place ... Only if you are very discreet – going out in the morning very early, and coming here very late at night – I will feed you and let you stay on me sofa for a couple of weeks so it is that you can look around ... But no one must know, not even me friend Trisha, or it is as I say, they will hound me off the street, so they will, and that will cause trouble for Trisha as she will try to defend me.'

The while she spoke, Martha worried that Peter might have the dreaded flu that was rife. What then? Neither Sally nor Trisha must be put in danger of catching that. It would surely kill them. The thought was unbearable.

'You would do that for me? Oh, Martha, you're an angel ... or ... well, can I hope that you have feelings for me? ... That you've felt what I have?'

A lovely smile lit his face, showing even white teeth that she marvelled at given the circumstances he'd lived for months now. Her heart melted. Her eyes connected with his. He made a movement towards her, but then stopped and grinned. 'I promised I would be a gentleman, and I will. Besides, as I said, I honk that much, I think you'd run a mile!'

She grinned back – a shaky grin ruled by the emotion flooding through her and the voice inside her telling her to be careful, that to have him in to her home at night was sinful enough, but to let him get close would surely render her at hell's gates. Turning, she went back into the kitchen.

With trembling hands, she reached for the bowl from behind the curtain around the sink and stood it on the tall stool that she'd pulled from under the worktop. Once she had the bowl filled with hot water, she scurried through the living room and up the stairs.

Checking on Sally and finding her fast asleep, she hurriedly found towels, one for Peter to dry himself on and one for him to wrap around himself which would give him the chance not to have to put his dirty clothes back on. As she turned and looked at her granny's bed, it came to her that Peter would be better sleeping in it and then she could keep him away from Sally.

When she got back downstairs, Peter stood from where he'd been sitting ... 'I'm sorry ... I – I couldn't eat the sandwich, me stomach ... Where's the lav? I need it quickly!'

'It's in the yard. The way we came in – the next door to the kitchen.'

Peter was doubled up as he followed her direction.

The muscles in Martha's own stomach clenched. She had to protect herself and Sally, but how? Sally, yes, she could manage that, but she would have to look after Peter, and that would mean close contact. But had she already put Sally in danger? *What should I do? Holy Mary Mother of God, be helping me! Sure, I was just being charitable. You wouldn't be punishing me for that now?*

When Peter came back in, he was as white as a sheet.

'Rest awhile. Your water is ready for you for when you'll be wanting it. I have to make a bottle for little Sally as soon she will wake for her night feed.'

When she passed by him with the hot bottle for Sally and a jug of cold water to cool it, having scrubbed her hands and arms before beginning to make it, Martha saw that Peter had closed his eyes and she was relieved to see that the colour had come back into his cheeks.

Creeping by, she left him, praying he had all he needed, but most of all that he would recover by morning from all that ailed him.

Sally woke not long after Martha had got into bed. Unable to relax and sleep, she was glad of the distraction which meant she didn't have to try.

This was a time that she loved with Sally. And yet her heart went out to Trisha for never having experienced it. It was a time when it seemed there was no one else on earth, only her and the tiny child snuggled into her making sucking noises and keeping her trusting eyes focused just on her alone. How she loved this little mite. And to think that she would be able to share her with Trisha until the time when Bobby returned left her heart filling with joy.

'Yes, and for many, many years, me wee darling, as wherever I land in the future, you will always be in me heart.' She sighed. 'Maybe it will be that I will be blessed with little ones of me own and they will be your sisters and brothers, so they will.' At this thought she lay her head back on the pillow and looked up at the ceiling. The unbidden thought came to her, *And I hope it is that Peter is being the daddy to them.*

The thought flushed her cheeks with embarrassment, and she was glad of the distraction of Sally protesting at having lost her attention. 'It is all right, me wee darling, I was only thinking a wee while there . . . Nice thoughts, and yet impossible ones, I'm afraid.'

But in her heart, she wished they could come true.

With Sally fed, burped and changed and now lying gurgling happily in a sleepy way, Martha found that her mind wouldn't let her rest. She had to find out if Peter was all right.

Every stair seemed to creak, when she'd never noticed them doing so before, but at last she was downstairs and faced with trying to open the latch of the door without making too much noise. To her amazement she did this, but the door then let her down as its hinges squeaked as she gently pushed it open.

None of it had disturbed Peter. She found him looking as fresh as a baby, with his hair a mass of damp curls and his long eyelashes sweeping his cheeks as he lay peacefully asleep.

For a moment she gazed down at him. As she did, she felt a love for him that she'd never felt for anyone in her life – a different love than that she'd had for her mammy, pappy and granny and from what she felt for Sally and Trisha. This was an overwhelming feeling that bound her soul to his and lit her body with feelings that urged her to be one with this man that she knew was hers – her God-given soulmate.

At that moment, Peter opened his eyes. His sleepy gaze gave him a confused look, but as his whereabouts dawned on him, so did her presence. He put his hand up to her. 'Martha? Oh, Martha.'

His hand pulled her down towards him. She bent her knees and knelt beside him. His fingers brushed through her hair, catching the ringlets, then stroking them. 'Martha . . .' His voice, thick with emotion, thrilled her.

'Peter . . . I – I just wondered how you are feeling?'

'Better. And that's down to you. I've drunk a whole glass of water and managed half of the sandwich. Feel my brow, I've cooled down and no longer feel feverish.'

'I so worried that it was that you had the flu.'

'No, I had that when I first landed back in England. It was rife on the boat. Many soldiers returning injured or unfit in some way came down with it. Most of them died – a travesty. But Blackpool seems unscathed.'

Relief flooded Martha. 'Sure, it must have been a bug you caught. Not surprising with the state of you. What is it you have been eating?'

Peter looked ashamed. 'I – I raided the bins before they were collected.'

'Oh, Peter.'

They didn't speak for a moment, just looked into each other's eyes. When Martha did start to tell him that he could sleep in her granny's room, he stopped her by placing his finger on her lips. 'Hush.'

His head came towards hers. She didn't move away; she couldn't. When their lips touched it was as if her world changed, that somehow she'd only been half a person and now she was whole. The freshness and taste of him gave her the knowledge that he had rinsed his mouth with salted water. But she wouldn't have cared as the feelings zinging through her – feelings she couldn't control – consumed her. 'Oh, Peter, Peter.'

'I love you, Martha, and have since I first set eyes on you, but I felt so unworthy.'

'You were never that. You're being down your luck just now, but I can help you.'

'Shush, let me kiss you.'

Martha was lost. She thrilled at his touch, his kisses, his caressing of her breast – all seemed so natural, as did his slipping off the sofa and lying with her on the rug and holding her close, his body entwined with hers. Feeling every bone, every muscle of him, she knew his desire. His closeness heightened her own.

It was as his hand touched her knee and then her bare thigh that she woke to what was happening. She stiffened. Peter immediately withdrew his touch. 'I'm sorry, Martha. I shouldn't have. But don't recoil from me. Let me lie next to you, just for a while. I promise I'll be good but tell me you have feelings for me and there is hope for me.'

'I do. It is that I love you too, and want you so much, but I am afraid . . . I've never . . . well, it isn't just for being that. I have many things holding me back. Me Catholic upbringing for one. Me fear of the consequences for another . . . Look, I'll be taking meself back to me bed just now.'

'No, stay a little while longer.'

Martha couldn't resist. She snuggled into him knowing that this was where she belonged for the rest of her life. He held her gently – undemandingly. Giving her love that encased her and settled in her heart that her future would be with him for ever.

When she woke, she didn't know how much later, Peter was on his elbow gazing down at her.

She shivered, not from cold but from the emotion of the moment.

'It's getting towards morning, me arm is dead, and I have to be on my way before I disgrace you, darling Martha.'

'Oh? What time is it?'

He bent and kissed her nose. 'Five a.m. And I thought I heard Sally gurgling upstairs, so one kiss and then I must dress and go.'

Moving off his arm, Martha felt the loneliness of his words. 'No, stay. You can go upstairs to me granny's room. Sure, there is a chair up there and no one will know you are there. And you can be sleeping in her bed from now on.'

'But what about your neighbours?'

They must not be for finding out, so you must move around quietly.' She giggled. 'There's a guzunder, as they call the piddle pot around here, under the bed. It is that you should use that when I am out and then you can be emptying it after dark when the neighbours know I am in and will assume it is me.'

'Ha! You think of everything. For sure it is that I will be using the piddle pot!' They both giggled at how he mimicked her. But then Peter became serious. 'Are you sure you want me to stay?'

'Yes, I cannot turn you out now, me love.'

'Oh, Martha.' His lips came on hers. She responded with all that was her as she clung to him.

'Don't . . . I so want to . . .'

Martha silenced him with a kiss. It was as if she'd woken a different person. For now she found that she wanted so much to be his.

As he rolled onto her, she didn't protest. She couldn't. She wanted this. Wanted to be his, to feel him closer than any other human being had been to her, for he was her – an extension of her.

For a moment after he entered her, she felt a stretching and discomfort, but his gentle movements soon took that away and she thrilled with his every movement, feeling sensations she never knew she could, or were even possible.

His love took her into him, making him hers, binding them together for the rest of their lives. His kisses lit every part of her.

When it was over, she lay in his arms, feeling at peace and at one with her world.

It was a cry from Sally that made her come to her senses. Sitting up and then standing in one movement, guilt flooded her – how could she have done what she just did? *Jesus, Mary and Joseph, forgive me!*

'Don't look like that, Martha . . . I'm sorry. I thought . . .'

'No, I was for realising, but don't be sorry. For a moment, I felt the guilt of my actions, but now I feel nothing but joy.'

Peter stood in all his glory. Beads of sweat stood out on his skin and trickled down his lovely but too thin body. Martha had the urge to catch them, but instead she went to him, snuggling her naked body into his, and hugged him. 'I love you, Peter. I am for regretting nothing and have banished the guilt that attacked me. But now, I must away to Sally and prepare her to go back to her mammy.'

As she left him, he bent to pick up the towel. 'Shall I come now and get into your granny's old room?'

'Yes, me darling . . . By the way, is it that you have recovered fully, do you think?'

'From my sickness, or from making love?'

His grin warmed her heart.

'From your sickness.' This came out on a little giggle. It seemed to Martha that she and Peter were a couple now – not two people who had met as strangers and still were in many ways, but as if they had known each other for ever.

'Yes, I think fully so now. I'm hungry, in fact.'

'Well, I am for making porridge and letting it soak overnight. It's in a pan in the pantry. Put it on to boil and help yourself. I'll be getting on, but when it is that you've finished, then take yourself to Granny's room. It's the one with the chair.'

At that moment, Sally let out a determined 'someone come and see to me' squeal. Martha turned away from the mesmerising sight of Peter and scooted up the stairs.

Picking Sally up and dancing around the room with her gave her the pong of why Sally was so bad-tempered. 'Sorry, me wee darling. It is that I had something on me mind . . . I'm in love, Sally! I'm in love with a wonderful man! Just you be waiting till it is that this happens to you, and you will understand.' Sally gurgled. 'Now, smelly bum, let's be getting you cleaned up before I take you to your mammy . . .

I know, it is that both ends of you are needing attention, but bottom end first as that is the most offensive, then I will get you to your mammy for your feed.'

Sally gurgled her approval.

When she opened Trisha's door, she was surprised to find her sitting on her sofa. 'Trish, me darling, are you all right? You should have been staying in your bed till I came.'

'I'm fine, lass. Now don't be making an invalid of me. I took me time and got meself down . . . Eeh, me little Sally.'

As she handed Sally over to Trisha, Sally looked up at her mammy and, to Martha, it was as if the baby knew she was home, such was the look that came over her face.

'Aw, me little lass. Ma is trying to get stronger so I can care for you.' Trisha snuggled her baby into her and kissed her hair. When she looked up, Martha thought that though thinner and with dark circles around her eyes, Trisha had never looked more beautiful.

'It is that you will get stronger, Trish.'

'Aw, Martha, please move in sooner. I could keep me babby with me all the time then.'

Martha didn't know what to say. On the face of it she could and would have done, but now she had Peter. What excuse could she make? A sudden inspiration came to her. 'I am for finding it difficult to leave the last place me granny was . . . I know I must, but it is that I need time to adjust, Trish.'

As the words came out, Martha felt selfish and unkind. She hung her head.

'Naw, don't be guilty, lass. I understand . . . What if we tried me having Sally with me and I knock on the wall if I need you, eh?'

Cheering up and feeling relieved, Martha said, 'Sure, that would be for working. When she has had her last feed in the evening and settled down, I could sit with you for a while. I'll bring the little gown I made up over the last couple of days and sit and hem it. Then before I go, I'll be making her bottle up. We could wrap it in towels to keep it warm till she wakes. But it is that you can knock if you have any difficulty, me darling.'

'Aye, I think that would work.' Trish laid Sally down, ignoring her protests, and put her arms out to Martha. Martha went into them. For all the world she wanted to tell Trisha about Peter but thought it best not to yet. She clung to her friend's thin, frail body. 'I'll always be here for you, Trish, and I will be moving in soon, just not yet. Sure, in another week, though, I'll have me bags on the step.'

'Ta, Martha, for all you do for me. I love you, lass. You and Sally are all I have right now.'

'And I love you, and am for feeling a powerful love surround me. It is for making me able to cope. We'll get through everything we have to face, Trish. We will. Sure, aren't I the one to know that?'

They both giggled and Martha felt a happiness inside her like none other. She had the best friend in the world and Peter – her Peter who she loved as if she had known him for ever.

SIXTEEN

Trisha

The elated and secure feeling left Trisha an hour later. She'd sat a while with Sally lying asleep on the sofa next to her, stroking her babby's hand and dreaming of what life would be like when she felt stronger and could take Sally for walks and play with her. And how it would be when she and Martha lived together.

It was when she was thinking of the time that they'd be able to have a stall together and wondering if Bobby would approve that there came a tap on the door and it opened.

'It's only me.' Edna popped her head around the door. 'Postie was about to drop a letter through for you, lass, so I thought I'd take it off him and bring it in. It's a military one, so from your Bobby, love . . . Aw, look at her, me little darling. Such a pretty girl in lemon . . . Eeh, I say sommat for you, lass, yours and Martha's talent in making her clothes is a marvel. I've never seen a better dressed little babby.'

'Ta, Edna.' Trisha felt sick. *A letter from Bobby . . . Oh, God, has he heard about me?*

'Here, open your letter, lass. I'll put the kettle on as I saw Martha pop out a few minutes ago and head towards the prom.'

Martha? She didn't say owt to me! But then the thought came to Trisha that she didn't want to open her letter in front of anyone.

'Eeh, I would love a cuppa, ta, Edna, but I'll wait a while to open me letter.'

'Naw good putting off the worst, Trisha, love. Better to face it while you have someone with you.'

Trisha felt like telling Edna she was a nosy old cow but bit her tongue and tucked the letter under the cushion. Forcing a smile, she said, 'Naw, I'd rather be alone.'

Edna shrugged. 'Well, I hope it's not bad news then, love. Now, let me get that tea. I'm wanting a cuppa meself, I've naw milk round mine.'

Trisha wanted to laugh out loud, but she held it back in. Lovely as Edna could be, she did have a little streak in her that wasn't likeable.

Left alone with Edna having disappeared into the kitchen, what Martha was doing going out and not saying – which was really unusual – occupied Trisha's thoughts more than the letter did. And the more she thought about it, the more it occurred to her that there had been something different about Martha this morning.

Sally stirring took her attention. As she went to lift her, she felt so weak all of a sudden and had to call Edna to lift her for her. This added to the depression that had clothed her and a tear trickled down her cheek.

'Don't be worrying, lass. You'll be right, I promise you. Whatever is coming, we can't change, so worrying and getting upset ain't naw use. Look at this little mite. Don't she lift your heart? All will be well, you'll see.'

This was Edna's good side, and Trisha welcomed it. She brushed the tear aside and smiled at Sally.

'There, she's grand now and me kettle will be boiling its head off, so I'll pop her back down beside you.'

By the time Edna came back with the tea, Sally had settled again.

When she'd drunk her very welcome tea while listening to the latest gossip – Phyllis down the road had been awake all night as her young Alf had toothache, Rita's lazy old sod of a husband, who hadn't been accepted for war duty because he had flat feet, hadn't got up for work again, and much more – Edna took a breath and said, 'You look tired, love. How about I put Sally in her pram and take her up and down the street, eh? I'll never be far away. You can pop your head out if you need me . . . Come on, babby, let's put a blanket around you to keep you warm. Though the sun is shining today, you haven't the means of keeping yourself warm.'

Trisha didn't object. She welcomed the chance to be alone for a moment – alone, that is, without Edna – but she wished that Martha was with her while she opened Bobby's letter. Where could Martha have gone and why didn't she say? This was so unlike her.

Once on her own, Trisha's nerves clenched her stomach as she opened the letter. The first word she read was: *Bitch!*

Gasping, she refolded the paper and held it on her lap. Bobby had judged her. His ma had told him her version and he'd taken it. In her heart, she knew it to be the truth, that she had betrayed him, but a big part of her had so wanted him to believe the story she'd made up and to stand by her. She knew she didn't deserve that but had hoped for it.

With a sinking heart she read the rest.

Me ma weren't fooled, and neither am I. Rape? There's no such thing and you know it, Trisha. If a bloke did jump you, you've only to kick him in the balls, or scream for help. You're never far from a house in Blackpool on your way home. You're no good and never have been. I'll sort you out when I get home and your bastard child an' all.

You're me wife and from now on you're going to do as I tell you. It's the only way to treat you. I tried being good to you and loving you, but that weren't good enough. Well, you prepare yourself, as this war is coming to an end, and I'll be home soon. You'll know it then. I'll have you on your knees begging me for mercy. Well, it's up to you. If you don't want your bastard to suffer, get rid of it before I come home.

That's all I have to say, except watch yourself as I have folk keeping an eye on you.

You mind me words,

Bobby

By the time she'd finished reading, tears were streaming down her face. How would he be when he knew that she couldn't give him children because of what she'd done? But then she straightened. Never would he part her and

Sally. Nor would she ever let him hurt her. She would swing for him first.

Screwing the letter up, she threw it into the fire then watched it burst into flames. As the last of it was beginning to smoulder, the door opened.

'Eeh, you didn't stay long, Edna.'

'Naw, she's off to sleep now. I'll leave her outside for a bit, babbies always sleep well in the fresh air. So? What did Bobby have to say? . . . By, it were that bad you've had to burn it! Well, that'll be his ma and her nasty tongue, lass.'

Aye, Trisha thought, *and you're not above that yourself, Edna*. But she bit her tongue and didn't let herself say so.

'He'll be all right when he gets home. It was a shock to him, that's all.'

'Naw, lass, he won't, this'll fester in him and what about when he finds out what it's brought on you? Men like to father a young 'un, even if they never take any further notice of their kids. A babby is testament to them being up to it. That they're as manly as the next.'

Trisha felt defeated. She could see in Edna's eyes and hear in her voice that she didn't believe the lie about the rape. For a moment, she felt like confessing all as the strain on her was too much, but she knew she mustn't ever do that.

'Right, love, if you're all right, I'll leave you for a while. I put me copper on to boil before I came out – it's me day for doing me whites. Babby's fine, I'll keep me eye on her.' She opened the door. 'Eeh, here's Martha, and it looks like she's been shopping . . . Hello, Martha. What you been buying then, lass?'

'Oh, it is that it's nothing, Edna. Just some material and I've had to go and pay me rent on me pitch. I'm hoping to get back to me work soon, so I am.'

'You'll be losing your powers at this rate, love. And what it is that you sew all the time, I don't knaw. Sally's the best dressed young 'un in Blackpool as it is. Let me take a look then.'

Trisha couldn't see Martha, but judging by the way she reacted to this, it seemed that there was something she needed to hide.

'No, that isn't for being possible as it is a surprise that I am planning.'

Trisha heard Martha's door open and then close in a hurry.

'Well, did you hear that? What's she up to, eh? . . . Surprise? A surprise for who, I'd like to knaw. Anyroad, me copper'll boil over at this rate. I'll see you later, Trisha, lass.'

Trisha didn't have to wait long for Martha to appear. Her flushed face showed there was a secret. 'Martha, love, you can share anything with me. I'd never judge you. I made the mistake of hiding me pregnancy from you and that caused a sort of rift between us and put a strain on me. I don't want you to go through that, lass.'

Martha moved towards her. 'I need a hug, Trish.'

Holding her as best she could in her weak state, Trisha stroked Martha's hair. 'Let it out, love. I'm here for you. Ma always said, a trouble shared is a trouble halved.'

'It's Peter . . . It is that I am hiding him so that I can help him.'

'What? Oh, Martha, lass, you could be in danger. You

don't knaw him. Eeh, I knaw as you were attracted to him, but at the end of the day, he's a vagabond.'

'Not by choice, Trish . . . Anyway, it is that you need to sit down, me darling. I'll sit beside you and tell you Peter's story and what it is that I plan.'

As she sat and held Martha's hand, Trisha let the whole story be told. Misgivings filled her, but she knew that to voice them would be the worst thing she could do. Besides, she felt there was more. Something Martha was ashamed to tell. She decided a little prompting might help. 'And you've fallen for him, haven't you, lass?'

Martha smiled. 'It is that you know me better than I know myself, but yes, Trish. I love him. I did from the moment he entered my tent and I looked into his eyes.'

'Has he taken advantage of that, love?'

'No! I mean, well, he didn't force me. I – I don't know why, but I find myself unable to resist, and even . . . Oh, Trish, it was for being me who initiated it.'

'Eeh, Martha, lass. I understand, I do, but you knaw where this could lead you.'

Martha lowered her head.

'By, we could be double trouble me and you, love. But allus remember, I'm here for you and will allus be so. Just like you are for me. Nowt may come of it. It don't allus happen. Anyroad, he might marry you, so then you won't have a problem.'

'I know it is that he will, Trish. With being fed and cleaned up, he will be strong enough to go out looking for work, and then to get himself a place. He knows he only has three weeks for that to happen.'

'There's a place on Coronation Street that only takes men workers in. A lot come during the season. But I don't recommend seasonal work. Has Peter any special skills?'

'I'm not for knowing. He went to war at age sixteen.'

'Well, he must have done sommat between leaving the orphanage and then.'

'He drifted. He hadn't a home, so couldn't get a job, then war began, and he lied about his age. He wasn't for having a birth certificate, so no questions were asked.'

'And you say it was a medical discharge due to being chesty and it was the fumes from the big guns that did it?'

'Yes. It is that you can hear a rattle in his chest . . . well, when you're close to him.'

Trisha giggled. 'You're as daft as me for getting so close . . . Eeh, Martha. I pray you ain't going to get trouble from all of this.'

Again, Martha lowered her head.

'Lass, that ain't me judging you. It was just me saying. Anyroad, we can ask around as regards a job for Peter, but we have to keep him secret, so coming and going ain't going to be easy. What if we put together to get him a room for a week, and then put all our effort into getting him a job? I knaw I can't do owt for a couple of weeks, but I could give you a note to take to folk who knaw me and see what they say.'

'What kind of job, Trish?'

'The fish gutting huts for one. They've been taking on women, but allus need men. Bobby did it to get extra pay when he couldn't get on a trawler. It ain't big money and it makes you stink, but it's a job. I knaw the foreman an' all.'

Trisha could see hope light up Martha's eyes.

'Then there's the railway. By, you'd be able to wave to him if he got took on as a stoker or sommat, but there's allus men working on the repairing, or as porters. And they're all old men as the young are at war, so that'll be a chance for him. Me da's mate works as a porter. I ain't seen him in a good while, but he'd knaw if owt were going that would be suitable for Peter.'

'Oh, Trish, that's amazing. I am thinking the railway rather than the fishing industry. It is that poor Peter has been stinking this good while and I've only just been for cleaning him up.'

They burst out laughing. And Trisha thought it a healing laughter. She hadn't yet told Martha about her letter, but though she'd vowed no secrets, she knew this wasn't the time.

'And, Trish, if I could move in with you sooner, sure, I could be helping him out more with only half the rent to pay.'

'You don't have to pay rent, lass.'

'I'm knowing that, but I want to. Half of everything is only fair.'

'All right, lass. It would be a help now I'm not able to work. Besides, it might affect me dependence money having you lodge with me, so I'll need it.'

'The only thing that is for worrying me is when I can be getting back to work.'

'I think you can go soon, Martha. I have Edna . . . I don't like her nosying around, but she is a good sort and will do owt for me and me Sally. She's been caring for her all morning.'

'Oh, Trish, I am sorry. It was torn that I was, but I had to get those clothes for Peter.'

'Just be telling me next time. You had me worried.'

'Sure, I will. No secrets between us, not ever . . . Which is bringing me to ask, what is it that has happened while I was out? I had a powerful feeling of foreboding when I came in here, so I did.'

Trisha decided she too must keep to the no secret rule. At the end of her telling, Martha gasped. 'But it is that you have to move from here, Trish.'

'I can't. Who would have me, eh? And you an' all. We're stuck. Our first aim is to get you settled before Bobby comes home. Then I'll take me chances with him. He mellowed once, he might again.'

'But he will be having so much to take . . . not just little Sally, but you not being . . . I mean . . .'

'Aye, I knaw. But what alternative do I have, eh? I reckon that if I stay, I might stand a chance of him accepting Sally, but if I go . . . Eeh, Martha, I'm trapped.'

The enormity of this hit Trisha. She lay back her head as tiredness swept over her.

'Don't be for worrying. It is that something will turn up. I see a good future for you, Trisha. And for me too. Once we are ready and you are well, we should use me pitch to put up our stall and take our chances. There's room enough at the front of me tent. Then you can be selling what we make while I carry on with the fortune telling.'

'It sounds grand, but what do you see for me when Bobby comes home?'

Martha hesitated, then smiled. 'I only know that in the end it will come right, me darling. Sure, weren't you one for blocking me looking into your future? Well, it is only when it is entwined with mine that I am for knowing it now.'

Trisha didn't believe this, but she didn't press Martha.

'So, when are you going back to work then?'

'I'll start in three days. I'm thinking I will go to this boarding house tomorrow; I'll tell them it is for a friend I am securing a room and that he arrives that evening. And then I'll be going to the railway. Then if it is that Peter is settled, I'll be taking a day to move into here and for getting Lil to come sooner. There's a few pieces she is keen to get her hands on after she was visiting to take a look.'

'Aye, Lil will give you a fair price – not what your stuff's worth, mind, but it is peace of mind to knaw as she'll get everything collected an' all. Eeh, I hope tomorrow goes well. The sooner you give your notice to Hattie Hargreaves, the better, as she'll charge you rent till the day you do.'

Martha nodded. Then asked, 'Is it that you need to eat your midday meal, Trish, for I have cooked an Irish stew and there's plenty of it for you too?'

'Aye, lass. That'd be good. I'll rest me eyes while you get it ready. I'll be fine till then.'

'Well, I'm thinking that Sally will be wanting a bottle. So I'll prepare that before I go, and all you'll need to make her comfortable after. Edna will soon be bringing her to you if she cries.'

* * *

When Martha left, having put all she'd need to see to Sally on the end of the sofa, Trisha leaned back and allowed her fear in. Martha had a look on her face when she'd asked how it was going to go with Bobby, which made her know that it wasn't going to be that she could persuade him to accept the situation. That wasn't good. Bobby could be cruel, and she was no match for him. As she closed her eyes, she told herself that she would practise kicking a man where it hurt, so that she could defend herself. And she might put a few weapons around the place to be able to get hold of quickly – not that she knew if she could hurt Bobby. The thought made her feel sick. Maybe she would just take her punishment and hope he got tired of giving it when he could see that nothing was going to change her mind. As long as he never hurt Sally – she couldn't see him doing so, but if he did . . .

A tear trickled down her cheek. She closed her eyes, causing more tears to run from them. For a moment, she almost wished something would happen to Bobby for she didn't know how she could face what he'd threatened.

SEVENTEEN

Martha

Martha snuggled into Peter. His arm lay under her head and his body was damp with sweat, as was her own nakedness. Their lovemaking had made her cry out with the ecstasy, and she hoped that Mrs Higginbottom next door hadn't heard her. If Trisha had, she would understand and, in any case, Martha, having told all to Trish, no longer felt the need to keep anything from her.

'I'll miss you tomorrow night, Martha. How will I be able to see you when I'm staying at the boarding house? Not that I'm not grateful for what you've done for me today – a home and a job – but I can't imagine not being able to make love to you . . . I – I'd never done it with anyone else, ever. You're me one and only girl.'

'I am knowing how you're feeling, but it is hopeless in our situation. Maybe Trisha will let you be visiting late at night for a couple of hours, but it is a huge thing to ask of her. Better it is that we both save to get a place of our own.'

'Are you saying you would marry me, if I did that?'

'I am, Peter, me darling man. I am, if it is that you be asking me?'

Peter untangled his body from hers and slid off the bed. There he went down on one knee. 'Will you marry me, me lovely Irish lass?'

'I will. I love you with all me heart, so I do.'

'Then with me first week's wage, I'll put the banns up and one month from now, we'll be wed!'

'Oh, Peter. It is our destiny.'

His kisses didn't allow her to say more. His lovemaking of her this second time was a frantic taking of her, but she didn't mind. To her, he was sealing his claim on her and for all his hurry, she still enjoyed every moment.

When he lay back spent, it wasn't long before she heard his breathing steady and then deepen. She lay listening to the sound of his slight wheeziness and worried that it may one day worsen once more but comforted herself that for now it seemed a lot better.

Her own eyes closed, but then shot open as a voice startled her. *Martha, what you dream of will be many a year from now. But never give up, keep the faith.*

Feeling stiff with fright, she lay there staring at the fading light of the gas lamp on the ceiling. What could it mean? *Please, Jesus, Mary and Joseph, don't let it refer to me and Peter – maybe the business I'm planning?* Again, she hoped it wasn't that.

Not able to conclude what was meant, Martha gave herself to thinking about the business. Would it work? Was there the custom for the lovely garments she and Trisha had made?

She forced herself to leave these thoughts as it disturbed her too much to delve into what should be the unknown. She'd always known that she would never see her own future clearly. This puzzled her; Granny hadn't been able to either. Only the odd premonition, like just now. But then, like Granny, she wouldn't want to know as life would be all about trying to change your own destiny.

Dear Granny, I miss you so much. Was that you just now? How I would love to be in touch with you and to be guided by your wisdom. I still feel your love encasing me and it comforts me to know that will stay for ever. Rest in peace, Granny.

The next thing she knew, she was opening her eyes to the dim morning light filtering through the curtains. Reaching out her arm gave her an empty space next to her. She sat up as panic gripped her. *Sally!* Then she remembered that Trisha had insisted on keeping Sally with her, and that was why Peter had come to her bed. *Peter! Where is he?*

Listening for any sound, she heard nothing. Throwing back the covers, she braved the cold lino and skipped across to the door. Opening it, she called out, 'Peter!'

Only silence met her. Why she felt so bereft and lonely she didn't know. *Sure*, she told herself, *he'll be in the lav.* But in her heart, she knew there was no one other than herself in the house. Donning her slippers and grabbing a cardigan to put over her nightdress, she ran down the stairs. A cold blast of air met her. The front door was wide open!

'Peter . . . Peter!'

The street was empty. Running to the yard to check the lav didn't help. Peter was nowhere to be found. *Why? Why has he gone? Did I push him too much to be settled and to get a job? Could it be that he couldn't cope?*

Tears of desolation filled her eyes. 'Peter, Peter . . . No! Don't leave me.'

Slumping down on the sofa, a feeling took her that her world had turned black. Fear and loneliness cloyed her and though the cold air made her shiver, she couldn't bring herself to close the door – that would be like making it a truth that Peter had gone.

As full daylight dawned and the street began to wake, Martha managed to close the door. She didn't want anyone prying into why she had let the elements in so early. But how was she to live if Peter never came back to her? The thought split her heart in two.

It was then that the idea occurred to her to see if Peter's clothes had gone. Dashing back upstairs, she found they had. She threw herself onto the bed and wept. Peter had left her. He'd taken everything she'd bought him and gone.

Wandering from room to room, not knowing why, Martha cried out her anguish. *How could this have happened?* Peter's whispers of his love for her, the plans he'd made – asking her to marry him. It was all so he could have his way with her and when he had, he'd left. How could he be so callous, so cold, and have no thought for her?

These thoughts didn't last long before they turned to worry for him. Something must have happened to him.

With this thought a new determination entered her. She would search for him, make enquiries. He had to be somewhere! Maybe he was ill? But though she went over and over the possible reasons for his disappearance, nothing settled her.

Hearing Sally crying gave her the knowledge that Trisha must be up. Finding the key to Trisha's house, she ran around there and let herself in. Trisha's voice came to her. 'There, there, me little lass. Your ma will soon have your bottle made. Hush now, the kettle is on.'

'Trish, Trish!'

'Martha? Is that you? I'm in the kitchen ... What's wrong? Eeh, Martha, lass, what's happened?'

'He's gone ... gone!'

Trish stood holding on to the side of the pot sink with Sally propped on her hip. She looked frail and shaky. The sight of her pulled Martha up. 'I'm sorry, me darling, I shouldn't have barged in. Here, let me hold the wee one for you.'

'Naw, it's all right. Sommat's happened, ain't it? Did you and Peter have a row?'

Martha could only shake her head.

Sally whimpered.

'I'll be making the bottle. You go and sit down. Let's get Sally seen to, then it is I'll tell you.'

'By, Martha, I'm worried over you. You look awful.'

'It is that Peter has gone. I woke and he had dressed and left. No note, nothing. He ... he even left the door open. Oh, Trish, something has happened to him, it must have. Why is it he would do this to me?'

'You daft ha'peth, he probably ran out of fags or sommat. He'll be back.'

A little hope entered Martha. This could be the answer – but why leave the door open?

Brushing this thought away, she beckoned Trisha to sit down and took over the task of making the bottle.

The process didn't stop her mind working. *Has he left me for ever? No! I couldn't bear that! What if he thought me too forward and that I would go with any man? And I was! Oh, Jesus, Mary and Joseph, what possessed me to behave in such a manner? Please, please don't let me have lost him. I love him. He's for being the completion of me.*

How this had happened in the instant way it had, and how the feeling had made her behave as she did, giving herself wholly and completely to a man she hardly knew, was beyond her understanding. All her teaching as a child, that marriage was a sacrament that bound a man and woman and only within its boundaries did sexual relationships take place, with the wife bowing to her husband's needs and bearing him children, had meant nothing when faced with the power of the feeling of love.

Shame washed over her once more – a feeling that after the first time of lying with Peter had visited her but had then vanished from the emotions she'd felt. Only the need to be joined with him had meant anything.

When she took the bottle through to Trisha, she was surprised by what Trisha said. 'You knaw, Martha, I've never been in love. I knaw that now. I miss Bobby, but . . . eeh, I don't knaw, I seem to be driven by a different need to what you've experienced – an attraction, or sommat like that. I didn't love . . . and now I knaw that I have never been in love with Bobby either – just sort of obsessed with him as a young girl and that led to me giving him what he wanted. Then, well, once I had known the feeling, I wanted more of it.'

Martha knew this wasn't how it was for her. Her heart broke to think of it, but if Peter was gone for ever, she could never give herself to another man. She would never fall in love again.

'Oh, Trish . . . I – I feel lost, abandoned, helpless.' She slumped into the seat next to Trisha.

'Naw, lass. Stop this now. Peter's only been gone five minutes – more than likely on an errand – and you're acting as if you are a grieving widow! He'll be back, I tell you, love. Now come on. Stop being daft.'

Martha couldn't stop the tears as she knew in her heart that Peter wasn't coming back. She closed her eyes and leaned back. Visions came to her of Peter. Hazy visions of a man lost, wandering, unsure.

Was she just clutching at straws? Finding a reason? She couldn't bear to think of him just abandoning her.

Trisha broke into her thoughts. 'Martha, love, don't hurt yourself like this. Just wait and see, eh?'

After all the surety, Martha could now detect a note of uncertainty in Trisha's voice, and this deepened her anxiety.

Laying Sally on the cushion next to her, Trisha turned towards Martha. Her arm came around her. 'Eeh, lass, lass.'

Martha leaned her head on Trisha's shoulder, feeling an even stronger affinity to her as now she understood. Trisha needed love. Since her father died, no man had ever loved her as he had, and she'd been looking for that love – mistaking it for attraction and paying the consequences. *I've known love – me pappy, me grandpappy and Peter.*

It came to her then that always she'd lost those she loved, but at least she had known them – been cherished by them.

'I love you, Trish. You're the best thing in me life.'

'By, lass, that's a bit deep. But I love you an' all. I love you like you're the sister I never had. We'll be all right, Martha, love. We'll help each other. Let's get you moved in – at least till you can get on your feet, lass. We have to aim for that, as I'm in enough trouble when Bobby comes home as it is. But it won't mean we ain't going to be a support to each other just because we ain't living together.'

'I am for knowing that, Trish. You're always going to be by me side, and me by yours.'

They sat quietly for a while, Martha with her head rested on Trisha's shoulder and Trisha's head resting on hers.

Martha's heart was broken, but her solace would always be the love she had for Trisha and little Sally. She'd care for them and try to make their lives better.

Thinking of this, she determined to tackle Cissy about letting her add a stall to her pitch. They had enough garments made to make a start – just to see how the land lay before the season really came to an end and Bobby returned. For when he did, their lives would change drastically.

A shudder went through her as the premonition she'd always had about what would happen when Bobby came home revisited her. She wanted to save Trisha but knew she couldn't. It was this that she hated about her gift – having the knowledge of bad things and not being able to prevent them. Just as she knew Peter had left.

The voice she'd heard in the night came back to her. *Martha, what you dream of will be many a year from now. But never give up, keep the faith.*

It comforted her – told her that one day her dream of being with Peter would come true.

'Eeh, me arm's aching.' Trisha sighed. 'Will I ever feel strong again, Martha?'

'It is that you will, me darling. But until then I'll be your strength.' With this, Martha determined that she wouldn't put her troubles onto Trisha's shoulders, but to find her solace in looking after her and Sally.

The rest of the day went into a blur of hoping and looking both ways up the street whenever she could as she went about moving in with Trisha. The only piece of furniture needed was a bed, as Trisha had sold her ma's now.

Martha had decided she would take her granny's. Though it was a double and would leave her very little space, she would find it a comfort as her granny and Peter had both slept in it. She hoped, too, to take Granny's bedroom chair – a wicker rocking chair – with her. And, she thought, of course, her precious sewing machine.

As it turned out, she managed to get both in, helped by Lil's men.

By the evening all was sorted, and Martha felt exhausted, if a little relieved that tonight she would be with others and feel safe as no one could put her out on the streets.

She sat on her bed and looked over at the eleven pounds lying on the dresser – the total she had been paid for all her furniture, cooker, mangle, cleaning brushes, carpet beater, rugs, ornaments and curtains, and thought, *My starting capital. The means to changing me life.*

As her heart dropped with the thought that she hadn't wanted her life to change as much as it would, she quickly started to plan how she would make things happen. *Always I must be doing this – finding a distraction. If I don't, how am I to be Trisha's strength if I lose my own?*

Making a determined effort, she retrieved a writing pad and pen from the top drawer of the dresser and wrote a list.

Get permission from Cissy to have the stall.
Find a carpenter to make the stall.

This led her to drawing a design as she needed it to have a roof with a rainproof curtain that could be closed around it. Their stock, she decided, would have to be taken home each evening. This led to item three – clean the trunks she and Granny had brought from Ireland carrying their belongings and which were now stashed under the bed. The lining of both needed replacing.

And finally, to buy more material and wool and encourage Trisha to take up her knitting again as in the beginning, she wouldn't be able to come and help on the stall.

A host of problems kicked in then – what to do about trying to run the stall and to continue with her fortune telling? How was she to manage? It was then that she had the idea of not going for a stall just yet, but a kind of display unit that would fit into her tent, then she could do both. Hopefully, she could sell her wares to her clients. With this, ideas tumbled. Maybe something could be constructed so that on a fine day she could hang some garments on the outside of her tent – and as the hot day they'd had today proved, there were always some nice weather days in September and even in October.

Excitement began to build as more ideas occurred. Not just for how she would sell their products but make more too – always she had her quiet times. If she could do her machining in the evening, she could leave the hand sewing for the daytime. After all, her machine was now in the living room, so she and Trisha could still work together as they always had done.

Hope began to seep into her. Not only for her financial future as she made herself remember the voice of the night. *Me dream of being with Peter will come true in the future. I must hang on to that and let it be me prop to get me through.*

Feeling better, Martha tucked her writing pad back in the drawer and stretched her body. The sound of Sally crying had her running down the stairs. Trisha, too, would be feeling really tired, so now was a good time to take charge.

In the living room, Trisha sat on the sofa, her face white and sunken. The air held the pong of Sally having filled her nappy – which reminded Martha that there was a bucket full of nappies soaking under the sink in the scullery. On top of that, they'd barely eaten today!

'Trish, if I be changing and cleaning up, then making her a bottle, would it be that you could feed her? I'm thinking of going to the chippy and treating us to fish and chips.'

'Eeh, that sounds grand, lass . . . Only, well, if I rest me eyes a while, I'd like to walk with you – Sally would sleep in her pram, and the evening's still warm. We could eat our fish and chips on the sea wall – there's nowt like eating them out of newspaper with the sea breeze on your face.'

'Oooh, I'd be loving that. Are you for being sure?'

'I am. Like I say, I'll rest a while, then sort meself out. I've still got one of Ma's cardigans that I ain't yet unravelled – the blue one. I'll wear that. Me ma'll be hugging me then.'

'Ah, to be sure, that's a lovely saying. Right, I'll soon scoot around. Then tomorrow, I'll put the copper on and catch up with all the washing, but in the afternoon, I'll go and see Cissy. I am for having a lot of plans. I'll tell you about them when we are eating our chips.'

Once they got to the seafront, Arthur pulled up. 'So, where are you two off to?'

Martha looked up at him. 'Are you able to be getting the pram on board, Arthur?'

'Aye. Though you two will have to sit up front with me. You see, I've adapted the back seat to put it on hinges, so now I only have to lift it up to make room for all manner of things – perambulators being one of them.'

Trisha giggled. 'Eeh, that's a posh word, Arthur.'

'Well, I deal with posh folk, Trisha, lass – though, they're not me favourite customers. You two lasses top me list of favourites.'

This made Martha feel warm inside. Arthur had been a constant in their life since that first ride to see the gypsies.

'Well then, you'll be giving us a discount, lad.'

Martha burst out laughing at this from Trisha – something she thought she'd never do again. But then, Trisha was so funny – not just what she'd said, but calling middle-aged Arthur 'lad'!

'Seeing as I've missed you, Trisha, and how good it is to see you up and about – as I don't mind telling you, you had me worried – then this ride is on me.'

'Ta, Arthur. This is the first time I've felt able to come out, but by, I'm feeling it in me tired bones.'

'I'll help you up. Come on, lass.'

To Martha, it felt as though Arthur was like a father to them and it was a nice feeling. No one could replace her pappy, or Trisha's da, but having Arthur felt good.

'So, where to, now you're all aboard?'

Martha spoke up. 'I'm thinking now we have a ride, Trisha, we could go and check on me tent?'

'By, that'd be grand. We could sit on our bit of wall then, and we can buy our fish and chips at Macie's. She sells the best and it'd be good to see her and show Sally to her.'

'Reet! Hold on, girls, Macie's it is. It's getting a bit dark now, so I'll have to weave in and out of the folk. For some reason, they love to take a stroll in the evenings as the dusk descends and as the promenade lights begin to come on. They seem to criss-cross the road at will.'

'You knaw, Martha, I loved the donkeys. It were the best job ever.' Trisha was gazing wistfully along the beach. 'The young 'uns were funny and joyful, though a few were afraid. I liked helping them gain their confidence and seeing them come back again for another ride.'

They were sitting on the wall. Martha wiped some vinegar that had dripped down her chin. Checking her tent had given her so many emotions and pain for the two people who'd occupied it and she loved dearly – both gone. *Granny and Peter.* Just saying their names in her mind made her catch her breath.

'Martha, you ain't listening to me, lass.'

'What? Oh . . . yes, I am. You were talking of loving the donkeys . . . Well, one day they might be yours.'

'Ha, what a thing to say! Where am I going to get the money to buy the donkeys, let alone a field to keep them in and a stable? Eeh, Martha, you daft ha'peth.'

'When we make our fortune. We will, I'm sure of it. Sure, it is that mammies won't be able to resist our wares, you'll see.'

Martha didn't think that Trisha had the same faith as herself in their business venture, or maybe her heart wasn't in it, but despite that she felt determined to make a go of it and knew that though Trisha wasn't believing it, she would put her heart and soul into it just the same.

They were quiet for a while. The peace around them soothed Martha. She loved listening to the lapping of the water against the wall and loved, too, the salty smell of the sea. To feel the wind in her hair, caressing her and giving her pure air to breathe. Tonight, though, they did little to soothe the pain of her broken heart, but nothing could do that.

Sighing, she screwed up the remaining chips into the greasy newspaper, not able to finish them all. 'Is it that you're for finishing your chips, Trisha?'

'I can't eat them all. I've ate me fish, it was delicious. But here, give me your leftovers. We'll empty them onto the ground as the seagulls love them.'

Within seconds they were crowded by squawking seagulls, flapping their wings, going for each other in their battle to get the juiciest morsel, swooping, ducking and diving, making Martha cringe away from them.

'Ha, scaredy-cat, they're lovely. Look how big they are and how white.'

'I'm beginning to think your calling is the animal and bird world, Trish.'

'Aye, I've always loved them . . . Right, Arthur should be along in a mo. Be a good 'un and put the paper in the bin, love. I'm whacked out – in a nice way, though. I've loved it tonight, Martha. Ta, lass.'

To see Trisha's lovely smile warmed a little of the coldness from Martha's heart. Whatever happened, she'd always have Trisha by her side, she was certain of that.

Giving her a hand down, she told her, 'We're going to be all right, Trish. It is that I can feel it. But I also feel we've a lot to go through.'

'Well, we'll go through it together, Martha, lass. Hand in hand, hearts entwined in friendship that naw one can break, so we'll always cope, eh?'

'We will, me darling. To be sure, we will.'

EIGHTEEN

Martha

Christmas had come and gone. With the sorrow she and Trisha both felt at missing loved ones, especially Granny, and the shock of Peter's disappearance still fresh for Martha, and Trisha still coming to terms with all she'd been through, they hadn't made much fuss. Sally had slept through most of the day, her first Christmas.

Not feeling festive, she and Trisha had enjoyed a peaceful lunch, Trisha having been given a couple of nice pork chops by the butcher who'd always done business with Bobby.

And so, after what was a non-event, the last two months had seemed to pass Martha by, and now, here she was back in the tent, with Easter soon to be upon them.

Her client's voice breaking into her thoughts brought Martha's attention back to her work.

'I want you to tell me if I am going to have children.'

Martha dealt the tarot cards. 'Choose a card to know your destiny.'

Always relieved to give good news, Martha smiled when the lady chose the ace of cups.

'Sure, it is that you are destined to find emotionally fulfilling relationships. An abundance of good things is to come your way – your cup really does runneth over, madam, so yes, as the cups are also associated with fertility, it is that you will have a family.'

The lady, who Martha judged as being in her mid-twenties, was beautiful with fair hair cut fashionably to just below her ears, parted in the middle and bunching into curls. Her eyes were hazel – honest eyes, Martha would call them, as she gave an air of innocence when she gazed at you. Her smile at this news faded for a moment as she said, 'Oh, thank you, but, well, my husband is in France . . . He will come home safely, won't he?'

Martha laughed. This she knew for certain. 'Yes, how else is it that your cup will brim to the top?'

The lady let out a little giggle of delight.

Martha, who always felt a little intimidated when dealing with the rich, warmed to her.

'Thank you. You have made my day. As has all this talk of us making many gains over the Germans now and it looking as though victory will soon be ours.'

Martha had mixed feelings about this. The elation she felt was tempered by her worries – Trisha's coming ordeal when Bobby returned and, on a lesser scale, where she would live.

She loved living with Trisha and didn't want that to end. They'd been so happy, watching Sally grow, teaching her new things, celebrating her every milestone and sharing her care – Trisha in the daytime and herself in the evening. Bath time was hers and Sally's special moment while Trisha rested with a cup of tea. Always there was laughter. Or if either of them did feel the pain of their grief, they comforted each other.

Things would change soon for them. Trisha had decided to do another season running the donkeys, while Martha had built their layette business from her tent – something she'd already started. Not that she'd sold much yet as there weren't many visitors at this time of year.

'Is there anything else? You have gone very quiet, Martha.'

Martha thought it funny how the rich felt they could use her name as seen on the board outside, but if a working-class woman came in, they would call her 'miss'.

Martha quickly covered up her momentary silence. 'No, it is that with the mention of war coming to an end a host of things came into my mind – the joy of that and the sorrow, too, for those families of boys who won't return.'

'Yes, I know what you mean.' Her eyes cast downwards. 'We have lost three young men from our family.'

'Yes, I detected the sadness. It is that I am sorry.'

'Well, I am on a happy mission today, so we won't dwell on it . . . I have wanted to ask you about the baby clothes and shawls you are displaying. They are beautiful.'

She listened with interest, rising and examining the garments closely as Martha told of hers and Trisha's plans.

'That's a wonderful idea, my dear, and would you consider making to order?'

'To be sure, that is one of our aims. We're building up the stock and I am for selling them from here to get our capital together. But the winters are long, and all promenade work dries up then, so we haven't been for making much progress yet. Though it is that the summer months are not for being a problem to us as many visitors come, but to take on a shop, we will be needing to trade all year.

'It can be done. I and many of my friends and associates buy from adverts in our magazines. You could sell that way. What we buy is delivered and charged to our account or paid for by cash on delivery.'

Martha had never heard of shopping this way. She had seen advertising in old magazines, but always she'd imagined you had to go to the shop to buy anything you liked.

Suddenly, she latched on to the positive outlook this lady had. She felt her stomach muscles tickle with anticipation, even though it all sounded beyond her and Trisha.

They could learn how it all worked. She listened carefully to everything the lady had to say and made a mental note of it all.

'It is for sounding just what we need to be doing, and yet not something we are having the capability of, especially, the bit about having to have a telephone!'

'Leave it with me. I will find out what I can for you … and, if you would allow, I would be glad to help. I have faith in you, Martha.' She put out a gloved hand. 'My name is Lady Rebecca Portlend. I have a friend, Lady Darcy Smythe. We champion women's rights and campaign for them. I just know she will find your layettes delightful. She has three girls and a boy and is wanting clothes for … Oh, you would make clothes for older children, I presume?'

'It is that we would. We would do anything asked of us.'

She fumbled in her bag. 'Here is my card. Do you have one I can have?'

Martha took the beautifully engraved card. 'No, I am not for having anything like this.'

'An address then, where I can contact you?'

'Cissy will take any business post. She's the owner of the guest house. I rent me plot from her.'

'I'll ring her bell and ask her for a card. Then, when I return to London, I will write to you. Suddenly, I am full of ideas and will try to help you all I can. I know many influential people, my dear. I feel I have a new cause to champion. And a worthy one. I really love yours and your friend's work and I think you deserve help for trying to better yourself.'

'Ta, that is so good of you. Oh, and me surname's O'Hara, not Lee as it says outside. That's a family name used by all the fortune tellers who are descendants of the Lees.'

'Oh, I see. Yes, I have seen that often, usually with "Gypsy" in front of the Christian name.'

'Me granny was a gypsy who found love with a farmer and left to marry him. I have never been for knowing that life. I was brought up in Dublin.'

'What an interesting life. It has been a pleasure meeting you and you will be hearing from me, Martha. And thank you for the good news. My husband and I hope to have a family when he's home. Only, as it hadn't happened by the time he left . . . We were married a year by then, and I have an older sister who is barren, I feared that I might be too.'

'There is nothing coming to me to say that you are.'

'Thank you . . . Well, my dear.' Once more, she opened her purse. 'I must pay you.'

'No, it is that it was a pleasure to be putting your mind at rest.'

'Not at all, dear, I owe you a debt.'

Martha couldn't believe her eyes when Lady Rebecca put a crisp pound note on her table. The sight of it made her bite her tongue as to refusing. It would be such a help.

As she left, Lady Rebecca turned and smiled. 'Check your post in a week or two, my dear, and I wish you good luck with your venture.'

Then she was gone.

Martha lifted the pound note and sat back in her granny's chair. Her face creased into a smile as she looked at it, an excitement bubbled up in her at the thought of the offer made by Lady Rebecca. *All my dreams could come true! Though I am wondering how it will work out.*

There wasn't long to ponder as Martha had only just arranged her embroidering stand on her table, intending to continue with the smocking she was doing on a baby dress, when the door flap opened again. Framed in the opening was a gypsy girl who she'd seen selling lucky heather on the promenade.

'Hello. Is it that I can help you?'

'I'm Cilla, great-granddaughter of Gypsy Rosa Lee who has now passed and gone to her rest. Before she did, she made me see that I must use my gift more than I do. I'm looking for you to test me and to maybe take me on a few hours.'

Martha went to say that she couldn't do that but stopped herself as it came to her that she may need an assistant. Before she could say anything, though, the girl said, 'I can tell you your fortune, if you like? I have a reading of you.'

'Really! That is for being amazing, so it is. But no. I prefer not to be knowing. How does your guiding spirit be working within you?'

'Visions, mainly. I look a person in the eyes, and then I close mine. It is then that the visions come. I – I . . . well, I have told folk things for them buying lucky heather – I wasn't taking your business, only to entice them to buy. I've seen them come into you after, as if they want to verify me. Many have come back and told me that you told them the same thing that I did . . . There was a lady a while back that came out of your tent. I saw immediately that she was going to die. She ran across the road and was knocked down by a tram and killed instantly.'

'Oh, I remember her. It is that this is amazing me. But then sure, we are relations, are we not?'

'Aye, your granny was a cousin of mine. But what that makes us, I haven't a clue.'

They both giggled.

'Sure, it is that our being related will be good grounds for us to start to work together.'

'You'll take me on then?'

'I'd be thinking it an honour, only, well, for a start, I'm not able to be giving you much by way of a wage. You will have to accept a small cut, but it is that I have plans . . .'

'Your layette shop?'

'You are for knowing that?'

'Ha, of course, I have the gift.'

Again, they were laughing. And for the second time that day, Martha knew she'd met someone who was going to be very important in her life and who would bring changes to it.

'So, I think if it is you could come to sit with me and take a few of me clients through their readings, that will be giving me a good knowledge of what you are capable of. After that, you can be having a few of your own. But I have a golden rule, so I have. It is as me granny said, we cannot be changing people's destiny, so if you see disaster, you mustn't be telling them. Most come in with something special they are needing to know. Address that, and tell them so much, but we have to be kind. Hearing bad news could send some to their deaths.'

'Kill themselves, you mean?'

'I do. So, we must always use discretion in the predictions we see.'

'But what if we can save them?'

'That is not for us to do. We aren't God.'

'So, you only tell good news?'

'No, not always, but it is careful that I am. On only one occasion did I slip up and predict a client's death, the very same lady you spoke of, but I was for turning it around, so she left not feeling fear. Telling her was wrong of me. There is plenty that you can be telling them, though, but just be careful.'

'I don't understand. Surely we have a duty to tell them?'

'No. As I say, we cannot play God with people's lives. Say that it is that someone has a decision to make, and they ask you to tell them if it is right for them, then if you see it isn't, that is what you can tell.'

'I think I understand. Can I come in tomorrow? I won't want paying but just to read a few in front of you so you can see if our readings match . . . Oh, I see you have the tarot cards. I'm not much on them, but I am skilled at reading them. I like to bring the things I see from my soul.'

Martha smiled. 'You are for being more like me granny than I am. She, too, liked to speak from her heart. She was for leaving the tarots to me. I see them as a relief – as if it is their responsibility, not mine, what comes up for the client. It is that I've never been happy with seeing the future for others and am never seeing my own.'

'No, nor me. But I'm glad as I wouldn't want to know. Me aunt said that is why it won't come through to us. But you must see what it is that I am in for.'

'I do.'

'Go on then, seeing as you don't tell the bad news, I'd like to know the good coming to me.'

'You are to become a very well-known fortune teller. The famous will pay you well, but that is long in the future. Before that . . . well, you will know happiness, but many things may set you back. Your strength will bring you through and you will live a long and happy life, feted by all.'

'Really? That's grand – well, not the bit about the trials, but then, life is full of them anyroad, so you have to take the good with the bad.'

'You do. Now before it is you want to tell me mine, I don't want to be knowing.'

'Just to say, the sadness in you will one day lift, Martha, and you will know happiness that is supreme – and so will your child, though she will be called upon to be very brave before she knows that peace.'

Martha gaped at Cilla. 'My child?'

'Yes. You are with child – a daughter.'

'Oh, Jesus, Mary and Joseph.' Martha did a quick calculation. But still could not believe it as she had seen her monthly, if only scantily, each month. Or had she? When was the last time? Doing a quick calculation, it dawned on her that if Cilla was right, she'd be five and half months pregnant now! How could that be?

'I see I have flustered you. Did you not have an inkling?'

'No. I – I didn't. I – I haven't been for having any signs. I was for thinking the thickening of my waist was me over-indulging on me friend's delicious pastries.'

'Are you upset?'

'Shocked . . . but no. Not upset . . . elated it is that I am as I loved the father so very much and still do, with all my heart.'

It was a relief to be able to say it out loud.

A smile creased her face – Peter's child! And a girl to play with Sally. 'This is for being wonderful!'

But then, it hit her. *How am I to cope? What if it is that the war ends sooner than I am thinking? Oh, God, where will I live? Where will I be bringing up my baby?*

'Don't look distressed, Martha, all will come right. This daughter will bring you great joy from the moment you give birth to her.'

Martha clasped her hands to her breasts. Today had been a good day, full of hope and now brimming with happiness – a daughter. Peter's daughter. Nothing of the shame of being unmarried entered her, only complete joy at having part of Peter with her for ever.

NINETEEN

Trisha

Martha's excitement when she came home overshadowed Trisha's own news, but she didn't mind. It was all so wonderful, though she did worry about the pregnancy bit. 'But, lass, are you ready for the name calling, the shunning of you, and the enormity of having a babby out of wedlock?'

'I am, love. You've been through it – well, it is that we have together, and that is how it is going to be for me. With you by me side, I can do this, me darling.'

'Aw, Martha. We'll be known as them two floozies, or worse! But who cares, eh?'

They giggled at this.

When they calmed, Trisha said, 'Give me a hug, love.'

'Oh, Trish, I needed that. I might sound as though I'm all right with everything, but it is a little scary.'

'Aye, well, get yourself to the doctor, eh? He'll be able to confirm it for you.'

'I don't know. I feel embarrassed. You're a married

woman, Trish, and that is for being a different thing to me. I'll see how it is this progresses.'

'Well, as long as you keep well. The doctors don't do much, anyroad. Examine you and confirm it, but then you have to get on with it for the most part. I'll always be here for you, lass.'

'Ta, love.'

'So, we might be given a chance to have help with our business then? Eeh, it all sounds a bit much, don't it – a telephone! The likes of us don't have such things, it's letters or nowt!'

'I know, but it is that Lady Rebecca made everything sound possible. And sure, it is that with her help it might be so, Trish.'

'By, I wouldn't knaw one end of a telephone from the other. If it happens, that'll be your job, as I'd make a muck up of it for sure.'

'No, you won't, Trish. You're for being as intelligent as the next one. It is confidence that you lack. But that is something that will be coming to you in time.'

'We need that shop, lass, but how? Mind, I've done sommat today that might help. I went to see Benny.'

'Oh? Is it that you think you can begin to work again?'

'It is. And he says he'll be glad to have me. Aw, it were lovely seeing the donkeys again, though they looked freezing, poor things . . . I came to your tent, but I heard voices and crept away. It was too cold to hang around. By, that Blackpool wind can cut you in two when it starts.'

'Sorry, love, it would have been lovely to see you, but I was glad to be busy. Lady Rebecca gave me a pound note!'

'What? Eeh, lass, you're rich!'

'Ha! You eejit. But it does help.'

'It does. You've had quite a day, lass.'

'I haven't told you it all yet.'

'You mean, there's more than Lady Rebecca, Cilla and you having a babby!'

'No, it is that I haven't told you everything about Cilla, only that she visited me and told me about my baby.'

Trisha wasn't sure at all about what Martha told her of Cilla going to be a sort of partner in the fortune telling. 'But what if she pinches your business?'

'No, that won't be happening. She's family – well, sort of. It is that she will be a help to keep it going for me. Especially when we get a shop. She can do so many hours and make her money and then I can do so many hours. Sure, the three of us will work it all between us, Trish.'

'Well, if you think so, but watch out for folk and don't be so trusting all the time. Look at how you took Pet . . . Eeh, I'm sorry, lass. I shouldn't have said that.'

'It's all right. Sure, Peter is for proving you right. Except . . . well, I'm convinced something happened to him. I just cannot see him walking out on me.'

Trisha didn't argue with this, she knew it was this belief that had kept Martha going – that and the hope that Peter would one day turn up again. Trisha wished with all her heart he would. She was worried, and she knew that Martha was too, about where Martha would live after Bobby came home. Bobby would never accept her living with them. And now, poor lass had a babby to think about too.

'Well, I hope you're right as that gives us hope. Especially you, love.'

Martha sighed. Trisha was glad to see that she was coping. She could have bitten her tongue off for mentioning Peter like that.

'So, where is that little Sally? She's late still being in her bed. I was thinking to bath her when I got in.'

'She's out for a walk with Edna. But she should be back now, it's getting dark.'

A worry set up in Trisha. She hadn't thought until Martha had said, but it was gone three now. 'I'll put me coat on and go and have a look. You get your feet up, love. The fire will toast your toes for you. You must be cold walking back in this. I think it might snow later.'

It hardly ever snowed in Blackpool and, if it did, it rarely settled. It was said the salty air prevented it, but Trisha remembered her da telling her that being surrounded by mountains with the Lake District, the Welsh mountains and the Pennines helped.

Hurrying along Enfield Road, Trisha's heart thumped against her chest. This wasn't like Edna. She usually kept Sally out for half an hour at the most, but she'd been gone over an hour. *If only I hadn't fallen asleep, but I'm still dogged by tiredness after all these months!*

Once she'd turned off the street and there was still no sign of them, Trisha began to panic. A woman came out of her door. Trisha didn't know her name as she hadn't long moved in. 'Excuse me, have you see a middle-aged lady with a pram pass by, love?'

'Naw. No one's been past here that I've seen. Sorry, lass. But it's a bit late to have a babby out. It's going to freeze later, I reckon.'

'Ta, love. I'll get on as I want to find them.'

Pulling her coat around her, Trisha began to run. She hadn't gone far when she was so breathless that she had to stop and lean on a gate post. The door of the house opened. 'Are you all right, Trisha, lass?'

'Eeh, Bett, have you seen Edna?'

'Aye, she went by with your babby a good while since, love. Ain't she back then?'

'Naw. I just got a bit worried. I'll get on to see if I can find them.'

'Hope you do, love.'

Knowing she couldn't run any further, Trisha slowed her pace. When she reached the corner shop she went inside. Edna was sat on a chair looking pale and shaky. 'Where's me babby?'

'It's all right, Trish, love. She's in me living room. Edna had a funny turn, so I thought I'd bring babby in while I see to her.'

'Aw, Edna, love. What happened?'

'I don't knaw, Trish. Me legs suddenly went wobbly. I was down the road a bit and it took me ages to get here. I'm sorry, lass. I didn't knaw what else to do . . . We were going to send the next customer to get you, but naw one's been in since.'

'Well, you gave me a fright as I knew sommat were wrong. Do you want me to help you home, love? You can hang on to the pram and link in with me an all.'

'I were just going to pop next door and get their lad to go for the doctor, Trisha. I reckon she should be checked over before she tries to go further.'

'Eeh, Edna. I hope it's nowt serious. I should do as Mrs Philpot says and be checked out. I'll get Sally home but let me knaw how you go on. I'll pop around to yours later, eh?'

Edna looked up and tried to smile. But then as she said, 'Little lass . . . she's been . . . grand . . . I . . .' she slumped forward and fell off the chair.

'Oh, God, Trisha! What's to do with her, eh? Come on, Edna, love . . . Edna . . . Edna!' Mrs Philpot looked up, her face ashen. 'She . . . she's gone!'

Trisha stupidly said, 'Gone? Gone where?'

'Passed on. She ain't breathing, Trisha. Look at her. She's dead!'

Shock held Trisha rigid. She couldn't take this in. Edna? Dead? Here, at her feet . . . 'How? I mean, why? Oh, God . . . What shall we do?'

'We need the doctor, and now! Go on, go and fetch the lad. I'll cover poor Edna over. Eeh, I'll have to close me shop. I've naw choice.'

When Trisha came back it all seemed so surreal to see the shape of Edna covered by a blanket. Edna, who'd been for ever in her life, who had helped and annoyed her in equal measure, but was always one to rely on . . . Edna, dead!

It just wouldn't sink in.

'Trisha, lass. You fetch babby through and get on your way home. There's nowt you can do. By, I'll have to scrub me shop from top to bottom having had a dead body in it!'

Trisha knew that shock was prompting Mrs Philpot to think like this. She was strait-laced, but kindly too.

'Are you sure, love?'

'Aye, I am. There's naw point in stopping here. There ain't much room as it is and the doctor will need to get round to check Edna . . . poor lass. I shall miss her popping in.'

Trisha knew she would miss her too. Almost as much as she missed her ma. Edna had come to mean so much to her. Even in her nosy times.

As she left the shop, she was glad that Sally was sleeping. She didn't feel she could cope with a fractious Sally as well.

As she walked home, her own legs felt wobbly. Was it real? Was Edna gone? Just like that? Snuffed out?

Trisha felt her cheeks dampen without consciously knowing she was crying. A sob caught in her throat. She had to stop a moment and wipe her face with her hanky. She couldn't imagine life without Edna.

When she reached home the door flung open. 'Oh, Trish, it is that I was going out of me mind . . . Trish! Trish, love, what is it? . . . Where's Edna?'

Martha was just as shocked when she told her. 'Oh, me poor darling. It is that you were so close to Edna. She were a lovely woman. Come and be sitting yourself down by the fire. I'll be seeing to getting you a cup of tea, and then see to Sally.'

They manoeuvred the pram inside, always a cumbersome thing to do. They'd found that it just fitted by the wall at the end of the sofa, but somehow tonight, it was acting awkward.

'You be leaving it to me, Trish. You're all sixes and sevens, as is being understandable. I'm for shaking from head to toe meself with the shock, so I am.'

The hot tea tasted strange, and yet was welcome. At this moment, Trisha wondered if anything would be the same again. Everything seemed to be changing. And soon she could have Bobby to contend with. 'Martha, love. Have you been hearing the news?'

'Yes, it is that Russia has surrendered, poor things, and well, just as we were thinking that things were going well, it is that Germany is attacking us again! Poor Lady Rebecca couldn't have been for hearing it as she was of the mind that we were gaining ground.'

'Well, didn't you say her husband was an officer? Maybe he knaws differently and has been in touch. I hope so. Just how long can it all go on?'

'Trish, are you mindful that when it's over, it is that I will have to be moving out?'

'I am, love. And I don't have the answer. Let's hope we have sommat sorted by the time Bobby comes home – a shop with a flat for you, eh?'

'That would be the best thing ever. Oh, Trish, that I should be worrying you over this at such a time, love. I'm heart sorry, so I am.'

'Naw, it helps to talk of everyday things, lass. I'm getting used to the idea now. There's nowt I can do.'

'Well, is it that I should see to Sally now and her feed while you get our tea on? Keeping busy is for helping when bad things happen.'

'Aye. That's a good idea. I have a meat pie ready for the oven – though there ain't much meat in it, so I should be calling it a root veg pie.'

'Root veg?'

'Swede, spuds, carrots, onions – you knaw, all the veg that grows under the earth.'

Martha laughed. 'Sure, I've never heard that saying before. But I know it will be delicious, your cooking always is.'

Trisha went into the kitchen and turned the gas on. The pie would take a good forty-five minutes to cook through. With this done, she leaned on the cupboard and hung her head. This change in her life was sudden and hard to cope with, but how much harder it would be to adjust to Bobby coming home – not living with Martha was going to be a wrench. She just didn't want to think about it.

The next day the street gossipers were out with their arms folded. All spoke in hushed, shocked tones. Mrs Higginbottom's voice came to her before she opened the door to her.

'Eeh, lass, what a shock. I'm collecting for Edna. Have you and Martha got owt to put into me pot?'

'Aye. Hold on a mo.' When she dropped the coins in, Trisha wished that it could be more.

Mrs Higginbottom cocked her head towards the house Martha used to live in. 'They won't give owt. Mean buggers. She said they didn't knaw the lady in question. I tell you, I'd rather have the gypsies next to me than them stuck-up lot.'

Trisha closed the door saying, 'Sorry, Mrs Higginbottom, I've to get ready. I start back at work this afternoon.'

With the cold air gushing in, Trisha wondered at her own sanity starting back before the season began, but Benny wanted her to. He said he wanted her to reacquaint with the donkeys before Easter. Easter was just a week away on the thirty-first of March.

Martha had already left to go to work as she had an early client booked in, so Trisha scooted around, not wanting to be in the house long on her own. She thought she would walk all the way and take it steady. The day was a grey one but not as cold as the day before. She'd buy some chips and take them to Martha's tent before she went on the beach – Martha was always quiet at dinner time.

They were sitting on the wall, their coats and scarves shielding them from the wind, Sally gurgling happily in her pram.

'I can be taking Sally into the tent with me, Trish. Sure, we can take turns in having her with us. But today, it is that it's best she is with me as you will have to be getting to know the donkeys again.'

Trish was grateful for this. She knew she would have to have Sally with her a lot while she worked, but today, her first day back, it was a bit daunting to do so.

The donkeys all seemed to remember her, which warmed Trisha's heart. She did love them and had missed them.

'Well, they won't take any getting used to you, lass.'

Trisha laughed at Benny as one after the other of the donkeys nudged her. A happiness came to her, which dispelled the sadness for now and gave her hope. *Everything'll work out for me, I'm sure. I'll miss Edna, but I have me future as a businesswoman to look forward to.*

But even as she thought this, the time when Bobby came home hung like a cloud around her.

Daisy nudged her.

'Eeh, lazy madam. I knew you'd be the last to greet me, lass.'

The donkey looked up at her and then began to bray in the way that donkeys do that make them sound as though they are laughing. Trisha giggled and snuggled her head into Daisy's. 'It's good to see you an' all, lass. Ha, you should be called Edna. You're like her in many ways.'

She brushed away the tears that threatened and took solace in patting and talking to the donkeys. This was where she loved to be. With these lovely characters on the beach of her beloved Blackpool.

TWENTY

Martha

Three weeks had passed since Edna's funeral had taken place, everyone in the street attending. Martha had stood by Trisha's side, trying to comfort her, but needing comfort herself as she'd become fond of Edna too – though, like Trisha, her grief had been broken and her tears were for her granny, her mammy and her pa as much as, if not more than, they were for the loss of Edna, just as she knew Trisha's were for her lost ones too.

Still no letter had arrived from Lady Rebecca, and she wondered if it would.

Suddenly, the confines of her tent seemed to bear down on her. No one had called in for a reading all morning, nor so far this afternoon. It had been like this since the last of the Easter guests had left just over a week ago.

Martha wriggled in her chair. Sitting in the same position hemming a gown for a baby boy was giving her cramp.

Standing, she stretched. As she did, she felt a movement. Her hands shot to the small mound of her stomach. Joy spread through her. Cradling her bump, she gasped as the movement happened again, only stronger. *My baby! I'm here, wee one. Oh, me darling wee girl, I love you.*

An urge came over her to tell Trisha. Running outside and quickly turning her board around to read *Back soon*, Martha ran across the road, dodging in and out of the landaus. Bending over the wall, she looked towards the North Shore, saw Trisha and waved like mad.

Trisha and her herd of donkeys trotted towards her, making her giggle as Trisha seemed to be one in the way she was leading them by the rope and keeping pace with them.

'What is it, lass? Are you all right? Have you heard from Peter at last?'

'No, but something much better has happened. Me baby moved – she moved, Trisha!'

Trisha burst out laughing. 'Well, you're in for it now, love. You wait until she gets stronger. By, she'll give you some sleepless nights. Sally played football in me tummy every night.'

They laughed so much, Martha said, 'Whist, you've made me want to pee now! See you later, love . . . Oh, is Sally all right?'

'She is. The fresh air is making her sleep, but she was active all morning, playing on the rug, kicking and gurgling, so it's not surprising. Now, go and have that pee before you do it and cause a tidal wave.'

Martha felt the urgency now, as she laughed once more and this sent her scooting back around to the rear of the guest house where there was a loo for her use.

As she came out, adjusting her long navy skirt over her petticoats, the kitchen door opened.

'Martha, I've a letter for you, love.'

'Ooh. Ta, Cissy. Is it that it came today?'

Cissy looked shamefaced. 'Naw, I'm sorry, lass. Judging by the postmark, it came a week ago, only it must have fallen behind me little desk in me hall. I never noticed it, then I got the woman who cleans for me to bottom me hall after me rush at Easter when it didn't get done, and she found it and one for me that was important an' all . . . I'm really sorry, lass.'

Although feeling angry, Martha understood. 'It is that these things happen. Ta, Cissy, I'll take it now.'

'It looks a bit posh, I must say. It has one of them wax stamps on the back. Who do you knaw who would write a letter like that?'

'I – I'm not for knowing until I open it but it could just be from a grateful client.'

'Aye, there were one a bit back who asked for me card. Well, I'll love you and leave you. I've a million and one things to do.'

Once in her tent, Martha carefully opened the letter, not wanting to spoil the lovely crisp cream-coloured envelope. The paper inside was just as lovely, and the handwriting exquisite.

Dear Martha,

How nice it was to meet you. And to discover your many talents, in particular the layettes you and your friend make. They are so beautiful. Here in London, we have many shops selling layettes, but none that I have seen with the individual touches you give to the garments, and most are manufactured, not handmade.

I have been speaking to my friend Lady Darcy and she is as excited as I am to help you to progress – two women with no support, making good, really appeals to us. We both support the cause of women being allowed more freedom of choice.

And we feel that among our many friends we can generate a lot of custom for you and help you to set up your business.

I have found that you need a premises that is near to telephone posts that are already in situ as at this time of monetary cuts no new ones are planned or will be erected especially for you. This fits in with your idea to have a shop.

Darcy and I know this won't be easy for you but would like to help. Darcy's husband is, amongst other things, a property owner and the last time they were in Blackpool, before the war, he talked of adding properties there to his portfolio. He works in the War Office, so isn't away fighting. He has shown a great interest in visiting Blackpool and taking up his idea. He specifically deals in business premises and has been in touch with a selling agent who has several shops for him to consider. One of these is on the North Promenade!

I have written the address at the bottom of this letter. He would like you to go along and to view it as a prospective shop for your business. If it is suitable, get back to me quickly, as the agent says there is interest being shown from other buyers.

Of course, if you do like it, nothing will happen quickly as surveys will have to be carried out to ascertain that the value matches the price and that the building is sound.

This will give you time to get a deposit together and be in a position to pay the rental which will be advised at a later date, both of which he assured Lady Darcy will be set at what you feel you can afford until your business is on its feet.

A kind of panic gripped Martha – Lady Rebecca had said she was to get back quickly, and the letter had been lying behind a desk for a week! But then, she thought, it had been the Easter holidays and no post from herself would have reached Lady Rebecca quickly. Feeling relieved, she read on:

So, this is the first step. It will be your task to find a photographer and a printer to print brochures for you. I am sure you will only need to ask around as I saw many posters up in and around Blackpool, and some leaflets were put through the door of my holiday home – quite a pile of them, so there must be someone local doing this work. Once all this is in place, you will be ready to begin.

Now, my dear, we understand that it isn't going to be easy for you, but we hope and pray that you can achieve it all over the coming months. One little hint, make sure you price your garments at the highest price possible for the London market. As you won't appreciate, but I can tell you, unless it costs the earth there are many ladies and gentlemen that won't even look at a product! Sounds silly, doesn't it, but it is true. But then, I am a good judge of quality and what you are producing is just that – the highest of quality.

Martha smiled to herself. Always she'd loved Lisa Mathew's stall, and now she was grateful to her too, for despite just being a stall on Blackpool Promenade, she stocked some lovely silks and brocades for a fraction of the prices of many outlets and was always looking out for new stock for her, telling her, 'You're me best customer, Martha, lass. If ever you need owt special, let me knaw and I'll move heaven and earth to track it down for you.' She had a feeling that those kinds of purchases were not too far in the future.

Clasping the letter to her breast, Martha gave an excited giggle. All at once, everything seemed possible!

The letter went on to say that because of this, she would advise having different brochures with different prices to suit individual areas and she finished by saying that she was eager to receive a reply and really hoped that all of this that she and her friend could offer would encourage them to chase and to catch their dream and make it a reality.

Martha sat a moment before reacting, but when she did, everything was a hive of activity as she packed away her sewing and her crystal ball and tarot cards into the crate she had for them, locked it and dragged it to Cissy's cellar, where she had been storing it for some time now, having been warned by other traders that more and more vagabonds were on the streets at night.

This had saddened her, as it seemed from what she'd heard most were casualties of war who were unable to fight any more and had been returned home. Only to find everything changed and that they were no longer welcome, there was no work they could manage and there was very little government help.

Thinking this made her, for the first time, feel a little pity for Bobby, as he would return to massive changes that would be hard for him to adjust to . . . But then . . .

A shudder went through her as she stopped the thought. She wanted to save Trisha. But she knew she had to heed her granny's words.

With everything now safe, Martha donned the shawl she'd taken to wearing over her coat and went in search of Trisha.

As she sat on the beach, the cold cut through her. 'How do you stand it, Trish, love? And what about Sally?'

'She's as warm as toast. And I'm used to whatever Blackpool can throw at me. Now, stop worrying about me and tell me the news you're so excited about.'

Trisha was sceptical. 'We don't have the kind of money this will take, Martha, lass. What are you thinking? We can't accept. It's a pity, but—'

'But we have time. Sure, we can be taking one step, then recover from that and be taking another.'

'How?'

'Firstly, it is that we need to view the shop. Then if it is that it is suitable, we start to save – and that is for being possible. We're marred out with stock. Not only of garments, but wool, silks and cottons too. Sure, it is that we can stop buying and save the money.'

'But will it be enough?'

'Together with what I am having left of the sale of my furniture and what we have from the sale of baby clothes from my tent, I'm thinking we could scrape enough. But I am not knowing altogether. It is a powerful big thing we are asking of ourselves, but we must try. Let's begin by doing the viewing, eh?'

'All right. Eeh, it's not that I ain't excited, or longing to do it, it's just that it seems an impossible dream.'

'I know. I'm having all the same fears, but I ain't for giving up without trying, Trish. I am thinking we need to find a photographer and see what he would charge, and it is that we need to do the same with the printer, then we will know.'

'Well, that makes sense.'

'Good. Oh, me darling Trish, I am for having a feeling this is going to work. Look, it's only three and the estate agent is just around the corner. I'll go and make an appointment for us to view ... I'll call on the little people to be making it so everything is going in our favour.'

'The little people? Who are they, lass?'

'Ha, they are only to be found in Ireland, but they won't be letting me down.'

Martha laughed out loud at Trisha's expression and with the excitement she felt. *This can happen for me, can't it? It must!* Patting her tummy, she told her child, *I'll be making it happen for you, me wee girl.*

★ ★ ★

'Well, you've called just in time, miss. I knew your visit was imminent, but I do have an offer on the table, which I was about to take. So, depending on your decision, your buyer will have to better it.'

'But it is that I can only write and that takes an age.'

'Ha. Never heard of the telephone, miss? I have instructions to telephone the gentleman interested the moment you say it is suitable.'

Suddenly, Martha was besieged with doubts that she couldn't brush away as she had been doing – what if she committed Lady Darcy's husband to buying and then she couldn't get the money together?

'How long is it it takes for a sale to go through, sir?'

'Oh, that can vary from weeks to months. In this case, I'd say you'd be looking at around eight to ten weeks, though that isn't the end of it, there will be repairs as the surveyor will point out – often a sale falls through at that stage as the buyer finds there is too much work to be carried out. But that depends on how foreseeing the buyer is. Yours already has a potential tenant in yourself, so that could make it worthwhile.'

Not understanding how everything worked, Martha asked, 'But what if it is that you take an offer and then later they decline to buy?'

Mr Green, the agent, looked at her quizzically. 'Why are you bothering your head with such things?'

'Oh, I – I'm always wanting to know how it is that everything works. I'm sorry.'

'No, it's all right. Well, to put your mind at rest, my client, whose offer is accepted, will lay down a deposit, most of which he will lose if the sale falls through. So, it is important, young lady, that you are sure the shop is right for you as this will be what my client bases his choices on.'

Martha felt the weight of this responsibility but was glad to know as she had been of the mind to say it was just right, no matter what. Now, she knew she must approach this in a businesslike way.

'Now, I can show you around as soon as I close my shop today. How would that be?'

'Oh, really? Sure, that will be fine. Ta very much. I'll be with me friend as it is that we will both be the tenants.'

When they met at the shop, which was in prime position near to the tower, Martha's nerves jangled. She so wanted it to be right, and yet did wonder if such a shop as hers would fit in with the intensity of traders here and with barrows on the prom, selling everything from hot spuds to having a go on a coconut shy. But then, this was where most of the visitors made for, so hopefully they would attract customers too.

Thankfully, Sally had been fed and was now fast asleep, leaving Trisha to give all her attention to looking around with Martha.

They both loved it. The shop area was small and yet big enough. There was a kitchen and a stockroom-cum-workroom at the back and a loo in the yard. But, best of all, there was a flat above, which though it needed painting and new oil cloth on the floor was plenty big enough for them both, if ever the need arose.

As Martha walked through the two good-sized bedrooms and one smaller, she could see this latter as a room for her child to share with Sally.

She pulled herself up. Yes, it was a nice dream, but she hadn't seen it for real. Not as a prediction, as she had stopped herself before that could happen.

'It gets better and better, lass. Just look at the kitchen, it's so cosy. But then, Ma Featherton was like that herself. This was her shop. She sold toys mainly and rented out chairs for the beach. She was a nice old girl. She died last year.'

'Yes, it is that I remember that. It has been closed for a long time and I've never been for asking you why.' Martha closed her eyes. When she opened them, she said, 'It is that she is welcoming us, Trish. She's happy that we will take her shop.'

'You've decided then?'

'Oh . . . no, I didn't mean . . .'

'You daft ha'peth. I knew the minute we got here that this was for us, I was just waiting for you to say how you felt. And, lass, I've been thinking we can do it . . . Maybe not all the stuff about photos and brochures, but if we pull our horns in, we could get enough together for the renting of this. That's if, like you say, that bloke fixes it to what we can afford in the beginning.'

'Oh, Trish, I'm so glad. It is that we are being smiled on. Ma Featherton is happy.'

'Good. Give her me love, seeing as you're in contact with her.' Trisha giggled. But then stopped herself. 'Aw, I'm sorry, Martha, I weren't meaning to mock you, lass.'

'I know, and I didn't take it like that. Sure, you are a one for having a joking way of looking at life and I am loving that, so I was only amused.'

Trisha let out a sigh.

'Well, we should be telling Mr Green. Come on, let's hurry downstairs to speak to him.'

When they met Mr Green in the main shop, he had some papers spread out on the windowsill. He turned. 'Now then, ladies, I have been hearing a lot of good comments. Are you happy with the place?'

'We are. It's perfect for us, so it is.'

'Good, good. I'll contact the buyer tomorrow, first thing. Hopefully he will contact you with his decision, but feel free to drop into the office to enquire how everything is progressing ... My, for lasses as young as you two, you're very ambitious. I like that and I wish you good luck with everything.'

He doffed his cap, then indicated they go before him to leave the shop.

Just as they did, an idea occurred to Martha. 'Will you mind me asking you a question, sir?'

'Not at all, I've already noted that you are an inquisitive one. How can I help?'

'It's your brochures. How is it we can get some showing our layettes, their prices and the options of sizes and colour we are for being able to offer?'

'Well, I can help you with that. My son does mine for me and a lovely job he does. He takes a job on from start to finish, so he takes the photographs, then typesets the wording and prints as many leaflets as I want.'

'Is it for costing a lot of money?'

'Look, I can see how the land lies. You're two talented young women with a dream and somehow you've met a benefactor, but that's only the start of it for you. I believe in you. I'll talk to my son. I'll get him to give you a very fair price. So, how will you use your brochures?'

Martha told him.

'Well, I must say, this all sounds exciting for you. So, you tell fortunes on the prom and that is how you met this lady who is helping you.'

'It is.'

'And the garments et cetera that you have in your tent she really loved?'

Martha nodded.

'I would say you've an excellent chance. A good start with this lady's help, and it's something you can do now. You needn't wait for the shop to be ready. If my son does the brochures for you and it sounds as though this lady can sell your wares, and at a good price, then you will soon have the rent together.'

Martha hadn't thought of this. She looked at a smiling Trisha. 'It is that it's all for being possible, Trish?'

'Aye, Mr Green's right. We've loads to sell already and can start posting orders off!'

Martha felt like cheering. Why hadn't she thought of this? 'May I be asking you one more thing, Mr Green?'

'Ask away, Martha.'

'Do you know how it is that we can send parcels cash on delivery?'

'I believe the post office have such a service, but occasionally I use a courier as there can be a large cheque to pick up on the signing of documents. Let me think . . . you would need one in London. Then you could send your parcel by rail and the courier pick it up and deliver it. But you will need a bank account for the money to be paid into.'

Martha hadn't ever thought of having a bank account, but it seemed that there was a service for everything, it was just a matter of finding out about it.

She looked at Trisha. 'Sure, we can be doing all of this, Trish. It is that we are beginning a new journey, me darling.'

Trisha beamed.

'Good. Now, young ladies, come into my office tomorrow evening and I shall have news on whether my son can take the job and what he'll charge. You're on your way, ladies, and it's my pleasure to be a part of that.'

Once he'd left them, Trisha took one hand off the pram and clasped Martha's. 'Eeh, love, I can't believe it . . . You knaw, I have no idea how Bobby will take all of this, and I fear he won't agree. He won't like me being better than him.'

Martha didn't know what to say to this. She squeezed Trisha's hand. 'He'll be all right, I'm sure of it.'

But inside, she wondered herself what would happen. Part of her dreaded Bobby coming home, but she'd never wish anything else for him. He'd done his bit to save the country and he deserved to have things how he wanted them when he returned – but would that mean him not wanting little Sally and refusing to let Trisha be part of the business?

She hoped not. With all her heart she hoped he'd accept both – though deep down, she did know the answer.

To have the news the next day that Joshua Green, son of the estate agent, would photograph, design and print the brochures for them made all these worries go away as no matter what concerns they had, Trisha and she were determined to go ahead with their dream. Joshua had also sent word that he could come that afternoon to the tent at two o'clock to take the photographs.

When he arrived, Joshua was so unlike his father, a portly man with blond hair and blue eyes and of average height, as Joshua was dark-haired and had very dark 'thinking man's' eyes that seemed to weigh you up in a glance. And being handsome, tall and lean left nothing to associate him at all with Mr Green.

His smile made her think his assessment of her was favourable. Hers of him was that he was a determined young man destined to succeed and to have all he desired. The look that went with his smile told her that she was part of that. She didn't want to be . . . She couldn't be.

Standing not hiding her bump, she greeted him. 'I'm Martha. Sure, it is that me friend and I are very grateful to you for offering us your services.'

His eyes went to her stomach. 'Oh . . . I – I didn't realise you were married. So, it's Mrs O'Hara?'

Somehow, Martha didn't want to lie to him directly by confirming this, so she just said, 'Martha.'

'Martha it is.' She loved the little nervous giggle he had. It made her smile.

'So, first things first. My charges. I produce my father's brochures for a penny each and charge him tuppence each. So, how does that sound to you?'

Martha had thought this through before he came and had decided that she would start with around twenty. This would make the total cost three shillings and fourpence. A huge sum for them at this time.

'Is that too much?'

'No . . . no, it is for being a good price, but I'm thinking I can only be affording ten until I make some money.'

'Ten paid for and ten on account, how would that be?'

'That's for being very generous, ta, Joshua.'

He looked taken aback for a moment, then recovered and said, 'For that smile, I would do them all for nothing.' His giggle took the edge off this being a pass at her and made her giggle with him, but immediately colour as she realised that this may make him feel she welcomed his attention. But then, did she? Surely it couldn't be so after giving her heart and soul to Peter? This thought dispelled any such inklings about Joshua. From then on, she was friendly but kept everything on a business footing. Thankfully, Joshua picked up on this and did the same. A small part of her was sorry about this, but it had to be this way. She had to wait for Peter, the father of her child, to return. Anything else would be a betrayal of him and she could never do that.

TWENTY-ONE

Trisha

Now that July was almost here, Trisha was getting more and more nervous. Martha was near to her time and next week they would have the keys to the shop! Was she doing right, going ahead without Bobby's permission? She felt in her bones that he wouldn't be happy with it all.

Picking up the boiling kettle, she was just going to pour it onto the leaves in the teapot when a cry made her jump. *Martha!*

Running to the bottom of the stairs she shouted, 'Are you all right, love? Is Sally all right?'

'Sally is, but, ooh, Trisha, it is the cramp I have in me belly.'

Trisha took the stairs two at a time. One look at the writhing Martha told her this wasn't the cramp. 'Eeh, lass, I think you've started your labour. I'll run to fetch that nurse the doctor told you to contact . . . By, I wish you had been to see her, Martha. Let's hope she'll come now as she hasn't been tending to you, she might refuse. Hold on, love, take deep breaths.'

Grabbing Sally, who was now crawling towards her, she ran back down the stairs, not heeding that she was still only in her housecoat.

'Come on, me little lass, let's strap you into your new carriage. There, you like that, don't you, eh?'

The baby carriage was a lot less cumbersome than the pram, which they managed to store in the lean-to in the yard now that it was summertime. Small and made of cane, it had a fixed hood woven into it and was the same shape as the pram. Sally could only sit up in it, though once when tired, she had made Trisha smile by going to sleep on her front with her bum stuck up in the air. She'd found a way, bless her.

Now, it looked as though the pram would soon be brought out for Martha's baby – what they would do for room then God only knew, as they had planned to stay together until they were forced to live separately, rather than Martha moving into the flat above the shop immediately.

Hurrying as much as she could, Trisha arrived at the address in Fielding Road.

'All right, all right, I'm coming.'

A stout woman opened the door. 'Who are you and what can I do for you? . . . Good God, girl, you're not dressed!'

Trisha coloured as it impacted on her that she'd hurried through the streets almost naked! 'I – I couldn't stop to dress, it's urgent. It's me friend, she were meant to be on your books but she's been too busy, now she's in labour!'

'All right, lass, let me get me bag. Is it far?'

'Naw, Enfield Road. Ta, Nurse. I thought you'd refuse me on account of her not seeing you before.'

'Naw, lass. I can't turn me back on a mum in labour. Hold on a mo.'

She was soon back wearing a cloak over her frock and carrying a small case. 'Right, let's get the little mite into the world . . . What's your name, love, and what's the mum-to-be's name?'

Trisha introduced herself and told her a little about Martha.

'Aye, I remember the referral coming through now, and did call once, but there was no one in. Sorry, but I'm a busy woman and had to leave it at that. So, what about her hubby? It being Sunday, is he going to under me feet, or is he at war like most others?'

Trisha felt tongue-tied. The nurse turned her head and looked at her. 'No father then?'

'Naw . . .'

She couldn't think want to say.

'I'm sorry. Has he copped it recently?'

'He left.'

'Oh, one of them, eh? There's a few do a runner when a babby's on the way.'

When they arrived, all was quiet. Then a baby's cry could be heard.

'Good God, you left it late, didn't you? Sounds as though mum's delivered on her own.'

Almost running to the stair door, Nurse disappeared through it before Trisha could gather herself. She looked down at Sally, unsure what to do. But then grabbed her and the teddy that she'd knitted for her, and told her, 'Sally go into her cot with Teddy, eh?'

Sally looked bewildered, but luckily, when they reached Trisha's bedroom, she accepted being placed in her cot. As Trisha moved away towards the door, though, she knew this was the testing time. If Sally didn't want to stay put, she would scream the house down. Luckily, she grabbed the rails, stood herself up and gurgled away as she did a little dance, her smile filling Trisha with joy. 'Good girl, your ma will only be in the next room, me little lass . . . We've a new babby in the house!' She couldn't help giving a little giggle. Sally responded by giggling with her.

'Aw, I love you, Sallykins . . . Ha! I've never called you that before! Don't knaw where it came from, but it suits you, babby. See you in a mo, eh?'

Creeping away with fingers crossed, to the sound of Sally calling, 'Ma-ma, Ma-ma,' Trisha opened Martha's door. 'Eeh, lass.'

Martha sat up beaming, her face glowing, flushed with the effort she'd made.

'She was for not waiting, Trish.'

'Aw, love . . . aw.'

'I've known some quick births, lass, but from what Martha's been telling me, this was the quickest ever – and for a first, a bloody miracle. They can take days as most think the first niggles of pain mean babby will be here any minute, but it's rarely like this. Haven't you felt owt till this morning?'

'I've only been having a wee back pain. But I wasn't for thinking it was me baby coming.'

'Ah! That'll be it then. Some feel it more in their back.'

'You never said owt, Martha, lass.'

'Well, never mind. I'm sorry I snapped at you, Trisha. As it turns out, love, you didn't have a chance to get me here sooner.'

'That's all right, it were the panic of the moment, Nurse.'

'Well, I'm all done here. No complications, no tears that need stitching, just a happy mum who needs bed rest. So, I'll take me payment, which I'll halve as I ain't done much and leave you both to it. You seems to me to be two very capable lasses. Only, it's a pity you were left to do this on your own. Life ain't going to be easy for you. Bloody men! But I wish you luck and my advice would be to move away somewhere and make out to your new neighbours that your men copped it in the war.'

Trisha wanted to go to Martha as she saw her hang her head, but the nurse had reached the door and Trisha's purse was downstairs. 'Be back in a mo, love.'

As soon as she closed the door on the nurse, Trisha once more took the stairs two at a time. Grabbing Sally, she went in to Martha. 'Aw, lass, lass, she's here! Your little lass is here!'

'Ha, she came like a bat out of hell, so she did. I'm for thinking this wee one is on a mission, Trish.'

'Aw, let me look at her . . . Eeh, she has your hair, love her heart. She's going to take after you – a beautiful auburn-haired girl. What are you going to call her? You've never made your mind up between Barbara and Jeannie?'

'Now she's here, Barbara will be her first name, though it is that she'll be known as Bonnie, and Jeannie her second.

Oh, and as I was always for planning, Patricia will be her third name.'

'Aw, ta, love, I'm honoured and'll allus look out for her as if she were me own . . . But Bonnie, why Bonnie?'

'I had a friend when I was little called that . . . It was that she was killed by a tractor running her over.'

'Eeh, that's awful, poor little mite. But now she's been honoured and remembered. That's a grand gesture, lass . . . So, is Aunty Trish allowed to hold her then?'

Martha giggled as she handed over the tiny bundle.

'By, she makes Sally look like a giant now!'

Sally crawled across the bed grabbing Trisha's arm to help herself get onto her knees. Her eyes were fixed on Bonnie. Trisha leaned towards her so that she could see. Sally pointed, then giggled, hitched herself nearer and touched Bonnie's face. Her eyes held wonderment as she looked up at Trisha.

'This is Bonnie, me wee lass. You must look after her – be a big sister to her. You can do that, can't you, Sallykins?'

'Sallykins? It is that I haven't heard that before? Ha, it is for suiting her, though . . . Sallykins. Me wee Sallykins. Come and be giving your Aunty Martha a hug, me wee darling.'

Sally gurgled as she crawled towards Martha, then lunged herself at her, impatient for the promised hug. As they came out of it, Sally pointed towards the baby. 'Babba!'

'Yes! Babba. Our babba, me wee darling.'

Sally smiled. 'Babba.'

They all ended up giggling as little Bonnie slept through without a care.

'Well, she's here now, lass, and she's started life by putting a spanner in the works!' Trisha looked down at Bonnie. 'You have, you knaw. You weren't supposed to come for another three weeks! Now what are we to do, eh?'

She looked up at Martha. 'I'll have to go and see Mr Green, love. Tell him that your babby's arrived so he'll have to delay signing the tenancy agreement.'

'No, that ain't to happen, Trish. Remember, I'm for having gypsy blood in me. No taking to me bed for fourteen days for us! Granny was for telling me that a gypsy mother gets straight out of bed and gets on with it, and that's what I'm for doing. Be a wee darling and fill a tub for me, eh? I'm in need of a cup of tea, a bath and to get dressed.'

'Naw, Martha, naw!'

'Yes! It is that it's no good arguing with me. Sure, I'm a strong young woman. Me labour was over with almost before it began. There is nothing to keep me in bed. It is work that we need to be doing.'

Trisha didn't know what to say. All she'd ever known was that a mother had to have a lying-in period after the birth. 'But, lass, what if you become ill? How will I cope?'

'I'm for being as fit as a fiddle, so I am. Stop your worrying, me darling, and get me that nice cup of tea you promised.'

Trisha grinned. 'Well, I've had me orders.' Handing the baby back, she stood a moment and looked lovingly at her friend. Never, she thought, was there a more beautiful sight than a mother and her newborn. But then, Sally leaned her head on the baby, and tears sprang to Trisha's eyes. 'Aw, Martha, look at them.'

Martha smiled. 'They are going to be the closest friends ever – their bond will be stronger even than ours, more so than if they were sisters.'

'That's nice to knaw, lass. One of your better predictions. Makes me feel all warm inside . . . Eeh, I bless the day you came to live next door, lass.'

When Trisha got downstairs, a knock came on the door and it opened. Mrs Higginbottom popped her head around. 'I saw the nurse. Has she dropped her babby then?'

'She ain't the cat's mother, Mrs Higginbottom! Martha had a little lass.'

'Look, I reckon we've tolerated enough in this street, and all from this house. I've not said owt, but I ain't happy with the situation.'

Incensed, Trisha forgot herself for the moment. 'Well, it's none of your bloody business, is it, so don't come poking your nose in where it ain't wanted.'

Her anger almost dissipated as she heard the familiar humph and wanted to laugh out loud, but instead, she said, 'And humph to you an' all!'

It was almost dinner time with their appointment at two-thirty when the door knocked again. Martha was sitting feeding Bonnie with Sally on the sofa next to her watching it all going on and every now and again stroking Bonnie's head, or leaning her own head gently on hers. She hadn't tried to speak since meeting Bonnie, just sat in awe of her.

'Now what?' Trisha raised her eyes to heaven.

'Ha, you seem to be expecting the firing squad, so you do.'

To Trisha, it was almost as bad, when she opened the door and Hattie stood there – arms folded, face like a smacked arse. 'Is it true, Trisha? Is there another little bastard living in me house?'

'Naw, it ain't true! There's naw bastards living here.'

'You knaw what I mean, lass. You two have brought enough trouble into my street. Besides, me contract says no lodgers, so I've been lenient with you even though you're nowt but common floozies. And I've had enough of the complaints I receive. Shame on you both.'

'We ain't floozies. We've made our mistakes but we're respectable folk. We're starting our own business soon on the prom, so put that in your pipe and smoke it!'

'As prossies, naw doubt. Sluts! Well, I want you out! Both of you, though where you're concerned, Trisha, me hands are tied, as you have a man at war, poor bloody sod! But she's got to go. If you don't put her out in the next week, then you'll go an' all, but then, where will Bobby be, poor lad, to have fought in the war, then to be homeless, eh?'

Incensed but near to tears, Trisha folded her own arms to steady her and give her strength. 'Don't worry, none of us'll stay here a minute longer than we have to.'

'Good, because once Bobby's home, I'll want assurances from him that he'll keep you in order, or you're both out on your arses!'

Trisha slammed the door shut. Shaking from head to toe, she sat down heavily on one of the dining chairs.

She could see that Martha was silently crying and Sally's bottom lip was quivering. Gathering all her strength, she stood up. 'Well, that's made our minds up. We'll move into the flat.' She swept Sally into her arms, then bent and touched Martha's head, stroking her hair. 'It'll be all right, lass, we've dealt with worse.'

Though tears streamed down her face, Martha said, 'I'll go, Trish, you must stay. Sure, it is that you need to provide a home for Bobby returning. He doesn't deserve to have gone through what he has and not have his home to come back to, so he doesn't.'

Trisha sighed. She knew Martha was right. Bobby had enough to contend with when he came home and none of it his fault. He weren't the best of husbands in the beginning, but he was sorry and tried to change. It would be like she'd kicked him in the face as it was without adding to it.

She bobbed Sally up and down on her hip. 'You're right. Though it will break me heart to have you move out, I don't see that we have any choice.'

'Though where it is we're to get the money from to furnish the flat, I'm at a loss for knowing. None of our cash on delivery money has landed in our post office account yet.'

'Aw, Martha, love. You can take your granny's bed and chair, and all the linen you brought with you an' all. And we can go to Lil's second-hand shop and get you some pots and pans and a sofa. And you've got your cot that the gypsies wove for you . . . Cilla has turned up trumps on that one, and I love the baby basket she made for you herself. The pram you can store in the kitchen of the shop. It's big enough . . . Aw, I'm sorry, lass . . .'

Trisha could be strong no longer. Tears flooded her face. 'I can't think of life without you with me, or at least living next door.'

Martha seemed to be the one who grew in strength then. With Bonnie fed, she lay her on the sofa and came towards Trisha. Her arm came around her as she told her, 'We'll get through, so we will.' She enclosed the crying Sally in her arms at the same time. 'It is that we three have little Bonnie to think of now. And at least I will have a home, and a nice one. Sure, it is that I'll have a sea view, something the visitors pay through the nose for.'

This cheered Trisha and with her smiling, Sally stopped crying too. Trisha kissed her on the forehead. 'Well, little Sallykins, we women love a good cry, don't we? So, that's our daily tears over with. Come on, we've got a new life to start, we need to get on with it.' She stood and held Sally high above her and twizzled her around. 'We're going to be in business, lass. Eh, you're going to be rich!'

Sally's last tear plopped onto her face as she giggled, kicked her legs and then let out a squeal of delight as Trisha saw in her face that her little world had righted itself. Her yell, though, made little Bonnie jump and she let out a cry to rival Sally's. Martha laughed out loud. 'Well, it is that the youngest little lady needs to join in with the tears too.'

They all laughed together.

When they reached Mr Green's office, they nervously went inside.

'Well, when did this happen? Your babby has arrived then? Have you been able to let the father know? I could ring the War Office for you, if you like?'

Trisha froze. The lie they'd told about both their men being at war had come back to bite them on the bum.

'Is something wrong, girls?'

'Naw, except, well . . . Martha's man ain't coming back.'

'Oh. I'm mortally sorry, dear.'

Martha just nodded.

Trisha jumped in. 'So, the day has come. We can't tell you how much we've longed for it to.'

'Yes . . . hmm, well, all is in order. We just need you to sign the paperwork and pay over the deposit of the first quarter's rent – a very generous discount, might I add.'

'Just the rent – not a deposit an' all?'

'Yes. You see, being in advance, the rent acts as a deposit, though it is our normal practice to take both. I'm acting on a new instruction from Lord Smythe. He explained that it is due to the fact that the garments you have already sold to their friends arrived promptly and were of excellent quality. And so, his wife told him you deserved more help to get your shop ready. And you won't have to paint it yourselves now as he has hired painters and decorators to whitewash it all through. It looks like new.'

'But that's grand. Eeh, Martha, lass, we'll be able to afford more furniture for you now.'

'Oh, have your plans changed?'

'Aye, now the babby's here, Martha will live in the flat.'

'Good. The insurance company don't like the premises to be lock-ups – this will save you money on that score, too. I will contact them and get an amended quote . . . Well, girls, I can only wish you luck. I've never met a braver pair of young women in my life, and now with two children to care for and no man to help either of you, you are going to find it even more difficult. You amaze me.'

As they went to leave, he said, 'And, Martha, I'm very, very sorry for your loss.'

Martha nodded again. Trisha could see she was lost for words at this new turn of events, which they both should have been ready for, but somehow they got caught up in the tangle of lies they had told to cover for themselves.

Neither of them spoke as they walked towards the prom, and yet this should have been a happy occasion – one of the happiest in their lives.

When they reached the shop, they both stopped and stared. It was as if the full impact of what they had taken on hit them.

'Jesus, Mary and Joseph, what have we been thinking of, Trisha?'

'It were your idea, love. Don't chicken out on me now.'

'But to have got it on a lie, as sure it is that is what has happened. I wasn't for thinking when we did that, but declaring I was a married lady on legal papers, it is that I could go to prison!'

Trisha felt her heart stop. Martha had only done that just to hide the shame. *Yet where are the bloody men that put us in this position? Not that they forced themselves on us, but how come they get to live their lives without any stigma, and as if they haven't a care in the world? Praised even, as if they were found to have made a conquest!* 'Bloody conquest!'

'Pardon? What conquest is it you are talking of, Trisha?'

'Ha, I didn't mean to say that out loud. I were on me soapbox in me head about how men get away with everything, and it came out.'

Martha began to giggle. The giggle turned to a belly laugh, but soon she was laughing and sobbing as if the world had come to an end.

'Eeh, me little lass. Let's get you inside . . . What a day – giving birth in the morning and then being thrown out of house and home, finding out you're a criminal in the afternoon . . . by, it's too much for anyone to take.'

The tears turned to laughter again as Trisha opened the door. Helpless laughter that bent Martha double, only real laughter, not hysterics, Trisha was pleased to see. 'What? What are you laughing at, Martha? Tears I can understand, but bloody laughing!'

'It . . . it's you . . . Ooh, it is that you don't know how funny you are . . . summing up me day! Ha, did anyone have such a disastrous one as that?'

'Naw, I doubt it.' Trisha saw the funny side and joined in the laughter. When she sobered, she said, 'Well, welcome to our layette shop. Which we haven't even got a name for yet . . . Is there such a thing as the layettateers?'

Drying her eyes, Martha shook her head. 'No. Not that I am knowing of.'

'Eeh, that had better be our first job then. We should have given attention to it long before now. The signwriters are coming tomorrow.'

'I know, it is that I have been so tired lately me brain was not for giving me any idea.'

'Let's have a cuppa, eh? Get the kettle and stuff out from the bottom of the pram and we'll start with that . . . Eeh, look at Sally, she'll be as black as coal crawling around, I didn't think when I let her out of the pushchair.'

'Ha, you Blackpudlians are for being proper tea bellies, it is your cure for all. Here you go.'

As Martha took the kettle, Trisha didn't deny this except to say, 'I beg your pardon, madam, I'm a Sandgronian! Born and bred. A Blackpudlian is for folk who settled here, like yourself.'

As if the mood had changed, Martha came back with, 'Ooh, it is that I bow to you, madam!'

Once more they were giggling as they came into the kitchen and Trisha was glad of it. She had a heavy feeling in her stomach put there the moment Mr Green had asked about Martha's man. Making it even heavier was the truth of how much trouble they might be in if it was ever discovered.

By the time they had drunk their tea, they had come up with and discarded several names, until suddenly Martha said, 'The Layette Lasses.'

'Eeh, I love it, Martha. It has your posh word for baby things, and a Lancashire way of saying "girls". I can see it now, standing out on our shop sign in blue, with pink baby things painted around it. What do you think?'

'Perfect. It is that we have made our first business decision together, Trish – the first of many.'

They were open the following week, with all their stock displayed beautifully – the white background of the walls giving a dreamy feel to everything, especially with Martha's touch of genius in draping pink and blue silk swathes between some of their many shelves.

They stood back to admire it all before they opened their front door for the first time. Martha took hold of her hand and squeezed it. 'We did it.'

'We did that, lass.'

The rush of warm air they let in with the opening of the door seemed to say, *You've arrived*. 'Here's one Blackpool lass who never thought to see such a day. Eeh, me ma, pa and gran would be proud of me at this moment.'

'Mine too. Good luck, Trish.'

'Aye, and good luck to you, me lovely lass. You did this for me. You changed me whole life.' They hugged. 'We'll be for being all right, won't we, Trish?'

'We will, lass. We're strong, and we can face whatever life throws at us ... Naw, don't start to tell me what that is now!' She laughed and Martha laughed with her.

Trisha took a deep breath. *By, I've done well for meself.* She looked at Martha. 'It all begins today, lass.'

They both gave an excited little giggle.

TWENTY-TWO

Martha

By the time they closed that evening, Martha felt shattered.

'You have to rest, love. You must. Here's your babby just ten days old and you haven't taken hardly a moment off your feet. You should still be thinking about not putting your feet to the floor, not running around like you are.'

'I know, but it is that it had to be done. Now we are open and are for having lots of stock, I will rest more. I am promising you, me darling . . . Oh, I'm hating this moment when it is you and Sally have to go home and I go up to me flat.'

'Me too. I tell you what, why don't we set up the second bedroom for me and Sally? Lil had a few single beds and cots in, then I could stay over a few evenings – well, two at least. I daren't stop more than that or that nosy old cow, Mrs Higginbottom, will be reporting me for not living there. But just visiting a friend is all right.'

'Sure, that would be wonderful, but why are there such rules when it is that you're paying the rent?'

'I don't knaw, but I read the contract Bobby signed recently, and there's loads – one is that the property cannot be left vacant for more than two weeks unless due to hospitalisation.'

Martha shook her head. She remembered such fears her pappy had, but then, he never went anywhere so it didn't make any odds, but it was like folk who rented were prisoners to rules.

'Anyroad, on them two nights we can open the shop late in the season. You knaw yourself how the ladies and gentlemen that visit take a walk in the evening. It might be worth it. A lot of the stalls do it.'

'That's for being a good idea, yes. I don't know why it is that I didn't be thinking of it. Oh, Trish, I feel so much better.'

'Me too. Now, hop on upstairs, and get you and Bonnie settled for the night, Martha. And have a good night's sleep.'

As she went to the door with Trisha, Trisha said, 'We did all right today, didn't we, love?'

'We did. We were for having a few sales but a lot of interest, which is looking good for our future, so it is.'

Going upstairs carrying Bonnie, Martha felt the loneliness she'd had these last days creep over her again. She thought of Peter. What would he think of little Bonnie? But then, she knew he would love her. Her heart longed for him. Though this wasn't always the case. Sometimes she ranted and raved at anything about him leaving her – it was one of her cushions last time and she ended up throwing it across the room in temper.

But despite her loneliness, she felt comforted when she opened the door and stepped into her living room.

The walls were white just the same as they were downstairs, but Granny's chair looked lovely by the window and often she sat there, watching the sea, rocking gently, with Bonnie on her knee. Peaceful moments that she loved. The sofa she'd bought had taken some getting up the stairs. It was a big, plumped-up one, in a soft grey colour with a faded red rose pattern woven into it. She knew it had come from a happy home and she loved it. Her rag rug matched it – well, it was mostly black, but it had splashes of red and grey too. And they'd managed to run to a small table and two chairs that stood in the corner. And a small dresser that stood next to it. Her sewing machine and all the stock of material and wools were in the stockroom downstairs, so she didn't have to make room for them, but the only other item of furniture she had bought was a huge chest of drawers – which had been another struggle to get upstairs – and that stood in her bedroom.

Thinking of furnishing the second bedroom filled her with joy. She would live for the two nights that Trisha stayed with her.

Next day, with Trisha looking after the shop, Martha walked down to see Cilla. Over the months they'd become very close and found they worked well together. Having her had been a blessing towards the end of her pregnancy, and now, with the shop, Cilla was doing most of the readings. But today, Martha had a lady booked in who came to see her each year when she visited to take the waters – something Blackpool was known for.

Listening outside the tent and finding everything quiet, Martha called, 'I'm for bringing me wee one to show you, Cilla.'

The flap opened immediately. 'Eeh, Martha, I have been dying to see little Bonnie. I have had visions of how brave she is going to be and how she will look after Sally. And that a man, whose name begins with J, will also be in her life and yours.'

This, and all of what Cilla came out with each time they met, told Martha that Cilla was so much more like her granny than ever she was. Granny would have known Bonnie's future. Maybe, she thought, it was because they really opened to their spirit guide, whereas she fought against knowing so many things, and often only let in half of what she knew was trying to be conveyed to her.

'Sure, it is that you are a miracle, if all that is to come true, Cilla, which I am not for doubting. I just wish it was that me granny could have met you.'

'She did. Well, at least, I was there when she called. We were all in awe of her. You should come to the camp to be having your babby blessed in the brook.'

Martha didn't like the sound of this: 'I'll be having a christening in the church, Cilla. And it is that you are welcome, as is the elder, but I'm not for the rituals of the clan. I have never been taught your ways.'

'That's what happens when one of us marries a *gorger* – mind, your granny, being a princess, was forgiven a long time ago.'

'I wasn't meaning to offend, love.'

'Naw, I knaw that. Don't worry about it and we're all of the Catholic faith too, so I would be honoured to attend. Now, let me look at little Bonnie.'

Cilla cooed over Bonnie and the moment of embarrassment passed.

'She's adorable, and like I was telling you, she will be a very brave young woman and will make you proud, Martha. I tell you what, while you see your client, I'll take Bonnie for a walk. What time is her next feed?'

'It's all for working out well as it is she was fed before I set out so she'll be going another three hours and I would be grateful to you, so I would.'

'I will love it. I'll take her to meet me friend who's selling pegs on the prom today.'

'Ta very much, Cilla, but be mindful that it is that I must be back at the shop by three as Trisha has promised to work the donkeys today.'

'I will.'

When Cilla left, Martha sat down in her granny's chair. She thought how nice it was that she had two chairs of Granny's to use, the one that had been in Granny's bedroom and this one. Both gave her comfort.

While she waited, she thought about the gypsy family she had. None of them were close relatives, but still, they were family. Maybe she should visit them and take Bonnie along to have the blessing Cilla was talking of. She remembered Handsi as a nice gentleman, who would now be the elder of the camp.

The flap opened. 'Ah, it is Mrs Wild. It is for being good to see you.'

The lady smiled. Always she looked nervous, but during the reading Martha was able to put her mind at rest. 'It is a good year you are in for. Your husband is to return to you, and I see happiness for you.'

'What about my mother?'

Martha turned another card. As she did, she knew. The black flag with the five-petal rose faced her.

'Please tell me. I am ready to hear.'

'The mother you love and nurse will go to heaven soon.'

'Thank you. I want that for my mother. I nearly didn't come to Blackpool as Mother's nurse warned me that the end is near. I have been praying for her peace from pain. When?'

'Very soon.'

'I will return to London today then. Thank you, Martha.'

As she said this, she put two crowns on the table. 'For being honest with me. Good day.'

As the flap closed behind her, Martha knew she never wanted to do this work again.

'Mrs Wild!' Jumping up, she managed to catch the lady before she got into a landau. 'I – I am wanting to tell you that I won't be here next year.' Feeling proud of being able to hand her a lovely card, she said, 'This is where I will be, but no longer telling fortunes. It is that my cousin is taking over. She is for being better than me. Please, be kind enough to be giving her your custom.'

'A layette shop? I love the name. Well, you didn't say, but I am hoping that with my husband home I will be able to add to my family. I will pay you a visit when I am next here, and yes, I will give your cousin a try. I saw on your board that it said and Gypsy Cilla Rosa Lee.'

'Ta. Next time it is you come, I think it is that you will need to visit me shop.'

'Oh, an extra foretelling. Thank you, dear. Good and bad news for me, but I am ready for both.'

When Martha arrived back at the shop, Mr Green stood just inside. Trisha looked upset and afraid.

'Now then, young lady, I have had a visitor – Hattie Hargreaves.'

'Oh?'

'Now, don't play the innocent. You have lied on a legal document. I trusted you. I should have asked for supporting evidence of all of your statements, but I was lax in not doing so. Hattie is a member of the landlord association, as I am, and she felt it her duty to tell me.'

'I am mortally sorry, and so ashamed to be finding meself unmarried with a baby. I – I thought you would judge me as a – a floozie if you knew. What – what is it that will happen to me?'

Mr Green stared at her, and then looked at Trisha and around the shop.

'Look. I haven't yet sent a copy of the papers off, but knowing this, I can't send them to Lord Smythe as they are. It's against all my principles. All I can do is to draw up new ones and you write in your proper status. Does Lord or Lady Smythe know that you have a child?'

Hope lightened the fear in Martha's heart.

'No, they are not knowing. I have no means of getting in contact, but if you think that it is that I should tell them, I will tell Lady Rebecca Portlend. I have her address to write to.'

'No, don't do that. She may never find out. Hattie can be mean at times; most women can about this sort of thing. She told me about you too, Trisha, but as you are married and I didn't ask who the father of your child was, there isn't a problem. However, Martha, think twice about doing this sort of thing again. It is a very serious offence to make a false declaration.'

'I'm sorry to the heart of me, sir.'

Mr Green shook his head. 'I expect you are, but well, you must be proud of yourself too. One mistake doesn't mark you as no good. You have achieved a lot and are a very talented lady. As you are too, Trisha . . . Now, I'll take my leave. As always, I wish you good luck.'

When he'd gone Trisha ran to her and held out her arms. 'Eeh, Martha, I've never been so scared in all me life . . . Eeh, lass, you're shaking even more than me.'

'I – I was for seeing meself in jail, Trish.'

'I knaw, I was too. Look, it's unlikely that Lady Rebecca or Lady Darcy will ever find out you have a babby, so let's forget it, eh?'

Martha thought for a moment but then decided, 'No, Trish, it is that I can't go through with the deceit any longer, nor is it that I can deny me little Bonnie. I'm going to write to them both and be for telling them the truth. It is for them to decide.'

'But we may lose the shop, lass.'

'Sure, if we do, we'll be getting a stall, and we are for having our brochures. They bring in business, so much so that we've had to place another order with Joshua. And it is that we can afford, once the cash on delivery money is credited to us, to put a deposit down on a flat to rent, so we can.'

'Aye, I can see as you're set on this course, lass. I would advise against it, but for peace of mind, I can see it is for the best. We'll do all right, won't we, eh?'

Feeling that she should lighten the fear they were feeling, Martha said, 'To be sure, I am for knowing a good fortune teller we could consult.'

Trisha let her go and stood back and looked at her. Martha kept an innocent expression. This made Trisha burst out laughing. 'You daft ha'peth. Ha, you had me going there! Anyroad, you said you would never look into your own future, and though you knaw mine, you'll only tell me the good bits.'

'Which it is what I have done. It is mostly good for you, me darling. To be sure, that is something I can promise.'

'Well then, it will be for you an' all as I'll make sure of that, lass.'

'Talking of fortune tellers, I made another decision today.' Martha explained to Trish what it was. 'And so, I have agreed to sign over me pitch to Cilla. It is for being her destiny but, well . . . I did talk to her about something else.'

'By, you've had a busy morning of decisions, lass. Slow down, you might come up with the idea that I'm a hindrance or sommat.'

Martha laughed. 'Oh, it is that I came to that conclusion a long time ago!'

They both laughed again then. To Martha, just being with Trisha was a joy. She could always cheer her up. And didn't miss the funny side of any quip she made herself, and despite everything that hit them, they spent much of their time having a giggle which made life easier.

'Come on then, what else has been on your big agenda?'

'I was for thinking that when telling fortunes there is a lot of time to spare, and how it is that Cilla is skilled in wicker weaving – look at the lovely cot and basket she made for me. So, it is that I suggested she do that alongside the fortune telling and that we would buy a sample of a cot and a basket, and then sell them at a profit.'

'Genius! I love the idea. Eeh, we're going to end up with an emporium, with babby clothes, babby equipment, toddler clothes and even toys!'

'Ha, steady on, we haven't been for having a customer through the door this last hour or so. That is not for pointing to an emporium! But, sure enough, the cots will be another attraction for our business, Trish.'

'Aye, they will. Eeh, I feel that excited, though we're to get over the hurdle of you confessing all. I wish you wouldn't . . . Anyroad, I'll take the pram into the kitchen and nip up and check on Sally. I thought I heard her rattling her cot, so she's woken from her nap.'

As Trisha steered the pram through the shop, the door opened. A well-dressed lady, with a mound of a tummy, walked in.

'Good afternoon, madam. Is it that I can be of help to you?'

'You're Irish! My husband owns land in Ireland, just outside Dublin. Very pretty. We visit often.'

Martha had an impulse to ask, *And who was it he stole that from?* But she bit her tongue and smiled. 'I was for leaving there a few years ago, but one day I am making plans to visit.'

'Are your parents still living there?'

'No, me mammy and pappy were . . . they have passed, so they have.'

'I'm sorry. That is sad.'

'Ta. It is good of you to be caring . . . Was there something special that you were after looking for?'

'I need to choose a complete layette. My friend had a brochure from her friend and knew that I was visiting Blackpool, so recommended you to me.'

All antagonism left Martha. She couldn't undo the injustice and didn't see any sense in letting the hurt of yesteryear interfere with what may be a godsend to them – a personal recommendation was the very best way of getting new business. 'That's for being nice to know. Please feel free to be having a look around and asking any questions. As our brochure says, it is that we can supply any colours, sizes and be doing different embroidery patterns for you.'

The lady smiled and began to browse the shelves.

Martha took some deep breaths. It was a funny day with everything, but now to be faced with one of the people who directly sacked Ireland and caused the unrest that killed her mammy and pappy was a trial almost beyond her endurance.

To distract herself, she thought to begin the letter to Lady Rebecca. Taking her writing pad from under the counter, she lifted her pen from the ink pot and wrote:

Dear Lady Rebecca,

It is that I have a confession to make . . .

She immediately struck this through. She wasn't going to treat her love for Peter, or the birth of her beloved daughter, like a sin or a crime. *But how should I write it?*

There was no time to try again as the lady called her over. 'I love so much in your shop, I am finding it hard to choose, and then, one doesn't know whether to buy for a girl or a boy.'

Thinking to take more interest, Martha asked, 'May I be asking, when it is that you are due, madam?'

'November.' She giggled. 'My husband came home on leave in February.' But then she sighed. 'I wish this war would end. I fear every day that my baby will never know his father.'

Despite everything, Martha felt sorrow for her and decided she wasn't responsible for what her husband did and was probably unaware of the suffering caused.

The woman turned away to touch some more of the garments. Martha closed her eyes and allowed the vision that pestered her. Smiling with relief, she said, 'Please don't be worrying yourself, your husband will return. I am for seeing the future, due to me gypsy heritage, and I see happiness lying ahead for you.'

The lady smiled once more, and Martha realised, now that her pre-judgement had altered, just how beautiful she was – radiant, with her true English peaches and cream complexion. Happiness shone from her, and her voice had a gentle tone. 'I know you are a fortune teller, my friend said that is how Lady Rebecca met you.'

At that moment, Trisha returned carrying both babies. She went to speak, but then saw there was a customer. 'Oh, I'll take them upstairs again.'

'How adorable. Do let me say hello.'

Martha's heart thumped. Her premonition earlier that she hadn't spoken of – that if she didn't tell lady Rebecca, she would find out anyway – was going to come true!

Trisha seemed to latch on to Martha's distress as she didn't move but looked at her as if asking for approval.

Martha swallowed; the moment of truth was on her much sooner than she wanted it to be. 'Of course it is that you can greet our children. The little one is mine; she's after being called Bonnie. And Sally is Trisha's. Trisha and I are partners.'

'Oh, I know, I saw that on the brochure, but you mentioned nothing about being mothers. You should, it gives us new mums more confidence than dealing with girls who know nothing about the trials of pregnancy and motherhood. I'm surprised Lady Rebecca hasn't advised you to do that . . . Hello, little ones . . . Ah, you are beautiful.'

Martha caught Trisha's glance and read the message she was trying to convey to her not to tell, but ignored it. 'Lady Rebecca doesn't know about my child.'

'Oh, I will tell her! She will be thrilled . . . Such beautiful children, they make me long for mine, and how wonderfully dressed they are . . . I so want that matinee jacket, but in lemon for a safe bet.'

As the lady cooed with the babies, Martha had a vision that she was to have a son but didn't tell her. The vision was hazy, made so by Martha's distress, and therefore could be wrong.

'I will write down all you order, and can post it to you.'

The lady turned and looked intently at Martha. 'You look troubled, dear. Are you all right?'

'Yes . . . yes, sorry, it is that I was distracted for a moment.'

'You take the babbies back upstairs, Martha. I'll serve Madam.'

Martha was glad to leave the room. When she got upstairs, she sat Sally down and lay Bonnie on a blanket on the floor before sinking into the sofa. Her mind raced nineteen to the dozen, then it occurred to her that tomorrow was a day they had both looked forward to – even if a little nervously – as their new telephone was to be installed. Neither knew how to use one, but it looked simple enough – you picked up the receiver, dialled zero and asked the operator to connect you. She would make her first call to the number on Lady Rebecca's card – but then, would the lady in the shop ring before then? She would just have to hope that she didn't.

Sitting back, she closed her eyes. All that had happened today had left her weary. Thankfully, it was nearly closing time. She decided she would ask Trisha to come back and to stay tonight. She needed company, or her worry would drive her mad. She could make a bed up on the sofa, and one with the cushions on the floor for Sally. She was sure she could make them comfortable – she so hoped Trisha would agree.

TWENTY-THREE

Trisha

Trisha's voice called up the stairs, 'The coast's clear, lass, but hey, we're better off by two quid!'

Martha clapped her hands together, telling Trish as she gathered the babies up, 'That's for being fifteen shillings more than me pappy earned a week for toiling on the farm for twelve to fourteen hours a day, God rest his soul.'

'Aye, it's a fortune! And sommat else. If you can see Cilla and make a firm arrangement about making cots for us to stock, Lady Joanne Runkin, as the lady was called, would be very interested. I told her we'd send a new brochure with her parcel showing one. I thought that you could go and see Joshua and get him to do that for the new order using yours as it looks lovely with the pink satin lining you gave it.'

'Ooh, Trish, yes. I spoke to Cilla, and she was liking the idea. I told her we would give her a fair price and then sell at a profit, and she agreed to that.'

Trisha beamed. 'Well, let's get on to it, lass. I think it could give our trade a real boost.'

'I will, but there is something I need to be asking of you, Trish. Would you think about staying tonight? Only, it is that I am shaken by all that has happened, and don't want to be alone.'

She explained how she could make them both comfortable.

'Aw, I would love that. But remember how we used to unscrew the body of the pram to store it in the lean-to? We could do that as Sally still fits into it easily. And then, if she gets a bit upset at all, I can rock her as if she's in a boat.'

'Ta, Trish. I knew it was that we could sort something out.'

'Aye, well, I could do with your company an' all. There's nowt I hate more than going back to me house on me own. Curtains twitch, or if me neighbours are on their doorsteps there's the odd remark like, "Think yourself somebody with a shop on the prom, don't you?"'

'I'm not for understanding them. For the most part, Blackpool folk are lovely, but it is that in your street you have a few rotten eggs.'

'I miss Edna. She could cut with her tongue at times if she got on her high horse, but mostly she stuck up for me. But you knaw, I don't blame them. I've done wrong and to them I've brought shame on the street. Anyroad, I'll still have to run the gauntlet this evening as there's things I need.' She sighed. 'Mind, when we get the room ready, I could have some things here and wouldn't need to face them all on the nights I stay.'

Martha's heart felt heavy for Trisha. To have to contend with the wrath of those she'd known all her life and who'd looked out for her hurt her. But it was their loss, for to her, no matter what she'd done, Trisha was worth her weight in gold compared to any one of them!

'Let us be having one of our hugs, eh? They're always bringing the smiles back to our faces.'

'Aye, I don't knaw what I'd do without you, Martha.'

As they came out of the hug, Trisha said, 'Eeh, we should be celebrating! Look! Two crisp one-pound notes!' Trisha did a little dance waving the money. Sally giggled, 'Mamma.'

Martha decided to join in as her cares seemed to shed from her. Yes, a lot had happened today – no more sitting in that draughty tent doing something she hated, no more living a lie, a possibility of helping Cilla and the gypsy clan to earn more money and, best of all, Trisha was going to stay the night! *If only Peter would walk through the door. How happy that would make me.*

Brushing this thought away, she told Trisha, 'While it is that you go home to fetch what you need, I will be going along to see Cilla, then Joshua as he only lives around the corner from me old tent in Waterloo Road.'

Cilla greeted her with, 'Martha, you are troubled. Let me be putting your mind at rest. Speak to me about what is on your mind. I knaw it's insecurity about your future. I could give you the answers.'

'No, Cilla, don't you be worrying. Now, I am coming with news on what we talked of – the making of cots like you made for me . . . Oh, Cilla, it is for being a wonderful skill your clan taught you.'

'They're your clan an' all, Martha.'

'I – I . . . it is hard for me to be getting me head around that. I'm sorry. It is that I'm not rejecting them but have never known the feeling of being one of them . . . I'm not for knowing the ways of that side of me family.'

'Well, at least you have acknowledged that's what we are – family . . . Anyroad, I'll not give up on you. But what you've come about excites me. Tell me more about it, eh?'

The atmosphere relaxed as they chatted, agreed a price and got carried away with thinking of the different styles they could be made in.

'Getting the cane isn't easy, though. There is a clan in Somerset that supplies the willow. They will be at the horse fair in July, so we can get some then. We have enough to make one cot for now, but that's all.'

'Well, it is that we will stick with the one design, then when you have a supply, you can make others.'

'I can get seagrass readily enough if you want baskets. I've got some drying out now as I thought to sell them here as a sideline to supplement me income.'

'Oh, that is for being a good idea. I love me basket you made for me with a wee lid for all the things I need handy for Bonnie, so I do. What is it you charge for them?'

'Well, I thought here I would sell them for thruppence, but if you're buying a few, I could drop that a bit.'

'I'll be giving it some thought. We could be for making sets – line a basket and a cot with the same material. How lovely that would be. Now, it is that I must away as I have to make another call and Bonnie will be wanting her tea.'

Cilla came outside and cooed over Bonnie for a few minutes before saying, 'Make sure she knaws of her family, Martha.'

'I will, it is a promise. And one day I will be for bringing her to meet you all.'

With this Martha made a hasty exit. She had such mixed feelings about being part of Granny's clan and just didn't feel ready to embrace them as her family yet, even though she'd loved the visit she'd made with her granny. She didn't know why, but an inner voice seemed to stop her, telling her that if she did, then the powers she possessed would come to the fore again, and she didn't want that.

Guilt visited her at this. She knew she was denying her own heritage and, by doing so, her granny. But then she settled herself with thinking that Granny had rejected the clan too and had only gone back when she had to. *Maybe a time will come when I need to, but until then, I will be as Granny was – a* gorger *and not a gypsy.*

When she pressed Joshua's bell, he took a while to answer. She'd seen him peep out of his curtain.

Filling with shame at the reason, she decided to turn away and thought to send Trisha on the errand tomorrow, but as she went to, the door opened. Joshua's expression cut her heart.

'I can see you are for judging me and have found me wanting. I'll not be darkening your doorstep; I'll be sending Trisha on me errand.'

As she turned, he said, 'No ... I mean, I'm sorry. I shouldn't have judged you. I was just so shocked by what my father told me.'

'Well, it is that women don't have the luxury of walking away from their sins. They have to be facing the punishment of others for ever. But it is also that we have choices. I could have been going to the nuns. But me wee baby is for being mine and deserves for her mammy to care for her. Nothing of what happened is her fault, so it isn't.'

Joshua hung his head.

Martha waited for a moment before asking, 'So, is it to be that I am not welcome?'

'No, no, of course not . . . but why didn't you tell me? Why lie if you feel how you do?'

'I wasn't for lying, I just didn't confirm what you called me as the truth.' She held her head up the while she spoke and looked him in the eyes. 'I think I was for making the right judgement as you have shown your feelings about me situation. I doubt it is that you would have been taking me business.'

'Oh, no, it isn't like that, Martha. It's that suddenly, you weren't who I thought you were . . . But if anything, well, I have to admit, a part of me is glad you're not married.'

Reading his meaning, but not welcoming it knowing her heart was given to another, and yet feeling a little twitch in the pit of her stomach, Martha didn't reply to this.

'Come in, come in. We can't stand here and do business. It is business I presume you are here about?'

'It is so.'

'Well, you know where my office is. Go through and I'll be with you in a moment. I need to make sure I have closed the dark room door – the room where I develop my photographs, I mean.'

Martha picked up the still sleeping Bonnie and carried her inside. Joshua glanced at her then away and went to turn from her but changed his mind. 'So, this is the little one. May I have a peep? Oh, she has your hair. How lovely . . . You're right, Martha, she is innocent, and it is the right thing to care for her.' He looked up and gazed into her eyes. 'Thinking about it, I would expect no less of you. I shouldn't have behaved how I did. If I can ever do anything to help, I will.'

Martha's heart flipped over. She couldn't understand why and immediately thought of Peter and felt ashamed. 'Ta, Joshua, but it is that me and Trisha manage well.'

'Good, good. Well, that way. Sit down and I'll be with you in a moment.'

When he came into the office, it wasn't in a businesslike way, but his words surprised Martha.

'You know, I do know what it is like to be looked down on. I suffer that, and the snide remarks people think it is all right to bander about within your earshot – words like "coward".' Joshua sat down in the seat on the other side of his desk to her. 'To tell the truth, I sometimes feel like hanging a plaque around my neck declaring, "I am flat-footed", and I've lived in fear of being sent down the mine to replace men who have gone to war, or some other tasks that would be beyond me, but it never happened, thank God.'

'I'm sorry, I wasn't for realising.'

'And I don't think it will stop when the war ends, only get worse as when the men come home, they won't be happy to know I wasn't one of them.'

Martha could see his fear and hear it in his voice. 'It's sorry I am as I know too well what it is you are going through. As well as the stigma of having a child out of wedlock, I am Irish and many pin the consequences of the struggles on me. I am feeling it in their glances when I speak . . . But I was for doing it meself just today, so I was. A lady came into me shop, whose husband is one of the English who have sacked land from us Irish. I did judge her the moment I was for knowing. And yet, it cannot be her fault. Women are for having no say in the buying of property, or the evicting of the rightful owners.'

'I'm sorry, I have read about the Troubles in Ireland. I lean towards our ways as being the cause of it, but it happened many years ago.'

'It is true enough, but families don't forget losing the land that should rightfully be theirs. Me own grandpappy was for losing his farm.'

'Oh? So, where is your family now? Did you all come over to England?'

Martha hung her head as a pain shot through her heart.

'I'm sorry. Have . . . I mean, are you alone?'

Martha nodded.

There was a silence for a moment, then Joshua stood and came around the desk to be next to her. He put his arm around her. 'I get the feeling that you have been through such a lot, Martha, my dear. I'm truly sorry. Would you like to talk about it?'

Without realising what she was doing, Martha leaned her head on his strong chest and poured out her story. By the time she'd finished, the tears were streaming down her face and Joshua was stroking her hair. His arm had tightened around her, making her feel great comfort and, yes, love. She knew he loved her.

Confusion swept through her. She couldn't deny returning his feelings, and yet wanted to deny it. Panicking, she told herself that this wasn't real. It was just that Joshua was here for her now. She didn't love him, she was mistaken. She loved Peter.

Unconsciously, she stiffened.

Joshua let her go and stepped away. Martha felt strangely bereft, and yet, welcomed being out of the aura of him.

'Are you all right now, Martha? Your story is harrowing. I cannot imagine what you are going through, and now, having no one to turn to with having your child and caring for her ... I know you said you think that Peter was taken ill, but I'm inclined to think of him as a cad! Accepting all you had, taking what he shouldn't then, once he felt like it, buggering off – excuse my language. But I'd like to wring his bloody neck!'

Martha came out of the feeling that had taken her and jumped to Peter's defence. 'It wasn't for being like that, Peter loved me. I know it in the bones of me, and I have visions of him lost, not knowing where he is or why.'

'I can see, my dear, that would be a comfort to you, but I can't come to the same conclusion. What could cause such a thing to happen? You said he had a chest problem, not a head one. But I understand. No one wants to think they have been duped, especially when ... well, you fell under his spell and did things I don't think are you ... I mean, what you were brought up to do, or know in your heart is right.'

'I feel accused. I could be saying that you are using your flat feet to avoid going to war, but it is something I don't think, or wouldn't say if I did. It is that you think you are for having the right to say similar things to me. But it wasn't for being like that. It wasn't.'

The tears he'd comforted, returned.

Joshua hung his head. 'I'm sorry, Martha, forgive me. I am judging again, when I know how hurtful that can be. I'm so sorry . . . Please may I hold you again – as a friend?'

Martha looked up. Saw again the love in his eyes and felt herself yearn to allow it. He rose. She didn't protest. Both his arms came around her, hugging her to him as best he could with her having the baby on her knee. His voice no more than a whisper, he told her, 'Martha, I love you and will always be here for you. I know I shouldn't speak of it given what you have told me – that your heart is given to another – but I have loved you from the moment I set eyes on you and would take second best if you would have me.'

'Oh, Joshua, it is that I am torn. I am for having feelings for you, but you are deserving of more than I can give.'

'I need to hold you properly, my darling.'

The endearment sent a tingle down her spine. The confusion she'd felt earlier returned. She tried to bring Peter to mind but at this moment, she couldn't. Why? Why was this happening? She loved Peter with all that she was. She couldn't allow this, it was unfair to Joshua. And yet, when he gently took her sleeping child and lay her lovingly on the sofa against the wall, she didn't object but allowed him to help her to rise. Not being a tall person, she had to put back her head to look up at him. His head lowered. His lips came onto hers for a brief moment, then he lifted his head and looked deeply into her eyes before holding her tightly to him.

Coming to her senses, she pushed him away. 'So, you think to use me in the same way you say Peter did! You are for thinking that I am a loose woman. I'm not . . . Please, let us be doing our business and I will leave!'

He looked shocked and then ashamed. Sitting back down, he shifted some things about on his desk before looking up and holding her gaze. 'I didn't think that at all, Martha. I am in love with you, and it breaks my heart that you cannot return my love. But I can see how my actions led you to believe what you do. Please, Martha . . . I – I will always be here. I want to be with you, but I should have taken things more slowly. I just need you to know that I would never take advantage of you. When I say that I love you, it is the truth. You occupy my every waking hour. And my dreams when I am asleep. But with my love comes respect for you. I just wanted to hold you close to me, just once.'

Martha softened. 'It was for being what you said. When in your arms I was for being in a place I wanted to be, but then Peter came to my mind and how you had said he'd taken advantage of me. I was for thinking you were wanting to do the same.'

'Never. If we never touched again, I would feel bereaved, but would still love you. And . . . well, when I held your baby, I felt a love for her too. She is part of you and so part of me.'

Martha so wanted all he offered, but what would that mean? That she stopped loving Peter? Could she? Could she love two men? What if she never, ever saw Peter again?

'Take your time, Martha. I understand. Let's remain friends and see how things go, eh? I am willing to wait for you.' He gave his lovely grin. 'What we just shared will keep me going for a long time. I want to do it again with all my heart, but if I never, then I will always hold the memory of it.'

He was so lovely, Martha thought. If only things had been different when he came into her life. But then would she have wanted them to have been – never to have known Peter's love, not to have her precious child? No, she wouldn't want that. 'Yes, it is that I would like us to be friends.'

A flash of disappointment crossed his face, but he soon smiled. 'Well then, I haven't even asked you why you are here, my new friend.' He giggled then and Martha giggled with him. The tension broke and they were soon back to the easy way they had with each other from the day he came to her tent.

When she left, Martha had a sense of bewilderment. She hadn't liked leaving, hadn't wanted to – felt disappointment at the same time as relief that Joshua hadn't treated her any different than he would a friend when he'd said goodbye with a casual 'See you soon, Martha' before closing the door on her. *Why does that matter to me? Oh, Jesus, Mary and Joseph, help me. How is it that I am feeling this way? . . . Please be bringing Peter back to me. I love him so much.*

With this thought she had the sense of having betrayed him and that didn't sit comfortably with her. But should she take what Joshua offered? She wouldn't let the answer in.

* * *

Trisha was already back from her home when Martha arrived. She greeted her with a hug and took the pram from her. 'Eeh, I thought you'd got lost, lass.' Picking Bonnie up out of the pram when she'd pushed it into the shop kitchen, she turned and looked at Martha. 'Has sommat happened, love?'

'It has.'

'Bad?'

'No . . . well, it is for being complicated. Let's away upstairs and I'll be telling you all. I'm in need of advice. And yet, it is that I know what I should do.'

'Eeh, you're talking in riddles, but though I'm curious, I can see that whatever it is, you have nice choices to make. Let's get upstairs. I'm hungry, so I turned the casserole up. It smells delicious.'

'Well, as it is that Bonnie is sleeping, we'll eat before I feed her, though I can feel me milk is in, so will be needing a towel to pad me breasts with, so I will.'

'Ha, Bonnie would sleep through an earthquake. She's too placid for her own good, but it's nice for you to have such a contented babby. She's adorable, such a love. I can see Sally being the boss of these two. She allus demands attention.'

As they ate their meal with chunks of bread to dip into the gravy, Sally, who'd been fed, played happily on the floor.

'Well, come on, what's happened to give you choices so you're not sure what to do, lass?'

Trisha listened without comment, and yet her expressions told all. They went from surprise, to astonishment, to sheer disbelief.

'Well, lass, I let you out for five minutes and you get into all sorts of trouble. Let's take it one at a time. That's how me da always dealt with problems. So, your gypsy family is the least of your concerns. You're free to choose when, or if, you pick up with them. It's not for Cilla to put pressure on you, or to add guilt to your shoulders. I'll have a word with her. She wants to think on. Would she like to have a family she knew nothing about and feel that she must mix with them? I doubt it. But to me your other problem isn't one. Joshua is lovely. He is here. He is willing to, and wants to, take you both on by the sound of things.'

'I know, but . . . Peter . . .'

'Peter is gone, love. Gone. And I ain't thinking, like you, that he'll come back. Take what Joshua is offering, lass. Jump at it . . . I mean, take your time. Not jump into bed with him, but get to know him, see what this respect he says he has for you is, 'cause neither of us knaw what that is from a man. It might be a prize worth having, you knaw.'

Martha smiled. She didn't feel that she'd gained anything from her chat, but it had been good to open up about it all. 'We'll see. It is for now that we are to be friends. And I think that is for being the best thing. I love Peter. I cannot be giving my love to another man at the same time.'

Trisha sighed but didn't answer. It was a relief for Martha to get up from the table and begin to feed Bonnie. Something she loved doing as it bound her and her baby together. As usual, Sally crawled over and demanded to be lifted up to sit by the side of her. With Trisha doing this, Sally sat watching, occasionally gently touching Bonnie's head. Martha felt strangely content and happy, as if something good had come into her life. *Who knows*, she told herself, *maybe one day I will let meself love Joshua*. But until then, she'd make herself happy. Something would turn up. She had Bonnie, Trisha and Sally and they were sure things in her life. She wouldn't dwell on the 'maybes'.

TWENTY-FOUR

Trisha

The summer months had been good to them. Trisha had loved her days, with the mornings in the shop and the afternoons on the beach with the donkeys that she so loved, but she found it easier now it was the beginning of October and the donkeys were stabled for the winter. For though she missed them, she could work full-time in the shop with Martha.

Everything was going well though they weren't making a fortune, just managing to pay their bills and have a small wage each and keep some reserves in the bank account.

Seeing him and Martha together, with Martha not realising how much she was coming to depend on Joshua, was a joy and yet frustrating. Joshua was perfect for her, but still she dreamed of Peter turning up one day and longed to know what had happened to him. To Trisha, Peter was a dream Martha was hanging on to and she prayed that one day she would let go of it.

The business had developed too. They had the

stockroom-cum-workroom all kitted out now and spent a lot of their time in there, fulfilling orders and only tending to the shop when the bell rang – a clanging that would wake the dead and had them giggling as it often made the customers jump and that broke the ice as they then giggled with a stranger and made a friend of them before they'd even looked at what was on offer. The bell gave them security as well as alerting them to tend to the shop – no one could get past it to creep in if they were thinking to help themselves.

Not that it was the only bell that made them jump as both still stared in fear when the telephone bell rang. Martha more than herself. Always she feared it would be Lady Rebecca, Lady Darcy or, worse, Lady Darcy's husband, Lord Smythe. None of them had ever got back to her despite her telephoning Lady Rebecca twice. She'd given up after the second time as just with the first call, a haughty voice had told her that Lady Portlend didn't take personal calls from those she didn't know.

Even telling who Martha thought must be the butler that Lady Portlend had given her card to her hadn't persuaded him. He'd merely said he would take her number and pass on the message that she had rung, and then, 'If Lady Portlend wishes to speak to you, she will return the call.'

Telling Martha to write hadn't helped, as try as she might, she couldn't put what she had to say into words. In the end they just had to hope that Lady Runkin hadn't told Lady Rebecca about Bonnie. But that didn't stop Martha worrying.

As Trisha worked on sewing a matinee jacket together and Martha sat embroidering, they were both deep in their own thoughts.

Trisha's mind was taking her to the time when Bobby came home. She'd written to him and told him about the shop but hadn't had a reply.

Guilt clothed her as she thought that she really didn't want to pick up her life with him again. She was the happiest she'd ever been.

She and Martha had settled into a routine with the little ones. At the moment, both were sleeping, but when they woke, they took it in turns to take a few hours off to see to them, taking them for walks if the weather was nice or sitting upstairs with their knitting or sewing and caring for them.

Bonnie, at four months, was growing more and more to look like Martha and was a joy, rarely making a fuss. Her christening had never happened as Father O'Leary had insisted that Martha confess her sins first. Martha was stubborn on this. She didn't consider what happened to be a sin. But she felt she was coming round to just going through the ritual for Bonnie's sake. No doubt, Bonnie would sleep through the whole process – she was still a lazy madam. Not like Sally – she'd screamed the place down when the priest poured the water on her head at hers. Trisha too had had the awful experience of having to confess her sin. But she'd gritted her teeth and got on with it, having to take the priest's innuendoes and sexual remarks, glad that he was behind the grid of the confessional.

Martha had never taken Bonnie to the gypsies either. And Cilla had stopped asking. Martha always said that maybe she still would take Bonnie to the camp one day, so she hadn't given up on the idea.

Sometimes, they wished Bonnie would demand more attention. Even feeding times were dictated by Martha's milk coming in rather than Bonnie squealing her head off as Sally did when anything wasn't right in her world. Not that Sally acted like a spoiled child, she just wanted you to know she had a problem, but soon showed patience once she saw you were preparing her bottle or mashing a little food for her.

She was into everything too, crawling around that fast you had a job to catch her at times.

In looks, she'd taken more after her father, which frightened and pleased Trisha. Frightened her as she would be a constant reminder that she didn't belong to Bobby, and pleased her as she'd never felt herself beautiful, or pretty even – 'passable' was what she'd term herself. She wanted her daughter to be beautiful and not to have to seek love as she had done – the wrong kind of love. She knew that now. She wanted Sally to have all the attention, so that she didn't lack confidence and could make the right choices.

But no matter what, she would be by her side. She had to accept, though, that life would change, and she didn't want it to. The thought came to her that she never wanted Bobby to come home again. The shock of this admission made her gasp.

'Trish?'

'Sorry, love, I got so deep in thought and sommat awful came to me.'

'I am knowing that you are worrying about Bobby coming home, Trish.'

'I am, and you once told me that it was going to be a bad time for me . . . I just don't knaw what to do. I fear he'll turn nasty again – not that I could blame him with what he has to face and after what he must be going through. I just wish he'd write and tell me his thinking on all I told him about the shop . . . I knaw how he feels about Sally, but he ain't winning on that one.'

Martha was quiet. Trisha knew she had more to tell her of what would happen. Part of her wanted to know, but she could do nothing about anything, only face it.

'Luckily, Bobby don't knaw that Sally's father has passed and about Ricky telling us that he thinks the family would want Sally . . . I hardly dare think what he'd do if ever he found out!'

'Then it is that you don't let him know, Trish. But I don't see that happening.'

The bell resounding around the shop had them both jumping up. Martha got there first. Trisha knew she was hoping it would be Joshua as he hadn't called round for a few days. It was. He was wondering if she was the one to have the babbies this afternoon and if she fancied taking them for a walk and for an ice cream with him.

Trisha felt her heart warm. Joshua was different to any man she'd ever known. Already they knew the meaning of the word respect. Joshua had shown them both that.

'That's fine by me, lass. I can have a peaceful afternoon.'

'Hello, Trisha. How are you?'

'I'm fine, ta, lad. Eeh, it's all right for some abandoning work when they feel like it.'

Joshua grinned. 'Playing truant actually. I have a pile of stuff to process for the *Blackpool Gazette*. I've been taking shots of Blackpool and loving it. Our town is something to be proud of. The best seaside in Britain.'

Trisha hadn't thought of it in this way, it had just been the town she lived in and loved, but a pride entered her at this. Yes, they were unique with their lovely tower, theatres, Ferris wheel and the miles of sandy beach, besides what was considered to be a sea with properties that promoted good health.

Suddenly, she felt like taking all her clothes off and running into it, despite the freezing cold, thinking that it might heal how she was thinking about her own future. But the postie arriving with a bunch of letters took the thought away as he said, 'There's one for you, from your Bobby I reckon, as it's postmarked "France". I thought to drop it off here for you, Trisha. You'll be waiting for news. He'll be coming home soon no doubt, lass. It's almost over but for the shouting, I hear.'

Trisha felt rooted to the spot. 'I'll take it for her, Jack. It's a big thing for her.'

'Aye, it is that, Joshua. Mind, there's a lot who won't receive such a letter. Meself included.' Jack coughed. Joshua patted him on the back. 'I'm sorry, Jack. Your Terry was a fine young man. We'll always be grateful to him and all the young men of this country who went to save us . . . I only wish that I could have gone.'

'Well, the town knows now that you tried to enlist but weren't accepted, I've made sure of that, and can't apologise enough for what I said just after me lad copped it.'

'Don't even think about it. I understood. And what you've done for me since has eased my life for me. No one has called me a coward since. I can't thank you enough for that.'

Jack wiped his hand over his eyes and sniffed.

'I know it's no consolation, Jack, but Father sits on the council, as you know, and though nothing is official yet, they are talking of a memorial being built on the prom, hopefully for the anniversary of the armistice which we all know will take place soon. Your lad's name will go on that and will mean he is remembered for ever for his bravery.'

'By, that's grand. Wait till I tell me wife. That'll cheer her up.'

'Well, just keep it between the two of you for now.'

Jack was smiling as he doffed his cap and left them.

Martha took hold of Trisha's hand. 'Is it that you want us to stay while you read your letter, Trish, love?'

'Naw, Martha, I'd rather be on me own. You get the babbies ready and get off.'

As she watched them a few minutes later walk off down the promenade, Martha pushing the pram and Joshua pushing Sally in the carriage, Trisha thought what a lovely sight they were. How she wished Martha could feel for Joshua what was obvious he felt for her. But then, to her mind, she did, but was in denial of it.

Eeh, Peter, lad, for all you only being in our lives such a short time, you caused us some disruption. But then, you gave us little Bonnie, so we can forgive you. But where the hell are you? By, I wish you'd turn up so that Martha can find peace with whichever one of you she chooses.

These thoughts soon left Trisha when she opened the envelope.

Dear Trisha,

I am hoping to be home by December. Everything is looking that way, though it may be a bit after. Cannot wait to see you. You know I love you. And I hope you understood why I couldn't face meeting your young 'un. But that won't happen, will it?

Trisha's heart sank.

I ain't heard from me ma in a long time. I hope she's all right. Not that you would care. I wish you'd made the effort to get to know her.

At this Trisha scoffed. The bad feeling with her ma-in-law was none of her doing.

We'll talk about this shop you're on about. I ain't liking the sound of it. It ain't for folk like us to be running our own business but I can see you had to do sommat while I were away after you lost your job on the rock stall. You can give it up when I'm home, at least you can when you start to have more babbies. I want you at home then, looking after me and our young 'uns.

Fear gripped her and despair settled in her heart. How was she to tell Bobby that having babbies could never happen? How would he react? With this question, her fear deepened. Yes, he'd said he loved her, and that he'd changed and would no longer be violent towards her, but when he learned that her unfaithfulness had not only produced a babby but had made her no longer able to conceive, what then?

She began to dread the end of the war that everyone was certain was imminent.

TWENTY-FIVE

Martha

Even though the October wind had that first chilly autumnal feel, Martha felt a deep warmth inside her as she and Joshua walked and chatted, interspersed by Sally sitting in her carriage pointing out something she loved with any sound she'd mastered – most were 'ga-ga' but said insistently until she received an acknowledgement.

Sally was wrapped up warmly in her rose and black coat, which Trisha had knitted using an ingenious idea she had of knitting with two skeins of wool at the same time to give extra thickness to it – a three-ply rose colour and a two-ply black had created a lovely effect. The collar and cuffs being black set off the matching single-coloured rose of the mittens and leggings.

Many passers-by stopped to admire her, with two ladies, after greeting them, asking about her outfit.

Martha directed them to the shop, omitting that she was part owner.

When they'd left, Joshua gave one of his giggles. 'I think

I should walk with my camera around my neck and carry my tripod. I might drum up business then, too!'

'Or it is that you could be wearing a billboard advertising your trade.'

This made them both laugh, with Sally joining in giving a squeal of delight as if she'd understood every word!

'She has a lovely way with her. I've never yet seen her miserable, she sees the joyfulness in life.'

'I was for seeing an all-singing and all-dancing girl when it was that Trisha was still carrying her, and I think the meaning is that she is destined for the stage.'

'Ooh, a star in our midst. Well, it wouldn't surprise me. She attracts so much attention – more than any child I've known – not that that has been many, having no brothers or sisters to make me an uncle.'

'Sure, I'm after being an only child too. It was a lonely life at times. I used to have make-believe friends after the only girl within miles, Bonnie, me lovely friend, died.'

'It's sad and shocking how much you've been through, Martha. I can't imagine it all, or how you've coped and got through it. I only remember losing a grandfather that I knew and loved, and that hurt so much.'

'If trouble is given to you, it is that you have no choice but to cope. But that's not for making it easy to do. Each time a piece of your heart seems to be torn away from you . . . You'll be knowing that, though. It's sad you lost your grandfather. Have you other grandparents living?'

'No, I didn't know the other three. They died when I was very little, but even so, I sensed the grief that my mother and father went through.'

Before Martha could answer, Joshua said, 'Ah, my favourite ice cream vendor. Look, over there with the bicycle. His name is Arturo, which means Arthur in English, but I much prefer the Italian version. He's a lovely man and his ices are wonderful. I never come down to the beach without buying one. Come on, I promise they're very special.'

Martha shook her head. 'It is that I am feeling too chilly for ice cream, I'm having a doughnut. But sure enough, I'll come down with you. I'd like to be meeting a man with such a lovely name.'

'I can't resist an icee no matter what the weather. Especially Arturo's. He has six daughters, you know, and he makes all his ice cream himself. Shall I get Sally one?'

'No! She'll be getting it all down her, so she will. I'll be giving her a little of me doughnut.'

When they reached Arturo Naventi, a handsome man who wore his black hair parted and neatly kept in place with Brylcreem, Martha saw his twinkly, almost black eyes as, in his lovely Italian accent, he made his queue of customers laugh while deftly filling cone after cone.

'Ah, Joshua! So, today you bring your girl to see me, eh? She *bellissima*! I see she maker you very happy.'

Martha blushed. Though she wasn't sure what the Italian word meant, she knew Arturo was complimenting her. She wanted to say she wasn't Joshua's girl. Joshua forestalled her.

'This is Martha. She's just my friend, Arturo.'

A fleeting feeling of disappointment came to Martha. She couldn't understand it.

Arturo grinned and gave a little wink. 'So, just a friend, eh?'

Joshua laughed out loud.

Arturo was a real character who added so much to life in Blackpool, Martha thought. She sighed. When she looked back to her growing-up years in Ireland, they seemed sort of grey now. But then, with all the injustices of the English, they were. How she wished her pappy and mammy hadn't got involved in the uprising. She missed them so much.

Arturo gestured towards where they had left Sally's baby carriage and Bonnie's pram parked by the steps. '*Bambine*? Aw.'

'We borrowed them.'

Arturo grinned, before saying a cheerful, '*Ciao*, my friend.' Then he patted his nose with his finger in a gesture that conveyed that he knew different to them just being friends.

This made Martha forget yesteryear and laugh with them.

'He is for being a tonic, Josh. I've seen him here, so I have, and heard the laughter surrounding him, but haven't yet had an ice cream from him.'

'You don't know what you're missing, love.'

Sally clapped her hands when they got back to her, her eyes fixed on the ice cream.

'Just a little, eh?' Joshua looked appealingly at Martha.

'Go on then, but don't get it on her new coat or Trisha will go spare!'

With Martha's doughnut purchased, they sat on a bench eating and watching the crashing waves. She'd lifted Bonnie and cradled her to her. Bonnie lay looking up at her, holding her forefinger as if it was lifeline. Martha flooded with love.

Droplets of seawater sprayed them now and again. Martha was in awe of the sound and the sight of the power the water could generate. But she giggled as Bonnie seemed to love it and though she appeared to cringe when the cold spray landed on her face, she gurgled as if she was chuckling.

As she watched her baby, enjoying the moment with her, she became aware of Joshua once more and she turned her head. He was watching her and Bonnie with a look of wonderment on his face. He smiled as he caught her eye and made a joke to cover his embarrassment at being caught in such an adoring pose. 'Ha, you've got sugar on your nose and look at the mess Sally's made with the piece you gave her . . . You'll be in trouble!'

This last Joshua said in a sing-song voice as he got a pristine white handkerchief out of his pocket. As he came towards Martha with it, she turned her head giggling. 'No, don't be wiping me nose, you eejit.'

'Eejit! What's one of those?'

'A daft ha'peth, as Trisha calls it.'

She'd turned to him as she said this; he took his chance and wiped the sugar away, his face close to hers. They stayed like that for a moment and Martha longed for him to kiss her. Then, shocked at this thought, she looked away.

'Don't, Martha.'

The pleading note in his voice compelled her to look at him. His love for her shone in his eyes.

'Don't push me away. You know how I feel.'

Unsure, Martha hesitated. Since she'd visited his house that day, he'd never spoken of his feelings. She'd come to feel relaxed with him and think of him as a dear friend. Now, something more than what friendship demanded stirred inside her as she gazed into his eyes.

'Is there still no chance? Are you still hankering after Peter?'

Peter! The man who occupied most of her wakeful night hours . . . but then, hadn't she also lain thinking of Joshua? Thinking that though her feelings for Peter were so very strong, so was what she felt for Joshua. Peter was gone. Would he ever come back?

'Martha?'

'I – I need more time, so I do. It is that to be fair to you, I want to be sure.'

'What do you think will make you sure?'

At that moment, Cilla came along the prom. 'Eeh, Martha, I see that you've found your destiny, lass . . . Hello, pleased to meet you, future relation.'

Martha was aghast. Her face burned. Joshua's surprise matched her own. Though he knew about her gypsy heritage she didn't think it had sunk in. Seeing Cilla in the traditional dress she favoured with her dark hair almost covered by a black scarf bordered with sequins and tied at the back, her white silky blouse topped with a sequined bolero and her long red skirt hemmed with sequins, it seemed reality had dawned on him. But just as quickly, he smiled his lovely smile. 'So, I am to win my fair lady, then?'

Cilla laughed. 'Yes, and if you cross me hand with silver, sir, I will be telling you more.'

'Cilla!'

'No, don't be cross, Martha, I want to know.'

Martha cringed. 'Please don't. I have never known my own future and sure, it is that I don't want to . . . Cilla, it is that you know that. And I am wanting to bring the wrath of the devil down on your head for ignoring it.'

Cilla looked afraid. Mortified, Martha stood. 'I wasn't for meaning it, I'm sorry. I was just for being cross with you. I want you to be respecting my wish.'

'No, I'm sorry, Martha, lass. Me tongue wagged before I could stop it.'

It always amused Martha to hear Cilla speak in the Lancashire dialect, but then, she had spent most of her young life in Blackpool.

Taking her cold hands in hers, Martha looked into Cilla's eyes. 'Sure enough, I forgive you. Give me a wee hug now. Only, please don't be doing it again.'

'I promise.'

Changing the subject, Martha told her, 'This is me friend Joshua.'

'The photography man! Well, lad, you will get your wish.'

Joshua smiled, but Martha felt as though she was going to blow her top.

'You didn't say that I couldn't tell his future, Martha, lass.'

From behind her, Martha heard Joshua's giggle. Seeing the funny side, she joined him, as did Cilla, and the atmosphere lightened.

'Well, I'm on an errand. I'm to get some candles to take back to camp with me tonight, so I'll see you soon.'

After leaning over and cooing with Bonnie for a moment, Cilla had a little chat with Sally, then waved as she went on her way.

The relief Martha felt left her with Joshua saying, 'That's the best news I've heard – and no denying it. I know you believe in the predictions of yourself and your family, Martha, so I'm a very happy man hearing what your cousin had to say.'

'Oh, Joshua, please don't be setting store by it, predictions can be wrong. Many factors can be put in the way . . . Sure, it is that I knew my destiny lay with Peter when I first met him, but it wasn't for turning out that way.'

'I disagree. You had a child together, that may be the involvement you knew he had in your destiny.'

Martha couldn't deny this. Having a child with someone was a fulfilment of your destinies being linked, but she hadn't thought of it in this way – the longing for Peter had clouded her judgement.

But then, Joshua said something he'd said before, but that seemed to have more meaning for her this time.

'Martha, even though I haven't fathered Bonnie, I love her as my own and always will. I'll always be there for her even if you never come to love me.'

This statement gave Martha the thought that she did love him. She looked down at Bonnie, knew that she was deserving of having a pappy in her life. And as if she understood, Bonnie put her hand up towards Joshua. When he gently took hold of it, he said, 'Bonnie has just accepted my offer.'

Martha smiled; it was as if all barriers were being removed. But still she had to admit that her yearning for

Peter did exist. It couldn't be wiped out by theories. It wouldn't be right to go to any man while she still hankered after another. What Cilla had said had only confirmed her own prediction of many months ago, but that didn't mean she had to go through with it.

Granny's words came to her. Well, that meant her own destiny couldn't be changed too. Once again, as she did whenever with Joshua, she felt the bewilderment of her situation.

'I can see you are unsure still, Martha. Let's not speak of it for a while. Let's give you this time you say you need. But I will never give up. I can't, I love you so much.'

Martha's heart warmed. She turned her head and smiled at him. 'Thank you. It is that I need to be sure.'

'You do have feelings for me, I know that, so I will be patient – patience will be easier after what Cilla said . . . No, don't get cross with me . . . though, on the other hand, you can if you like.' He laughed. 'You never look more beautiful than when you're cross.'

Martha shook her head. 'You're for having the gift of the gab, I'll be saying that for you.'

'Ha, me granddad used to say that to me. I could always smooth talk my mother around – still can. I would love you to meet my mother. She's lovely. Very scatterbrained, though. She's always making us laugh – looking for her specs when she is wearing them, that kind of thing. And yet she can be very confident and supports Dad in all he does.'

'One day, it may be that I do. But for sure, we said we'll take things slowly.'

Joshua sighed, but it wasn't a sigh that said he was exasperated, just a wishful one.

'Sure, it is that we need to get back now, Josh.'

'Josh? No one ever calls me that, well, not since I left school. You said it a while ago and I thought it a slip of the tongue, but I like it. I like it very much. It has a familiar sound to it.'

'We were forever being the ones for shortening names in our family. I am after being the only one to call Trisha "Trish" and Bonnie is really Barbara. And me family sometimes called me Mar, but it wouldn't be sounding right here as it is how Trisha and others address their mammies.'

'I like Martha for you. It is how I dream of talking to you.'

Martha gave him a playful slap and, in a mock-strict voice, said, 'That's not for being patient!'

Sally's bottom lip quivered. Her large eyes stared at them. 'Oh, me wee babba, we were only playing.' But this didn't appease Sally. Tears plopped onto her cheeks as she looked adoringly at Joshua.

Martha sighed. 'It is that I'm going to have to kiss you better, Josh, or we'll be having the floodgates opening.'

'Mmm. Thanks, Sally.'

Martha laughed out loud as she put Bonnie back into her pram and then bent to kiss Joshua's forehead, but he put his lips up and she caught him smack on them. A feeling zinged through her. She ignored it and whispered, 'That is not respecting me, Josh, but I forgive you.'

A couple walked by. The woman humphed, the man clicked his tongue. Martha felt her cheeks redden. But Joshua's endearing giggle had her forgetting her embarrassment and joining in. Sally, too, gave a watery giggle and Martha knew with a deep sense of relief that all was right with Sally's world again – and that became even more so when Joshua lifted her out of her carriage and swung her around at the great height of his outstretched arms.

A lovely sound of squeals and giggles filled the air. It lifted Martha and deepened the feeling she had for Joshua.

But once home and with Joshua out of sight, her feelings returned to not being sure and to thinking of Peter once more.

This was soon forgotten as she detected anguish in Trisha, even though she was full of two ladies having called and ordered two-tone coats for their children. 'They said they saw one of ours on the prom.' She picked Sally up. 'Eeh, me little lass, you've been a model for our business.'

Sally put her head on Trisha's shoulder and yawned. A reluctant star at the moment, as she just wanted to close her eyes.

'The fresh air has fair worn her out, so it has.'

'Aye. I'll just go and have five minutes with her and let her have a nap. Shall we close a little earlier, or will you stay down here? Only, it's time for Bonnie's feed an' all.'

'So it is. The time is for running away with me today. Look, it is dark already. Yes, there's only five minutes to go. I'll put the latch on . . . Oh, it is glad I am that you are staying the night, Trish. I've a lot to talk about.'

'Haven't you always? Your chin wags nineteen to the dozen most of the time, lass.'

'Go on with you, it's not for being like that!'

As Trisha disappeared having taken an unprotesting Bonnie out of her pram and balanced her on her free hip,

Martha prepared to close the shop – clicking the lock over, putting the pram in the kitchen, tidying stock on the shelves and taking the drawer that they put their transactions, orders and any little notes and ideas in out of the desk – before, satisfied all was well, going up herself.

She hadn't allowed herself to think of anything other than the task in hand while doing these chores, even though her heart wanted to ponder it all.

As she climbed the stairs, she suddenly felt tired herself, but the tingling sensation of her milk coming in gave her an urgency that carried her forward.

It seemed no time at all before their tea was cooking, both little ones were bathed and settled, though they'd had tears and giggles, and protests from Sally, who wanted to stay with her mammy and not go to her bed.

When peace finally reigned, Martha and Trisha gave a simultaneous sigh of relief. Trisha still seemed full of the anguish Martha had felt present and so put her own worries to bed and asked, 'What is it that is worrying you, me darling?'

Trisha told of the fears her letter had given her.

Martha trembled. The premonitions that she'd never let fully in vibrated through her senses.

As she dished up a mound of mashed potato for each of them, followed by a slice of meat pie and gravy, Martha asked, 'Would it help if it was that I took Sally? You could be saying that I offered for her to be company to me wee Bonnie rather than having Bobby send her away. Sure, it could be that he would not object to you visiting your own child, as long as it is he doesn't have to have anything to do with her?'

Trisha cheered up, picked up her knife and fork and smiled. 'That could work. Would you? I mean, it will be a lot of work for you when I'm not here and . . . and, eeh, but I don't knaw as I can do it.' Without having eaten a morsel, her knife and fork were placed on the table again. The anguish returned to her face. 'How would I walk out of here without her? How would I bear not having her with me? I would miss even going through the evening ritual we have of late, of her not wanting to go to bed. How would you soothe her when it is her ma she wants to stay with her?'

Martha felt at a loss, except to say, 'Maybe, just until it is that you can get Bobby accepting Sally? I – I, well, I'm powerfully afraid that he may hurt her. Think about it, Trish, love. Bobby has so much to contend with that is upsetting, so he has. What if it is that he reacts badly?'

Trisha bent her head. But then her spirit returned. When she looked up her expression showed her determination. 'Sally ain't negotiable, Martha. If Bobby ain't accepting of her, then I leave with her. I'll give him one night to decide if he meets her and keeps her or not. So, for the night when I knaw he's coming home, I'd gladly leave her here to keep her safe.'

'Sure, it is that you're making the right choice, me darling. And it is that you have a home here if it turns out that Bobby can't be accepting of Sally.'

'I knaw, and'll be glad of it, whichever way it goes. I loved it when we lived together, lass. I knew a peace – a freedom that I've never known in me life. I didn't even get that before you moved in as I were lonely and haunted by the ghosts of me life – and me sins an' all. But all that vanished when you came . . . You knaw . . . I mean, I ain't saying this is me and you, far from it, but there are women who prefer to live with women and how I feel about men now, I think I may be one of them.'

This shocked Martha to the core, but she didn't remark on the implication of it, just put an understanding smile on her face. 'You haven't been treated well by any man, apart from your pappy, and that is for being why you feel like you do. It is a way of not taking that risk again. Sure, time will tell.'

'Or you could, Martha, lass.'

'No, don't ask that of me. Besides, we are so close, sharing our troubles and happiness alike, that it is that me spirit won't be able to help. Everything will be clouded by what it is I know of you and that is so very much.'

'Cilla then?'

'Yes, Cilla is gifted far more than me. If it is that you really need to know, you must be visiting her.'

'I'll see. Anyroad, I'm starving. All this delving into maybes has upset me. I allus eat when I'm upset.'

Martha didn't feel a bit hungry now, but she smiled and tucked in as Trisha did.

Between mouthfuls, Trisha put everything right again by saying, 'I love you, Martha. What would I do without you?'

Martha felt her heart warm. 'I love you too, Trish.'

Trisha's eyes filled with tears. They both rose and went towards each other. The hug they found themselves in gave

Martha the strength to face her own troubles – her pain over the loss of her family. Her confusion over Peter and Joshua and, yes, the insecurities she felt where Lady Rebecca and Lady Darcy were concerned. She still dreaded the telephone ringing and one of them being on the end of the line, condemning her.

Well, she decided she could put that right now! 'It is that I'm going to write that letter, Trish. To be sure, I'm going to do it this very minute!'

With shaking hands, she wrote a simple note, telling how she'd tried to inform them both on a number of occasions. That she was sorry if they both felt let down by her, but that she was happy to have her child born out of love. And how she hoped that this wouldn't affect the agreement over the shop as they were doing so well.

Not giving herself a chance to change her mind, she grabbed her shawl and ran outside. Arthur was coming along the prom, his horse ambling along. He took the letter and promised he would post it for her, and she could give him the cost of it next time he saw her.

As she went back inside, she had a feeling of dread and knew no letter could help their fears as now her nervousness increased and that dread settled deep in her stomach.

TWENTY-SIX

Trisha

Trisha let her knitting fall onto her lap. How she wished it was just another day and she was at the shop as normal. The mantelshelf clock loudly ticked every second.

A knock on the door had her stiffening. When it opened, a gust of freezing December weather chilled her, and the sound of clapping could be heard. Mrs Higginbottom popped her head around, her voice not concealing her excitement, or her expected triumph.

'He's coming! Your Bobby is walking down the street, lass. You better be ready with a good story.'

Trisha's heart stopped.

'Come on. Make the effort. One or two have put flags up, and all are on their doorsteps to welcome our own hero home. Surely you can do the same? . . . Where's the young 'un then?'

'She's stopping with Martha for the night.' Trisha rose.

'Your partner in crime, eh? It were a bad day when them gypsies moved into our street. That one's influence on you has led you into all sorts of trouble, lass. She's no good – a kid of her own an' all, and not married!'

'I don't want to listen to this, Mrs Higginbottom. I've enough on me plate, ta.'

'Well, you should think on and I reckon you should prepare yourself, me girl.'

The glee in her face made Trisha feel sick. Her fear increased with every step. It was as if this was her day of reckoning.

The joy that greeted her when she got to the door took Trisha aback as she looked along the row of houses. Her neighbours giving Bobby a hero's welcome home, which made it seem as though Armistice Day was being celebrated all over again – what a day that was. A joyful day with everyone out in the street, just like today, laughing and chatting. Though today they weren't drinking, dancing and singing as they had been on the eleventh of November. Relief and happiness had shone from everyone.

Now, many were shaking Bobby's hand as he walked by them. Others waved small bunting flags. It all seeped into Trisha, lifting her spirits.

When Bobby saw her, he grinned. On impulse, she ran towards him. He didn't deserve to be treated any differently by her to how the neighbours were greeting him. He was a hero. All the lads returning from France were.

When he dropped his rucksack and spread his arms, she went into them. He picked her up and swung her around. Everyone cheered. To Trisha, it felt as though all was forgiven and would be all right. Her emotions were mixed as to how she felt – resigned, hopeful, but still unsure and a little afraid.

'You look beautiful, Trisha. By, I've missed you, lass . . . Is that a new frock?'

She'd made an effort this morning and dressed in the same frock she'd worn to the tower. As she'd put it on, she hoped it would bring her more luck than it did the last time she'd worn it.

'It were one of me ma's but I don't think you ever saw her in it. She got it from a jumble.'

'Well, it suits you . . . Eeh, I'm exhausted, lass.'

She could see he was, and in a state too, with open sores around his mouth that looked nasty. She suddenly wanted to care for him, to try to make up for her sins.

'You'll be right, Bobby. I've water on for a bath for you and I've got a stew cooking for tea. You've been through a lot, but you're home now.'

He looked deeply into her eyes. It was to Trisha as if he was scrutinising her soul. Her fear came back. He shook his head then smiled again. In a low voice he said, 'We'll be all right, won't we, lass?'

She could only nod. Her tears released from her eyes as she prayed, *Please God, let it be so.*

At last, they had made it back to their home. Bobby waved to all as he closed the door.

'By, that were a fine welcome. It seemed for a moment that it was all worthwhile.'

'It was, Bobby. You helped to keep everyone free.'

'Naw, it were never that. Aye, the freedom bit, but never

worth all the lost lives, the broken men, families going through trauma, loneliness and fear.'

His body trembled.

'You did well, Bobby. I'm proud of you. Let's get you that bath, eh?'

'What about that kid you had first?'

His tone had changed. Trisha stiffened. She stared at him.

'You didn't keep that little bastard, did you?'

'We'll talk about it, Bobby, but not now. Get settled first, eh?'

'Tell me. Tell me now! 'Cause I couldn't take that, Trisha. I told you to get rid of her!' His anger sounded in his voice. His eyes glared at her as he threw down his cap with a smack on the table. Trisha jumped.

'I – I never said I would do it . . . I couldn't, Bobby. Nowt were her fault. She's just a babby. I knaw as you'll love her.'

'I hate the thought of her. I can't take it, Trisha . . . It's her or me!'

This came out through gritted teeth. His body trembled; his fists clenched. Sweat trickled from his forehead.

Trisha stood as if turned to stone, not sure how to deal with this change in him. Memories of painful punches came to her – the one that caused her to lose their child being the most vivid. Without thinking, the words voicing this came out. 'You lost me one babby, and you ain't losing me another, Bobby.'

His mouth went slack. His eyes looked at her in disbelief. 'I made that right, Trisha.'

'Naw, you could never make that right, and you never will!'

She wanted to stop herself but couldn't. She didn't want to be saying these things to him, but they were the truth. They burned in her every day till she wanted to beat Bobby with her fists.

Only having Sally had helped her with her grief, and she was never going to give her up. She could never go through what she did when she lost little Patricia. She would end up in the madhouse if that happened.

Suddenly, Bobby slumped forward and held on to one of the dining chairs. His face seemed to have lost all colour. His sweating increased, as did his shivering. This wasn't anger.

'Bobby! Bobby, what's wrong, lad?'

'I – I don't feel well . . . I'm scared, Trisha . . . I'm scared of catching the flu . . . I – I lost mates . . . Oh, Trisha.'

Bobby's knees gave way. He tried to cling on but landed at her feet.

'Eeh, Bobby, naw!' Her anguish for him mixed with her fear for herself and Sally. Millions were dying of the flu. *Please don't let it be that!*

'Maybe you're just exhausted. We shouldn't have talked about everything till you were rested. Let me help you to get up, love. Then I'll get you that bath, sommat to eat and help you get to bed, eh?'

How she accomplished this, Trisha didn't know as Bobby's strength seemed to ebb out of him, but at last, though he'd only had a sip of his tea and refused any food, she had managed to get him upstairs and into bed.

'Ta . . . Trisha, lass . . . I – I . . .'

Whatever Bobby was going to say went into a fit of coughing. 'I'll get the doctor, Bobby, lad. Try to sleep.'

As she went to go out of the room, Trisha thought she'd open the window first, then shut the door. She hoped that way the germs Bobby breathed would escape outside instead of into the house.

As she crossed to the window, Bobby moaned. The sound cut into her heart. How could he have become so ill in such a short space of time? 'Don't worry, love, we'll get you sorted.'

But as she looked at him, she wondered if that was possible. She didn't want him to die. 'Hold on, Bobby. I won't be long, love.'

Running to the door, she opened it and screamed out, 'Help me, someone please help me.'

At her screams, several doors opened. Mrs Higginbottom was first to ask, 'Whatever's wrong, lass? Mind, I did warn you.'

'Naw, it ain't that! Bobby's sick! . . . Naw, don't come near me. I think it may be the Spanish flu.'

'Naw, lass, naw! Oh, God, most of the street shook his hand.'

'I knaw. Tell them all . . . Maybe if they wash? I don't knaw. But I need a doctor, Bobby's bad . . . Send someone for the doctor, ple-e-ase.'

'All right, love. Let me get me coat, it's freezing. You go back inside, lass.'

Once back indoors, Trisha stood still and she looked around her. For a moment, she felt helpless. Panic gripped her as she imagined herself and everything around her covered in the flu germs and the only place untouched was her old bedroom where Martha had slept, but was now empty.

Into her hysterical mind came the logic that opening the door and the windows and then cleaning everything was all she could do.

An hour later, Trisha put what was left of the block of carbolic soap she'd used back under the sink with the rest of her cleaning products and put the soaking wet scrubbing brush on the kitchen windowsill to dry. The bucket she emptied down the drain outside. When she straightened up, her whole body ached.

Wearily going back inside, she took the kettle off the hob, poured water into a bowl and set about washing herself and her hair with the smaller, less harsh bar of carbolic soap, then wrapped herself in one of her ma's coverall pinnies that she still kept hanging behind the kitchen door.

Feeling safe at last, Trisha shivered. The house was freezing. Closing the windows and door, she ran upstairs to look in on Bobby, hoping he was feeling better.

From the door, she called, 'Bobby, love, how are you?'

A groan told her he had worsened. 'I've sent for the doctor. At least, I asked them in the street to go. I'll get you a drink, eh?'

Another groan. This wasn't like she'd planned it at all. Her heart felt heavy with guilt, and it surprised her to realise that there was still something inside her that cared deeply for Bobby. He'd played a massive part in her growing-up years.

The doctor didn't go into the bedroom but stood outside the door. 'Keep giving him plenty of water and douse him in cold water every now and again.'

'Will I catch it, Doctor?'

'At the rate this flu is spreading, everyone will . . . Look, where's your little one?'

'She's with Martha.'

'Make sure she stays there and have no contact. I know it will be difficult, but you need to keep her safe. For yourself, take every precaution. You have a clean house, which will help, just keep washing everything with hot water. And try to cover your mouth and nose when tending to Bobby . . . Poor lad, after going through all he has . . . We owe them a great debt, you know.'

Trisha nodded. She couldn't speak, she felt full of tears.

When he'd gone, she called out again for someone to help her. One of the Blakey boys from a house at the other end of the street came towards her.

'Don't come any nearer, lad, but would you run me an errand, love?'

The boy agreed to deliver her message to Martha. 'Tell her she's to give you a ha'penny for going. She will, so don't be afraid to ask.'

'Ta, Trisha, I will. Hope Bobby gets better. Me and the lads wanted to talk to him. Find out what it were like over there.'

'I'm sure he will. He's strong, is Bobby. You keep yourself safe, lad. Keep washing your hands, eh?'

The grubbiest boy she'd ever seen looked up and grinned.

'Aye, well, you've probably built up a resistance to infection, you wallow in it all the time from what I've heard of your ma's ways.'

'Me ma's all right.'

'I knaw. She has a lot to contend with. Good lad. Hurry along, won't you. And if Martha wants to send me a message, tell her to write it down so that you can post it and not hand it to me.'

'Aye, I will, Trisha. See ya.'

Getting a tea towel, Trisha tied it around her face, letting it hang over her mouth, then filled a glass with water. When she got upstairs, she could hear Bobby wheezing. She couldn't believe how quickly the flu was taking hold of him. 'Drink this, Bobby.'

'I'm dying, Trisha.'

'Naw, love. You're strong. Put up a fight and you'll get better, I promise.'

'Hold me hand, Trisha. I – I'm sorry I said what I did.'

'I knaw. Don't worry, love.'

'I – I mean, about your kid. You're right, it ain't her fault she were born . . . If I could get me hands on him as raped you, I'd kill him!'

'Don't, Bobby. Let's leave it, eh?'

Now she had to face up to her lie about the circumstances that brought Sally into the world, she cringed against doing so, but couldn't tell him the truth.

'Aye. All right, love. I just can't get me head around it, but anyroad, if I get well, we'll have a family of our own, won't we?'

Trisha swallowed. Everything was piling onto her shoulders at once. She had to lie about this too. He didn't deserve to know the truth about anything at this moment.

'Aye. Hopefully. Try to rest now, Bobby. Your voice is getting croaky.'

'It hurts like hell.'

He began to shiver in a way that Trisha had never seen before. His whole body shook. For a moment, she thought he was going to have a fit, but it calmed down.

'Help me, Trisha.'

'What can I do, love?'

'So hot. And me head!'

Trisha felt at a loss. Remembering the doctor said to douse him in cold water, she hurried downstairs and filled a bowl. The action of swabbing him down helped him. He calmed and closed his eyes. Rubbing him dry brought memories to her. Not many of them were pleasant from after they were wed, but before, they'd been good together. How she wished she could get those days back. The only fear she'd had then was of her ma being cross with her. By, she wished she'd listened to her ma, as the adventure she'd felt she was on then had turned sour beyond words now.

Covering the now sleeping Bobby, Trisha wiped away the tears that had never been far away since this morning. She feared for Bobby. Would he recover? And if he did, what then?

A banging on the door made her jump. She covered Bobby and tucked him in, fearful of his laboured breathing, and went to go downstairs, but the stair door at the bottom opened and her ma-in-law stood there. Trisha immediately thought Mrs Higginbottom would have sent for her.

'Where's me Bobby? Oh, God, is he all right? Why didn't you send for me, you bitch? I didn't even knaw he were due home!'

'I – I'm sorry, I thought he'd have written to you. I had naw idea you didn't knaw.' This bewildered Trisha. Bobby wrote to his ma more than to her, and surely Mrs Higginbottom would have told her of his homecoming?

'You wouldn't, little miss never-does-owt-wrong! Huh, you want to look to yourself and how you behave. I've kept me Bobby informed.'

'Well, he didn't seem to knaw that I still had Sally.'

'Naw, well . . . anyroad, get out of me way. Me Bobby ain't well and he needs his ma, not a floozy who don't care a jot about him.'

'I do care . . . Anyroad, you mustn't come up, it's the flu, you don't want to catch it.'

She stopped in her tracks. Then sank down onto the stairs. 'Naw, naw, tell me it ain't that.'

Her sobs tore at Trisha's heart and gave her the reality of the awfulness of what had struck Bobby down. As even though she'd been afraid and taken all precautions, till this moment she hadn't let the consequences sink in. Bobby could die! She could catch it and die!

Trembling, she told her ma-in-law, 'Take yourself downstairs, you'll be all right down there. I've scrubbed everything with carbolic. Just let me get down and through to the scullery so that I can wash meself after tending to Bobby and I'll make you a cup of tea, eh?'

To her surprise, her ma-in-law obeyed. She looked defeated and half the woman she was as she did so. Trisha didn't want that for her.

When Trisha took the tea to her, her ma-in-law looked up. Her tear-stained face had an evil expression. 'You've dragged me Bobby into the gutter, Trisha, and I'll never forgive you.'

Trisha bent her head. The accusation and hatred in her ma-in-law's eyes was too much to bear. She couldn't defend herself. She hadn't behaved like a wife to Bobby when he went away.

'I don't believe naw rape story, so don't come that . . . How could you, eh?'

Trisha had no defence. At this moment, she knew she had behaved as these women saw her – like a slag. Would she ever be forgiven?

'I could kill you with me bare hands, I hate you that much.'

Not wanting to take any more of this, Trisha stood. 'I think you should leave my house now, Mrs Rathbone.'

Just saying the woman's name made her realise the gulf between them that had always been there. She'd never called this woman Ma.

Trisha gasped with this thought as it brought to her her own lovely ma. How she would love to be held by her at this moment.

'You're kicking me out of me own son's house?'

'Not kicking you out but telling you to go. I ain't going to sit here and listen to you calling me names. I've Bobby to look after, I don't need you grinding me down.' Trisha couldn't believe she was saying these things, but suddenly she knew she had to make a stand. 'Either you stop getting at me, or you go.'

Mrs Rathbone rose. 'I ain't even started yet, girl.' She flew at Trisha. Her punch in Trisha's stomach had her bending double.

In this weakened state, Trisha felt herself being dragged to the door, then thrown through it. She landed on the pavement outside, banging her head on the kerb.

Mrs Rathbone's screamed abuse brought the neighbours out. But before anyone could get to Trisha, Mrs Rathbone gave her a vicious kick in her side.

Winded and in extreme pain, Trisha gasped for breath, then went into the blessed blackness that had started with a zinging noise in her ears as it descended on her.

TWENTY-SEVEN

Martha

Martha's head ached and she felt exhausted as she went to close the latch on the shop door.

Sally had been fractious all day to the point where a lady customer had left in a huff, asking what kind of business-woman she was. And saying that she would not have a very good report for her friend, Lady Darcy, who had recommended she visit the shop when she came to Blackpool to spend Christmas.

This had mortified Martha and added greatly to the anxiety she felt around the issue of the reaction of Lady Rebecca and Lady Darcy. Had they received her letter? If so, what did they think to hearing she was now an unmarried mother – a shameful state to most and one not to be associated with?

She sighed. There was nothing to be gained by worrying, and at last, Sally was settled and playing happily on the floor of the shop as Martha slid the bolt into place. A frantic knocking made her slide it back. In the dimness outside the glass door, she could just make out the young boy who'd told her his name was Ted when he'd brought the news to her earlier of Bobby being ill.

Opening the door, the lad's anguish immediately told her that the fears that wouldn't leave her all day were about to come true. 'Is it Trisha, Ted?'

'Aye! They took her to hospital! Her ma-in-law beat her up. Mind, the copper gave her what for. Told her if owt happened to Trisha, she'd find herself dangling from the end of a rope! She went mad. The copper had to restrain her . . . By, it were a sight. I saw Trisha's knickers!'

Martha just stared at him, the scene playing out in her head. Her anguish sending confused messages to her brain.

'Miss?'

'Oh, it's grateful I am to you for bringing me the message, Ted. Ta . . . Here. Hold on.' Martha hurried to the counter, collected a coin and wrote a note. 'It is that I want you to take this to the address I have written there for you. There's a ha'penny and there'll be another when you get back.'

'Owt for you, Martha, I'll do owt.'

'You're a good wee boy. Now be hurrying, please.'

By the time the bell rang, Martha had managed to calm herself enough to feed Bonnie, give Sally a boiled egg for her tea and give her a quick wash. She seemed a lot happier when she had Martha's undivided attention.

When she opened the door to Joshua and paid her dues to Ted, relief flooded her.

'Oh, Martha, the boy has been telling me what happened. I can't believe it. How can one woman beat up another so badly that she has to go to hospital?'

The question marked how different his life had been to her own, but she didn't dwell on it.

After greeting him, she told him, 'I need to go to the hospital to see Trisha. I have no one that I am being able to call on to stay with the children as Cilla has gone home to the gypsies' field. She only opens till lunchtime now and some days not at all.'

'I'll stay. It's not a problem. You must go and see what you can find out. Do you know how it happened?'

When she told him about Bobby, he looked wary. 'Maybe you shouldn't go near to Trisha, just find out how she is and leave her a message to say we are thinking about her, eh?'

'I must see her, Josh. Maybe it is that she is not infected. In her message to me she said it is that she was taking every precaution. But she needs me, so she does.'

'All right.'

'Look, I will hang me overall behind the door of the lav in the yard. When it is that I come back, I will come in that way through the gate, then be leaving me clothes outside. If you let me in, I will be sure to go into the shop's kitchen and wash before I am coming back up here.'

Joshua nodded. He didn't look convinced, but there was nothing Martha could say to make him feel any safer. The word 'flu' put the fear of God into everyone, including herself.

At the hospital Martha found Trisha barely conscious. She could do nothing but hold her hand. 'I will be taking care of you, me darling. You'll be all right.'

'B-o-obby?'

'His ma is caring for him, so she is. He's for being a strong young man.'

'Naw . . . he – he's weak. He might . . .'

'Trish, it is that you must try not to think of that . . . Where is it you are hurt, me darling?'

'Me side, and me leg . . . I think . . . Eeh, Martha, she kicked me so hard. I were in agony. When I tried to grab her, she bit me, and got me hair. She . . . she were like a savage!'

The curtain around Trisha swished back at that moment. 'Oh, hello, I'm the doctor. Are you a relation?'

'No, but I am all that Trisha has, except for her child. We are like sisters.'

'Well then, that's good that she has someone . . . Trisha, you have a broken leg, and we are going to set it into plaster for you. Nothing else appears to be broken, though you are badly bruised. You can go home once you are comfortable, but if you notice anything in your urine over the next few days, you need to seek medical help.'

'Is there sommat that might be wrong then, Doctor?'

'Well, by the look of the developing bruising, there is a possibility of kidney damage. We won't know until you have symptoms, such as passing blood, but hopefully that won't happen . . . Not that you will be fine, you've a long way to go to get strong again.' He turned to Martha. 'Are you able to care for her, young lady? I understand she cannot go home as her husband has the flu and her ma-in-law has taken over . . . A wicked woman by the sounds of things.'

Martha didn't comment on Bobby's mother. The doctor had been right in his description of her, and she had no words to add to that.

With Trisha tucked into bed some three hours later, Martha sipped the cocoa that Joshua had made, telling her he was a dab hand at doing so as he'd been taught by the matron when he had been in boarding school. 'She thought boys should have the same skills as girls, though the cocoa and bed making was all the parents would allow her to go ahead with, but both have stood me in good stead.'

'It's delicious, ta. And Trisha enjoyed what she was able to drink.'

'How are you going to manage, Martha? You can't possibly run the shop on your own with two little ones and Trisha to care for.'

'It is that I will ask Cilla, as she is due tomorrow, so she is. She was talking of closing her tent until it is Easter. Me needing her help may be for making her mind up to do that.'

'Oh, that would be ideal. Poor Trisha will be very sore for a while. Anyway, if you're sure you'll be all right now, I'll get home, but if there's anything I can do, I will. I'll call in at some point every day.' He kissed her cheek, then looked into her eyes. 'You look tired, Martha. Try to get some rest.'

His eyes spoke different words to her, and she wanted to fall against him and let herself love him to exclusion, but knew she wasn't ready yet to do so.

With the flat quiet as Trisha had fallen asleep, Martha looked at the letter she hadn't had time to open when it arrived and had dropped into the drawer where she put her takings – not that there had been many of them today as more than one customer had left without purchasing, so a pair of bootees and a shawl were her only sales.

When she picked the letter up, a vibe went through her that warned her this wasn't good news. Warily slitting it open, her heart sank when she saw it was from the bank.

Dear Miss O'Hara and Mrs Rathbone,

We have to inform you that the cheque you paid to Lord Smythe's estate in respect of your rent has bounced through insufficient funds. Please bring your account into order before drawing any further funds on it. Thank you.

Yours sincerely . . .

She couldn't read the signature, it was just a scrawl, but she paid no heed to it anyway as panic had settled into her, making her gasp and look around in bewilderment for the answer as to why this had happened.

Despite it being late, she ran down the stairs to the shop, lighting it up as she went, and scurried to the second drawer in her counter to retrieve her ledger.

But all seemed in order, so how could this have happened? According to her daily record, there should be money to spare in her account.

When she went back upstairs and sat staring into the dying embers of the fire her mind raced over the possibilities. She checked the figures again against the receipts pinned to the book on the relevant page. The last receipt before she wrote the cheque clearly stated that the money from a customer in Birmingham – a cash on delivery – had been transferred into their account ... It was a mystery! Nothing had ever gone wrong with the system in the months they had been sending items. But this one was a large order – a cot, which when they packed it they filled with blankets, baby clothes and a shawl, all made by her and Trisha and ordered at the same time.

They'd worked well into the night to complete them, knowing they needed to top up their bank account before the rent was due.

Not able to put the bounced cheque down to anything else in the ledger, as all other monies credited in her book in the same period they had paid into the account themselves, Martha sat back. Her head ached and her chest felt knotted with fear – it was a criminal offence to write a cheque with insufficient funds available. The bank manager had told them that when he'd accepted them on their business showing good profit and had issued them with the chequebook. *Oh, Jesus, Mary and Joseph, what will happen to me? To the shop? Isn't it also a clause in the rental agreement that no payment of rent can be missed and must be being paid within seven days of becoming due?*

They hadn't seen any difficulties ahead. They had begun with advance rent paid so had plenty of time to make the next payment. And they had, with capital to spare! Something must have gone wrong!

Tears tumbled down Martha's face as a feeling came to her that this was bad, really bad. She closed her eyes, going against her own rule and allowing her spirit guide to visit.

When she opened them again, she knew that in such a short time hers and Trisha's new and exciting world would crumble. But she also knew there was hope. What it all meant wasn't revealed to her, but she hung on to the hope as she went to see to Trisha.

The next day, after a restless night, and with Martha's help, Trisha was able to make painful progress to get to the sofa and sit with a blanket around her, her pot leg rested on a stool in front of her. Her face was etched with pain, but she managed a smile for Sally, and was able to cradle a crying Bonnie to soothe her while Martha washed, dressed and saw to everyone else doing the same, then feeding everyone.

She'd made up her mind not to share the worry they had with Trisha. She had enough on her plate to contend with. But that didn't make the problem go away, so she determined to visit the bank once Cilla arrived. She would close the shop whilst she was away, so that Cilla could concentrate on looking after Trisha and the children.

It was three hours later that she made the trip. The bank manager looked at her with disdain. 'A serious matter, Miss O'Hara, and one that I warned you of. What have you to say for yourself?'

Martha shook inside but determined to look as though she was confident all would be sorted out. 'I am for not knowing the reason and need to check the figures of me account, sir. I was thinking I had plenty of funds when it was that I wrote the cheque. And should have had according to my calculations.'

'Huh, that is something they all say, madam. Well, the facts don't lie. You wrote that cheque with insufficient funds to cover it.' He opened a huge thin ledger. 'There, this is your balance. It is the sum total of all that has been paid in.'

Martha opened her own ledger and showed him the receipts for the cash on delivery sales. 'Are you able to be showing me that all of these have been credited to me account, please?'

He sat in silence, ticking off receipts and putting them into one pile and not ticking off two and putting them onto another. Sighing, he said, 'These have not appeared in your account.'

Both were of goods sent to different customers in Birmingham.

'But I have the receipts . . . It is that I had no idea.'

'Ignorance is not an excuse. Each time money has been paid into your account on your behalf, you should have checked that it truly was!'

Martha felt at a loss.

'What will be happening to me? . . . It is for being a mistake! I didn't—'

'Ah, but you did, madam. Your cheque has bounced. You are responsible . . . I must say, I am not surprised. How you – a – a, well, a person who can have a child out of wedlock could even be considered a fit candidate for renting a business premises is beyond me. Since that came to my notice, I knew you would be capable of what you have done now and will be having harsh words with Mr Green over his judgement in even considering you!'

Martha hung her head. 'Will . . . will it be that I am prosecuted, sir? I – I am promising you that this wasn't deliberate.'

'That will be up to Lord Smythe. He is the one who has been duped here. I will be speaking to him later today . . . Did he know about you and what you are before he let his premises to you?'

'No.'

'Ah, I thought not. Well, those of us who care about our town were extremely proud to have such an investor in it. You have let us down, but then, you're Irish!'

This was too much for Martha. 'Yes, it is that I am Irish, sir, and proud I am to be. If it wasn't for the English, I would be being a landowner now, too! What it is I have done was for being a mistake. I was trusting that the receipt of my money meant the amount was in my account. I was not thinking to deceive.'

'I think I have answered that one – you cannot plead ignorance of the law in order to commit a crime, and that maxim applies in this case too. Before you promise to pay money to another, you should be certain you have that money to pay. Now, I will bid you good day, madam. You will be hearing from me as to your future with this bank and, no doubt, Mr Green as to your future in continuing to be allowed to rent the premises you now occupy. My advice would be to be looking towards making other arrangements.'

Martha felt defeated as she stepped outside. She looked this way and that along New Road, unsure of what her next move should be. She felt sick with nerves and her worries were like a ton weight on her shoulders. Panic grew in her as the thought of being branded a criminal filled her head. How would she cope in prison? How could she be without her precious Bonnie?

A tear plopped onto her cheek. Desperation filled her.

'Martha? Martha, are you all right?'

She looked up to see an anxious Joshua coming towards her. When he came up to her, he took hold of her arm and steadied her. 'Martha, darling, I went to the shop to see how you were and how Trisha was, and Cilla said you had gone on an errand of dire importance to your future ... Martha? Oh, Martha, you're shaking. What on earth has happened?'

Joshua held her firmly and steered her away from the bank towards the promenade, then across the road.

The icy wind cut through her. Her hair came loose and obscured her view as it flapped across her face. Without Joshua's support, she would have fallen on her face. She could feel his love and concern for her and at this moment wanted that with all her heart, but would he still want her after what she had done?

He steered her into the foyer of the Clifton Hotel. 'Let's get you warmed up, darling. Cilla is coping well so you have no need to return immediately. Trisha is all right, too, though she needs some help for the pain she is in. I called into my doctor before I came looking for you. He is going to call in to see her. I'll see to the cost of that, so don't worry ... Anyway, Sally is playing happily around Trisha's feet and Bonnie was just being Bonnie and lying quietly, happily kicking her feet and seeing amusement in that.'

The picture he painted made Martha long to be back there with them all in safety. But was it safe? *Oh, Jesus, Mary and Joseph, please let it be.*

They sat in chairs that seemed to hug you in grand surroundings of plush red and golds. Joshua ordered a pot of tea for them, though Martha wasn't sure she could stomach anything at the moment.

'Talk to me, Martha. Let me help you, darling.'

There it was again, the endearment that touched a small part of her frozen heart.

In a quiet, hesitant voice, she told him what had happened.

'Oh, Martha! These things happen in business. It's not good, but when it isn't deliberate and it is obvious you thought you had the funds, then it is looked on as careless rather than a crime. I cannot understand Brumble taking this attitude with you, the pompous old fart!'

This shocked Martha and despite everything made her want to giggle.

'Well, he is. He sets himself up as judge and jury of everyone, from his elevated and powerful position in the community. He has been the breaking of many a good man with the financial rod of iron he holds over them. And he is heartless in his decisions, seeing right and wrong as black and white. Nothing is given understanding. If I had known you wanted to bank with him, I would have advised against it.'

'Is it that he can make me go to prison?'

'No, he can't. He can advise your landlord to take that action, but he is a lot of talk, so . . .'

'But he seemed as though it was that he hated me . . . Me having had me child out of wedlock, and . . . and for being Irish.'

Joshua was quiet for a moment. His face paled.

'Josh?'

'Well . . . Oh, Martha, I must be honest with you. Having a child . . . well, look, I'm not judging you, just saying how it is. But it doesn't help your case. It makes you look like you are a certain kind of person . . . a – a . . . Oh, Martha. I have to admit, things are tricky for you, my darling . . . I think we should speak to my father.'

When they reached the estate agent's office, Mr Green, Joshua's father, greeted them sombrely. 'Well, Martha, you seem to have got yourself into very deep water and so soon after taking over what was to be your dream.'

'It is naive that I am for being, Mr Green. I did not try to deceive deliberately.'

He humphed. 'Well, that may well be, but Brumble can be a tricky customer. From what he has just been saying, he seems to revel in thinking he has a right to beat you with a stick because of . . . well, your circumstances. I am trying to get to speak with Lord Smythe. I have been promised that he will ring me the moment he is free.'

'What do you think the outcome will be, Father?'

'I don't know. I will do my best to put this in the light it is. After all, it was Lady Smythe's friend, Lady Portlend, who suggested the idea to you, Martha, of seeking and fulfilling orders from afar – a very good business idea, but one that takes a lot of skill and relies on others, especially delivery men, to handle your cash and to pay it into your account, less the company's commission for the transaction. Not everyone is scrupulous and as this is two amounts – one of them quite large – and from the same area, we may be looking at a thief being involved.'

Martha knew that this wasn't going to go well for her. She'd had no communication from Lady Rebecca, and yet she had been so very keen in the beginning and had said that she would support her. Lady Smythe, who she hadn't ever met, had sent customers to her, but nothing from Lady Rebecca. It all pointed to them not wanting to be associated with her – though for Lady Smythe, her husband may have insisted that she send custom as he had a vested interest in her business doing well.

A small part of her felt she'd lost something with losing the lovely Lady Rebecca as a friend. Shame washed over her. Such women didn't behave how she had. Whatever had possessed her to do so, she still didn't know. But yet, she didn't regret it. None of it. She couldn't imagine a world without her Bonnie, nor one in which she'd never known Peter. For still she knew that despite her growing feelings for Joshua, Peter was embedded in her heart.

The telephone on Mr Green's desk ringing made her jump. The sound seemed to hold her destiny.

As she listened to the one side of the conversation, she knew it did.

'Yes, an unfortunate incident, but one that can be explained if you will allow me to give you the facts of what happened, Your Lordship.'

After a moment, Mr Green began to tell what happened. Martha's heart thumped in her chest.

'Yes, if those circumstances prevail, it is unlikely that Miss O'Hara will regain the funds. We are hoping— No, I don't think she can, if that happens, but I can make arrangements with her to clear the backlog in instalments.'

Then an embarrassed Mr Green hanging his head, 'Yes, Your Lordship, those are the circumstances, but how they look aren't true. Miss O'Hara is a respectable— Well, yes, I understand, but . . .'

Martha knew she was doomed. It was obvious that Lord Smythe knew of Bonnie and wasn't happy about it. She didn't blame him, or any of them. She had done wrong, and her sin was coming back to haunt her.

'In her defence, Miss O'Hara and her partner have worked extremely hard, and the shop is looking beautiful, an asset to the promenade and to your investment. Well, no, on the face of it— But the circumstances—'

Martha could have hugged Mr Green. He was fighting a losing battle on her behalf, but not giving up.

'But this is her home and the home of her child. Please reconsider— Well, I beg of you, to at least give her . . . us more time to help her to find accommodation . . . Thank you. That is very generous. Goodbye, Lord Smythe, and I remain your hum— Well! He put the phone down on me, the pompous swine!'

'Father!'

'Well, he didn't budge in his views – him, a known philanderer with more than one child born the wrong side of the blanket! Hypocrite!'

Anger shone in beads of sweat on Mr Green's forehead. Martha had the urge to go to him and to hug him. He'd championed her despite everything. Like his son, he was a thoroughly nice man.

'So, Martha, my dear, things are not good for you. Lord Smythe has served notice on you . . . I am sorry, my dear. He did want it with immediate effect, but I persuaded him otherwise and so he has given you a month.'

'A month, is it? Oh, Mr Green, ta. But what is it he is going to do about the cheque?'

'He isn't going to take it to the police, but he does want his money and now . . . I'm sorry, Martha.'

'It is that I can get it together, but it is all that me and Trisha are having in our business, and we have other outstanding bills. Besides, where is it I am to live? Will I be needing a deposit for that?'

'You will.'

'Martha, I will help. I have that house with many rooms.'

'Joshua, my son, if you take Martha and her child in, you will bring scandal down on our family . . . I mean, well, not because it is you, Martha, but well, taking any woman into your home, son, will provoke outrage.'

'I'm not for letting you do that, Josh. There will be a way, there has to be.'

But at this moment, with Trisha put out of her home too, and their business having to go, Martha couldn't think of how she was to resolve it all. Her heart was breaking – to lose her dream so quickly after achieving it, but worse, to make her child homeless, left her feeling devastated.

TWENTY-EIGHT

Trisha

Trisha sat on Martha's sofa, staring at the crackling fire. She couldn't take in all that had happened.

Out of pain, but in the fuzzy world the pain relief had put her into, nothing had made any sense to her – not why she was in the flat above the shop, not why she had no news on how Bobby was, and not Martha saying they were losing the shop. It all seemed to be happening to others.

'Trisha, love, it is that I have made you some porridge. Eat it up. It will make you stronger.'

'Martha, I need to knaw how me Bobby is, lass.'

'I know. I will try to go to your house later. It is that there are so many things to see to. We have orders we are to fulfil; we have to find new premises – not least, somewhere for me to live. Maybe both of us.'

'I knaw, lass, but I can't take it all in. You say someone must have stolen our money? Well, what's the use of trusting our goods to the system of cash on delivery again, eh?'

'I know, I have been for thinking about that. It is costly too. But it is that our custom from our adverts is for being the mainstay of our business. I am thinking that if we only put our adverts in one area at a time, and then one of us be delivering them all to that area . . .'

'Eeh, Martha, Martha. I wish we could sell your hope, your belief. Here we are, lass, on our arses, as Edna would have said, and you're still thinking up schemes to make us rich. Ha, I have to admire you, love.'

'Sure, it is that I know there is hope . . . I – I allowed me guiding spirit in. We are in for a bad time, but we are for having hope.'

Trisha sighed. She couldn't believe like Martha, but she was glad that Martha did have that to sustain her. 'Martha, I can't think about all of that at the mo. I need to find out how me Bobby is. And we need to find you a home . . . well, me an' all, 'cause if owt happens to Bobby, Hattie Hargreaves won't let me keep the house. Not that I want to. I don't ever want to go back there again! It all changed after me da died and I became a bit wayward. I ain't known much but disdain from the neighbours since then, and now I've nowt but bad memories.'

'I know, the place holds nothing but a lot of sadness for you now, so it does. Let's hope Ted calls today. He does now and again, but surely so if there is news.'

As if they'd conjured him up, Cilla called up the stairs, 'There's a lad here to see you, Martha.'

This sent Martha running down the stairs. Trisha held her breath. Why would Ted call on them? What was happening?'

She didn't have long to wait. When Martha came back up the stairs, her face was white. 'Trish, I'm sorry, love, but Bobby's . . . he's in hospital, love, and . . . well, his mammy is dead.'

'What? Oh, naw, Martha, what can I do? What happened?'

'It appears that no one had been seeing Mrs Rathbone since she hurt you. She's not been for opening the door to anyone. And so, a couple of the men decided to break in . . . They found her lying on the bed with Bobby. He was for being barely alive, but sure enough, she was gone.'

'Oh, Martha, Martha . . . I don't want Bobby to die. I have to get to him. Help me to get to him, please, love.'

'Sure, it is that they may not be letting you go into the hospital to be with him, me darling.'

'Naw, Martha. Don't let this be happening. I – I should have been looking after him. I wanted to do that. I were scared, but . . .'

'And it is that you must think of yourself and Sally, me darling. It could have been you who was catching the flu. Thankfully, you didn't, but what use would it be for you to get it now and leave little Sally?'

Trisha knew that Martha was right. And yet it didn't feel right. Her husband was dying, and she should be by his side.

'Sure, it is that I can telephone the hospital. I'll just be a wee while. Try to relax, Trish. You have to get well yourself, me darling.'

Trisha felt far from well and wondered if she would do so again. Her leg throbbed, her head ached and her bruises still felt sore, though some were healing. Her mind went to the shocking news of her ma-in-law's death. She had mixed feelings about it. She wouldn't wish ill on anyone, but she couldn't feel sorry either. But Bobby. She didn't want Bobby to die.

At the sound of Martha's footsteps on the stairs, she held her breath.

Martha's expression told her nothing. 'Is he all right, lass?'

'He's not for being all right, Trish, but it is that he is holding his own. They've been getting fluids into him, and he was rallying, so he was.'

'Eeh, Martha, he's a strong lad, me Bobby. He could beat this now he's being looked after.'

'Trish . . . they were for saying he has a long way to go, and it is still not for being sure he will recover . . . They . . . Oh, me darling, it is that they found other things, but they weren't for saying. They need to be speaking to you. They said the doctor would be grateful if you would be making an appointment to go in to see him.'

'What other things? Bad things?'

'They weren't for saying, me darling. But I think it is that you must be preparing yourself.'

Martha came and sat next to her and held her hand. At that moment it felt like a lifeline to Trisha. She clung on to it wondering what she had to face on top of what they already were together.

'Trish, it is sorry that I am that this has happened, but it is that we must sort out our position too. If Bobby will be in need of care, is it that you will go to your home with him when you are well yourself?'

'I don't knaw, I hadn't thought, but, aye, I'm his wife till death do us part and in sickness and in health, so I must, Martha . . . And I'd want to. I owe him that much.'

'Yes, it is what I thought, Trish. But what of Sally?'

All of this was too much for Trisha to sort out in her mind. She understood Martha's concerns. So much had landed on her shoulders in such a short time and she could see she was frantic with worry over it all. 'If it's nowt catching, then me Sally will come with me. Bobby will have to accept that. But if it is, well, I just don't knaw, Martha . . . Oh, it's all a mess. Look at me. I feel broken and unable to care for meself, let alone anyone else.'

'Don't get despondent, love. The doctor was for saying that you are healing well. He said he would be contacting the hospital with his report and that it is that he thinks you'll be having your cast off in a few weeks.'

'Eeh, that'd be grand. I just wish I weren't in so much pain in me side where I was kicked.'

'It was sure the doctor was that it was only bruising, when it could have been real damage to your kidneys. So it is that all will heal, me darling. I will be caring for you and Sally while it does.'

'Oh, Martha, you've such a lot to sort out, lass.'

'It is just fulfilling the orders we already have and finding somewhere to live. Somewhere I am able to afford, and that is why it is that I spoke to you about continuing our business, Trish. Without it, I'm for being destitute. It'll be the workhouse that I will land in.'

This really hit home with Trisha. She hadn't fully taken in the seriousness of it all. Suddenly, a fear clenched her.

She was in the same situation. Bobby would be discharged from the army very soon, that's if he lived, so her payments from them would cease and he wouldn't be able to go to work for a while – if ever! Hers and Martha's business would have to fold – but would it? Realisation dawned. 'Eeh, lass, I ain't been with it. I've only just realised what the position is for us. And, aye, we will carry on. We'll find a way.'

Martha visibly relaxed. 'Oh, Trish. Together we can. It was that for a while there I faced prison as it was me that was for signing the cheque, but Lord Smythe said he wouldn't prosecute.'

Seeing the anguished tear fall onto Martha's cheek gave Trisha the enormity of what was happening. If it was possible, she clung on even tighter to Martha's hand, trying to latch on to the strength she was showing. 'By, Martha, how did this happen to us, eh? We've worked hard, sometimes long into the night, just for some bloody thief to benefit. What did Mr Green and Joshua say? Will they help us, lass?'

'They will. Joshua was for taking us into his home, but his father stopped that idea. He . . . well, it was their reputation he was thinking of.'

'Huh! That's it. We're tainted ladies now, love. Floozies, tarts, and yet the men who did this to us are free to go their own way with not a worry in sight of what they left behind.'

Although Martha didn't answer, Trisha knew that in her own case, she didn't agree. It seemed fixed in her mind that there was a reason that Peter went off and no one could alter that. Maybe it was a way she found she could cope with it all, 'cause to her mind, the bastard had had what he wanted then slunk off in the same way that Ralph had treated her. Though she had to admit, it wasn't the same. She and Ralph were just two people who had met, had an animal-like attraction to each other and enjoyed the moment. Where Ralph did wrong was in not protecting her when he said he would.

'That was for being a powerful sigh, me darling. Don't give up. I know it isn't for being easy, and more so for you when you are feeling unwell too, but it is that neither Joshua nor his pappy have given up on us. Mr Green is looking out for a flat, maybe above a shop like this one, but with the shop being occupied. He said they are for being the cheapest accommodation as it is only help with the rent of the premises that the shopkeeper is looking for.'

This cheered Trisha. 'And you're right, love, we can do our business anywhere as long as we have our hands to knit and sew with. Like you say, a stall would do us right an' all and the pitch that I worked on selling rock is still going, you knaw. I'm sure Cissy would rent it to us.'

Martha's smile lit her face. 'There, you see. It is the hope that you have in your heart that is making the world look a better place, even though it is that we have our worries mounting up.'

It was a week before Trisha could go to the hospital. Still Martha hadn't found anywhere to live, and it seemed that the clock was ticking down towards doomsday at times, but at others they were hopeful. Things had eased a little for them financially, as a payment had come in for some goods that they'd sold a while back. And Cilla had said that the gypsies would never let Martha go to the workhouse and though she didn't relish living with them, she did see it as a better option.

For now, Trisha's worries and concerns were all on what the doctor would tell her, and what the future looked like for Bobby.

The doctor was a young, gangly man, which surprised Trisha. She'd only ever seen older doctors. His glasses were as thick as the bottom of a beer bottle, his hair black and curly. His smile made up for anything else he was lacking in the way of good looks. Though why he was smiling, Trisha later thought, was because he was a mad-science-type, who took glee in having discovered something, as his words had chilled her.

'Mrs Rathbone, thank you for coming to see me. What I have to say is very unpleasant, but it is important that you know. You see, you may be at risk.'

'From catching the flu, you mean?'

'No. Syphilis.'

'What?'

'Yes, I am sorry to inform you that your husband is infected, and badly. Did you have sexual relations with him when he returned home?'

She'd never heard it called that and wondered at him asking such a thing of her. Her cheeks burned as she told him, 'Naw. He weren't well.'

'I'm not surprised. I would say he caught the disease when he first went to France, as it is advanced.'

Trisha didn't know what he was on about. 'What is it? Is it bad?'

The doctor cleared his throat. 'It is very bad if untreated, and your husband's hasn't been, or at least not in time. And in answer to what it is, it's a very serious sexually transmitted disease. Treatments for it are very new but are only effective if caught early.'

'Sexual?'

Trisha blushed even more at talking to this man about such things, even if he was a doctor. Without thinking, she said, 'So, he went with another woman? I – I . . . the rotter!'

'I'm sorry. But yes. And my only motive in telling you is to protect you. So, nothing happened between you on his return?'

'Naw, I told you, he were sick. And he stands need to be with what he's put me through, the bloody hypocrite!'

'Now, now, Mrs Rathbone. I can understand how you feel.'

'Naw, you can't. You're a man. Things are different for you, ain't they, eh? If you had sex, you can walk away and think of it as a conquest. Well, we women can't. We get left with a lifetime of being called names, having a kid to bring up on our own and being looked down on and passed over, all for doing the same thing.'

He coughed again. 'I'm sorry. I can see that you're upset, and it is understandable. But being cross with me because I am a man isn't going to help you. You need to know that you must never let your husband touch you again . . . and, well, that his life expectancy has been greatly shortened. I'm sorry. So very sorry.'

Feeling anger at everything – in particular Bobby and his ma – she blurted out, 'Well, I ain't. He bloody deserves it and if he don't die soon, I'll bloody well kill him!'

To her surprise, the doctor burst out laughing. 'Oh, I'm sorry, but do you know, that's exactly how I would feel. I understand fully. And I'm one for saying that you should vent your anger – I mean, don't kill Mr Rathbone, but let out how you are feeling.'

Trisha found that she liked him and could relate to him. For some unknown reason she wanted to tell him why she was so angry. He listened without commenting, then said, 'That's terrible. That another human being could put someone through that. And his mother did all this to you, too?'

'Aye, and all because of the rape of me.' She hung her head at this lie, as she hadn't wanted to lie to him, but shame made her do so.

'I'm sorry. You haven't had very good experiences with men, have you?'

She shook her head. At this moment she could have said that she hated them all.

'Well, we're in the same boat there – not that I've had bad experiences with women, but they never look at me in the first place. So, it is bad in a way.'

Trisha looked up. Suddenly, she saw beyond the glasses and the too thin face to a nice person, who she knew she already liked very much. 'I don't knaw why. If they got to knaw you, they would see a lovely caring man. It ain't all to do with looks, you knaw.'

She immediately regretted saying it as his face coloured and he looked away.

'I – I didn't mean, I – I . . .' It was then that she made things worse. 'I reckon you're a handsome man an' all.'

He looked aghast. 'I'm sorry, I have to go. I'm a very busy man, and I should not have allowed the conversation to go this way. Please forgive me and forget all we have said. I – I just need to say that your husband can come home, or we can arrange for him to go into a convalescent home for soldiers where he will be cared for for the rest of his life.'

'You mean, he ain't got long?'

'I can't say, no one can, but the disease has taken hold rapidly, and the sores are difficult to heal. We can only soothe them.'

'Sores? Them on his face, are they to do with it?'

'They are. But the worst ones are in his private area.'

Trisha felt repulsed for a moment, but then an overwhelming sorrow took her. A tear plopped onto her cheek. 'So, you don't all get away with doing it then?'

'No. There are risks.'

Somehow, this didn't give her the satisfied feeling she thought it would. So, Bobby had strayed as she had, and they'd both paid a heavy price for doing so. But poor Bobby had paid much more dearly than she had. Her punishment was a joy in the most part – not the name calling, or the being ostracised, but in little Sally she'd been given a gift for her bad behaviour.

'I want to take care of him meself.'

'Well, if you are sure? You will have to be scrupulous in cleaning your hands, not kissing him, and no relations whatsoever.'

'Eeh, what about me young 'un? Would she be in danger?'

'Well, possibly. We can't say for sure, but if she kissed him, or messed with his open sores, then there is that possibility.'

'I can't then, I'm sorry. Me heart wants to, but I don't mind putting meself in danger, I can take care, but me little Sally can't protect herself.'

'I understand and agree. I will make the arrangements and will make sure you are informed, Mrs Rathbone. Now, if there's anything else I can help you with, I gladly will.'

Trisha had the strangest feeling come over her that wanted her to say, *Yes, you could give me a hug.* She swallowed hard as at this moment, that's exactly what she would have liked to happen. She didn't know why, only that at him rising and preparing to leave, she felt somehow bereft.

'I – I didn't get your name.'

'Doctor Kennings.'

'Mine's Trisha, short for Patricia . . . Ta for what you've done today. It couldn't have been easy facing me with this news. I – I wouldn't have wanted anyone else to have told me. You were very kind to me.'

He stood and held her gaze. 'I hope you'll be all right, Trisha.'

She loved her name on his lips. He made it sound special.

'Aye, I will. I'm a strong lass whose been through stuff as would make your hair curl . . . Ha, it already does!'

He grinned. 'I take after my father; he has a head of curly hair.'

'It's lovely.'

He coughed again. She was learning he did that when embarrassed. 'Well, good day, Trisha. No doubt our paths will cross again as I will continue to care for your husband. I am head of the urology department.'

'Ta, doctor. I feel safe with you taking care of him . . . Before you go, can I see Bobby?'

'I would say yes, but Sister is the one who makes those decisions. I'll ask her. I can usually persuade her as I am one of her favourites.' He touched his nose. 'Always pays to be on the right side of the ward sister.' Then he grinned and left.

Trisha stood looking at the door that had closed behind him. She wanted to run after him but had no idea why. She couldn't be attracted to him – like he said, he wasn't the kind that women went for. Not in looks anyway. But there was something about him. She felt it in his look, his smile, his kind and gentle way.

Shaking herself mentally, she folded her arms as what she'd been told came to her. *So, me Bobby were at it all the time!*

Somehow, she no longer felt angry at him. Only sad at them both having been hurt.

The sister opening the door to the small office she was sitting in put a stop to these thoughts. 'Mrs Rathbone? This way.'

As she followed the sister, her heart was in her mouth. But nothing prepared her for seeing Bobby. He was skeletal, and his eyes glared out at her – not in an angry way, but because his sockets were so sunken. His teeth looked huge in his skull-like face.

'Bobby, love. Eeh, I'm sorry.'

In a weak voice, he asked, 'You ain't mad at me?'

'Naw. I was at first, after what you've put me through, but you've had more than your punishment for cheating on me, lad. Don't think about it.'

'I just want to come home, lass.'

Trisha lowered her head. 'It ain't possible, Bobby.'

'Aw, Trisha, don't say that. I knaw you've to have your babby with you. I'm all right about it. I – I should have been from the beginning, lass. I'm sorry . . . I'm sorry for how I've been.'

'I knaw. We both are. We were too young, Bobby. Anyroad, me fear is me babby catching . . . well, what you've got.'

'I'd keep away from her, Trisha, I promise.'

'And you knaw as we can't . . . well, can't have relations, or even kiss, don't you?'

'Aye.'

It broke Trisha's heart to see tears on his cheeks. She'd never seen Bobby cry.

'I can't think about all of that, I just want to be home . . . Did . . . did they bury me ma?'

Trisha's heart felt like breaking for him. 'They did, Bobby. I saw it in the *Gazette*. There was a few there.'

'She hurt you badly, Trisha, I'm sorry.'

'We can't keep saying sorry, love. We have to accept what's happened and that's that.'

'Aye . . . They tell me me ma's house has to be sorted. Me Aunt Betty's going to see to it.'

'That'll be a relief to you, love . . . Look, Bobby, I'm worried how we'll manage moneywise.'

'I've got a bit – enough to keep us going for a bit. And me aunt said she'll sell most of me ma's things and get some money for me an' all. And you can carry on working, I won't stop you doing that . . . Please, Trisha, don't let me go into a home.'

'All right, Bobby. It's what I told the doctor I would do as soon as he asked, but then he said me Sally would be in danger, so I changed me mind. But if you're sure you'll take every care not to go near to her, then I'll do it. I'd like to have you home, love.'

Again, his tears flowed. 'Ta, Trisha.'

She wanted to hold him. He looked so vulnerable, so lost and alone – he didn't deserve this. Instead, she chatted, telling him about the shop. He surprised her then by saying, 'Get Martha to move in with us, lass.'

'That's nice of you, Bobby, but I don't think it a good idea, not in the circumstances. If nothing resolves for her, then yes, we will do that, but only as a stopgap. I'd be too scared of her or her little one catching what you have.'

Bobby sighed.

'Well, love, I'll get going. I'll tell the sister what we've decided, and I'll come back at visiting time. I'll sort a few things before then, eh?'

She blew him a kiss and walked away, her heart heavy with fear and sorrow.

Once outside the hospital, Trisha decided to make her way to her home – not that it felt like that any more. She needed to see what state it was in and make a plan so that she was ready for Bobby.

Her crutches sounded hollow on the pavement as all was quiet in Enfield Road. She was glad of this and hoped that no one came out to greet her. It wasn't to be as Mrs Higginbottom's curtain twitched and her door opened seconds later. 'You're back then, lass?'

'Aye, I'm back.'

'How's Bobby?'

For a moment Trisha felt like screaming out what was wrong with Bobby and telling this hateful woman to stick that in her pipe and smoke it, but she just said, 'Not well. The flu has left complications. He's coming home soon, and I'll be looking after him.'

'No more than a wife's duty. Poor lad. Well, good. Glad to see you doing sommat you should.'

'Sod off, will you!'

'Well!' She crossed her arms. 'You're a bad apple, Trisha Rathbone. Allus have been and allus will be. I won't ask how you are, 'cause I don't bloody well care! I just feel sorry for your Bobby.' She went to go in, but stopped. 'So, if you're coming back here, what about that bastard of yours, is she coming an' all?'

Trisha bit her tongue as to what she wanted to say. This woman had thick skin, so it wasn't worth it. 'Where else would she go, eh?'

'It's Bobby I feel sorry for, poor lad, having a slag like you flaunting your kid in front of him every day when he ain't well.'

Trisha lifted one of her crutches. 'If you don't want a swipe with this, you'll sod off into your own home and shut your mouth!'

'Well!'

The door slammed shut.

Trisha made it to her house, unlocked the door, but was hit with the foul smell of death. She flung the door wide, opened the windows, then collapsed in a heap on the sofa.

Her tears flooded her face, her nose, her mouth. It seemed to her that every part of her was weeping as, filled with despair, she lay her head down and sobbed her heart out.

TWENTY-NINE

Martha

Martha had helped Trisha to get ready to go to the hospital to have her cast removed and to collect Bobby before making one final check that all was done. Satisfied it was, she prepared to await Arthur coming back from dropping Trisha off to pick her up too.

She looked around the empty shop. The last of the crates of stock and fixtures and fittings had gone to Joshua's for him to store in his cellar for them. She sighed. *At least it was that I had me dream, and how lovely it was at times.*

Sally tugged her skirt.

'It's all right, me wee Sally. Mama will be back to pick you up later.' Sally seemed content with this and stared out from her baby carriage through the window. She loved to watch the folk passing by.

Martha did the same, only one didn't pass by, but had obviously been making for the shop as her car pulled up outside. Martha watched, wondering if it was the new owner, but when a chauffeur alighted and opened the door, she saw it was Lady Rebecca. She felt her face colouring with shame.

'Martha! Oh, Martha, I am so sorry.'

She swept towards Martha as if gliding, her face full of concern. She stopped as she saw the pram and then Sally smiling up at her. 'Ah, two children?'

'No, Your Ladyship.' Martha gave a small curtsey. 'This is for being me friend's wee girl. Me Bonnie is in the pram.'

'Ah, she's adorable.' On cue, Bonnie gave one of her charming smiles. 'Now, my dear, I am so glad that I caught you. I wanted to say how sorry Lady Darcy and I are about what has happened. We had such wonderful reports of your shop and the work you were doing . . . And, well, we did hear about your child. But we both decided that something dreadful must have happened to your fiancé, and that this was awful for you – not having the baby but having to cope on your own.' She took hold of Martha's shoulders and looked into her eyes.

Martha felt confused. She was talking as if she'd never received her letter.

'And we both thought you so brave not to have given your baby away but to have soldiered on. Then that horrid bank manager got to Lord Smythe and that was that. We could do nothing to help. Oh, you may think it is only the working-class women who are downtrodden, but I can tell you that many of my class have no say in anything other than running their households, my dear. Though that will change. We are working towards it changing.'

She looked around.

'If only I could have seen it when you had all your stock out. I wanted to come often, but circumstances stopped me. But, Martha, I will still support you, I promise. I will take some leaflets with me and will still pass them around to my friends and anyone I can. Oh, you will still make layettes, won't you?'

Hardly over the surprise of Lady Rebecca turning up out of the blue like this, Martha took a moment to find her tongue. At first, she just nodded, but then told Lady Rebecca her plans. 'I will, and so will me partner, Trisha. We're going to rent a stall in the spring. It'll be by the side of me old tent, so it will.'

'But where will you live? You have a home, don't you?'

'Yes, it is that I am to rent a flat.'

'And will you have a telephone?'

'Yes. I have been able to keep the same number. It was for being a relief that I could as I have customers coming back for items as their babies grow.'

'Good! Well done, my dear. You know . . . Lady Darcy, who is also fighting for women's rights, and I, look on you as a heroine. A young woman of substance, who stood up for herself, kept her child against all the odds and opened a business of her own. You are a rare – a very rare young woman, Martha.'

'Ta. I ain't been for thinking of meself that way, and it nearly broke me spirit when I was for losing the shop, but I will fight back, and I did write to you to tell you about Bonnie. It wasn't me trying to deceive you, so it wasn't.'

'Oh? I never received it. If I had, I might have been able to save all this happening. Lord Darcy likes an honest, open person – not that he is himself at times! Anyway, Martha, we can't undo what has been done . . . But I so admire you.'

'Ta, Lady Rebecca, that is for meaning a lot to me.'

'Well, it's Christmas in a few days' time and we are going back to London tomorrow. I only came to oversee our holiday house closing – though, to be truthful, I could have left that to my trusted staff. I really did want to see you, my dear. I needed to put my mind at rest as to how you were and what was happening . . . Ah, is this your carriage?'

Arthur had pulled up outside.

'Yes, it is that I have to go, but ta for coming to see me, Lady Rebecca. It's meaning the world to me.'

'My pleasure. Now, if you do need to contact me, telephone, as one can never rely on the post.'

'I did try, but it is that your butler wouldn't put me through. He was for instructing me not to ring again.'

'Oh? Well, look, if you ring again, just give your name, and I will instruct my butler that I am to be given the option of taking the call. If I can't as I have visitors or something, I will ring you back. So, please, Martha, do call me if you need to.'

'Ta, I will be doing that, but only if I need to.'

'And send me half a dozen of your new brochures. Someone told me that they bought a wonderful baby cradle from you. I would love to see those.'

Not having time to tell her about the cradles being made by her cousin, Martha just bade Lady Rebecca farewell. Then stood looking after the car as it disappeared along the prom, wondering if that really happened or if it had just been a daydream. But she knew it wasn't and was left with a lovely warm feeling boosting the hope that she'd allowed to flag.

When she arrived at her flat on Waterloo Road, just a few doors away from where Joshua lived, she stood holding Bonnie in her arms and Sally's little hand as she looked around her. It seemed familiar as all her furniture was there to greet her, brought here over the few days leading up to today and put in place. Her bedroom furniture would come later, as would that for Trisha's room, as her second bedroom, wherever she lived, would always be known as.

Beside her stood her cases, and a box containing Bonnie's daily essentials. Her pram was to be stored downstairs at the back of the shop, which sold groceries and newspapers.

The owner, a Mr Piper, was a jolly man, whose wife sometimes came to the shop to help him out. They had no children and were looking forward to hearing one around during the day. They knew her circumstances but didn't let it worry them. So all in all, Martha thought, she'd dropped lucky and knew from the vibe she felt that she would be happy here, her only worry being how she was going to manage for money until the season began.

Going to the window, she looked out. A window opposite looked festive, with tinsel that caught the little sunlight and the holly hanging in it.

'Christmas. Oh, me wee ones, you're not to have much of a one this year. But it is that we will do our best.'

She and Trisha planned to have it at Trisha's. Bobby stayed in bed most of the day and said he would that day, as long as the door to the stairs was left open and he could hear everything.

They had a leg of a cockerel to share, and horse chestnuts to roast. Their knitting and sewing over the last week had been making rag dolls for the children, and they'd made some paper chains to put up. Neither had felt the least like doing any of it but knew they must for the children.

'Are you there, Martha? I saw you arrive.'

Joshua seemed to be at the top of the stairs and opening the door as his voice reached her. She turned and smiled at him. 'It is that I am.'

'And how are you feeling? A big step, but I think you will be cosy here.'

'Oh, I will. And it is that I have a nosy neighbour to keep his eye on me.'

He grinned his lovely grin that melted her heart. As he came nearer, he told her, 'I'd be more than a neighbour if you would only consent to marrying me, Martha, darling.'

'Sure, you aren't for being good at proposing, are you not? Didn't I hear a note of blackmail in your voice?'

His laugh filled the room. She joined in with him. Then he became serious. 'Are you no nearer to saying yes, my darling?'

She'd become used to his endearment and loved hearing it. And she'd wished a million times that the curse of Peter, as she now looked on her love for him, would go away. For without that, she would willingly give herself to Joshua. But she knew it wouldn't be fair to do so.

'Oh, Josh, I am not for wanting to be a torment to you, but I promise that soon I will make my mind up.'

'I will pray every night that you choose to come to me, my darling. I love you so much that it hurts.'

He looked so beautiful as he lifted Sally, but kept his eyes on her, that she felt compelled to go towards him. His arms opened. Nothing in her stopped her wanting to go into them, no doubts, no fears – her heart suddenly felt ready.

Somehow, they hugged, with children pushing for prominence, Bonnie gurgling for her bit of attention and Sally saying, 'Me. Me want to hug.' They ended up in a fit of laughter.

'It is that we will have to see to them first. I am having a new pen for them to play in. It sounds bad, to pen them, but it's for them to play safely in. It's in Trisha's bedroom. Would you be a darling and get it set up for me, Josh?'

'Anything. Anything, if my prize is to be to hold you close.'

They giggled again.

But the atmosphere changed once the children were happy. A feeling took Martha that she was about to take a great step. She could see the same had taken hold of Joshua as they slowly moved closer. Once more, his arms opened to her. She did not hesitate. Her reward was to be bathed in a warmth so beautiful that as Joshua's lips came on hers, there was no one else in the whole world, only them.

Trisha

Trisha felt excited, as she hummed whilst peeling the potatoes. It was Christmas morning and any minute now Martha and Bonnie would arrive. Sally was chattering nineteen to the dozen in baby-speak, and when she'd looked in on Bobby he hadn't woken yet, which had added to the peace. Not that he disturbed it much when awake, but she felt her own mind rest when he rested.

It seemed to Trisha that everything was working out a lot better than she'd thought. Bobby was a good patient, and though very weak, he often managed a smile for her and never complained. Always he asked how Sally was and said that he loved to hear her playing.

Finishing off peeling the last of the spuds for dinner, she looked at the clock for the umpteenth time, willing it to strike ten o'clock as that was the time Martha was aiming to get here.

But there was still fifteen minutes to go. Lifting the skirt of her pinny, she wiped her hands and thought she would wake Bobby and see if he could manage something for his breakfast.

'Ooh, Sally, it's Christmas!'

Sally, who sat on the floor amusing herself with a ball that a neighbour had given her, looked up. 'Mas?'

'Yes, well, that's half of it, lass. Eeh, when Martha gets here, you'll have your present.'

'Press?'

'Yes, me little lass. By, we're going to have a lovely day. Now, sit still while I pop up to see Bobby, eh?'

Sally nodded.

As she passed the fireplace, Trisha checked the guard. It was hooked onto the wall and wouldn't budge. She'd run up the stairs quickly and would still be able to hear Sally.

All was so quiet upstairs, deathly so, that it put a dread

into Trisha. She didn't know why. Trepidation made her skin crawl to the point she hardly dared to open the bedroom door. When she did, she sighed with relief. Bobby was sleeping.

Crossing the room to open the curtains and let in the light of the street lamp, she found she still couldn't see properly. The room felt cold. She shivered. 'Come on, Bobby, love, wake up, it's Christmas morning!'

Nothing.

Feeling anxious once more, she lit the lamp next to the bed. Bobby's face was still – too still, and very pale. 'Bobby? Bobby, love?'

Bobby didn't move. Realisation dawned on Trisha. 'Bobby, naw. Naw, Bobby!'

As if to convince herself, she pulled back the covers. Bobby lay in a pool of blood. A slow and steady drip of blood dropped onto the floor. On a gasp, Trisha said his name. 'Bobby! Bobby, what have you done? Naw, naw.'

Pulling the blankets further back, she saw the penknife he'd kept from boyhood, and which was always in his sock drawer, lying near to his hand. His wrists were slashed into gaping holes.

'Oh, God!' She opened her mouth to scream, but nothing came. It was then that she saw the note written on the cover of a torn fag packet. Where that had come from, she had no idea as Bobby hadn't smoked since he'd been ill.

Trisha, I'm doing this because I love you, and because I cannot go on. Not like this. I can't face a Christmas Day like this, not sharing it with you and the kids we

dreamed of having – the kids we can never have
because of me sin. Have a happy life, Trisha. I didn't
give you that, but I want you to find one. Bobby x

'Oh, Bobby, Bobby.' Through her tears she told him that her own sin would have prevented them ever having another child. 'I did love you, Bobby. We could have been happy.'

'Trish, Trish, it is that we are here. Merry Christmas, me darling.'

The voice seemed alien. Trisha went on her knees and sobbed.

'Trish, Trish, me darling, what is it?'

The footsteps came closer. Martha was by her side gasping in horror and in shock. 'Jesus, Mary and Joseph, Bobby, what is it you have done?'

Three days later, Trisha stood shivering by the open grave that contained Bobby's ma's remains. Martha's arms were around her and Joshua's arms were around them both.

When her handful of earth landed on Bobby's coffin with a resounding thud, she said in her mind, *Goodbye, me Bobby, lad. We had our good times and I'll remember them when I think of you.*

As they went to walk away, she looked up. Doctor Kennings stood a few yards away. He stepped forward. 'I am so sorry, Trisha . . . May I call you that?'

She nodded. 'Ta, Doctor. And ta for coming. It means a lot to me.'

He took her hand. 'Just as you could call on me when Bobby was alive, you can still do so if you need anything, Trisha.'

As she gazed up at him, she wanted the words not to be the empty kind said at every funeral, she wanted him to mean them.

He seemed to read this and nodded. 'I do. I do mean it. I would like to be of help to you.' He caught sight of Joshua then. 'Joshua! I've been meaning to look you up since I took the post at Blackpool Victoria. How are you?'

'Good to see you, Walter. Only, not under these circumstances, of course. I heard you were back and had a post at the hospital. I thought to let you settle in and seek me out first as you'd be busy finding your feet.'

'I have been. There's a lot to setting up a new department.' He looked at Martha who was still enclosed in Joshua's hold.

'Let me introduce you to Martha, my fiancée.'

Trisha gasped.

'Oh, it is that I was to tell you, Trisha, but with everything happening . . .'

'But it's wonderful news, lass. I'm pleased for you.' She opened her arms and Martha came into them. 'I'm not planning to leave you, Trisha. It will be you and me for a long time, living together in me flat, so it will. I promise you.'

'Aw, don't even think about that. I'll be all right. I want you to be happy, Martha.'

'And that's all I want for you too, Trisha.'

Trisha looked up. Walter and Joshua were standing together watching them. She caught Walter's eye and smiled at him. He smiled his lovely smile back and a little of the coldness left Trisha's heart.

She snuggled into Martha.

'Everything is to turn out for you how you wish it, Trish. I see it now and I know for sure who it is that has captured your heart.'

Before Trisha could react to this, Joshua said, 'Shall we go to the pub to get warm, girls? I think they let prams and baby carriages into the back room. We can raise a toast to Bobby.' He turned to look at Walter. 'Will you join us, Walter?'

Walter nodded. 'I'll do more than that, I'll push the baby carriage. I can just about manage that, as I'm a learner. And I'm sure you're experienced enough to guide the pram, Joshua.'

Trisha felt as though she was being transported to another world as she followed and the four of them left the churchyard.

At the gate she hesitated and looked back. 'Bye, Bobby. Rest in peace. And I think I can go forward to that happy life you wished for me in your note. Ta for that, lad. I'll never forget you.'

Martha linked arms with her once more and she filled with the feeling that she'd always had since Martha had come into her life. The feeling of being safe.

EPILOGUE

Martha
1922

Martha watched four-year-old Bonnie run along the promenade towards Joshua, her arms open, her gleeful cry of, 'Da . . . Da!' ringing out. On her heels was Sally, yelling just as loudly, 'Uncle Josh, Uncle Josh!'

Josh laughed his lovely laugh as he caught Bonnie, always the winner in any race with Sally, who now plunged into him grabbing his free leg.

Though Sally was nine months older than Bonnie, Bonnie was the tallest, with long legs that enabled her to move like lightning at times.

'Girls, girls, I do love you, but you have to let me move. I need to hug my wife.'

Martha laughed at him as he untangled himself. Then she was in his arms, oblivious to all.

'Martha?'

Her name on a strange, and yet familiar, voice froze her. Josh let her go and she turned around to look at the man who called out.

'Peter! Oh, Peter . . . where is it you have been?'

Josh stiffened by her side. His arm came around her, protecting her. She could feel his fear.

'I – I don't know for the most part. I'm sorry.'

His eyes – his remembered, dark eyes – held hers.

'Come away inside.' They were stood outside the shop – the same one where four years ago, she and Trisha had begun their business. They had been regranted the lease after hers and Josh's wedding in March 1920. Her new father-in-law had set things in motion and backed them with sureties.

'Trish, is it that you will be all right if I go upstairs a while? . . . You are for remembering Peter?'

Trisha looked up from folding a shawl that a customer had just ordered. Her look held surprise and then concern. 'Aye, of course.' She nodded at Peter. Then smiled at the still shocked Josh.

'Can I come too, Mummy?'

'In a wee while. You and Sally are to be playing nicely and are to be good girls for Aunty Trisha.'

Out of character, Bonnie agreed. Usually assertive about what she wanted to do, and a very determined little girl, she could stand her ground for a good five minutes trying to win her own way.

Martha was grateful she didn't this time.

She climbed the stairs on shaky legs, holding on tightly to the rail. For all her calm exterior, inside an explosion of emotions were attacking her.

Once upstairs in the flat, which Trisha and Sally lived in until tomorrow – Trisha's wedding day – she motioned to an armchair. 'Sit down, Peter.'

As he did, the July sun shone through the window onto him. He looked different, and yet the same. He'd filled out and was cared for, and prosperous, by the look of his clothes.

'I came to find you, Martha.'

Joshua, who had followed them up, coughed.

Peter looked in his direction, then back at Martha.

'This is Joshua, me husband, Peter. He is for knowing all about you. You are able to speak in front of him.'

'I – I'm glad you are happy . . . I am too. I married Jenny, my nurse . . . Well, that night . . . I . . .' He looked at Joshua. 'I'm not here to cause trouble. Jenny sent me. She is waiting at our hotel. You see, when my memory came back – I lost it . . . I . . .'

Joshua moved towards him and placed his hand on his back. 'Don't be afraid, Peter. We are glad you have come. You have been like a ghost in our cupboard. It's good to know you didn't just walk out on Martha.'

'No . . . no. I remember that night now. I woke, sweating, and not knowing where I was. I got out of bed. The moon was bright and with the light from that and the street gas light, I was able to find my clothes. I felt that if I could get outside and cool down, then I would be all right. I went to wake you, Martha, but I didn't know . . . I couldn't remember your name, or even what you were to me, or how I got there. It was terrifying. Once dressed and outside, I thought to walk, but then couldn't remember where I was going or where I had come from. It wasn't until a year ago that I pieced everything together with the help of Jenny and the asylum staff in Manchester. How I got there, I still don't know, but they tell me that I was brought in by a couple who said they found me sitting in their garden not knowing who I was.

'I am still a mystery to them, as there doesn't seem to be anything physical that caused this, only extreme trauma . . . from the war . . . but others had that . . . Why me?'

Martha hadn't realised that she had tears running down her face until Joshua handed her his handkerchief.

'Are you all right, darling?' Joshua moved towards her as he said this. She could hear the fear in his voice.

She looked up at him. Saw his beloved smile – uncertain at this moment, but the smile that was for her only. The one she loved with all her heart.

As she took her eyes away and looked at Peter, she filled with pity for him. His eyes were full of tears. This was costing him dearly.

'Sure, it is that I don't want you to worry, Peter. I have been wondering all these years why it was you left me like you did. But I was always having faith that it was something you were not able to control. But . . . I – I was for having a child.'

Peter's mouth dropped open. 'My child?'

'Yes, Peter.'

'The little girl downstairs?'

'Yes.' To Martha, it was as if time had stopped. Fear, pain and relief vied inside her.

'Does she know?'

'No. It is that she is too young. She thinks Joshua is her pappy. We had been planning to tell her when she is older.'

Peter was quiet for a moment. His fingers were entwined, and they now showed signs of him gripping tightly as his knuckles turned white.

'I think that is how it should remain. I – I don't have any right to claim her. She . . . she's beautiful, and I know that I love her very much . . . It is a feeling that flooded me as soon as you told me. Will you tell her when she is older?'

It was Joshua who answered. 'We will. And, well, if Martha agrees, we will keep you informed of her progress . . . send you photos, that sort of thing, and tell her all about you when she is older. Would you like her to come to find you then?'

'Yes.' Peter hung his head. 'I will count the days. But I know this is the right thing for my child. I – I was an orphan, as you know, Martha. I would have given anything to live in a happy home with a mum and dad, with no complications – wanted and loved. I want that for my child.'

Martha felt compelled to go to him. He stood. She opened her arms. He willingly came into them. 'Oh, Martha. I caused you such a lot of hurt.'

'I never was for losing faith in you, Peter. And I am not feeling anger. I am for being happy that it is that you have found happiness as I have. And we will be doing as Josh says. But it is that I want to be thanking you for not disrupting Bonnie's life.'

As he came out of her hug, he asked, 'Bonnie? That's a lovely name. I, well, I do have another child. A son. He is three. And, yes, I am happy, very happy. Today, though, I feel that my world has been rocked.'

'I'm for being glad for you. And am understanding. Knowing you have another child, it is natural for you to want to be a parent to Bonnie and to be having her with you. It is a great sacrifice you are for making.' Martha felt a deep fear. Would he change his mind?'

'I am willing to make it for you, Martha, and especially for my daughter. I saw the love Bonnie had for Joshua, and he for her. I know he will be, and surely is, a good father to her . . . I should go. I need to be with Jenny.'

'Of course. I'll walk with you, Peter. You look a little unsteady.'

'Thank you, Joshua, I'd be grateful for that. Jenny and I are staying at the Metropole.'

'Ah, that isn't far. If you're feeling up to it, we can walk?'

'Yes, thank you . . . Goodbye, Martha. Thank you for understanding.'

'Goodbye, Peter. Be sure to give your address to Joshua. We were meaning it when we said we will send you news on Bonnie.'

'I will.'

The tear that trickled down his face matched her own.

'Will you be all right, darling?'

'It is that I will, Josh.'

And as the door closed behind them, she knew that she would. Her questions would no longer plague her. Her love for Joshua would no longer be marred by a shadow of the past. Her heart was free – free to give to him completely.

Trisha knew a great relief to flood her as Martha came running down the stairs, just as Joshua came back in. She was yet to find out what happened, but to see Martha and Joshua in a loving hug warmed her heart and laid her fears to rest.

Not so that it completely steadied her. Her heart still drummed other expectations around her – other needs and her own future happiness. Only one thing could calm that – her wedding, to be held the next day.

She smiled as the children joined Martha and Josh in a huggle and heard Martha say, 'I love you with all the world, Josh.' Then Bonnie and Sally repeated the words, making them all laugh.

'Aye, well, I may as well join in as I love you an' all. You're like a brother to me, Joshua.'

Joshua broke away from his adoring fans and came over to her. She loved the hug he gave her.

'I shall be honoured to give you away tomorrow, Trisha. Walter's a good man.'

'Aye, he is. The best. And I love him with all my heart an' all.'

The door opened and Walter stood there. 'Oh, who is this you love with all your heart, Trish?'

'Ha, you, you daft ha'peth!'

She ran to him, just getting there before Sally. His hug increased the beating of her heart and filled her with joy as he then picked Sally up and kissed her cheek, making her smile widen and, Sally being Sally, she did as she always did when happy and danced around the shop.

'Go away, Walter! It is that you shouldn't be for seeing Trisha today, it is for bringing bad luck!'

Trisha gasped. Had Martha seen something?

The atmosphere quietened. Martha blushed. 'Sure, it is an old wives' tale, for it is that you two are to be the happiest couple ever.'

'Phew, Martha, you had me worried then, though I can't see anything but happiness in the future through my crystal specs!'

Trisha burst out laughing. Walter treated his poor eyesight with such good humour, she'd ceased to feel sorry for him a long time ago.

As she looked at him, she couldn't believe that she was being given this second chance at happiness. How could anyone so lovely fall in love with her?

Walter had accepted fully that they wouldn't have children, saying Sally was all he needed, and that he would be a good father to her. She knew he would – he was already – and Sally adored him.

Tomorrow, they would be a proper family, moving into a house on St Anne's Road, just a few doors away from where Martha and Joshua lived.

These thoughts led her to wonder about Martha and Joshua's happiness and she knew that only one thing now could complete their married bliss – Martha having a babby. They so would love a child together. She prayed that would happen in the future for them.

Later that evening, Martha sat holding Trisha's hand. The girls were asleep at last, and this was their time together on this, Trisha's last evening before she became Mrs Kennings the following day.

Feeling happy and supported with having Martha and Bonnie stay for the night, Trisha first of all wanted to know everything in the latest turn of events. 'So, what happened today, Martha?'

Trisha listened in silence, allowing Martha to tell in her own good time what had gone on with Peter.

When she'd heard all, relief flooded her. 'Eeh, that's good. You allus said he was a good bloke and that he couldn't help leaving you. It seems you were right, but how do you feel, eh? I mean, you fell in love with him once.'

'It is that I feel free. Free to give my love to Joshua. And I do love him with all my heart. There wasn't for being a spark of love for Peter, only pity. Oh, and a feeling that I am at peace to know that he is safe, and more so, that he is happy.'

'And generous. Not many would sacrifice having their child with them.'

'No, there is that too. A good man. And yes, one it is that I am proud to have as the father of me child. But that is all he is for being to me. Like I am for saying, I am free.'

'I'm glad, Martha, lass.'

'And I am for being glad, too, that tomorrow you will be marrying your Walter.'

Trisha sighed as she said, 'We've been through the mill, lass.'

'It is that we have. But we came out the winners in the end, so we did.'

'We did, love.'

'And tomorrow, it is that you begin the happiest time of your life, Trish.'

'Eeh, Martha, I can't believe it. Me, a doctor's wife. How did such a thing happen? . . . And, well . . . Oh, Martha, I've never told you, but . . . well, we haven't . . . you know.'

Martha looked astonished for a moment. Then her eyes seemed as if they were looking at something Trish couldn't see, yet knew she was a part of.

'I – it is that that's how such folk as Walter have been brought up.'

Her forced smile didn't make what she'd said seem sincere. It was to Trish as if Martha was covering up something. Trisha didn't ask, she didn't want to know, but then Martha asked, 'But it is that you have felt his love and need of you?'

'His love, yes, but never the other. Eeh, I haven't minded, though. It's been a lovely respite. Different. Undemanding. Like being loved for you and who you are, and not anything to do with the other side of things.'

'That's beautiful. For sure, you are for being the loveliest person, and a good one, Trish. You deserve all the happiness in the world. Everything will happen, you see . . . Oh, Trish, you're everything to me and you know that it is that I am always here for you.'

As Trisha laid her head on Martha's shoulder, the feeling intensified that Martha was afraid for her, but then, she wouldn't let anything hurt her, would she?

Maybe it was with her mentioning the intimate side of marriage. Maybe it had deepened the hurt she knew Martha felt at not having become pregnant and given Josh a child of his own. For the umpteenth time she wondered why that was, but she had no answers.

But with this being a plausible reason for the strange way Martha had acted, Trisha felt her doubts to be stilled.

'And you to me, Martha. Without you, I don't knaw where I'd be.'

'Well, it is that you'll never be for knowing. As nothing will ever part us, Trish, nothing.'

A LETTER FROM MAGGIE

Dear Reader,

Hi. I hope you enjoyed reading *The Fortune Tellers* as much as I enjoyed writing it. Thank you from the bottom of my heart for choosing my work to curl up with.

And so you have begun Martha's and Trisha's stories, and lived their courageous fight back from poverty to rise and fall and rise again. I hope you are looking forward to their journey onwards in book two – *The Fortune Teller's Secret*.

This next instalment will see Martha holding many secrets that cause her much stress, knowing that the conclusion of them will mean heartache and pain for her dear friend Trisha.

Trisha's near perfect marriage to Walter unravels in a way no one would expect. But Martha cannot break the pact she and Trisha made that she would never tell anything she sees in her visions – Trisha wants to face what is coming her way without any pre-warnings of it. A decision that, in the end, proves to make Trisha stronger.

Through it all Martha suffers greatly too, as hers and

Josh's failure to have a family almost tears them apart. Can Martha and Trisha come through it all to find lasting happiness? Ahh, this I can't reveal, so look out for the book coming out in autumn 2023.

Now, I move on to write the third and final book, and my imagination is taking me on to the next generation – Bonnie and Sally, their lives, loves and losses. Their courage in wartime, and, hopefully, their ultimate happiness. Of course, I plan to weave Martha and Trisha into this, so an epic journey awaits me and them. Excited!

If you have enjoyed this first book in the trilogy, I would so appreciate you rating the book and leaving me a review on Amazon or the online bookstores you buy from, and on book group forums you belong to such as Goodreads and TikTok.

Oh, and a Facebook mention would be amazing too. Reviews are like I'm being hugged by the reader, they encourage me to write the next book and they further my career as they advise other readers about my work, and hopefully whet their appetite to also buy the book.

If you are new to my books and would like to read more, my backlist is listed in the front of this book. There are two trilogies available, and two standalone books for you to choose from. These are available from Amazon and other online stores.

I am always available to contact personally too, if you have any queries or just want to say hello, or maybe book me for a talk to a group you belong to. I love to interact with readers and would welcome your comments, your emails, and messages through . . .

My Facebook page: https://www.facebook.com/MaggieMasonAuthor
My Twitter: @Authormary
My website: www.authormarywood.com/contact

I will always reply. And if you subscribe to my newsletter on my website, you will receive a quarterly newsletter giving all the updates on my books and author life, and many chances of winning lovely prizes. I'd love to hear from you.

Take care of yourself and others,
Much love
Maggie xxx

A Research Note

Many Blackpudlians may be tripped up a little by me calling what we all know as Talbot Road, New Road. This is because Thomas Clifton, Squire of Lytham, didn't name this road after his son until 1924, when it became Talbot Road as we now know it.

ACKNOWLEDGEMENTS

Many people were involved in getting my book to the shelves and presenting it in the very best way to my readers – my commissioning editor, Rebecca Roy, who works tirelessly, advising on structure of the story, besides overseeing umpteen other processes my book goes through. My editorial team headed by Jon Appleton, whose work brings out the very best of my story to make it shine. My publicity team who seek out many opportunities for me to showcase my work. My cover designers who do an amazing job in bringing my story alive in picture form, producing covers that stand out from the crowd. The sales team who find outlets across the country for my books. My son, James Wood, who polishes my work before submission and works alongside me on the edits that come in. And last, but not least, my much loved and valued readers who encourage me as they await another book, support me by buying my books and warm my heart with praise in their reviews. My heartfelt thanks to you all.

A special thanks to two Blackpudlians: Vicky Gordon, the granddaughter of Arturo Naventi, an ice-cream vendor on Blackpool beach many years ago, for allowing me to base my character on her grandfather and giving me wonderful snippets about his life and his work. All served to help me bring my Arturo to life.

And to Steve Cross for helping my research into the streets of Blackpool I wanted to use as the setting, and confirming if they existed during this era. Thank you both very much.

But no one person stands alone. My family are amazing. They give me an abundance of love and support and when one of them says they are proud of me, then my world is complete. My special thanks to my darling Roy, my husband and very best friend. My children, Christine Martin, Julie Bowling, Rachel Gradwell and James Wood, my grandchildren, and great-grandchildren who all light up my life. And to my Olley and Wood families. You are all my rock and help me to climb my mountain. Thank you. I love you with all my heart.